For Dave —
So happy that you enjoyed
"Nightmare" —
Hope you like this one.
Best Regards

A Cold
Night in Hell

June
2020

Books by Beverley Armstrong-Rodman

Murder is a Family Matter

Baa Baa Black Death

I'll Be Killing You

Secrets Can Be Murder

Nightmare in the Everglades

A Cold Night in Hell

A Cold Night in Hell

BEVERLEY ARMSTRONG-RODMAN

A COLD NIGHT IN HELL

This is a work of fiction. All of the characters, names, incidents, organizations, and dialogue
in this novel are either the products of the author's imagination or are used fictitiously.

iUniverse books may be ordered through booksellers or by contacting:

iUniverse LLC
1663 Liberty Drive
Bloomington, IN 47403
www.iuniverse.com
1-800-Authors (1-800-288-4677)

ISBN: 978-1-4917-4596-0 (sc)
ISBN: 978-1-4917-4594-6 (hc)
ISBN: 978-1-4917-4595-3 (e)

Printed in the United States of America.

iUniverse rev. date: 09/17/2014

To take revenge is often to sacrifice oneself

(Kongo)

Time spent in getting even, would be better spent in getting ahead

(Unknown)

Cast of Characters

Kate Chandler – trapped in her cottage with a stalker

Angel Baby – aka Maddy – beautiful, but vengeful

Dr. Patrick O'Neal – looking for revenge and redemption

Mark Duncan – looking to renew an old friendship

Nick DeLuca – a good hearted cop who went beyond the call of duty

Davey Chandler – a seven year old who was full of tricks

Paige Chandler – who grew up over night

Jill – Kate's best friend

Sonny and Lester – two young men who should have stayed home

Mac Chandler – Kate's husband, who chose a bad time to go to London

Bob Garland – the friendly mechanic

Walt Sr. and Walt Jr. – cottage caretakers

Tom, Dick and Harriet – the three Chandler cats

Kingsley – a new friend for Davey

Acknowledgements

This book is lovingly dedicated to my wonderful, supportive, patient husband, who has encouraged me with his humour, and his occasionally brilliant suggestions! I couldn't have done it without you, Ward, and wouldn't have wanted to!

To the rest of my family and friends, I say many thanks for your interest, patience, and constant pestering as to when the book would be finished. You are the ones who kept me going. Keep watching for number seven, because it's definitely coming.

Prologue

The redhead sitting at the bar was a beauty, absolutely drop dead gorgeous. In the common vernacular, she was "a knock-out." That was why the eyes of every man, and almost every woman in the upscale Toronto bar, were fixed on her, as she sat sipping her martini, without a glance to right or left.

This was one of the "snazzy-jazzy" lounges so prevalent in Toronto. It was "ritzy-glitzy," and super noisy. Instead of a quiet, laid back, unassuming bar, which she usually chose, this one had a wild and crazy feel to it.

It was full of a lot of happy people having fun, a lot of bored people wishing they were having fun, and a lot of unhappy people, hating the fact that others were having more fun than they were.

Tonight she was in a "what the hell" sort of mood, and wondered what kind of clientele she might encounter.

It seemed that she was oblivious to the many admiring male glances, (along with several deadly female glares), all directed her way. Anyone who knew her, however, (and there were precious few in that club), would understand that she was, in fact, very aware of the stir she was causing, and was loving every moment of it.

Taking another sip of her drink, she casually peeked at her image in the mirror behind the bar. Yes, she was still gorgeous! It wasn't just a dream. She really was the most attractive woman in the place, and she intended to stay that way for the rest of her life.

The woman who had once been happy to be cute, perky and pretty, was now ecstatic at being chic, sultry and beautiful. The doctor had done a wonderful job, and she promised herself that she would never grow old and ugly.

Surprisingly, just about everything to do with her appearance, was new. Her rebuilt nose gave her a patrician look. Her reconstructed cheekbones gave her character. Her widened eyes offered more depths into which a man could fall. The refashioned, puffy lips were unbelievably kissable, and the already smooth skin, had been tweaked and pulled just enough, to give that flawless appearance. Even her chin had been remodeled, to give her an exquisite heart shaped face.

The biggest disappointment was that she was still relatively short. There wasn't a darn thing the doctor was able to do about that. She had asked him if he couldn't stretch her legs somehow, but he just laughed and shook his head. "My talents only go so far, Angel Baby, so enjoy your new beauty, and forget about your height. You're tall enough for any man."

"Angel Baby" she purred softly, as she smiled at her image.

She had taken the doctor's advice, and was now wearing six inch red stiletto heels. They gave her sufficient height to be taken seriously – very seriously.

The fat man sitting a few stools away, thought she was smiling at him, and he grinned hopefully. He would never know just how lucky he was, that Angel Baby had already noticed and discarded him. That also went for the redhead with pimples on his chin. He looked to be about seven feet tall, so he wasn't even a contender.

As she continued to gaze at her image, as well as checking out the people around her, she told herself that the best part of her miraculous transformation, was that anyone who had known her before, would never recognize her now. Even her own mother and father wouldn't recognize their wayward, troublesome daughter.

Well, she had paid plenty for these results. She had paid in pain and suffering and fear, if not in actual cash, and she was enjoying every moment of her beauty. Appearing cool and nonchalant, she secretly basked in the attention. If Mac could only see her now! She could hardly wait for his reaction.

Dan Taylor was sitting at the curve of the bar, shamelessly staring, and assessing his chances. His piercing brown eyes started with the red stiletto shoes, which were really the only things about her he didn't like. Why did women think they had to wear those ugly-ass shoes – specially red ones? They were downright dangerous – more so for men than for the women who wore them. They could be great weapons. An irate woman could put a guy's eye out with one of them.

Anyway, starting with the offending shoes, his eager eyes moved slowly along the sheer black stockings. Dan loved the sexiness of black stockings. His wife wore some kind of mud coloured ones, which were not appealing.

He lingered on the way her short black skirt clung to that voluptuous ass, then on to the silvery top, which gave only an enticing hint of the fully rounded breasts beneath.

Dan paused over the red waves of hair, which reached her shoulders, picturing his hands moving softly through them. He almost shuddered with anticipation. Finally, he stopped for another long, lingering look at that perfect face.

She looked like a high class call girl, which, of course, was the picture she wanted to present. In actual fact, however, she was nothing more than a cheap little thief, a budding con artist with a mean streak a mile wide.

A man not usually given to philosophical thoughts, Dan couldn't help wondering why the God who had created all women, had made only one specimen who looked like this one. He would likely have fallen off his bar stool, if he had known that in this particular case, the patrician nose, the smooth creamy skin, the high cheek bones, the puffy lips, and the small, slightly pointed chin, which completed the heart shaped face, were mostly the work of the magic fingers of a renowned cosmetic surgeon, who lived and worked in Switzerland.

Dan, however, had no way of knowing this, so his fantasy continued. Not being a man with much vocabulary at his fingertips, "wowee" was all he could think to say to himself. She was a beauty, and he wanted her. In fact he simply had to have her. Suddenly his wife and kids were just a distant memory, actually a rather unpleasant distant memory!

The beautiful woman preferred to call herself "Angel Baby," but even "Angela" or "Angel" were better than her real name, (and, of course, she couldn't use it any more).

Continuing to assess the prospects, she determined that there were only a couple of men sitting at the bar, who deserved her interest or attention. Although the place was crowded, the pickings were slim.

Maybe she should give up here, and go to another bar. Maybe she should give up the con completely for tonight, and just go back to her hotel. A good night's sleep wouldn't hurt, and it actually sounded rather appealing.

No way! Giving up wasn't even an alternative. She felt all pumped and ready for action. She had to find herself a patsy – that word was so much better than "victim."

The fellow sitting to her right, just where the bar curved, was okay, although there was something tough about his face. He looked to be the type with more brawn than brains. She didn't mind that, as long as he wasn't too tough. She didn't want to tangle with anyone who might get rough with her. There was no way she was putting this beautiful face in any danger!

Unfortunately, at the moment, he was staring so hard, that his mouth was gaping a bit. Not too attractive, but he was wearing an expensive watch, and his clothes looked expensive. That likely meant a fat wallet!

The guy sitting three stools over to her left, was an obvious loser. She could see his image in the mirror. He looked intelligent, but he had a stupid little moustache which was too "Hitleresque" for her liking. Also, she could see that there were a lot of broken capillaries on his bulbous red nose. That meant that he was a drinker. That was okay, maybe even a good quality in some cases. The problem was, that she didn't like them too smart, and she didn't like big red noses. They reminded her of clowns, and she hated clowns. They frightened her more than just about anything. So, that guy was definitely not a contender.

There was a perfect candidate also sitting to her left, but just as she was about to make a move on him, his tall, blonde girlfriend with the big hooters, made her way back from the restroom, and slithered onto the stool beside him. Bummer!

It looked as if "Mr. Brawn but no Brains" was going to be "it" for tonight. Sighing, she gazed once more at her wonderful reflection. In her own mind, she had always been a beauty, but now she was "over the top beautiful."

Even more important, she no longer looked anything at all like the woman she had been before. The only things which hadn't changed, were her sparkling brown eyes. Even her naturally brown hair was now a soft shade of red.

The obliging mirror reflected the little smile which she had been practicing for two months. It was alluring and demure, and it was pouty enough to be promising. Best of all, so far it seemed to work very well.

"Okay, boys," she muttered as she downed the last of the martini, "hang on to your hats, because Lulu's back in town."

Chapter One

Kate Chandler and her husband Mac, were enjoying a happy afternoon on the golf course. Because it had been threatening rain all day, there weren't too many people playing. That was the way Kate preferred it. She was an erratic player, and didn't like to be crowded or hurried. She was good at most sports, and was sure that if she had the time, she could become a pretty good golfer, but there were so many other interesting things to do.

This afternoon was one of the really good golf days for her. She was full of energy and enthusiasm, and was hitting that mean little ball a country mile. Her ability to chip and putt, however, was another story.

Mac smiled, as he waited for her to chip onto the green. In his eyes, she was still gorgeous, even though she was the mother of twin teenagers, and a seven year old son. She had long shapely legs which just didn't quit. After a week in the Florida sun, they were tanned a nice toasty brown.

Her reddish blond hair was pulled back in a loose ponytail, and she had a golf cap pulled forward, to protect her face from too much sun. What a great looking package, he thought, as his eyes ran up and down her body. After coming so close to losing her two years ago, every day with Kate was a good day for Mac.

He knew from experience that Kate could do just about anything to which she set her mind. She had a determination and a "joie de vivre" which allowed her to not only enjoy life to the fullest, but also to assess a situation, and quickly decide how to handle it. She was both artistic and athletic – an unusual combination, and he loved her with all his heart.

In some ways she had changed, since her lonely weeks on that tiny island in the Everglades. First, of course, she was much more self-sufficient. There was no disputing that.

There was something else though. He couldn't quite put his finger on it, but it made him somewhat uneasy. She could be laughing and kidding with him one minute, then quiet and withdrawn the next. It was almost as if she had gone to a different place in her mind, a place where Mac couldn't reach her, a place which Mac couldn't understand. Thankfully, those moments were becoming more rare now, as she came to accept that she really was safely home again, surrounded by friends and family.

On an impulse, they had flown down to their condo in Panama City Beach, for one lovely little week in January. Kate's long time friend Jill, had gladly moved into their house in Toronto, to keep an eye on the kids and cats. They had hastily thrown a few things in a suitcase, and taken off.

Since Kate's terrible misadventure two years ago, which had started right here in Florida, they had made the most of every possible opportunity to relax, have fun, and enjoy themselves. Life was just too darn short and unpredictable, to risk putting things off into a nebulous future.

In the past two years they had taken the kids to Disney World, and they had done a family cruise to the Mediterranean. They had also done a fun trip to Las Vegas, for a little gambling and relaxation, just the two of them.

It was only last week, once the New Year's festivities had come and gone, that Kate mentioned how tired Mac looked. She suggested that they fly down to their condo at Edgewater Beach Resort, and enjoy a little special time together, beside the pool, and on the golf course. It sounded too good to resist, so here they were, tanned and relaxed, and almost ready to return to a cold winter in Toronto.

Kate was an author and illustrator of children's books, and she had an important book reading and signing in a couple of weeks. She was really looking forward to that.

Mac was a marine biologist, and had a convention in England, at which he was giving a paper. Unfortunately, because of some snafu, the two engagements were scheduled for the same week, so Mac was going to miss Kate's book signing and reading, and she was going to miss the presentation of his paper.

That was another reason why this short little trip had seemed like such a good idea. They would at least have this time together, before heading back to their hectic lives.

For Kate, part of the fun of golfing, was watching for animals and birds. This afternoon she had already seen two small Florida deer, a skunk who waddled along behind them for a while, and a few squirrels.

There were a couple of ponds on this course, which were reputed to entertain a large old alligator. Kate had never seen him, but figured if there was one alligator around, there could be more, so she was trying to keep a watchful eye on her surroundings.

She knew that alligators usually hibernated at this time of year, but there were always exceptions, and she wasn't taking any chances.

Actually she wasn't really seeing much of what was around her. Instead, her mind had gone back to the lonely days and nights she had spent in the Everglades, wondering whether she would ever see her family again.

They were now on the sixteenth hole, and Mac was in the bushes looking for golf balls. There was hardly another soul on the course, so they were just taking their time. Kate left the cart at the point where Mac had gone into the thick brush, and began walking down the fairway.

The warmth of the afternoon, (it was unexpectedly warm for January), and the quiet of her surroundings, gave Kate time to remember the situation in which she had found herself two years ago.

She had been kidnapped by a psychopath, who had left her without food or water, on a tiny island in the Florida Everglades. Never knowing at what moment he might reappear, she had fought for survival, and for a chance to get herself off that island.

Snakes, stinging and biting insects, a tropical storm, and a Florida panther, had just been some of her problems. She had also had to evade a couple of murderous drunks, her psycho captor, and a crazy ex-girlfriend of Mac's, who wanted to kill her. Coming out of all that in one piece had been a miracle, and now she cherished every moment of every day.

She was thinking happy thoughts, as she strolled down the fairway, but then the wheels fell off!

Enjoying the peaceful and quiet surroundings, Kate was suddenly startled to hear Mac let out a cross between a scream and a shout. Whirling, she looked back to see her husband leap into the golf cart, and gun the engine, as he waved frantically at her.

What was wrong? Had he been bitten by a snake in the bushes? Surely not. Snakes should all be hibernating in January, just like alligators.

Meanwhile, it was obvious that Mac was frantic. He had lost track of time in the bushes, finding two golf balls in good condition, and one throw-away. The only bad news was that he had backed into a strange thorny bush, which had put hurtful stickers all over his golf pants. Trying to brush them off was useless, as they simply clung to his trousers, and stung his fingers.

When he came out of the bushes, however, and looked around for Kate, he immediately saw the possible danger. Way down the fairway, he could see that his beloved wife was walking right toward what looked to be a dog, or possibly a coyote! As he watched, the animal stumbled, then slowly struggled back to its feet. What in the world was Kate doing? She was walking right toward him, but her head was down. She apparently didn't even see him.

The dog, or more likely coyote, was close enough now that Mac could see what looked like froth coming from its mouth.

"Oh God please no," he muttered, as he yelled at Kate to stop.

When she turned, looked back at Mac, and saw his frightened face, her heart gave a jump. What was wrong? She quickly glanced over her shoulder, back the other way, to see what could be scaring him. Because of her bad experience two years ago, her first thought was that there was a psycho about to pull her into the bushes. Wrong!

Now her heart gave a huge jump, when she realized that she was within about ten feet of a drooling coyote. As her mind registered the situation, the unfortunate creature staggered, and almost fell.

It was one of those "what do I do now" moments, as Kate and the coyote stared at each other.

It's amazing how the human brain can assess and disregard several ideas in a matter of seconds. She first thought of turning and running back to Mac, and the safety of the cart. But, would that encourage the animal to run after her? Yes, more than likely.

Next she considered standing perfectly still, and looking it right in the eye. Maybe that would encourage it to stop as well. On the other hand, maybe not!

Should she shout, and wave her arms frantically, to scare it into running away? Doubtful.

While processing these possibilities, she heard Mac yelling, "It's rabid, Kate."

Well duh, that was pretty obvious! Coyotes don't usually froth at the mouth and stagger around! Not even realizing that she had made a decision, she began backing up very slowly, never breaking contact with the rheumy eyes of the sick beast.

Kate didn't have to hear Mac's warning, to understand that the coyote was sick, and undoubtedly rabid. One look into those pathetic, watery eyes, might have been enough, but the thick, white, frothy foam, all around its mouth, and a long string of saliva hanging loosely from its bottom jaw, really told the tale.

The coyote suddenly tried to lunge at Kate, but didn't have enough strength. It fell to its knees, then, getting up, and apparently losing interest, or possibly being scared by Mac's frantic shouts, it staggered into the nearby bushes.

To Kate it all seemed to happen in slow motion. Once the coyote had disappeared, however, she felt so sorry for it, that she wondered what she could do to help.

Mac almost ran over her, in his anxiety to get the cart between her and the coyote, which had now disappeared. Thank God for that. The poor animal had looked emaciated, and there was little doubt that it was in the advanced stages of rabies. In that condition, there was no telling what it might have done. There was even the chance that it might get its second wind, and come rushing out of the bushes at them.

Whether it was Mac's yelling, the noise of the golf cart, or Kate's decision to back up very slowly, there was really no way of knowing why the coyote had stumbled off into the thick underbrush, rather than trying again to lunge at a possible victim. Maybe its den was hidden there, and the poor thing would just stay in it until he died.

Taking no chances, Mac hugged his wife tightly, as she gratefully jumped into the golf cart, then he took off at full speed.

"Whew, that was a close one. Why in the world did you walk right up to him like that?" he asked, more sharply than he had intended.

"Mac, I'm not stupid enough to deliberately walk right up to a rabid animal. Give me a break. I was thinking about illustrations for the next book, and I really wasn't paying attention to my surroundings. I was just enjoying a wonderful afternoon out with my husband, with no cares or worries.

"I'm glad you came out of those bushes when you did, though," she grinned. "I'd likely be heading for rabies shots right about now, if you had kept looking for those damn lost balls. I think it was your shouts which scared him."

Her husband just shook his head, and grinned back at her.

All thoughts of finishing the game were forgotten, as they headed to the club house to report what had happened. The unfortunate coyote was a danger not only to himself, but to any other golfers who might encounter him accidentally.

After explaining the incident to the man behind the desk, who didn't seem too interested in the problem, they packed their clubs into the car, and headed back to their condo at Edgewater.

"What next?" groaned Mac. "It wasn't enough that you went through hell on that island, but now you come home and go looking for trouble on a lovely, peaceful golf course!" He was teasing her, and was prepared for the playful swat she gave him.

"Trouble just seems to find me these days. I'm going to have to start wearing a good luck charm." The incident had scared her more than she wanted to admit.

"No, that's the end of it. That's the end of any more 'Kate adventures,'" Mac declared, shaking his head. "You don't need any foolish good luck charm. What you need is to mind your own business, keep alert," (this was said with emphasis), "and leave the excitement to someone else!

"Dammit, that was a close call, Katie-girl, and you've got to stop day-dreaming. There are bad things and bad people out there. Let's just hope all those dark clouds and other shit are behind us.

"That psycho who nabbed you, is dead, Maddy is tucked away safely in the psychiatric hospital, and the rabid coyote is hiding in the bushes. There can't be anything but blue skies from now on."

He hugged her again as he said this, and gave her a kiss on the cheek.

Kate thought that it sounded very much as if Mac was trying to convince himself of this rosy picture. Unfortunately, he had forgotten that the Fates, or evil spirits, or anything else you might want to call them, are always lurking around, watching and listening.

They're like mean spirited, sometimes mischievous, but more often malevolent godparents, always ready to teach these puny humans a lesson, when they get too cocky or sure of themselves, or just too happy.

She believed in an evil presence in life, and she winced, and gave a little shudder, when Mac made his comment about that being the end of her adventures. If any evil spirits were listening, they would surely try to make Mac eat his words. She wondered with trepidation what might happen next, and resolved to be extra careful in the weeks to come. Life was too good right now, to let anything spoil it.

If Kate had only known what lay ahead, she might have decided to stay in Florida forever, rather than returning to their Toronto home. She, however, had no way of knowing what those malicious Fates had in store for her, so she and Mac went on happily enjoying their vacation in the sunny south.

Chapter Two

Another beautiful Florida day – another adventure. That seemed to be the way this week was going.

Both Kate and Mac were already sorry that they had come down for only the one week.

"We've hardly had time to unpack," complained Kate, to herself, as she gazed out at the amazingly calm waters of the Gulf. This morning they were a beautiful turquoise, streaked with cobalt blue.

Staring at the peaceful water, had a strangely soporific effect on Kate. She felt slightly hypnotized.

Just then a flock of pelicans flew by, playing their favourite game, "follow the leader."

Kate and Mac were now watching something in the water. It looked like a school of black manta-rays, or possibly sting-rays. Kate could never remember which was which, but they seemed to be having a great time, swimming very close to shore. She wouldn't want to be out there, wading or swimming at the moment.

Mac had come out to the balcony in his tighty-whities to survey the scene, when Kate called him.

Laughing at him, she said, "Oh my goodness, Mr. Chandler. I do declare I'm feeling quite faint. You make such a tempting picture in the clothes you're almost wearing! Did you have anything particular on your mind?"

Mac guffawed, and shook a finger at her.

"Naughty lady. Get your mind out of the gutter, and come and get dressed. I don't want to distract you from your mission today. But, hold on to that thought for later," he added, waggling his eyebrows at her.

They were heading out to Destin, which was less than an hour's drive from Panama City Beach. Kate wanted to do some shopping for herself and the kids.

For a special treat, they planned to stop at Dusty's on the way back.

Dusty's was an interesting little oyster bar, right on Front Beach Road. The first time Mac had taken Kate there, was the year they were living in PCB. It was actually shortly before Kate had been kidnapped. She had been quite hesitant when they first walked through the door, and saw the line-up of people waiting for a table.

It had that fishy smell of all oyster bars, it was crowded and noisy, and there were dollar bills stuck all over the walls and ceiling. Fortunately, they didn't have long to wait, and after ordering and devouring a dozen of Dusty's famous baked oysters, Kate had been hooked.

The oysters were absolutely delicious – large, succulent, spicy. No wonder the little pub, or diner, or whatever it called itself, was so popular. It was full of people laughing, shouting, cheering, eating, drinking, and making new friends. It was indeed a "happening" place.

Every time the hard working men behind the actual "oyster bar" finished shucking another pail full, they would whack the large iron triangle which hung over the sink. It resounded throughout the pub, and everyone cheered, effectively adding to the mayhem.

This time, after their successful shopping spree in Destin, Kate and Mac were eventually seated at the large round table right in the center of all the excitement. It could seat six or possibly eight people, and it was a great way to meet someone new.

They each ordered a dozen of "Dusty's Special Oysters." Cold, frosty beer was absolutely "de rigueur" in this party atmosphere. Somehow, wine just didn't cut it. It had to be the golden beer at $1.00 a glass!

As they waited for their order, they chatted with the other people at the table. One couple said they were on vacation from Cleveland. Another said they were from Virginia. One couple finished, paid their bill, and left without saying much of anything.

Almost immediately, two more people were seated. Kate looked at them as they sat down, and nearly choked on her beer. She couldn't believe her eyes. There, sitting across the table was a well known Toronto practitioner, a family doctor, along with a very young, very busty, very pretty blond, who definitely was not his wife.

The trouble was that this particular family doctor, was the man to whom the entire Chandler family had entrusted their health over the years. Kate knew Dr. John Weatherston's wife Marge very well. They had both done hospital volunteer work together. Not only was John Weatherston apparently cheating on his wife, but, while he was in his early fifties, this dolly wasn't a day over twenty, if that!

Kate knew that this was not one of his two children, since he had two boys. He certainly wasn't treating her like a niece or a cousin or a long lost sister. Kate readily jumped to that conclusion, after seeing the way he was caressing her tight little butt, and whispering in her ear, with a lecherous grin.

When the couple had seated themselves on the stools, and began looking around at their table companions, Dr. John's eyes came to focus on Kate, and his face turned the colour of cranberries. The usually calm, gentle, knowledgeable family doctor, now appeared as nervous as a cat in a room full of rocking chairs. He didn't know where to look or what to say. He was obviously shaken at the realization that he had been found out – caught without any possible explanation.

Kate thought he looked as if he was going to have a stroke. Talk about an embarrassing situation. She felt as embarrassed as he did. She was also disgusted. His wife Marge was a lovely woman, smart, pretty, and devoted to her husband and two kids. She didn't deserve this.

When Mac gave a sudden sharp intake of breath, and then glanced quickly at Kate, she realized that he had also recognized their family doctor. Now what? What does one do in such a circumstance? What can one possibly say?

Well, it appeared that Dr. Weatherston knew what to do. As people were introducing themselves, he simply said "I'm Dr. Weatherston, and this is Cathy Newell." He gave no sign of recognition, nor did Kate and Mac. It was extremely awkward.

Big boobs Cathy seemed totally unaware of the situation, and was soon ordering a beer and a burger, after confessing to everyone at the table that she hated oysters. Dr. John kept his eyes down, as if he was a naughty kid, who had been caught feeding his pet at the table. He made no more eye contact with Kate or Mac.

This would have made a great scene for a movie, Kate thought, as she ate her oysters without really tasting them. She was upset that this cheater was here in PCB, having a great time with Catharine and her "boobsey twins," aka her twin boobs, while his unsuspecting wife waited at home.

She was sorely tempted to ask, "How's Marge doing these days, John?" Or, even better, she could have inquired, "How's your dear wife these days, John?" Of course she didn't, but part of her wished that she had.

They were barely back into the car, before they looked at each other and laughed. "Well, that was fun," said Mac, shaking his head.

"That old fool. Actually, he isn't even that old. I doubt that he's fifty-five yet. It must be the post mid-life crisis raising its ugly head."

"I just don't know how I'll be able to face Marge. It puts me in a heck of a position. I'm certainly not going to be the one to tell her, but how will I ever look her in the eyes again, knowing what I know. Do you think there's any possibility at all that it's innocent?"

"Are you kidding? Didn't you see them just before they sat down? His hands were all over her. He was playing doctor for real!"

"Well that really spoiled the whole day for me. I couldn't stand to be home with the kids, doing the laundry and washing the floors, while you were making a fool of me with some floozy. I think I'd do a Lorena Bobbit on you!"

"Ouch. I believe you. That's why I'm always so good, and keep my eyes averted like a nervous monk, when there are good looking women around."

Kate punched him playfully on the arm, but found it difficult to change the subject. It was just too bizarre, and rather delicious in an awful way.

"You know, maybe we shouldn't be so judgemental," suggested Mac, as they drove back through the Edgewater gates.

"We don't know anything about his home life. Maybe his wife is a totally cold fish, and won't give him any loving. Or maybe she's sick, and has told him it's okay to find solace elsewhere."

"Oh, don't be a goose," exclaimed Kate.

"No matter what his reasons, he should not be playing around with a girl less than half his age. Shame on him. Shame, shame, shame. Do you think this means we'll have to get another doctor? I just can't picture going to him again. We would both be too embarrassed."

Back at the condo, Kate placed all her purchases on the bed, to look them over before packing them away. She was pleased with what she had found, and was sure that the twins and Davey would also be happy. With the new clothes for each of them, plus the fudge which she intended to buy at the Pier Park fudge shop, she felt that her shopping was finished for this trip.

Now she could just relax and have fun the next few days. Unfortunately, at the moment she didn't feel like having fun. She just felt like punching Dr. John Weatherston in his handsome face.

Mac wanted to go to the hot tub before dinner. They donned their bathing suits, poured a couple of glasses of wine in plastic cups, and headed down to the comfortably hot and bubbly tub.

"This is the life for sure," muttered Mac, closing his eyes and leaning back.

"Do you realize that it's likely snowing and blowing back in Toronto right now? How about staying here till springtime?"

He, of course, was kidding, but Kate could see a lot of merit in the idea.

"It must be wonderful to be retired, and be able to come and go as you please," she mused, as she sipped her wine.

"Do you think we'll spend our entire winters down here when we do retire?"

"I don't see why not. We could spend our summers at the cottage, then head down here, and really, you know, we wouldn't even need the Toronto house. Maybe we'll just sell it. It would be a bit difficult having all three places to maintain."

"Oh no. I couldn't sell our home. I'd miss it terribly. Wouldn't you?"

That idea had never really occurred to her, and it seemed alarming.

"Tell me we won't do that, Mac. I'd hate to leave Toronto and all our friends. Surely we can figure out something."

"Calm down. It was just an idea. We've got lots of time to think about it. Just remember, though, we've always said we wanted to travel extensively when we retire. How does that fit into all your plans?"

Kate just grinned at him.

"As you say, my darling, we'll figure out something."

Chapter Three

Going up in the elevator, Angel Baby and Dan were quiet, both staring stiffly at the numbers, as the elevator made its way to the twelfth floor. There were two other men and a woman in the car with them, and the silence was uncomfortable.

Angel wondered whether maybe they were a threesome, but the woman got off by herself. Actually, she was quite attractive, and it seemed ironic that she would be by herself on a Saturday night. Of course there might be a man waiting for her in a hotel room on that floor. That was always a good possibility.

Maybe there was a woman waiting for her! These days it could just as easily be a woman. Life was strange, Angel thought, as she clutched her little silver purse, with its valuable contents.

Finally reaching their floor, Angel walked out of the elevator first, and gave him a bewitching, "come hither" look over her shoulder. Dan didn't seem to notice, as he pushed slightly ahead, fumbling for his key. He was obviously nervous, and Angel wondered whether this was the first time he had picked up a woman in a hotel bar, or any kind of bar for that matter. He certainly couldn't be accused of being overly suave.

She smiled inwardly. This was going to be a piece of cake. She figured she'd be in and out of there within the hour, although maybe she should give him something for his money. Sure, she'd let him do a little kissing, before she gave him the Rohypnol. Kissing was okay, and she could use the practice with her new lips.

As she scanned the hotel room, she wasn't too impressed. It was L-shaped, so that you couldn't see the bed section from the door. That was nice. The colour scheme, however, put her right off. It was all done in beige and a rather sickly green. She had always considered green to be her unlucky colour, and she wondered whether she should perhaps abort the mission right now.

The other thing which gave her pause, was that the bathroom was to the right, just as you entered the front door, and she felt that was really tacky. The bathroom should be in the most unobtrusive and inconspicuous spot in a hotel room, certainly not right at the front door! Who designed these places anyway?

Oh well, at least there was a bar, small, but well stocked. Hopefully, she hadn't been wrong about Dan. Hopefully his wallet would be stuffed with big bills! Hopefully she could get them all without too much fuss or muss!

She sighed a little, as she smiled coyly at him. This wasn't going to be a whole lot of fun. Actually, so far this guy had been about as much fun as a week old corpse! There was a faint whiff of body odour about him, which turned her stomach. She would have to breathe through her mouth, so as not to be overpowered by his strange aroma. What was he using as after shave cologne – "Eau de Sewer?"

If only she had noticed the odour sooner, she never would have come upstairs with him. She had a very sensitive nose, and bad smells made her gag. Damn - she should probably have left the bar downstairs, and tried another hotel. Surely she could have found a more attractive man! Still, she wouldn't be here that long, so she would just have to put up with him for a short time.

"Would you like a drink?" Dan asked. He couldn't believe his good luck in landing this dishy dame, but her extreme good looks were making him nervous.

Good God, yes, she thought. I'll need at least three to get me through this.

There was something earnest and pathetic about him, and it made her want to slap him. He deserved what he was about to get. Why didn't he know enough to stay home with his wife and kids, and stop trying to play in the big leagues?

"I'd love a drink" she replied, giving him her devastating smile.

Dan was happy to have something to do, as he fumbled with the drinks. He was excited, but he was scared too. He had never hooked up with a girl this good looking. What if he couldn't perform? What if he made a total fool of himself?

Well, in that case he'd tell her he was just recovering from major surgery. That would be a good excuse. No, wait a minute. He didn't have any scars, so how could he blame non-existent surgery for his failure to perform?

Maybe he could plead a case of malaria or yellow fever. No, that wouldn't be believable. He just had to calm down, have a couple of stiff drinks, and hope that they weren't the only things that were stiff.

As they clinked their glasses, Angel took a pretend stumble, and spilled her glass of wine all over Dan's shirt and pants.

"Oh no. Oh I'm so sorry," she exclaimed in fake horror.

"Oh how could I have been so clumsy? I guess I'm just nervous." She kept babbling, as she tried wiping his shirt with a napkin from the top of the mini bar. She had really made a mess of the shirt with the red wine.

She had practiced that fake stumble over and over with a glass of water, until she could do it effortlessly. It really had looked like an accident.

"That wine is going to stain," she exclaimed.

"You'd better go into the bathroom, take your shirt off, and rinse it. Might as well take off your pants too," she added suggestively.

"Rinse that spot well, and I'll use the hair dryer on it. I'm so sorry, but I promise I'll make it up to you."

As she said this, she was pushing him gently toward the bathroom. She gave him the little pout she had been practicing, and Dan's knees melted. His initial shock and annoyance at her clumsiness, had quickly turned to excitement, when she mentioned taking off his pants.

Angel, of course, needed a ruse to get him into the bathroom, while she did her "magic." She had discovered that it was impossible to get the few drops of Rohypnol stirred into a victim's drink, if he was standing right there in the room. So far she had been having great success with her "spilling the wine" trick.

While Dan was in the bathroom, she didn't waste a moment. Putting down her almost empty glass of wine, she removed a small, unlabelled bottle from her silver purse.

Quickly she poured a few drops into his drink, and stirred it with her finger. Hesitating a moment, she added another two drops, then returned the bottle to her purse, hiding it under a lace hanky.

It was just about then, that she had a strange feeling of regret, or maybe even shame. Why was she doing this? She hadn't always been this way. She had once been a lovely, sincere, genuine girl, full of wit and fun. She had once had a wonderful boyfriend named Mac. Where and when had she gone off the rails?

She knew very well when it had been. It had started shortly after Mac announced that he was going to Europe alone, for one last jaunt before settling down. She was sure that when he returned, he would ask her to marry him.

True, she did experience a few little "spells" that month before he left. She knew that it was actually the fact that he was taking that European trip without her, that had precipitated the sudden bouts of anger and nervousness. It was during that time that she actually had a few blackouts – hallucinating or dreaming things, which got all mixed up with reality.

When Mac returned, and confessed to her, that he had met someone else, the true love of his life, Angel (whose real name was Madison), slipped into a strange, quasi dreamlike state. There were days when she didn't know whether she was awake or dreaming. She stopped eating, and her hair started falling out – maybe because she kept twisting it and pulling at it. She had always been petite, but she became positively skeletal those next weeks and months.

She had taken to stalking Max, calling him constantly, going to his place of business, and begging him to reconsider. It was all to no avail. Mac and Kate were married, and Madison had been kicked to the curb.

In actual fact, Mac had felt terrible about dumping her. He had tried to let her down as gently as possible, but that hadn't worked. Madison had become cunning, and the police were never able to prove that she was the stalker. She had slashed tires, sent threatening notes, and tried to scare Kate in a dozen different ways. Nothing had worked. Kate and Mac had mostly just ignored her, and gone on with their blissful marriage.

Finally, she had realized that her aggressive attitude wasn't working, so she gave up, at least temporarily. She got herself physically healthy again, became marginally stable, and tried to pick up the shattered pieces of her own life. It had been a struggle, but for several years she managed to put Mac in a little compartment at the back of her head, and left him alone.

Then had come the time when Kate was kidnapped, and Madison - (this was before she had reinvented herself as Angel Baby) – got herself involved again. She saw a chance to kill Kate, and ingratiate herself with Mac, but it didn't quite work the way she had planned. She suddenly found herself being shipped to a Draconian psychiatric hospital in British Columbia, where she spent her days plotting her escape.

When she did find freedom again, (she had always had faith that she would), with the help of her long suffering parents, she managed to get herself to Switzerland, to start "Madison's Life – Part Two."

That was when, to her own surprise, Madison had morphed into Angel Baby. She had fallen madly in love with Dr. Patrick O'Neal, and had forgotten all about Mac, at least for a couple of years. It was only when Patrick rejected her, that she had crumbled like a stale cookie. She had gone berserk, and destroyed not only his office and clinic, but more importantly, his marriage.

That life was all behind her though. Now her mission was to have some fun, and to get together a good pile of money. This would allow her to fly out of the country at a moment's notice, and live comfortably in some far off place.

After a short while, she would return to Canada, and start working on getting Mac back in her life. Of course the only happy ending would be contingent upon her success with Mac. If her attempts failed, or if the police came after her again, she needed to be able to escape quickly, but she certainly wouldn't be happy without Mac at her side.

There were many days when Angel didn't know what the heck she was doing or trying to do. Then there were days when she was quite clear headed, and had some sort of plan, faulty as it may have been.

Angel had stumbled on the idea of picking up men in hotel bars, slipping them the date rape drug, and stealing their money, always managing to get away before they wakened. It was so simple, and so easy, that she quite enjoyed it. She liked getting all dressed up, and sitting at a bar, basking in the admiring glances from just about every man in the place. She actually enjoyed going up to the various hotel rooms, and practicing her charms on the unsuspecting men.

She had discovered that she really didn't like to be touched much, so she concentrated on becoming the best kisser possible. There were so many ways to kiss. She could have her eyes open, or eyes closed. Her lips could be parted slightly or held close together. Were her hands better around the man's neck, or running through his hair? All these little things were important. She would use them when Kate was out of the picture, and she was once again wooing Mac, her one true love.

With Mac she had always been herself – no subterfuge. She had been real. Now she was just playing a part – learning as she went along. She knew there would be no room for mistakes this time. As soon as she was rid of Kate, she would start her campaign to get Mac back in her life. And, if everything went wrong, she would have the money to get the heck out of Dodge, and start a new life in the islands, somewhere warm and sunny, with a long, beautiful beach.

She could quite easily picture herself in an eye-popping bikini, lying on a beach lounge, sipping a piña colada, and looking at the world from beneath a big picture hat, and from behind fashionable dark glasses. She quite liked that picture, and, of course, it was just that much better, when she was able to conjure up a tanned and beautiful, recently bereaved Mac, lying there beside her.

She was close now, she could feel it. And that "oh so perfect" Kate Chandler, who had stolen Mac from under her nose, had no idea of the avalanche which was about to come down on her head.

Chapter Four

————————————————————————————

Angel Baby was sitting demurely, sipping from her replenished wine glass, when Dan eventually came out of the bathroom, wearing only his jockey shorts, his sox, and a foolish grin.

"Hey, that's not fair. I'm almost naked, and you're still dressed," he said, taking a big gulp of the drink she offered him.

She had planned to practice some kissing, but Dan got to his drink too quickly. Oh well, she thought. That's okay. I'll be out of here earlier than I expected. Just show me the money, she grinned to herself.

They chatted for a few minutes, before Dan insisted that it was time for her to "get naked."

"I've got an idea," she suggested.

"While you refresh your drink, I'll do a little strip tease for you. Would you like that?"

"You bet," he grinned, finishing off his drink too quickly, and pouring himself another.

She started slowly, first removing her shoes, then her top, wondering when the darn drug was going to kick in. Maybe she hadn't given him enough. She discarded the loathsome thought of actually getting into bed with him. So far, every time she had played this little con game, she had been lucky.

The victims had all fallen unconscious before she actually had to remove all her clothes, and get into bed with them. A girl had to draw certain limits, and Angel Baby never let a man touch her intimately, unless it was Patrick or Mac. Her secret motto was "you can look, and you can kiss, but don't try touching this gorgeous miss."

She knew that was totally goofy, but it made her giggle secretly, as she said it in her head.

Drugging them required perfect timing, and so far she had become very good at it. She had not yet had to actually get into bed with any of the men.

Just as she was fiddling with her bra, Dan's lecherous grin disappeared, and he put his head in his hands.

"Wow, I don't feel right. Guess I drank that too fast. Oh man, I'm really dizzy."

Angel played her part perfectly.

"Dan, you don't look so good. I hope you're not having a heart attack." That suggestion always seemed to scare a man, and with his heart beating faster, the drug moved through his system much more quickly. Dan became noticeably more pale, as she helped him to lie back.

He fell onto the bedspread, and she lifted his legs, so that he was lying flat out. All the while she acted very concerned.

Seconds before he passed out, he seemed to realize what had happened. With a horrified look he mumbled "You bi-bitch, you put something, you put something into - - into - - the - - drink."

"You bet I did, you moron," she muttered, as she stood there, watching and waiting.

When she was sure that he was really out cold, she quickly looked for his wallet. Where the heck was it?

After a futile search on the dresser, beside the tv, and on the floor, she realized that it must be in his pants, which he had left in the washroom.

Hastily putting on her silver top, (later, she would be grateful to herself for doing that), she padded barefoot to the bathroom. She would get the money, put on her shoes and jacket, and be out of there in a flash. From force of habit, she shut the bathroom door behind her, even though Dan was now out cold, and there was no chance of him barging in on her.

Time was of the essence. The sooner she made her escape, the better. All she had to do, was finish dressing, make sure the hall was clear, and take the elevator down. She always managed to walk briskly, yet look casual, as she went through the hotel lobbies, and out into the cold, dark streets. She had done this several times now, and was getting better each time.

The trick, of course, was to choose the right man in the right bar. No point in going up to a chintzy room with some bozo who had $30 in his pocket. Actually, any money she made this way was just icing on the cake. She had access to quite a lot of money, which her parents were always willing to supply. They would do anything to keep her as far away as possible. For many years now Madison Ramsay's parents had been frightened of their daughter.

The beauty of the con was that 99% of the men would not report her to the police. They wouldn't want their wives to find out what they had been doing. They would do anything to keep their names out of the paper, so she felt safe in pulling the same stunt at least three times in a city before moving on. She had started in Halifax right after coming back to Canada, and was slowly making her way across the country.

The "game" as she called it, had a twofold purpose. First, she was making pretty good money, money which she could always use in the weeks ahead. After all, a girl needed pretty baubles to keep up her spirits!

Secondly, pure and simple, it was a kick! She loved the feeling of being smarter than someone else. She loved to punish these creeps, who were always so willing to cheat on their wives or girlfriends, as soon as someone better looking came along. She was punishing all men, because one man had done that to her.

Men were basically pigs. Well, most men were. There were always a few exceptions, of course, and her beloved Mac was one of them. Yes, he had made one really bad mistake, throwing her over for someone else, but she had forgiven him, and she was going to fix that for him. She was going to get him out of a bad marriage – well, it was bad in her eyes, and then they would live in wedded bliss forever.

That was her plan, and so far it was working. Soon the hard part would start, and she had to be ready. Until she could find the perfect opportunity to carry out her nefarious scheme, she felt that she might as well keep scamming the cheating husbands. She loved excitement, and what could be more fun and exciting than tricking some bozo, who was hoping to cheat on his unsuspecting wife! The money was good too, and what girl couldn't use a little extra cash!

These thoughts were all running through her head, as she tried to find Dan's money.

She was just extricating the wad of bills, when she heard a noise at the hotel door.

Oh God, surely it wasn't Dan creeping around. Was he trying to get out to call for help? No, that was impossible. She had given him plenty of the Rohypnol. He was out cold. Well, if it wasn't Dan, then who was it?

Could the night maid be coming in to change the towels, or put chocolates on the pillows?

What the hell was she going to do? Her heart was beating so rapidly that it was hard to breathe. She felt as if there was a small bird caught in her chest, flapping its wings hysterically.

At least she had closed the bathroom door. That was one piece of luck for her side. Listening carefully, she heard a woman's voice say, "I've caught you this time, you cheating bastard. Get up and face me like a man. Trouble is, you're not a man are you? You're nothing but a cockroach! Come on, Dan. You can't fool me, I know you're awake."

Shoot! It must be Dan's wife! Who else would sound so angry?

Angel heard the woman – whoever she was, slam the outside door, and hurry past the bathroom, as she approached the bed.

"Dan, I can't believe you'd do this to me again. Where is she? Where's the tramp this time? She can't have gone far. I see she's left her red hooker shoes and her silver purse behind! Well, she won't get very far without them."

Angel's heart sank. Had she really left her shoes and her purse in the bedroom? Shit! How was she going to get out of here? She couldn't very well waltz out of the bathroom, hurry over to the chair and say "excuse me, I think these are mine." Things could turn nasty pretty quickly.

She'd simply have to make a run for it in her stocking feet. Damn it! She hated to leave her good luck silver purse behind, and those gorgeous red shoes had cost her a fortune!

Angel Baby realized with disgust that tonight she had picked the wrong man and the wrong time. The bad smell emanating from him, should have been her warning. This was turning into a fiasco.

Dan's wife Clara, had been suspicious of him for some time. More than once, he had come home smelling of perfume, always a little drunk, and a little sheepish. She didn't think that he had a mistress, because these occasions were too far apart. He was just a silly, pathetic, middle-aged man, looking for a little occasional excitement in his otherwise dull life.

She didn't think he could handle much more sex than he was getting at home, but apparently her foolish husband thought he could. Men were such dreamers!

Clara sat home and watched movies all day and most nights. She loved the ones in which the wronged wife took her revenge – sometimes on the woman, but usually on the husband. She had seen movies in which the wronged wife had stabbed him, shot him, burned him to a crisp, framed him for murder, and even one in which the wife had pushed her errant husband off a cliff.

She wasn't ready to do any of these things, because, if the sad truth were known, Clara still loved Dan. He wasn't much, but he made a good living, and he was good to her and the kids.

Maybe if she could take off a few pounds – well, maybe 50 or so, she could find herself a boyfriend and do a "tit for tat" sort of thing. That wasn't too likely though, and she knew it. She thought about it every night, as she tore open another bag of chips, or opened another box of chocolates. Dan was hers, and all she really wanted, was to bring him home, and make him promise never to stray again.

Tonight, however, she was too angry to think straight. She had been hoping that she would find that Dan was totally innocent. She hoped that maybe he had been telling the truth, when he called and said that he was just too tired to make the long drive home. He claimed that the traffic was heavy, and it was a blustery winter night.

He told her he had taken a room to get a good night's sleep, because he had another important meeting early in the morning. Far-fetched – yes – but that would have been so nice, and so acceptable, if it had been true.

Instead, she had found all the evidence she needed. The purse and those awful red hooker shoes told the tale. They made her want to punch him, and that was exactly what she did.

Leaning over, she began shaking him, and yelling obscenities. She was using words she hadn't realized were even in her vocabulary. Then, looking over her shoulder for a glass of water she could throw at him, she saw those damn red shoes again. Somehow they seemed to be mocking her.

She looked down at the tired, scuffed old winter boots she was wearing, and something snapped. With a sob of despair and anger, she pulled back her fist, and smacked dear Danny boy as hard as she could, right on his drunken face.

Because of the ruckus she was making, sobbing and shrieking and punching all at the same time, she didn't hear the noise of the hotel room door closing, as Angel Baby made her escape.

Chapter Five

While Angel Baby was enduring her misadventures in Toronto, Kate and Mac were enjoying the rest of their stay at their EBR condo, totally unaware that a tornado was building up in their lives.

They had started their day with breakfast at Oceans. The skies were blue, the gulf was calm, and there were several couples walking the beach, holding hands, as seniors love to do. It was a scene right out of a travel magazine.

After breakfast, they had headed up Front Beach Rd to Pier Park. Starting at the entrance, they had slowly walked along the colourful streets, wandering into every quaint shop along the way. They had stopped at the fudge shop to bring home treats for the kids, as well as some for themselves.

Kate had tried on several tops in some of the boutiques, and had bought herself two colourful ones because they were "cute" – not because she needed them. "After all," she grinned at Mac, "you can't come to Florida without buying at least one new piece of clothing to bring home."

Eventually they stopped at Margaritaville to sit on the deck, do more people watching, and enjoy a cool drink, before heading back to the condo. They certainly didn't need any more food, but the ambiance at the popular restaurant was fun, and the view was great.

Now, an hour or so later, they made their way down to the exotic Lagoon pool. It wasn't long before Mac wandered into Oceans to get them a couple of fancy drinks. They were taking good advantage of their last day of vacation. Kate had most of their clothes and things packed, so that they could enjoy every last moment of this short little holiday.

She looked up from her book, which wasn't exactly captivating, and gazed around.

Although she was sitting in the shade beside the pool, there were several people basking in the sun on the pool deck. For January in the Florida panhandle, it was a surprisingly warm day, a bonus of sorts, before they had to head north again.

Every once in a while, a cool little breeze would ripple past, disturbing the palm trees sufficiently to cause their fronds to twist and twirl like cancan dancers shaking their ruffles.

Visions of the kids and cats at home caused Kate to grin. This had been a fun week, but she would be glad to be home with her family.

Just as she picked up her book again, a woman sat on the lounge next to her, and accidentally upturned her large beach bag. Several items escaped and rolled around the concrete under Kate's lounge chair.

"Damn, what a klutz I am today," exclaimed the gal, smiling at Kate, who somewhat reluctantly stood up and moved her chaise a bit, so that all the errant treasures could be retrieved.

After lotion, sunglasses, a paperback novel, and a bag of chips, were tucked back safely into the seemingly bottomless beach bag, the women began to chat.

"You look familiar to me," remarked the self proclaimed klutz. "I'm Sandy Jarvis from Toronto. Have we met?"

"No, I don't think so," replied Kate.

"I'm Kate Chandler, and I'm from Toronto too, but I'm pretty sure I don't know you."

"Kate Chandler" squealed her new companion.

"Of course, you're the author and illustrator of those wonderful kids' books. Oh, my girls adore your books – specially the latest one. They're absolutely in love with Shadow, and have actually been campaigning for us to take them down to that little island, to see if we could spot him! Your illustrations are so perfect. They make him come alive."

Kate couldn't get a word in, so she just sat there quietly, while the woman continued her excited rant.

"I can't believe I'm actually talking with you. Oh, it would be so perfect if I could have my picture taken with you to take home to my kids. Otherwise they'll never believe me."

Kate laughed good-naturedly, and thought to herself that the woman's name should be Chatty Cathy rather than Sandy. Being in a good mood, however, she graciously agreed to a picture.

"My husband Charlie is in Oceans getting us a couple of margaritas," explained Sandy.

"I think he's got the camera in his pocket."

"That's funny. My husband Mac is in there getting us a couple of rum swizzles. Come to think of it, though, I wonder whether he's forgotten all about me. He may have met someone in there and is chatting at the bar. Mac makes friends wherever he goes."

"Isn't this a gorgeous place? We've never been here before," said Sandy, putting on her sunglasses, "but friends of ours were down last year, and were raving about the Edgewater Beach Resort in Panama City Beach. I had never even heard about this area, so we decided to take their advice and come down for a week.

"We usually go to Key West, which is such a fun place. We haven't been disappointed here though. We just can't get over the glorious beaches. Charlie and I have been walking down to Pineapple Willy's every morning before breakfast, and I'll tell you it really works up an appetite! All I've done since we got here is eat!"

"Well, we certainly haven't been that ambitious, although we always say that we're going to go walking before breakfast. In other words, we have good intentions, but bad follow through." Kate grinned ruefully.

"Two years ago, we spent an entire twelve months living here, and it certainly isn't difficult to get used to it. Still, I know I'd miss Toronto and Muskoka in the summer. There's no place on earth more beautiful than Muskoka, but I guess I'm prejudiced. We've just bought a cottage up there."

Sandy was nodding her head, but didn't really seem to be listening. Suddenly, staring at Kate, and pointing a finger at her, she cried, "Wait a minute. You're not only the writer and illustrator, you're the gal who had that terrible experience a couple of years ago. You're the one who was kidnapped, and left to die on that deserted island, aren't you?"

Kate had become accustomed to people recognizing her, and being fascinated by her "adventure," so she didn't take offence. She knew all too well what a really interesting story it was.

"Yes, I'm the gal. I'm very lucky to be sitting here today, and I know it. I thank God every day for being back with my family."

"It must have been hell on wheels for you," said Sandy sympathetically.

"Does it bother you to talk about it?"

"No, actually it doesn't. I realize how intriguing it is to people, and when I talk about it, it's as if it happened to someone else. Maybe that's crazy, but that's how it feels. I can't even imagine now, how I made it through some of the things that happened to me."

"How did your family cope while you were missing?"

"As far as I can understand, Mac and the kids were great. I'm so proud of them. They put out flyers, co-operated with the police, did a lot of actual searching themselves, did television spots to keep the public aware of the situation, and were just marvelous. I'm blessed with a wonderful family."

"I can't imagine being all alone on a little island, never knowing when my captor might come back, or whether he was coming back at all, or what he would do to me when he did reappear. I would have been totally paralyzed with fear. My imagination is too colourful for my own good. How did you manage to keep going day after day?"

Kate gazed off toward the shimmering gulf waters for a moment. How had she managed to keep going?

"Well, to begin with, I'm pretty strong-willed. I was torn between my anger at the monster who took me away from my family, and my determination to get back to them. I never really let myself think for a moment that I wouldn't make it. I had an extraordinary husband and three great kids waiting for me, and I couldn't let them down.

"Also, I prayed a lot, and most of the time I felt as if God wasn't too far away. There were times, though, when I would give in to a little despair and self-pity, but I forced myself to keep going.

"Sometimes I even pretended that I was on that "Survivor" program, and that there were television cameras following me around. You'd be surprised how helpful that was. It smartened me up in a hurry, whenever I started feeling sorry for myself. I'd just tell myself that this was a "made for television" movie, and I had to make it entertaining and realistic. It certainly wasn't difficult to make it realistic," she laughed.

Sandy was about to ask something else, but Kate interrupted, "Oh, here come the guys now with our drinks. At least I assume that's your Charlie. I guess they must have met at the bar. Sorry we didn't have more time to chat. I don't mind answering questions, because it really is a pretty good story, and I like stories with happy endings."

"Well, I think you should be writing a book, so that people could read about everything that you endured. It would be a best seller for sure."

"Funny you should say that. There are two publishers who have both suggested that I write a book, and I'm in the process of writing down every last thing I can remember about those awful days. That's why I don't mind talking about it.

"Actually I wish I had been able to put my hands on some paper and a pen while I was there. Then I could have kept a daily diary. It's amazing how much stuff I've forgotten, and how much I can remember, once I start talking and reminiscing.

"Luckily my kids are always hounding me with questions, so it keeps it fresh in my mind. It would have been super to have a camera with me, although I was so busy scrounging and foraging for food, and fighting the wildlife, that there wasn't much time for picture taking." She laughed at this, and shook her head. Sometimes it just didn't seem real to her.

After the two men returned with the drinks, the subject of Kate's hair-raising adventure was dropped, and they spent a fun-filled hour together. Sandy's husband Charlie, was not only good-looking in an outdoorsy sort of way, but he proved to be a funny man, with a quick wit and an infectious laugh. He was one of those people you just can't help liking.

"Are you going to karaoke tomorrow night?" asked Sandy, as they eventually prepared to head back up to their respective condos.

"No, we can't. We're flying home tomorrow."

"Oh really? Why aren't you staying until Saturday?"

"Well, there's a big fraternity reunion dance at the Royal York on Saturday night, and I wouldn't miss it for the world. The Royal York is my favourite hotel, and I haven't been there for a very long time.

"We'll be seeing lots of our old friends – frat brothers of Mac's, and it's going to be a great event. We've got a room booked, so that we can stay overnight. I'm really excited about it, but it means that we have to leave for home a day early."

"Lucky you. It sounds like a wonderful evening."

"I guess we'll be going to karaoke anyway, in spite of what Charlie says."

Charlie interrupted. "I've never been able to get enthusiastic about karaoke. It always seems to be obnoxious people with horrible voices. There's nothing worse than someone who's been drinking too much, and who thinks that he or she can actually sing."

Kate couldn't help grinning. "I know what you mean, but karaoke here at Oceans isn't much like that. We went a few times the winter we lived here. It's mostly snowbirds, and some of them have excellent voices. I've only once seen a drunk get up there, and he was a spring breaker, so he doesn't count. It's actually a nice way to put in an evening. If we hadn't been flying home, we'd be going for sure.

"There's a bonus too, when you go to karaoke. The chap who runs it so well, who's name is Paul, has the most beautiful voice you'll ever hear. He's got an incredible range. I'd be happy to just listen to him all night, and forget the others."

"Oh, will he be here this week?" Sandy looked enthusiastic.

"Yes, I imagine so. He's here almost every Friday night during the winter months. I'm sorry that we're missing him this trip. He's a very interesting man, and so patient with the seniors. I'm sure you'll enjoy him, and if you get the chance, please tell him that Kate says 'Hi.'"

"Oh, I will. We'll definitely go, now that we know about Paul, and we'll be sure to speak to him.

"I've made Charlie promise not to get up and sing. That would be going too far." Sandy grimaced at Kate and Mac, and shook her head.

"In our wedding vows Charlie promised he would never sing in public."

They all laughed at that, and Charlie good-naturedly said he would be quiet, and not even hum along.

To satisfy his wife, he took a few pictures of the two women together, and after saying their good-byes, they finally went their separate ways.

Kate had just a few more things to organize and to pack. She was strangely ambivalent, however, about going home. She missed the kids and her life in Toronto, but it was cold and snowy at home, and the sun always seemed to be shining here in PCB.

If it hadn't been for the big dance at the Royal York, she would have been very reluctant to leave.

Somewhere in the back of her mind, she was waiting for the other shoe to fall. Life had been almost too good since her miraculous return from "the great adventure." It just seemed almost inevitable that something else equally bad, was waiting for her.

Little did she know just how soon her fears would come to fruition.

Chapter Six

Angel Baby slipped out of the hotel room, and sprinted down the hall in her bare feet. Well, she was wearing sheer black nylons, but she might as well have been in bare feet, for all the protection the stockings gave her.

One good thing, was that she could run much faster down the stairs, without the encumbrance of those beautiful red "throw me down and hurt me" stiletto shoes. Damn, she hated to lose those shoes. She had bought them in Montreal, and wore them every time she went out "trick or treating."

She had come to think of them as her lucky shoes, and now they were gone. Maybe Dan's angry wife would take them home and keep them – wearing them occasionally as a reminder to Dan of his transgressions. No, she likely had big feet and chunky legs. Still, she might keep them in an obvious place, just to tease and shame her wayward husband.

Actually, Angel Baby couldn't help grinning, as she thought about her shoes. If she ever caught a husband or boyfriend cheating, she would likely put those beautiful red shoes on his pillow every damn night, just to remind him that two could play that game! Angel Baby didn't have a single forgiving bone in her body. She pretty well ran on the fuel of revenge.

Reaching the main floor, she had to stop and catch her breath. Closing her eyes, she tried to picture the layout. She was pretty sure that there was an outside door just a short way down the hall from the stairwell. She had checked it out when she first came in to the hotel, but she was so flustered at the moment that her mind felt wobbly. She had to really concentrate, because she could barely remember where she was.

Peeking out, she saw with relief that there was indeed an outside door just a few steps away. She wouldn't have to go through the main lobby at all. No need to draw attention to herself. At least she had her silver top on when she was trapped in the bathroom. Thank goodness for that. It would have been really difficult to be running around in just her bra and skirt! Not very easy to be anonymous that way!

A blast of freezing cold air hit her as soon as she opened the door a crack. This was not going to be easy!

In spite of her fears, it took only three minutes before she was able to flag down a cab. The driver was wearing a turban, and she hoped that maybe he wouldn't be able to speak much English. That way she could avoid any questions he might have, about her lack of a coat and shoes, and he wouldn't be able to tell the police much about her.

She gave him the name of her hotel, then sat back to catch her breath.

Suddenly she groaned, and sat up straight. How was she going to pay the cab driver? Her money was in her silver purse, and her silver purse was still in Dan's room. His cranky wife would undoubtedly take that too. Shit, shit and double shit! This little adventure was turning into an unmitigated disaster.

Calming herself, she remembered the little pocket sewn inside her panties. She always carried a couple of bills in that pocket – just in case. This was the first time she would have to use it, but she was very grateful for her foresight.

She had laughed at herself when she had sewed a tiny pocket into several pair of lacy panties, feeling sure that she would never need this "mad money." Well, tonight was certainly a "just in case" situation, and things couldn't get any more "mad" than they were at this moment.

Unfortunately she would have to pull up her skirt, and dig into the panties to retrieve the money. How was she going to do that without the driver seeing her? Oh well, who cared? Why not give the guy a thrill?

Squirming around, she managed to hike her skin-tight skirt, and get her fingers on the money. All the time she kept her eyes on the rear view mirror, and she could see the driver watching her with amazement, and a slightly lecherous, but guilty look. He obviously couldn't believe what he was seeing, or what he was hoping to see!

So much for trying to be inconspicuous! She was definitely going to have to get out of town quickly. She had overstayed her welcome in good old Toronto!

Not liking the idea of returning through the well-lit lobby in bare feet, and no coat or jacket, she asked the driver to take her around the block to a side door. At her request, he waited while she tried the door. To her relief, it was open, and giving him a little nod, she got herself inside and out of the cold.

The side door did not open directly into the lobby, so she was able to slip down the hall, and get into an elevator without being noticed. Thank the Lord for small mercies. She was going to be okay after all.

That calming thought changed in a hurry, however, when she reached the door of her hotel room and realized that she had NO KEY! Her room key was in that damned silver purse which was sitting in that damned room – likely about to be taken home by Dan's damned wife!

What now? "Stay calm, Angel Baby," she told herself. "Stay calm and think!"

Hopefully, she looked up and down the hall, thinking there might possibly be a late night chamber maid, turning down beds or bringing extra towels. If so, Angel could easily charm her into opening the door to Angel's room.

No such luck. The hall at the moment was totally empty, except for one bedraggled, cold, barefoot, desperate gal. There was no choice, but to go down to the lobby desk, and ask for another key.

She couldn't face taking a lot of stairs again, so she boldly stepped into the elevator and headed down. What the hell! Let them stare at her bare feet. Who cared?

She scanned the front desk before approaching it, and was relieved to see that there was only one clerk, and he looked to be quite young. Good. She could always manipulate the young ones.

What she didn't like, was that he was watching her, as she made her way toward him. He was staring at her shoeless feet with a puzzled expression.

Putting a frightened little smile on her face, she asked in a tiny voice, "Could I possibly have an extra key to my room? You won't believe what just happened to me. I was mugged, and the beast took my fur jacket and my purse, and even my shoes!"

Of course there had been no fur jacket, but she thought that was a nice added touch.

She managed to squeeze out a couple of tears as she continued.

"I'm so cold, and my feet are frozen. I just need to get into my room and have a nice hot shower."

"Do you want me to call the police?" asked the anxious young man, totally taken in by her good looks and her sad situation.

"No thank you. I'll do that the minute I get into my room." She gave a very good imitation of a woman shivering with cold (although her shivering was mostly from excitement), and the clerk hastily handed over the extra key.

"Call me if you need anything," he suggested hopefully, as he watched her head back to the elevators.

She was so beautiful – just like a movie star, he thought. His mind immediately turned to his favourite movie – "The Graduate." Suddenly he was Dustin Hoffman, and she was the luscious Mrs. Robinson. In his mind's eye, he was just watching her begin to undress, when his supervisor came out from the office, and asked what was happening.

The nervous clerk assured his boss that it had been a very quiet evening, and that nothing unusual had happened. For some reason, he just didn't want to tell about her. He had an annoying little suspicion that the gorgeous gal was up to something, but he couldn't quite figure what it could be.

Angel Baby was in the lovely hot shower when she began to giggle. How ridiculous the entire evening had been. She had experienced a little voice, which told her that she shouldn't go up to the room with Dan, but she had foolishly ignored it.

As the hot water cascaded over her body, she finally began to relax, and let her mind wander. She forgot all about Dan and his silly wife. The panicky run through the hotel in stocking feet, the crazy taxi ride, the pimply young desk clerk – all were forgotten. Suddenly she was back in Switzerland where this new chapter of her life had begun.

How happy she had been, until right near the end of her stay. She had gone there with the express purpose of having her face changed, so that no one would ever be able to recognize her, and drag her back to that awful hospital. She would have to win Mac's love all over again. She would never tell him who she really was, but she knew that she could make him love her just as she had done before, and they would be happy forever and ever.

That had been the plan. After months of many surgeries and painful recoveries, however, that plan had begun to fade. Her doctor,

Patrick O'Neal, had made her forget Mac, at least for a while. He was tall, with black curly hair, sparkling blue eyes and a mischievous grin. He was gorgeous, and so charmingly Irish.

At first he had been very much against doing all the changes she requested. She was good looking just as she was. Angel was determined, though, and could be very persuasive. Gradually he began to fall in love with her, as he made the drastic changes she wanted. She had become his Galatea, and he was her Pygmalion.

Somehow she had managed to put Mac aside in a separate compartment of her heart. Her focus then was on Patrick. Unfortunately he was married, and had two little girls. She hated the wife and children with a passion, even though she had never met them.

She knew that if only she could get Patrick to leave them, then she could be happy living in Europe forever. She became obsessed with this talented, caring, beautiful man, and her entire focus was on making him love her.

Dr. Patrick O'Neal was a happily married man. He was happy with all the money he had, and with the beautiful life he led. He wasn't looking for an affair, and was really blindsided by "Angel Baby," as she called herself.

He didn't know anything about her past, except what she chose to tell him, and what she told him was that she was being stalked by an evil man, who wanted to kill her, or lock her away forever.

Before he really understood what was happening, he had put her into a lovely condo, showered her with gifts, and was leading a double life. He couldn't help himself. He was totally smitten with this beautiful woman.

The fact that he had created her with his own two skilled hands, somehow made him love her, even though he didn't want to. Well, maybe it wasn't actually love, but he was certainly smitten, even infatuated. For the first time in his marriage, he was able to set aside his wife and children, and let himself go a little bit crazy over this charming and mysterious creature.

It was not until she began insisting that he leave his wife and kids, and devote himself to her, that Patrick realized what a mess he had made of things. There was no way he ever intended to leave Madelaine, or Lainey, as he called her. The very thought of leaving the children was abhorrent, and he began to see that he couldn't continue with the affair.

Cracks were showing in Angel Baby's personality, too, and he finally suspected that there was something seriously wrong with her. He had been blind and stupid, but now he understood.

One afternoon Angel had confronted him in his office, giving him an ultimatum. This was it. He had to leave his wife and children for good, or else.

Patrick was surprised, but he didn't hesitate. He told her the truth. There was no way that he would ever leave his family for her. He was leaving the next day for a skiing vacation with Lainey and the girls, so this was "good-bye."

Although she looked angry at first, she soon seemed to accept his response with great calm. That should have set off warning bells, but he had been relieved at her apparent acceptance, and had gone off with his family, with a false sense of well being.

There was so much more to the story, and Angel was still in the hot shower, reliving those wonderful days in Switzerland. Suddenly, however, something snapped in her head. She could almost hear the pop, and she shook her head to clear it. This was happening with more frequency, and she wondered with dread, whether she was once again slowly but surely losing her grip on reality.

She turned off the shower, and stood there, frozen in time. She almost choked as reality came rushing at her. Trying to put the Switzerland memories behind her, she stepped out and reached for a towel. Shaking her head again, this time in bewilderment, she asked herself whether all those lovely memories had really happened, or whether it had all been a dream.

Was Patrick real, or simply a figment of her overactive imagination? Had they gone skiing in the Alps? Had they made love in front of a roaring fire? Had they sipped hot chocolate at a little café, with a noisy cuckoo clock on the wall? Had she ever even been in Switzerland? Right now she wasn't sure.

What she was sure of, was that she was in some sort of serious trouble. What exactly was in the silver purse which she had been forced to leave behind? Well, there was her lipstick, a tissue, some money, and the bottle with the date rape drug.

The bottles were all unlabelled, though, and she had brought them from Switzerland, stolen from Patrick's office. This one would be untraceable, still, it could have her finger prints on it, and she was certainly on file somewhere. That was bad – really bad. She had to get through this without leaving any trace of herself.

Then, to make matters worse, she remembered the hotel key. Oh shit!!! Could the police trace her through the key? It was one of those little electronic cards, but did it have the name of the hotel on it? She didn't think so, but couldn't be sure. Where had she put the duplicate? Did the police have some way of tracing those cards? Yes, likely.

She had to get out of here – right now. They could already be on their way. Dan's angry wife had likely called them, when she realized that Dan had been drugged.

Not even bothering to dry herself properly, she raced into the bedroom and grabbed some clothes. Her jacket was back in Dan's room, and she had no other winter clothing with her. Well, a turtle-neck and a pullover with a pair of jeans would have to do. Did she have time to pack the rest of her things? No, absolutely not.

Grabbing her big tote bag, she stuffed it with anything she thought might be traceable to her, grabbed her stash of money, slipped into a pair of flat shoes, and, taking one last look around the room, she headed out into the cold.

Once again Angel Baby was on the run!

Chapter Seven

The flight from Panama City Beach to Atlanta was uneventful. Mac read, while Kate did some rough sketches for her next book.

Once they landed in Atlanta, they had only 25 minutes to catch their connecting flight. As they were hurrying along the concourse, they heard a woman begin screeching behind them.

Turning in unison, they saw an elderly woman picking herself up off the floor, pointing and screaming, "Stop him, stop him, he's got my purse."

Heading right towards them, was a 250 pound man, who could have been a player for any football team. He was running full tilt, looking neither right nor left.

Mac casually stuck out his foot just as the thief was passing them. The fellow fell flat on his face, like the proverbial ton of bricks. He fell so hard that he lost his breath momentarily, and blood squirted out of his broken nose. It was like a scene from a slapstick comedy.

In a total daze, he tried to stand up, but two travelers, a tall, skinny fellow, and a woman in an army uniform, pounced on him, and held him down until security guards arrived to cuff him. In all the melee, he had clung tightly to the old lady's purse.

While he was being put in cuffs, the irate woman grabbed her purse from him, and managed to give him two good kicks on the leg, before he was dragged away. She might have been old, but she was feisty.

Kate and Mac had no time to lose if they were going to catch their connecting flight. Mac grabbed his wife's arm, and dragged her along. She came reluctantly, for the moment, much more interested in watching the little scene play itself out. They were well settled on the plane, before they actually began to laugh at the ridiculous scenario which they had just witnessed.

"Did you see how hard he fell?" asked Kate with a grin.

"I thought you might have killed him. He likely cracked the floor."

"I'm lucky he didn't snap off my leg," chortled Mac.

"What a bruiser he was, but he was no match for that supposedly sweet little old lady. She got in a couple of good kicks."

"Good for her. Hopefully he'll think twice before attacking another elderly person. Some of them can be pretty spunky."

Shortly before their flight landed at Pearson International in Toronto, Mac asked, "Did I tell you about the golfer I met in the pro shop the other day?"

"No, I don't think so. Why?"

"Well, he told me an interesting little tale. He used to play at the Tyndall golf club before it was closed, and apparently one day he and his partner saw a cougar come charging out of the bush, chasing a squirrel. They were absolutely amazed, because they didn't think there were cougars or panthers that far north in Florida. Anyway, the cougar chased the squirrel right up a tall pine tree. Then the squirrel leaped over to another tree, and sat chattering at the cougar, who found himself stranded at the very top of the old pine.

"Apparently the cougar didn't fancy trying to make the same leap as the squirrel, or maybe he realized that the squirrel was just too fast for him. He looked down, saw how far up he had come, and very slowly and carefully made his way back down.

"As soon as they saw him coming down the tree, the golfer and his pal took off in their golf cart. They were scared that he might attack them!"

"I can hardly believe that," said Kate, shaking her head. "I didn't think there were any cougars in the Panama City area. Coyotes – yes, but cougars – I don't know. You never read anything about them in the newspaper."

There really wasn't time to debate the point, as the seat belt sign had come on, and they were beginning to make their descent.

After retrieving their luggage, and setting off in the airport limo, they were amazed at the piles of snow along the highway.

"Yep, it's been snowing all day," said the limo driver.

"Just stopped about an hour ago. We've had snow every day this week. You were darn lucky to be in Florida, and we were lucky that they were able to keep the runways cleared. Supposed to be getting more in the next few days too," he added glumly.

"You know, our kids kept us up to date on all the snow, and we knew that the schools had been closed for a couple of days, but I just hadn't pictured this much piled along the highway," Kate muttered in disbelief.

As the limousine approached their home, she exclaimed at how beautiful the house and yard looked. Jill and the kids had all the lights on, both inside and out. The lights gleaming on the pristine snow, had created a picturesque tableau. There were times when Canada was just too beautiful to be believed.

The boughs of the elegant fir trees were bent low with snow. They looked as if they were Southern belles, who had traded their summer green frocks for winter white. Kate had such an artist's eye, and the imagination to go with it, that she could picture them dancing at a cotillion. She wondered whether she could work a picture like this into her next book.

Of course the homecoming was a loud and joyful event. Davey and the twins, Peter and Paige, were trying to tell them about everything that had happened while they were away. The three cats, Tom, Dick and Harriet, were purring like motorboats, and winding themselves round and round their ankles. Jill was standing aside, grinning happily.

Jill had been Kate's best friend and confidante since their kindergarten days. Actually, the two young girls had been on a trip to Europe, when they met Mac, and the three of them had shared some wonderful adventures before coming back to Canada.

Over a delicious pot roast with hot crusty bread, Mac and Kate heard of all the "goings on" which had taken place in the past eight days. They, in turn, told of their vacation highlights, thrilling everyone with the tale of the rabid coyote.

Eventually the dishes were done, the kids were tucked in, and the three adults sat in front of the fireplace, to enjoy a drink before bedtime. Jill was staying the night, so one drink morphed into two, as they sat reminiscing about various holidays they had shared over the years.

Just before saying goodnight, Jill remembered something. "Kate, there've been a couple of strange phone calls. A woman rang twice asking for you, but she wouldn't leave her name. I said that you weren't here at the moment, but that I would be glad to take a message for you. She tried to pump me for info as to where you were, and when you would be back, but I played dumb, and didn't tell her anything.

"Then your publisher phoned, and said that some woman had called them a couple of times, looking for you. I guess someone there did tell her that you were away on vacation in PCB, and that you'd be home this weekend. I'm assuming it was one of your fans."

She didn't want to mention that the thought had occurred to her, that it could be Kate's former stalker and would-be killer, Madison Ramsay. She knew that Madison was supposedly safely locked away in a psychiatric hospital in British Columbia. Still, patients were sometimes released, or managed to escape, and Jill was definitely scared of Madison. She had stalked Kate and Mac for a long time after they were married, and she had been on her way to kill Kate, just before Kate was finally rescued in the Everglades.

Jill tended to be a pessimist, and had the life-long belief that if things could go wrong, they usually would. She could never quite forgive herself for not being with Kate in the Everglades, even though she hadn't even been in the country at the time of the abduction. She just hated the thought of Kate being there so alone and so vulnerable.

Now she didn't want to say Madison's name, but an ugly little fear kept niggling away at the back of her mind.

Trying to appear casual, Jill asked, "Have you ever heard any more about Madison since she was locked away in that old hospital?"

"No, thank God," replied Mac.

"The authorities promised to let us know if and when she's ever released. Of course, officials can screw up just like anyone else, so I guess she could finally get out, and we wouldn't know it. I don't think that will be any time soon, though. Poor woman. She's a real nut case. She apparently had quite a break-down after the Everglades incident. They won't be letting her out for a long, long time."

Jill was somewhat reassured to hear that, but there was still a nagging doubt in her mind. She wondered whether Mac was just trying to persuade himself that he and Kate were now safe from Maddy.

She decided that it wouldn't be a bad idea to maybe call the old hospital, and make sure that she was still safely tucked away there. For now, however, she wouldn't say anything. They seemed so happy these days, and they deserved that happiness after the terrible nightmare they had endured, when Kate had been kidnapped.

Finally the three friends said their good-nights. Both Kate and Mac hugged Jill again, and thanked her for taking such good care of the kids, the cats, and the house. Doors were locked, the alarm was set, the lights were turned off, and silence reigned in the Chandler home.

Jill, however, tossed and turned, unable to rid her mind of troubling thoughts.

Chapter Eight

The tall man with the curly black hair and flashing blue eyes, hurried through the Toronto airport. There was a look of sheer grim determination on his face. Sadly, it replaced the usual mischievous, happy-go-lucky grin, with which he met the world.

Dr. Patrick O'Neal was on a mission, and nothing would deter him until it was completed. Was he an avenger, seeking retribution for the crimes which had been perpetrated on him, or, was he an angel of mercy, trying to stop a crime before it happened? He decided that he was a little bit of both.

Although he had always hoped and planned to come to Canada some day, he hadn't expected that it would be under these special circumstances.

His return from the family vacation in Spain, had been shocking.

After his first feelings of rage, a profound sadness and sense of devastation had covered him like a heavy blanket. What he wanted to do, was look into Angel's lovely eyes, and simply ask "why?"

Eventually, as his life fell apart, thanks to her, and he realized the extent of the damage she had done, he knew that he would have to see her at some point. He had to make her look into his face, and explain her vindictiveness. She had to account for her wickedness. After all he had done for her, he needed some answers.

The idea of saving Kate had come later.

He had been searching for months now, and during those long, lonely days and nights, he had plenty of time to speculate about ways to exact revenge on the redoubtable Angel Baby.

His initial flood of anger, and need for revenge, knew no bounds. Common sense, however, gradually kicked in, and he realized that no matter how much time he spent contemplating clever and satisfying ways to kill her, the bottom line was that he was still a doctor, a man dedicated to saving lives, not taking them.

He might occasionally spend some time speculating about the gratification of strangling, or shooting, or stabbing, or poisoning, but when push came to shove, he just couldn't do it.

The return to his home that dreadful Sunday, had marked the beginning of the end of his life, as he had known it. Everything had blown up in his face.

Before leaving on vacation with Lainey and the two girls, the unfortunate affair with Angel Baby had come to a screeching halt. For some weeks he had been noticing a gradual but definite change in Angel's personality.

There had been cracks appearing in her carefully built façade. Every once in a while her mind seemed to slip a cog or two. He put it down to the pain and fear which she had suffered, during the many operations she had demanded over the past two years.

It was a long story, and a bad one, because at the end of the torrid affair, Patrick was left feeling extremely gullible and stupid. Mostly, however, after Angel had destroyed everything he loved, he felt a need for some form of revenge, and a new purpose in life.

He was so angry, so surprised, so hurt. How could she have done such a terrible thing? She had destroyed his clinic, his office, his marriage. They had loved each other. How could he have been so wrong about her?

Gradually a determined calm had set in. She couldn't be allowed to get away with the havoc she had caused. He had to find her, and get some answers. His thoughts hadn't really gone beyond that point.

Now, weeks later, after his head had cleared, he had done a lot of thinking on the long flight over the ocean.

He had begun to question this wild trip to Canada. What would he actually do when he found her? That was the burning question.

When Angel had first come to him, begging him to change her face completely, so that no one would ever recognize her, he had thought she was crazy. To consider cutting up that lovely, adorable face, had seemed a terrible desecration. Most of his patients came to him because they saw themselves as ugly or plain, or because they had always wanted to be truly beautiful. Here was a girl, however, who was already very good looking. Why try to improve on perfection?

Gradually, however, when he heard her story about the madman who had been stalking her relentlessly, with the declared intent to hurt and eventually kill her, he had been won over. It went against everything in which he believed as a doctor, but to all appearances this was a unique case. She seemed so terrified and so alone.

The good doctor was in the business of helping people, and he felt he had to help this poor girl, who apparently was all by herself in what could be a cold, cruel world.

It had taken months of surgeries and recuperations, before his patient was totally satisfied with the results, and in those months he had gradually and unknowingly fallen under her spell.

Angel Baby had seduced him very easily. She was charming and funny, waiflike in many ways. She was spontaneous and light-hearted, and somehow she made him feel like a god, - a god who had created perfection.

The doctor, who had been such a perfect husband – loving, generous, thoughtful, full of fun, had somehow lost his way. He had been bewitched and beguiled, and as he gazed with pride at the beauty he had created, he realized that he loved her.

She was the crowning achievement in his highly successful career, but it was as if he had walked willingly into a quagmire. He just kept being sucked in deeper and deeper, until he was way over his head.

Patrick was a skilled and caring doctor. He was also, (or at least he had been), a good husband and father, and he doted on his two little girls, Shannon and Maureen. Cheating on his wife had not even been a possibility or a consideration. That was until he fell under Angel Baby's spell.

Although he had helped many beautiful women over the years, doing face lifts, bust enhancements, tummy tucks etc., there had been no temptation to stray from the marital bed. He was never able to explain to himself or to Lainey, what it had been about Angel Baby that had enticed him.

The affair might have gone on indefinitely, until it burned itself out, but Angel made the mistake of challenging him with an ultimatum. One day she had come to his office in a feisty mood. She told him that it was time for him to make up his mind. He had to either leave his wife and kids for good, or else she was out the door.

The doctor had not seen this coming, and, although he was shocked, he was also a tiny bit relieved. True, he had been crazy about Angel, but she was beginning to wear a little thin.

All the intrigue, and secrecy, were becoming a nuisance, and they went against Patrick's natural disposition. He was an open, generous, friendly man. He had always been a family man. He had a multitude of friends, and an excellent reputation. It was the type of life most people dreamed of having.

All the hiding and furtiveness were becoming not only unpleasant, but just plain too much trouble. Besides, the idea of leaving Madelaine and the girls was preposterous, and he explained that to Angel. If he had to choose, he would always choose his family.

He called her bluff, and said the affair was over. He totally expected that she would crumple like an old tissue, and would pack her bags for Canada. Angel, however, surprised him.

After hearing his quick response, and seeing him actually laugh at her ultimatum, her face grew red, and she clenched her hands into fists. She looked around the room, as if searching for a weapon, and Patrick realized that he might be in danger. He was grateful that there was no scalpel near by.

She seemed to be having trouble breathing, and her eyes had darkened to a strange and scary black. Patrick stood up and actually backed away from her. She was like a firecracker about to explode.

Suddenly, however, she seemed to relax and become calm – too calm. She smiled at him sadly, and said that she understood.

He should have been suspicious of the abrupt change, but he was so relieved that she wasn't screaming or crying, and that she hadn't attacked him, that he didn't analyze her reaction. He just wanted to get her out of there as quickly as possible.

They eventually parted on what he thought were sad, but amicable terms, and he actually hugged her before she left. Then, with a relatively clear conscience, he departed with his family for their vacation in Spain.

Because he had never been unfaithful before, and because he had always been so dedicated to his work and his family, he had no idea what to expect from a discarded mistress. He was just thankful that Angel was taking it like a lady, and not making a fuss. Later he would look back and realize what a total idiot he had been.

The weekend he and his family returned from Spain, he faced complete, unmitigated disaster. Angel Baby was gone – disappeared. At the time, that was the good news.

Behind her, however, she had left such destruction, both emotional and physical, that his world simply collapsed. His clinic and the attached lab had been completely demolished. It was as if a bull-dozer had made its drunken way through the buildings. The chairs, cabinets, operating tables, recovery beds, had been hacked and sliced, till every bit of stuffing decorated the rooms like great gobs of snow.

Files had been ripped and scattered. In the lab, every beaker, test tube, jar and bottle had been either broken or stolen. There was glass everywhere, and noxious vapours hung in the air, clinging to the walls and counters. It must have taken hours for her to do such complete destruction. There was no doubt that it was the work of a mad woman – totally angry, totally crazy.

The physical damage was nothing, however, compared to the vicious letter which had been sent special delivery to his beloved Lainey. It was a malignant, malevolent letter full of vitriol, lies and madness. In it Angel had described the affair in great detail. She told of all the fun things they had done together, and of all the money he had spent on her. She graphically described their lovemaking, - enhancing the stories to the point that they sounded like pornographic movies.

She recounted what he had supposedly whispered to her, as he worked on her face, and made her "the most beautiful woman in the world," (at least in her mind). Worse still, she described all the plans (completely non-existent), which she and Patrick had made to "dump" Lainey and the girls, and leave them forever, as he and Angel made a new life far away from Switzerland.

Patrick's protestations were to no avail. After a day of weeping, shouting, and bitter recriminations, his beautiful Lainey had packed up the girls, and left for France. She had started divorce proceedings immediately, and with the malicious, splenetic letter as proof, she had been able to get full custody of the children.

Patrick's life as he had known it, was effectively over. After a short period of rage, and then depression, he had decided that for him, perhaps the best medicine would be revenge. He would spend every penny he had to find her. That was as far as he had really gone. The inchoate plan was to find her, talk with her, ask why she had done such a thing.

Oh, who was he kidding? At that point he still felt like strangling her with his bare hands! After that he didn't much care what happened.

He hired the best private investigators in Switzerland, New York, and Toronto, and the search began. If they couldn't find her, he would hire others. He had no intention of quitting until they either found her, or his money ran out. Because Angel had been in Switzerland under a false name, it had been more difficult and time consuming than expected, but knowing that she was from Canada had been a help. He felt that she would likely return to areas which she knew best.

After months of searching, one of his investigators had picked up her trail in Montreal, and had followed her to Hamilton and then Toronto. Once he was positive that he had the right woman, the retired detective contacted Patrick, and within hours the embittered, single-minded doctor was on a flight to Canada.

Dr. Patrick O'Neal had made Angel Baby into a very beautiful woman, just as she had requested. As a reward, she had ruined his life and everything he had loved. She owed him big time, and she was going to pay.

He had created her, and he told himself that he could just as easily destroy her!

The problem, of course, was that he hadn't really given much thought to what was meant by the term "destroy her." He just had the frantic, gut-wrenching feeling that he had to catch up with her. Somehow he had to make her pay. What would happen after that was still a blur.

Chapter Nine

Kate had been excited all day, thinking about the big dance that night. Her new dress, shoes and evening bag were all laid out carefully, and her little overnight bag was packed.

As usual, Jill, bless her heart, was staying over to be with the kids.

The two friends were having an afternoon cup of tea, when Jill said. "I wish I could find myself a decent man. I could be going to that dance tonight, if only I knew one of Mac's frat brothers. There might be one or two of them still available."

"Oh, Jill, maybe I should have tried to find you a date," laughed Kate.

"For a city this size, it's amazingly difficult to find an eligible guy."

"Tell me about it. I'm definitely not going on the internet to find someone. With my luck he'd be a serial killer for sure! I can't bring myself to go to bars, though. They were the big meeting places in the 80's and 90's, but that's not for me. I don't want a guy who hangs around bars all the time."

"I take it there's still no one at work who takes your fancy?" asked Kate, pouring more tea.

"There's no one at work, period. They're all married or way too young." Jill was an editor for one of the big book publishing houses in the city.

"Maybe I should go on a cruise, but you know you're always hearing stories of some single girl disappearing from a cruise ship. I don't think I'd want to take the chance. I don't suppose I could persuade you to go on a cruise with me?" she asked, only half kidding.

"If you get desperate enough, I definitely will. I promise. But then what would I do if you found yourself a guy, and wanted to spend all your time with him? I'd be wandering around like a lonely old lady."

They both giggled, and grinned at each other. These two were closer than sisters, and truly loved each other.

Jill's husband had been killed in a freak accident almost ten years previously. He had been hiking with two friends, when one of them was attacked by a black bear, who came out of the woods, with two cubs trailing behind her. The bear had attacked the nearest of the three men, and Jill's husband Seth, had tried to help his friend. The bear had turned on Seth, and with one powerful thrust of her claw, had ripped at his neck and head. Seth had bled to death before help could arrive.

It had taken Jill a long time to recover, but now she was ready for another romance, if only she could find a suitable guy.

That night, when Mac and Kate were ready to leave for the hotel, their kids and Jill all lined up to inspect them.

"You look like a princess, mom," said Davey admiringly.

"You do, mom," agreed Peter. "That dress is cool!"

Paige didn't say anything. She was thinking how nice she would look in that sea foam coloured dress. When would she ever be old enough to dress up like a princess, and go to the ball, she wondered. Her mom really did look good, but Paige just couldn't get the words out. She felt mad at the world these days, and she didn't know why.

"Have a wonderful time, you two, and be sure to get your pictures taken. Mac, it will be fun to see which of your frat brothers have gone bald, or fat, or doddery. You two will be the best looking couple there. Kate, don't let anyone step on those gorgeous silver shoes. I want to borrow them!"

On the way down in the car, Kate kept talking about the Royal York, and how she had always been fascinated by it.

"Did I ever tell you that I once wrote an essay about it?" she asked Mac.

"It was in high school English composition class. We had to do an essay about some building in Toronto which impressed us. Most of the kids chose Casa Loma, but I chose the Royal York.

"I went down to the hotel, and managed to talk one of the higher-up personnel into giving me a tour, and telling me about its history. It was terrific. I got an A+ for it. I likely still have it somewhere in a box in the basement. I should dig it out and see what I wrote.

"Anyway, it was a fun assignment, and I did a good job on it. I don't know what it is about the place, but it has always drawn me to it. Maybe I worked there in a previous life, or maybe I was murdered there!"

Mac snorted at that one.

"You're the craziest gal. You've got so many facets to your personality. I never stop discovering new things about you."

Kate just laughed and patted him on the arm. "I hope we get lucky and see the ghost tonight."

"The ghost?"

"Yep. There's supposed to be some guy who appears, and wanders around. I think it's on the 8th floor. He wears some type of a purple jacket, and he doesn't try to scare anyone, he just wanders."

"He's probably lost his room key," joked Mac.

"I just hope he doesn't wander into our room!"

Kate insisted on strolling through the enormous lobby before checking in. She looked at everything with great enjoyment. There was such a feeling of old world luxury, dignity, elegance, and refinement. There was a feeling of history there too.

The crystal chandeliers were just as she remembered them. The comfy chairs, huge four-faced clock, spiral type staircase – they were all there, just as Kate had remembered them.

As they made their way to their room, she muttered, "I wonder whether the old haunted Crystal Ballroom is still closed off to the public. Wouldn't it be great fun to get in to see it!"

"I don't think so," said Mac, shaking his head, as he unlocked the heavy door. "I seem to remember reading somewhere that at times they can hear music coming from the ballroom, even though it's been closed for years. I think it was closed because it didn't meet fire regulations. It would spook me to hear music coming from it. Wouldn't that scare you too?"

"I'm not sure," she laughed, "but I'd like to have the opportunity to find out!"

"Oh, this is lovely," she exclaimed, as she circled the room.

"We should have booked for two nights. I'll never get to see everything in the little time we have. I want to have a drink in that Library Bar, with its dark, intimate feeling, and I need to explore all the quaint little sitting areas with the beautiful antique furniture. Oh, Mac, thank you. This is so perfect!"

"You're easy to please, kiddo. We'll come down again for your birthday or our anniversary, and you can wallow in all the history and character!"

They soon found their table in the huge dining room, and had great fun trying to recognize many old school friends they hadn't seen for fifteen years. They had come from all parts of Canada for this big fraternity reunion.

The meal was exceptional, and Kate and Mac took the time to walk around the hotel some more, before the dancing began. Kate was in her glory, loving every moment of this trip down memory lane.

Meanwhile, a very beautiful woman in a ravishing dress, made her way unnoticed into the ballroom.

Angel Baby was good at stalking. She had stalked Mac and Kate when they were first married, and she had perfected her skills in her mind, while incarcerated in various psychiatric facilities over the years.

She had discovered, without much trouble, that the Chandlers were coming to this big fraternity reunion ball. It made her furious. She should have been going with Mac. After all, she knew many of his frat brothers. They had spent much of their time together, partying at the frat house. How awful that he was going with Kate! It hadn't taken her long to decide that she was going too.

Not only was she going to crash the party, but she was determined that she would dance with Mac at least once before the night was over.

After dinner, when people were milling around here and there, up and down the halls, it was supremely easy to slip in as one of the guests. Of course she didn't have a table at which she could sit, but she managed to look as if she belonged, as she wandered around the room, looking for Mac's table. Once she spotted it, she was able to keep an eye on them.

She grudgingly admitted that Kate looked beautiful tonight, but she felt confident that she looked even better.

When Mac finally made his way to the washroom, leaving Kate and their friends at the table, Angel made her move. She headed to the lady's lounge, and accosted Mac in the corridor.

"Hello, don't I know you? We met some place last year, didn't we? You're Mac Chandler, and your lovely wife's name is Kate.

"I never forget a handsome face, and yours is definitely unforgettable." Saying this, she made the little pouty-lipped smile which she knew was so attractive.

Mac looked puzzled. How did she know his name?

"I'm not sure that we've met," he said with a grin.

"I know I'd remember a lovely gal like you."

Oh what a line, thought Angel Baby.

What she said was, "Why, you silver-tongued rascal. You'll make me blush."

Mac couldn't help admiring her dress. It was black, high in front, and dipping right to her derriere in the back. The neck and cuffs were silver, embedded with flashing brilliants which looked like diamonds. She was a real knockout. He noticed too that she was wearing silver stiletto heels which must have been six inches high.

"Just give me a minute, and I'll remember where we met.

"I'm here without an escort tonight, and it's a huge disappointment. My boyfriend stood me up," she pouted.

"I had this great new dress to wear, and I just decided to come anyway. I don't suppose you'd like to do a lonely girl a favour, and give me one dance?"

She gave him another pouty, come-hither look, and Mac hesitated. He had no interest in dancing with her, but he was a gentleman, and she was charming, if a little too forward for his liking.

All men needed a little tweaking of their ego occasionally, and it was certainly flattering to Mac, that this gorgeous woman wanted to dance with him. Actually, how could he possibly refuse? He would appear churlish and gauche, if he walked away from her now.

Making a quick decision, and hoping that Kate wasn't looking, Mac gave her his thousand watt smile, and, taking her hand, they walked back into the ballroom.

Swallowing his doubts, he hoped that he would not live to regret it.

Chapter Ten

———·❦·——— ———·❦·——— ———·❦·———

The band was playing the "Theme From Picnic," and Angel snuggled right up close to Mac. It was so unbelievably wonderful to be back in his arms, after all these years. It was also such a kick to know that Mac had no idea who she really was.

"I guess if we're dancing, I should know your name," Mac said, trying, unsuccessfully, to put a little distance between their two bodies.

"Oh no, let's not do names. I'm only going to be in your life momentarily, unless something really strange happens, so let's just be two ships in the night."

"That's not fair. You know my name," replied Mac, intrigued in spite of himself.

"You can call me whatever you like. You pick a name which suits me." She smiled up at him, as she snuggled her head back against his chest.

Mac was trying to keep her dancing at the end of the ballroom, farthest from where Kate was sitting. His dance partner, however, seemed to be trying to drag him down right past his table. It was almost a battle of wills.

When the band had finished the "Theme From Picnic," they segued right into the old standard, "What are you Doing the Rest of My Life?" To Angel Baby it was prophetic. She could see the rest of her life being spent with Mac, and she absolutely had to dance this one with him. Mac, however, tried to break away.

"I really must get back to my wife. She'll wonder what's happened to me," he said, apologetically.

Angel Baby, however, wasn't going to relinquish him that easily. "Oh please dance this one with me, and then I'll be out of your life forever." (Not very likely, she thought to herself).

Mac reluctantly kept dancing, and was even more sorry when his partner said, "I hate being all alone like this. It was so awful of my boyfriend to let me down. You'd never let a girl down like that, or would you, Mac? Would you ever run off with some girl you just met, and leave your one true love behind?"

Mac was beginning to feel truly uncomfortable. Who was this beautiful woman, and what did she want? This dancing had been a mistake.

"Well I don't know your situation at all, so it's difficult to say. Was your boyfriend sick, or did he have to go out of town? What makes you think he went off with another woman?"

"Oh, I don't know, and I don't care. Let's not talk about him. He's a loser.

"By the way, is there any room at your table? I'd love to meet your wife."

That was it for Mac. This woman had to go. He couldn't afford to spend any more time with her, or she'd be asking him to take her home!

"No, I'm sorry, there really isn't any room, but it's been very nice having a dance with you. Can I escort you to your table?"

The music had stopped, and they were near the exit to the rest rooms.

"No, that's fine," she said crossly. "I can take care of myself."

Having said that, she reached up, gave him a rather lingering kiss on the cheek, and took off. He thought she had been aiming for his lips, but he had averted his head just in time.

Max stood there dumbfounded. "God I hope Kate didn't see that," he mumbled, as he hurried back to his table, never thinking that there might be some tell-tale lipstick on his cheek.

Kate had been watching her husband dancing with the stranger, and wondering who she could be. She was likely the girlfriend or wife of one of the fraternity brothers. Mac looked uncomfortable, though, as the woman snuggled right up to him.

She couldn't help grinning when she saw the long kiss on the cheek, and how flustered and annoyed Mac looked.

Kate couldn't wait to ask him who the redhead was, as she very carefully and deliberately wiped the lipstick from his cheek.

"I don't suppose you'd believe me if I told you that I don't know," he grinned, grabbing her hand.

"Come on, we have some dancing to do."

When the evening was over, Kate and Mac said their good-byes, then headed to the Library bar for a nightcap. Kate also insisted that they stroll around the lobby again, soaking in the elegance and beauty of the décor.

"This hotel is like a beautiful old dowager – graceful, tasteful, refined, full of history and old world ambiance. Just imagine the stories that have occurred here. I'm so glad you brought me tonight, Mac. I'll always cherish this evening, in spite of that little glitch, or should I say bitch!

"Now it's your turn to talk, and tell me who the heck that was. I couldn't see her face, but I loved her dress, and she certainly was clinging to you."

Mac just shook his head. "I thought she was going to molest me right on the dance floor. She was an excellent dancer, though. I got the feeling that she knew a secret which I didn't know, and she was getting a lot of fun out of it. Very bizarre!

"Anyway, she accosted me outside the men's room, and asked me to dance. I couldn't get out of it gracefully, so I danced! That's all there was to it. Just be glad I didn't bring her back to the table. She actually asked me if there was room for her to sit with us. I lied and said that unfortunately there wasn't."

"Well you sure know how to pick them, buddy. I loved her gorgeous red hair, and that dress. Wow, it must have cost a buck or two!"

"I'd love to see you in that dress. It would look better on you," smiled Mac, loyally.

Before heading back to their room, Kate suggested that they take a stroll on the 8th floor, in hopes of seeing the ghost in the purple jacket.

Mac figured he owed her one, so he acquiesced. Although they strolled quietly up and down the hall, sadly, no ghost appeared.

Finally they decided it was time for bed. Kate would have liked to do some more exploring, and she wondered what the stories were behind each of the over thirteen hundred guest rooms. What a dream vacation it would be to spend a month here, just exploring every nook and cranny. She thought about that, as they made their way back to the room.

"Could we do a bit more snooping tomorrow before we check out?" she asked hopefully, putting her arms around her husband.

"Sure, if that's what you'd like to do. We'll have breakfast sent up to the room first, then we'll don our Sherlock Holmes caps, grab our magnifying glasses, and away we'll go!"

"Very funny," laughed Kate, heading to the washroom.

When she next appeared, she was wearing a fancy pink and black lace nightie and peignoir set, which she had bought specially for this occasion.

Mac looked lovingly at her, thinking how lucky he was to have such an enchanting and beautiful wife.

"I love the nightie, Kate, but I suspect it would look really good on that chair over there," he suggested, waggling his eyebrows at her.

Kate laughed. "You are a hopelessly dirty old man, Mac. I paid a lot for this nightie, and need to get my money's worth out of it."

"Well, I paid a lot for this room, and need to get my money's worth out of it too," he replied.

Kate couldn't argue with that. Slowly removing the pink and black creation, she laid it out gracefully on the chair, then sashayed over to the bed.

All thoughts of ghost hunting, elegant rooms, and strange women were forgotten.

Chapter Eleven

Things were getting back to normal in the Chandler home. Yesterday Kate had taken Mac to the airport for his flight to England. She wished with all her heart that she was going with him, but there was no way. Her reading and book signing appearance was coming up in less than a week, and it was a big deal.

Her publisher was throwing an elaborate luncheon for her, and there was no possible way that she could have changed the date. It was just unfortunate that the dates for the Marine Biology convention in London, at which Mac was giving a paper, could not be changed either.

Kate had finished the laundry, and was just putting a pan of butter tarts into the oven. They would be ready for Davey's lunch. He was the only one of the three who still came home for lunch.

Having a few minutes to spare, while the tarts were baking, Kate made herself another cup of tea. While waiting for it to steep, she picked up two furry toy mice, which Tom and Dick had been batting around, in their version of kitchen hockey. She threw the mice into the cat toy box in the corner. It was full of catnip balls, furry mice, and feathery birds, all of which seemed to find their way around the house, after a full day of play by the three cats.

When she did sit down at the kitchen table, with a mug of steaming tea, and one shortbread cookie, little Harry (short for Harriet), lost no time in jumping onto her lap. She was the smallest of the three Chandler cats, and truly the most affectionate. She never saw a lap she didn't like, and began purring and kneading, before curling into a contented ball.

Kate smiled at the lovely little creature – one of God's true masterpieces. Her delicate wee face looked up at Kate, as if to say "I'm glad you're back home with us," before she closed her inquisitive eyes, and purred herself to sleep.

"I'm going to have to disturb you when that oven timer dings," Kate laughed, as she rubbed the cat between her ears.

"I wish I'd had you with me on the island," she whispered. "You would have kept me from being so lonely.

"I wonder how you would have liked meeting Shadow, though. I guess in a way, he's a distant cousin, so you might have become friends."

Little Harriet snoozed contentedly, the tarts baked and bubbled, and Kate sat quietly, looking out at the pristine snow in the back yard. At the moment, everything seemed perfect in her world.

As usual, when she sat quietly doing nothing, her mind flipped back to those haunted days she had spent alone on the little island in the Everglades. It hardly seemed real, now that she was home, where she felt so safe and comfortable.

She could barely imagine that she had really done all the things she had to do in order to survive. She could, however, always remember the ever constant fear that the kidnapper would return. She also remembered the nagging doubts and fears of what he might do to her, if and when he actually did come back to the remote island.

She knew that in some ways, the experience had changed her forever, and she felt that the changes had been good. She was much more self-sufficient now. She knew she could do things she wouldn't even have tried before the kidnapping. She hoped, however, that she would never again be put to the test.

Once the tarts were out of the oven, Kate went upstairs to have a shower, and get out of her working clothes, before Davey got home. She had an appointment for a hair cut at 1:30, after Davey had gone back to school. She had cancelled the appointment twice before they left on vacation, and there was no way she was going to cancel it again.

As she was brushing her hair, and applying her lipstick, she glanced around the bathroom. It was all done in shades of white and aqua, and looked quite tropical, with a large mural of a hibiscus plant on one wall.

After having spent weeks with nothing but rain water in which to bathe, and nothing but some vaguely minty tasting leaves with which to clean her teeth and mouth, Kate delighted in the lovely feminine accoutrements in her bathroom. Gently she ran her hand over the delicate silver and aqua perfume atomizer, which Mac had found in an antique shop.

She squeezed some hand cream from the white dispenser, and looked with pleasure at the small crystal dish, which contained her four favourite lipsticks.

She had never been one to obsess over possessions, but deprivation of the niceties of civilization had made her much more thankful, and appreciative, of what she had.

The house was a sprawling five bedroom, with lots of space for everyone. Each of the three kids had been allowed to choose the colours and decorations for his or her room. Strangely, Davey's was by far the most artistic. Kate was quite sure that he would be an artist – possibly much better than she was. It was a talent they shared, and it meant that they had a special bond.

She might have taken her home a bit for granted before the kidnapping, but that certainly wasn't the case now.

Life was good, and she was a very lucky woman – or so she thought.

When the phone rang, Kate answered it in the bedroom.

"Hello Mrs. Chandler. This is Walt Jr. I have some bad news."

"Oh, what is it Walt?" asked Kate with concern. Walt Jr. and his father had been hired to keep an eye on the Chandler cottage in Muskoka, when they weren't there. They checked it regularly, to make sure that no vandals had broken in, and no trees had fallen against it, etc.

Walt Jr., who was just sixteen, helped his father taking care of several cottages on the lake. The wife and mother had died the previous year, and the two Walters lived permanently on the lake, taking care of each other, as well as the cottages.

Kate and Mac had bought their cottage the previous fall, so this was the first winter for them.

"What is it, Walt?" Kate repeated. "What's happened?"

"Well, dad and I were over to check your place yesterday afternoon, and someone's broken into it. Your big kitchen window is shattered, and there was a lot of snow inside, as well as broken glass. It's obvious that there are a couple of televisions missing, but we couldn't tell what else might be gone.

"Anyway, we swept out all the snow and glass, and wiped the counters and stuff, and then we left, to go to the store for a big piece of plywood, to board it up till the spring. We didn't have anything with us that would fit it. That's a big window!"

Walt Jr. paused here, and Kate said impatiently, "Well, that sounds fine. So what's the problem? Weren't you able to get it fixed?"

"No, because, well because, my dad had a heart attack on the way to the store. He was really upset about your cottage, and because we're supposed to be taking good care of it, and, oh I don't know why, but he had a really bad heart attack. I got him to the hospital, and he's in the Intensive Care Unit. I don't know what to do.

"I'm calling from the hospital now, and I just can't get out to your cottage right away, so I thought I'd better tell you. I'm scared to leave my dad, and I'm sorry I didn't call sooner. I just forgot everything when he had his attack."

Young Walt was obviously distraught, and Kate needed to reassure him.

"Walt, I understand, and I'm so sorry about your father. I'm sure he'll be fine. He'll get good care, and he's a strong man. As far as the cottage is concerned, well, don't worry about that. We'll take care of it ourselves. You just stay with your dad, and help him to get well."

She didn't have any idea of how she was going to take care of the problem, with Mac away in England, but she was sure she could think of something. She felt so sorry for poor Walt Jr., who was all alone in the world, except for his dad.

"Thanks, Mrs. Chandler, I'm glad I called you. I didn't know what else to do, so I called the police, and they said they'd be out to take a look. Maybe you might want to call them, and see if they can help. I'm really sorry."

"Thanks, Walt. You just take good care of your dad, and leave the rest to me. Please call again, and let me know how he's doing."

After she got off the phone, she sat on the bed, staring into space. What the heck was she going to do? She didn't know anyone else in the area yet, so she would have to drive up there herself. She'd leave this afternoon – the sooner the better. Too bad she couldn't ask Jill to go up with her. That wouldn't work, though. Jill had a job, and she'd need her to come over and stay with the kids.

She'd have to check the cottage to see what had been stolen, and what other damage had been done, if any. She wasn't sure of what animals might be roaming around, and that was a very big kitchen window. Even a deer could easily get in, which wasn't a happy thought.

She sighed as she realized that this was just another test of her self-sufficiency. There's got to be an answer to this problem, she thought. There was always a solution, if you could just stay calm and think about it.

Mac always said that she could assess a situation, and figure out the problem or challenge before most people realized there was one! He claimed that there was now an iron bar where her spine used to be.

She smiled at that recollection, wishing he was here with her now. She would have to do her best without him, and she'd make him proud. It might be a challenge, but she would get that damn window boarded up before their lovely cottage was damaged any further.

Her mind was going like a computer. She made herself a mental checklist, and by the time Davey arrived home for lunch, she had made several calls, including one to the insurance company, and she had decided on a basic plan.

When Davey heard that she was going up to the cottage, he begged to go with her. This was Thursday, and he could afford to miss school for one day.

Kate was way ahead of him. She knew that the twins had mid-terms tomorrow, so they couldn't go with her, but Davey would be good company. Maybe once she got the window boarded, there might even be time for a little skidooing. He would love that.

After one quick call to Jill, to ask if she could come over and stay with the twins and the cats one more time, she began to throw a few things into a suitcase. Then she stopped and shook her head. She remembered that the car would have to be parked at the end of the long cottage road, just off the main road. That meant that she wouldn't be able to carry anything heavy through the snow. It was a long way by foot.

Using a garbage bag would be much smarter than using a suitcase. She had left some clothes up there, so she only needed to take the bare necessities. It was more difficult convincing Davey that he could not bring all the books and toys that he felt he would need.

She couldn't face the thought of canceling her hair appointment again, so she decided that they would leave right from the hair dresser's salon.

Leaving a note for the twins, and one for Jill, they were finally on their way. She hated to leave without seeing Peter and Paige, hugging them, and wishing them well on their exams, but she would call them from the cottage, and she knew they would be fine with Jill. Besides, they were at the age where they felt they could do quite well without their parents around! It was always much easier to wind "Aunt" Jill around their fingers!

Davey, being a friendly, outgoing little fellow, soon struck up a conversation with Kate's hairdresser. He began telling her all about where they were going, and why.

Mona, the hair dresser, was interested in Davey's tales, and asked him exactly where the cottage was located. She was impressed with the little guy, who seemed so smart. He was able to tell her which turnoff they had to take, and just how far along the cottage road they had to walk, to get in to the cottage in the winter.

Then he explained all about the window getting broken by some bad people, and maybe everything was stolen! Or maybe there were some animals planning to stay there for the rest of the winter! He was so excited and so knowledgeable, that he had everyone listening with interest.

It had started snowing by the time they left the salon, but Kate really had no choice. She felt that she had to make this trip. It was about a two and a half hour drive to the cottage, so she knew it would likely be dark before they got there. It got dark so early now in the middle of winter.

She had taken a lasagna and a few items out of the freezer, but would have to stop to buy some supplies such as milk and bread along the way. She just prayed that the snow wouldn't continue for too long. Trying to make their way through deep snow in the dark would be almost impossible, - specially if they were burdened with a lot of junk. Also, Davey's legs were short. It would be a tough trip for him if the snow was deep.

If only Kate had known what fate had in store for her, she and Davey would have stayed tucked up safely in their own home, leaving the cottage to fend for itself.

Chapter Twelve

Angel Baby kept going over and over that wonderful night at the Royal York. Somehow, in Angel's chaotic mind, memories of that night had morphed from the actual fact, that she had boldly crashed the party, to a beautiful, romantic fantasy, that it had been an actual date with Mac. She remembered dancing with him, and how close he had held her, and it was all perfect in her mind. It had been just like the old days.

She had accomplished what she set out to do. She had tested her new look on her ex- lover, and she had passed easily. Mac had no idea who she was. Even her voice hadn't given her away.

A normal person would have been horrified at how close she had come lately, to being caught. There was the most recent scary night with Dan, when she and his wife almost came face to face. Then there was the night at the Royal York, when the hotel police were supposedly watching for party crashers. There were also all those nights she had gone to hotel rooms with strange men, drugging them, stealing their money, and making a hasty retreat. Those had been "living on the edge" moments, and Angel Baby seemed to thrive on them.

With her mind ticking like a time bomb these days, she accepted the fact that she wasn't quite normal, and she wondered whether she ever had been. All she knew was that she loved danger, and close calls. Any time she could get the best of someone, was a good time for her.

Angel Baby knew that the situation was definitely getting worse. It seemed that reality and imagination were vying for her attention, and that was scary. She feared that if it happened too frequently, she'd have to go into hiding somewhere, at least for a while.

Her main hope was that she could hold things together, until she was done with Kate. At that point she'd make her escape to a lovely warm island. She would just relax, lie on the beach, and let the sunshine and the peaceful water restore her.

The only thing in the world she really feared, was being sent back to that psychiatric hospital. It was so old, that it was likely closed by now anyway, but she was never going back into any psychiatric facility – no matter what. If she was ever cornered, she would fight till she drew her last breath.

Those stupid doctors hadn't been able to diagnose her properly. They couldn't agree as to what was wrong with her, and their feeble ideas seemed to change from day to day. She had first been diagnosed as having a borderline personality disorder. That was bad enough. Then, however, as the months went by, they came up with new ideas. Maybe she was bi-polar, schizophrenic, psychotic, manic depressive, or just plain crazy. They simply couldn't make up their own confused minds. At least that was how Angel saw it.

No matter what they called it, they all agreed that she should be locked up for her own good, as well as for others. Of course Madison, (now Angel Baby) didn't quite agree with the so-called experts. She thought that maybe she was just more sensitive and intelligent than other people.

She had been keeping a close eye on Kate, since she and Mac had returned from their vacation in Florida, and today had been her lucky day. She had seen Kate go into the hair salon, and had waited patiently till she and Davey had come out and driven away.

As soon as Kate's car was out of sight, Angel had pranced into the salon, and pretended she wanted an appointment for the following week. Speaking with the woman in charge she said, "I thought I just saw Kate Chandler leaving here. She had darling little Davey with her."

"Oh, do you know Mrs. Chandler?" asked Mona, with interest. Like most hair dressers, she loved to talk, and she had a few moments before her next appointment arrived.

"Yes, we're old friends, but I've been out of the country, and haven't seen her for a while," lied Angel, with a straight face. She was excellent at lying – a trait which had helped her out of many bad situations. The lies seemed to fall from her mouth like petals from a dying rose.

"She seemed to be in quite a hurry. There's nothing wrong, is there?"

"Actually, there is. She and Davey were telling me, that their cottage in Muskoka has been vandalized, and the big kitchen window has been shattered. Her husband is in England at the moment, so she and Davey are driving up there this afternoon, to try to get the window repaired, and find out what's been stolen.

"I don't envy her. That's no place for a woman on her own. What if she gets stuck in the snow? Apparently they have quite a long, winding road in to the cottage, and this winter you never know when another snow storm will appear."

"Oh, how awful," said Angel, secretly delighted at this news.

"I wish I'd known. I could have gone along and helped her. I'm free this week, and we used to be so close. I don't suppose you know where their cottage is? I've been out of the country for a few years now," she repeated, "and we've lost touch. She'd be happy to see me though – specially if I could help her. We were closer than sisters at one time."

"Actually, I know exactly where it is," replied Mona, happy to help.

"Davey told us all about it. His directions were so good, I think I could drive right to the door myself," she laughed.

Ten minutes later, Angel was back in her car, writing down the directions to Kate's cottage. Lady Luck was certainly shining down on her today. She couldn't believe her good fortune. This was such a great omen.

She knew she'd be successful this time, in getting rid of the detested Kate. If she was going to be alone at a remote cottage, on an empty lake, that would be a perfect place to attack her. Too bad Davey was with her. She had liked Davey about as much as she liked any children, which wasn't very much. Still, although she didn't like him, she wouldn't enjoy hurting him. Oh well, she would just have to play that by ear.

Thinking of Davey, reminded her of the times she had spent with him, when they were all rushing around, looking for Kate in Florida. Davey would be able to recognize her voice immediately. She was sure of it.

One of the things Patrick had not been able to do, when he changed her appearance, was to change her voice. Davey was smart, and he had a good memory. Also, she remembered that he picked up on things very quickly. She had no worries about Kate. It had been years and years since Kate had once heard her voice on the phone. The first big test had been Mac, and she had passed it easily. Mac hadn't recognized her voice at all, that night at the dance.

Maybe Kate and Mac wouldn't recognize her voice, but it was likely that Davey could.

With that in mind, she had been practicing lowering her voice, and speaking much more slowly. She felt confident that it was working pretty well. When she was around Davey, she would just have to be extra careful. After all, she didn't want him to recognize her too soon. She wanted time to terrorize Kate a bit, before revealing who she really was.

Smiling to herself, she went back to the hotel to pack. Now that she knew where Kate's cottage was located, she would head north tomorrow morning. No way was she going to go stumbling around in the dark tonight. Tonight she would stay out of trouble, and get a good sleep. That would put her in top shape for tomorrow, when she would finally realize the culmination of all her plans and dreams, the final eradication of Kate Chandler.

The next morning, by the time she was on Highway 400, headed to the world renowned Muskoka cottage country, she could barely contain her excitement. Everything she owned at the moment was with her in the rental car, including the little gun. She certainly couldn't forget that little gun. There might come a time when it would be very handy.

She hadn't really decided how she was going to kill Kate, but the gun was certainly a good possibility. She had stolen it one night from a dimwitted fellow in Montreal, and it was now one of her cherished possessions.

It had been surprisingly cold in Toronto, and she could hardly believe that a few nights ago she had been running around outside in her stocking feet with no jacket. Lucky she hadn't caught pneumonia. She felt much more secure now, with a new jacket and boots, and she had a feeling that she was going to really need them where she was going.

As she drove along the highway, she was surprised at how much traffic there was. According to the radio, there was another big snow storm coming, and she hoped that she would be safely off the road, at Kate's summer home, before the storm hit.

She wondered whether Kate and Davey had run into any bad weather on their trip the previous day. She felt good. knowing that she was now driving along the same highway her prey had driven. Had Kate made the trip safely? She hoped so. She didn't want anything to spoil the pleasure she was anticipating, as she tortured, and eventually killed the woman she had hated for so many years.

She didn't even want to consider what she would do if, for some reason, she became stranded at the cottage. If she killed Kate too soon, she might be stuck there with a dead body. Then there was still the problem of Davey. It would be really difficult to kill a child, especially one as smart and cute as Davey, so maybe she would just leave him there with his dead mother, and hope that someone would find him.

"Wait a minute," she said out loud.

"I can't leave any witnesses. Davey would be able to tell everyone exactly who killed his mom." She knew that, as well as being very bright, Davey Chandler was an excellent budding artist. He would probably be able to draw a pretty good picture of her, as she looked now. No, that wasn't acceptable. Davey would just have to go. He was the one fly in the ointment. Too bad he was going up to the cottage with Kate.

She didn't feel at all good about the Davey problem, and it took the edge off the day, at least for a while.

To get her mind away from this dilemma, and onto something else, she began to take mental inventory of what was in her big tote bag. Almost all the money she had in the world was in that bag. She would have to carry it in to the cottage with her.

Her weapon of choice was the little bottle of Rohypnol. That was the date rape drug which she had stolen from Patrick's pharmacy. It was so clean and easy. Unfortunately, although she had taken several small bottles of the powerful drug, she had been using it all across the country, and now there was just this one bottle left.

She also had the gun, her little "Montreal special." There were no extra bullets for it, but, hopefully, one would be enough, if she decided to use it.

Angel had always suspected that Kate was prettier than she was. She had convinced herself a long time ago that this was the reason Kate had been able to steal Mac from her so easily. Now, though, she knew that her rival wasn't even in the same class as she was. Kate might be pretty and attractive, but Angel was beautiful!

She still wished she could think of some unique way to kill Kate. She knew one thing for sure. She would carve up that pretty face so that Kate would know before she died that no man – specially Mac, would ever look at her again, except with disgust and pity. She was going to be such an ugly corpse, that she would be happy to die, once Angel Baby was finished with her.

Angel Baby grinned at the thought.

Chapter Thirteen

Thinking of pretty women – and Angel had to admit that Kate was pretty – if you liked that kind of look, she took another quick glance at herself in the rear view mirror. Yes, her face was still gorgeous. Patrick had done an amazing job.

"Thank you most sincerely, Dr. Patrick O'Neal," she said in her new low voice. "You did one hell of a job on me, and I'll be eternally grateful to you, even though you turned out to be a first class disappointment." She grimaced, as she thought of how much she had loved him, or thought she had, and how much he had let her down.

Did all men disappoint you in the final analysis, she wondered. Mac certainly had. Still, she was willing to give him a second chance. She was so willing, that she would even kill his wife and his son for him. Now that was true love!!!

She didn't think she loved Patrick enough to kill his wife and kids, so that he could be free. She couldn't gather up much enthusiasm for that. She assumed that meant that she really loved Mac much more than she had ever loved Patrick. Still, Patrick was awfully attractive!

What was that old song? It was something about "If you can't be near the one you love, then love the one you're near!" Yes, that was a good philosophy. Of course she had fallen for Patrick. He was available, and Mac hadn't been.

As she drove along, her mind gradually drifted to a snowy afternoon in Switzerland, when she and Patrick had gone skiing. They had such fun together, and she wanted to sleep overnight in the ski chalet. Patrick, however, pointed out that there was no way he could stay over night, without Lainey becoming suspicious.

Angel had thrown a real tantrum, and Patrick had become angry with her. She had soon calmed down, however, but it made her realize that the time had come to do something about his marriage. If he wouldn't smarten up, and talk with his wife, then she would have to go to his precious Madelaine herself. Her plan was to marry Patrick, and go to Italy or Spain or maybe even Greece to live. Why not? Patrick had lots of money, and beautiful women are really appreciated in those countries.

How had it all gone so wrong? For a time there, she had been madly in love with him, almost forgetting about Mac. She had made up her mind that she would graciously let Kate have Mac all to herself. She, the new and beautiful Angel Baby, would stay somewhere in Europe forever, and be quite happy as Mrs. Patrick O'Neal.

It hadn't been until Pat told her that he would never leave his wife and those darn kids, that she realized he had just been a passing fling, and that Mac was still the love of her life.

His cruel words of rejection had been like killer waves crashing over her head. She had felt that she was drowning.

Well, Patrick was dead to her now. In spite of his lively, fun-filled blue eyes, his infectious smile, his curly black hair, and, of course, his money, he was no longer of any importance. She had erased him from her mind as easily as erasing inconsequential words from a blackboard.

True, she still thought about him occasionally, but her mind was concentrated again on Mac. Besides, Pat would be so angry with her, after he discovered the mischief she had done.

She couldn't help but giggle when she thought about what Madelaine, (she hated the way he always referred to his wife as Lainey), would have said, after she got the letter. Because of his Irish temper, she was quite thankful that good old Dr. O'Neal was still in Switzerland, with a big, wide ocean between them. At that point in time, it had never occurred to her that good old Dr. Patrick O'Neal might cross that big old ocean, and follow her to Canada!

Patrick was a terrific doctor, though. She had to give him full marks for that. He had made her even more beautiful, although he had been very doubtful at first. He had been so reluctant, because, as he had emphasized over and over, she was already lovely. "You don't tamper with beauty" he had said.

She had persuaded him, however, and now she still got a charge out of gazing at herself in the mirror, for five or ten minutes at a time. She would turn her face this way and that, feeling her nose, running her fingers down around her chin, trying various smiles.

Angel Baby loved herself, and Mac would love her too, even though he would never know that she was actually his old love Madison, hiding so cleverly behind the new face. She could never let him in on that little secret.

Although vaguely concentrating on the highway, Angel was still mainly preoccupied with her visions and memories of happy days in Switzerland. There was another time when they were again spending the afternoon in a little ski chalet.

Pat said he had to be home by 9 o'clock at the latest, so they had skipped the skiing, and were having a lovely time drinking wine in front of the little fireplace, and making love on the king sized bed.

She was even dropping grapes into his mouth, one at a time, kissing him between each grape.

Wait, though. Did that actually happen, or had she seen it in a movie? Her heart began to race, as she realized that she really didn't know. It was happening again. Reality and imagination were combining to form a muddy picture in her bruised mind.

She was concentrating so hard now, trying to get her renegade mind back on track, that she didn't realize her driving was becoming erratic. She was not only going too fast for the worsening conditions, (when had it started snowing so heavily?), but she was also veering more and more over into the next lane.

A large beer truck, coming right up behind her, gave her a long, loud honk. It scared her so much, that she jerked the car back into her lane, and shouted several curse words at him.

She was so interested in shouting at the beer truck, that she didn't notice a big van swerving wildly to avoid a collision. It was one of those vans which looks too tall for its wheel base, and as the frantic driver lost control, it rolled over onto the median.

Blissfully unaware of the accident she had just caused, Angel Baby continued on her mission. The interesting truth, however, is that even if she had realized that she was the cause of the accident behind her, she wouldn't have cared very much. She was no longer the responsible, sensible, fun loving, adorable Maddy with whom Mac Chandler had fallen in love so many years ago – long before he had even met Kate.

Instead, this woman's personality and character had deteriorated greatly in the past years. She was not, and could never again be the young girl Mac had loved. She didn't act the same. She didn't think the same, and she surely didn't look the same. Now even her voice was different.

When Mac had held her in his arms on the dance floor at the Royal York, he hadn't had a clue that she was his former lover Maddy.

That knowledge had given her a great sense of power. Actually, she had been ecstatic after that magic night.

Every few minutes, she continued to glance at herself in the rear view mirror. "Angel Baby" she purred, as she drove on, still remarkably oblivious to the worsening situation around her.

Eventually she decided she had better fill up the gas tank, so she pulled over at the next station along the highway. Going in to the store part, she immediately started flirting with the young man behind the counter. She even managed to persuade him to come out and fill the tank for her, even though the sign proclaimed "Self Serve."

Angel Baby loved young men or boys. They were so easy to manipulate – they really were putty in her hands, and she delighted in the power she had over them. This one reminded her slightly of the young desk clerk in the Toronto hotel. He would have done anything for her, of that she had been certain.

Undoing her heavy jacket, so that the young chap could enjoy the considerable cleavage showing in her pink sweater, she pouted prettily, and asked for his help with a map. She explained that she was going to a cottage for the first time, and had lost the directions her friend had given her, and wasn't quite sure how far she needed to go.

Remembering the directions which Davey had explained to the hairdresser, she got the young man to show her on the map where the cottage would be – or at least close enough. In her mind, she was confident that she could find it with just a little help from this guy.

The teenager was quite happy to lean over the map with her. She figured that if she hadn't been wearing the big parka, he would have been trying to accidentally on purpose lean against her breasts, or maybe even touch one with the back of his hand.

Actually, she didn't like to be touched, but she liked to know that someone wanted to touch her. Big difference!

If she couldn't find Kate's cottage, she might have to ask someone up there at the lake, but she didn't want to do that. To begin with, there might not be anyone around to ask. The less people seeing her, the better, but she certainly didn't want to get lost. She was pretty sure that she could find it, though, mostly because she knew that Davey was an unusually smart kid. That meant that the directions he had given the hairdresser would be accurate.

It wasn't until sometime later, when she was back in the car, that she realized she shouldn't have told that young gas attendant where she was going. He might remember her and her questions, once the news of the murder got out. Well, the damage was done now. There wasn't anything she could do about it. She certainly wasn't going to turn around and go back to the gas station. And even if she did, what would be the point? She wasn't about to kill him, as well as Kate. That would be just too darn risky, and the poor kid hadn't done anything to deserve to be murdered.

Anyway, she was definitely not a killer! She just had to remove Kate from the scene, because she had to free Mac from his marriage. It all made sense in her convoluted mind, although a saner individual would certainly not have been able to see the wisdom of her plan.

No, it had been a foolish mistake on her part, letting the gas kid know exactly where she was going. She was sure he would remember her, just because she was so good looking, but, hopefully she'd be long gone out of the country before the murder was discovered.

As always, Angel Baby would depend on her phenomenal luck and good looks to see her through.

Chapter Fourteen

The afternoon before Angel set out to catch up with Kate, Davey and his mom had a mostly enjoyable trip to the cottage, at least until they reached Bracebridge. That's when things began to get a little dicey.

Bracebridge is a bustling little town, right in the center of the summer paradise known as the Muskoka Lakes. It offers everything the camper or cottager needs for a happy vacation. The main street runs pretty well right through the town, from one end to the other. It boasts a movie house, a library, many restaurants, and clothing shops galore.

Close by, there are also shopping plazas, which offer grocery stores, hardware stores, drug stores, and camping equipment emporiums. Pretty well everything the tourist could possibly want, can be found in and around Bracebridge.

To take care of emergencies there are all the usual doctors, dentists and veterinarians.

Bracebridge is just a small version of a big city, and in the summer, it is bursting at the seams, with the tourists who come from far and near to cottages, cabins, and tenting grounds. In the winter, it welcomes the snowmobilers and skiers, who love to take advantage of the pristine snow and beauty of the forest trails.

Judging by the clouds that particular afternoon in January, there was definitely snow lurking around, waiting to pounce on unsuspecting drivers. As yet it hadn't attacked, but Kate knew it was coming. She wouldn't feel completely comfortable until they were actually inside their cottage.

She could see that it had already snowed a lot the day before, judging by the mounds of fresh snow everywhere. It occurred to her that snowshoes might have been the ideal method to get into the cottage, but it was too late for that possibility.

Davey was content, sitting in the back seat, and talking to his mom. She explained to him, that when they finally got there, they wouldn't be able to touch many things until the police arrived. Actually, it might be a good idea to keep their gloves and mitts on. They wouldn't want to wipe out any fingerprints which could lead the police to the vandals.

Davey was mesmerized. He was in the middle of a real life mystery! Wait till he told the twins. He would walk right behind his mom, and not touch anything which she didn't touch. That might be difficult, and he might forget, but he would try his best. Maybe he'd become a detective when he grew up, along with being an artist, and a water-skiing champ. His dad had promised that he would teach all three of them to water-ski this summer, and Davey was determined that he would be the first to learn.

In the meantime, if the police came, and if they got the window all boarded shut, he was hoping that they could take out one of the skidoos. Maybe they could have a winter picnic. He'd seen that on a movie once, and it looked like fun.

All in all, Davey was a happy boy. Getting an unexpected day off school, having this nice trip, helping to solve a mystery, and maybe meet a real detective, and maybe having a skidoo ride, added up to just about the best holiday he could imagine.

Kate was wondering how much damage had been done during the break-in. Had the vandals simply wanted to steal whatever they could? That wouldn't be too bad. At least it was all covered by insurance. If, however, they had done a lot of damage, it could be a real mess.

She had certainly heard enough stories about rotten young punks emptying things from the frig, and smearing them around, plugging the toilets, peeing and doing even worse on the carpets or beds etc. She was assuming that it was aimless, or drugged out teens who had broken in, and she hoped that they had limited themselves to simple thievery.

She also hoped that they hadn't taken or destroyed Davey's art supplies. She had persuaded him to leave a lot of his things at the cottage, so that they wouldn't have to always be dragging them back and forth. Since they had bought the cottage late in the fall, they had only been there a couple of times. Everything was very new to them.

She knew that her son was looking forward to drawing and painting with her. He had such a talent already, and she was encouraging it as much as possible. She could envision the two of them co-authoring a book somewhere down the line, and doing all the illustrations together. How much fun that would be!

Too bad Mac had to be away just now, but she was pretty confident that she could handle things. Hopefully, she and Davey could get out for a skidoo ride before heading home. He was too young to drive one himself, but they'd have fun riding through the woods with him hanging on behind her. Maybe they'd bring some hot chocolate and sandwiches. Then again – maybe not. She simply wouldn't be able to carry in much in the line of food extras.

Even if the snow wasn't very deep, (and she was sure that it was), it was quite a long jaunt from where they would park the car to the actual cottage. She wasn't going to be able to buy all the things they might want or need – not tonight anyway. She would do well to get the two of them in safely, with the small amount of stuff they had to carry.

If it was nice and clear tomorrow, though, she thought they could take the skidoo out to where the car would be parked, then drive back in to Bracebridge, to buy some treats, as well as ordering the plywood needed to fix the window. She would just have to play everything by ear. No sense making too many plans now, until they got to the cottage and could assess the damage.

"Mom, you and I have never been at the cottage all by ourselves. Will you be scared tonight?"

Kate had to laugh at that. In Davey's own little subtle way, he was admitting that he might be a bit scared to be all alone up here in the wilderness, with only his mother to protect him.

"No, I don't see why either one of us should be scared," answered Kate with a smile. "It will be really quiet, though, not like in the fall, when we were here. I suspect that all we'll hear will be the wind whispering through the trees."

"What do you think the wind whispers?" asked her inquisitive son.

"Well, what do you think you would whisper, if you were wind talking to your friends in the woods?"

That stumped Davey, and he was quiet for several miles, as he tried to imagine what it would be like to be the wind.

"Could we make fudge tonight?" he asked hopefully, finally tired of his own imaginings.

"That's doubtful, kiddo. We're there to work, and once we check out everything, and get the window covered, we'll need to get to bed. Of course, if there's no wood or cardboard or anything to fix it, I'm not sure what we'll do. That means there'll be lots of work tomorrow.

"There'll be no time for fudge I'm afraid. Besides, what happened to the fudge we brought home from PCB for you?"

Her son looked sheepish. "I guess I ate it all. But it wasn't very much. Really, it was a pretty small box," he added.

Kate laughed, and shook her head. "Since I didn't leave any supplies such as sugar or butter or cocoa, I guess the idea of fudge is out. Don't worry, we're going to have fun with or without fudge."

"Are we going to build a fire in the fireplace?" Davey figured it was time to change the subject.

"Yes, of course. Your dad left a fire all ready to light, and there's lots of wood in the box. Maybe, if we're not too scared, or too sleepy, we'll tell ghost stories."

He grinned at that. Nobody could tell a good ghost story like his mom, and what he liked even better, were the stories she told about her days and nights in the Everglades. He never tired of those tales.

As they passed the famous burger joint, beloved by all cottagers heading north, Davey was disappointed to see that it was all closed. "Why wouldn't they stay open, they're losing good money," complained the budding business man.

Kate snorted. "Are you kidding? Think of how much money it would cost to heat that place, buy all the hamburger meat and buns and fixings, pay at least two people to work, and then wait for the very occasional car to go by. This is winter, mister, and not too many cottagers are dumb enough to be going up on a blustery, cold afternoon."

"Well, we're dumb enough," sighed Davey contentedly, as he picked up one of his books which always stayed in the car. He loved having the back seat of the SUV all to himself. Usually he was sharing space with the twins. This was a real treat, having both the car and his mom to himself. When he was with the twins, they joked with him, played with him, but also teased him a lot – specially Peter. When he was alone with his mom, though, they joked together, and she made him feel important, and smart and protected.

When his mother had been kidnapped, Davey felt it might have been his fault. If he hadn't taken the cart back to Publix, maybe the man couldn't have grabbed her.

If he had only remembered sooner about the van parked next to them with "Take a chance on Chance" painted on the side. That had been such a good clue. If he had not listened to Maddy's warning, and if only he had told his dad what he knew right away, they would have found his mom much sooner.

Fortunately, however, in the final analysis, it had been Davey who was instrumental in helping his dad find his mom, and it was then that the guilt finally lifted from his little boy shoulders. That was also when the special bond between Kate and Davey became even stronger.

Eventually they stopped at the Harvey's in Bracebridge, and both had cheeseburgers and fries. Davey had a hot chocolate, and Kate had black coffee. She would have preferred tea, but coffee would be better at keeping her awake on this dull afternoon. It would soon be dark, and she really wasn't looking forward to making their way on foot, along that probably black, narrow road. Thank goodness she had remembered to bring two good flashlights.

As they sat there, quietly enjoying their burgers, Kate's mind flashed to the summer, when they would be going back and forth to the cottage pretty well every weekend. She wondered whether this Harvey's would become the family's favourite stopping spot.

Once April rolled around, they intended to start shopping for a big beautiful boat. It had to be strong enough to pull the kids on the skis, and big enough for the five of them to be comfortable, as they boated around the lake. They had already agreed that it had to be a bow-rider, but she wondered how they would ever agree on the right colour.

She could picture them all sitting down on the dock. Well, she and Mac might be sitting there sipping wine, while the three kids were out in the canoe, (which they also planned to buy). Then she pictured all of them swimming and fooling around in the water. It was going to be so great! Hopefully they would get to know some neighbours, and it would be a healthy, happy, fun-filled summer.

As they were finishing their burgers, a heavy man, dressed warmly in a big parka, came crashing through the door, stomping his boots to shake off the snow.

"Boy, that's a miserable afternoon," he said to all and sundry.

"I've just come from Sudbury, and it's a real blizzard up there. It's good here in comparison, but I think the damn storm is following me."

Kate wasn't happy to hear that. The sooner they got in to the safety of the cottage, the better it would be. She'd worry later about getting them out again.

Her plans to order some plywood in town, had to be revised, when she discovered that several of the stores were already closed. Apparently the approach of the big snow storm from the north had everyone spooked.

She would call them first thing in the morning, to order some wood or heavy plastic. Meantime, what was she going to use tonight? The more she thought about it, the more sure she was that Mac didn't have anything useable tucked away. She certainly couldn't remember seeing any big pieces of wood in the little shed.

Sure, tomorrow she could order all the supplies she was going to need, but tonight was the problem. She would have to use her imagination, and she was just getting a glimmer of what she thought might be a good idea.

Chapter Fifteen

It had started snowing heavily, while they were enjoying their cheeseburgers at Harvey's, and the visibility was now poor. Kate was becoming a bit uneasy at what they might be facing.

Obviously, they were going to have to park the car, and walk in to the cottage. In the summer time, it would likely be a beautiful walk, but of course they would be able to drive right up to the back door in the summer. On a snowmobile it would be a beautiful, fun-filled ride. On two feet, however, carrying supplies, it was going to be an onerous task.

She bought as little food as possible in town, already envisioning the tough trip. Everyone in the store seemed to be in a hurry. They were all looking apprehensively out the windows, as the harried clerks ran the groceries through check-out.

Kate was thankful that at least she had been able to persuade Davey not to bring any of his books, games or puzzles. There were enough entertainment things at the cottage, even if their televisions had been stolen. Hopefully the thieves wouldn't have bothered to take the board games or decks of cards. They had likely been after the things which could be easily fenced for cash.

When they arrived at the beginning of the cottage road, Kate made sure that Davey was bundled up well. The wind was biting, and her heart sank as she looked ahead into the darkness. This was really going to be a challenge.

She would have been much more worried, if she had known that the very next day, her old nemesis, Maddy, would be setting out to track her right to the cottage, where she and Davey would be very much alone.

They each had a small overnight bag of necessities. Kate also had the frozen lasagna she had brought for their dinner, plus the little bag of bread, milk and cookies. Plans were changed, however, concerning the lasagna.

They had just stuffed themselves on burgers and fries. That would be their dinner. She would make Davey cocoa and toast before he went to bed, and he would be happy with that. He wasn't usually too interested in food, unless it was French fries, pizza, or burgers.

The lasagna would stay in the car. It was cold enough that it should be fine, but if it did thaw, she would just pitch it. Saving the lasagna was the last thing on her mind.

Buying a jug of water had been a big decision point in the store, but reluctantly Kate had given up the idea. It would be way too heavy to carry. Besides, there was a heated water line at the cottage. By just turning on the switch, they could have running water within half an hour.

Of course, it came right out of the lake, and they couldn't drink it, without boiling it, but that was preferable to trying to drag a heavy jug along. She had to keep burdens as light as possible. She hoped that the storm had not taken out the power lines. A cottage with no heat, no light and no water, would be more of a challenge than she was prepared to face right now. Besides, she'd been there and done that two years ago.

Why had she been in such a rush to get up here? The cottage would have survived another few days. Why hadn't she waited to leave tomorrow morning, so that at least they would have had daylight to make this long walk? Even better, if she had waited till the weekend, Jill and the twins could have come too. It would have been a party, and much more fun.

Should she turn around now and head home, while they could still see the highway? Possibly yes, but Kate had a stubborn streak. Also, she usually had faith in herself and her abilities to cope. She just hated to give up, and leave the cottage unprotected.

What would Mac do? Mac, of course, would forge ahead. Okay, so be it. Packed like a couple of mules, she and Davey would continue on their way. At this point there was no turning back.

Strangely, she didn't really consider staying at a motel in Bracebridge over night, then going in to the cottage in the daylight. What a smart choice that might have been. Still, Davey would have been bored and disappointed, and she was focused on getting the kitchen window boarded up as quickly as possible. She wanted to keep the damage to a minimum.

She wanted to show Mac that she was totally capable of handling everything, while he was away. Maybe, subconsciously, she was trying to live up to the reputation she had earned, by surviving her ordeal in the treacherous Everglades.

Whatever the reason, she just didn't give much thought to staying overnight in a motel.

Once along the way, she looked back over her shoulder at the car, which was parked just off the township road. Already it was almost lost in the snow.

The roads would probably be ploughed tomorrow morning. She hoped that the car wouldn't be ploughed in, buried under mounds of snow. If that were the case, they'd be there until the spring! She had left enough room for a police cruiser or skidoo to get by. It would be nice to know that someone could come and rescue them, if they needed to be rescued!

Although it was just before six o'clock, it was already pitch dark. There was no moon to give them light, and no Mac to give them protection. All they had was each other, two flashlights, and a slightly dampened spirit of adventure.

The wind was amazing. It bullied them along. It pushed and shoved, showing no mercy. Then it would seem to shift, and suddenly it was blowing right in their faces, making it almost impossible to keep their eyes open.

Lights were visible in only one cottage along the way. It was right at the beginning of their trek, closest to the township road, but it had a long, unplowed driveway. Should she turn in there and ask for help, or should she keep going?

It was very tempting to ask for some assistance, but she decided that it was better to keep going. Why waste most of their energy trying to struggle through the snow at someone else's cottage? They might discover that whoever was in the lighted cottage was hostile or senile. Or maybe it was teenage kids doing drugs far away from their families back in town. Maybe it was the very people who had broken into her place, and stolen all their valuables.

Kate's imagination was always one step ahead of her. She decided they had to conserve their energy for making it along the length of their own road. She felt safer not disturbing the residents lurking in that first cottage, whoever they might be.

Little did she know how soon their paths would cross.

"Mom, do you think there are any wolves in these woods?" asked Davey, as he shone his flashlight here and there around him.

Kate had to laugh. She had been entertaining similar thoughts, but wasn't going to admit it to her son.

"Davey, there are no wolves in this part of the country, and all sensible bears are sleeping soundly in caves, all cuddled up to keep warm.

I'm pretty sure it's just you and your old mom on this little adventure," she added, turning to look at him. "Now let's save our strength and not talk so much. We'll get there faster, and we won't be so tired. As soon as we get there, we'll build a fire, and have some cocoa and cookies."

Silently they trudged along, with only the wind and the darkness as companions. Kate was in the lead, with Davey following in her footprints as much as possible. He was a good sport and a real little energizer bunny.

This was an adventure, but he had to admit that it was difficult trying to walk in the deep snow, with the wind blowing more snow in his face. He wasn't going to whine about it, though. This wasn't nearly as bad as what his mom had gone through in the Everglades, so he would not utter one word of complaint.

Kate kept looking over her shoulder, to be sure he was close behind her. Bless his heart, he was puffing, and doing his best to keep up with her, but when his tired legs caused him to stumble and fall face down into a big snow drift, she could sense that he was probably close to tears.

Helping him up, she wiped the snow from his face, gave him a kiss on the nose, and said, "We're almost there. See – there's the outline of the cottage just ahead. You've been amazing, Davey Doodle. My legs are a lot longer than yours, and they're really tired, so I can just imagine how tired yours are. Wait till I tell dad and the twins about how terrific you've been." She wasn't sure whether she could see the cottage or not, but hoped it would encourage her son.

That was all Davey needed. He would do anything to please her.

"It's a good thing Paige isn't here. She'd be all worried that the wind was messing her hair," he giggled, as he plodded on.

"I think you're right," laughed Kate, thinking of her beautiful daughter, who was going through the terrible teens. This morning she had begged not to have to go to school because a small zit – hardly noticeable without a magnifying glass – had appeared on her chin. Paige had become the family drama queen.

They trundled along in silence, except for their heavy breathing.

Every once in a while Kate would mumble, "Please God keep us safe, and stay with us." It made her feel a bit calmer and more resolute. They were almost there, and they were going to be fine, at least that's what she kept telling herself.

It was snowing harder now, and the wind was really howling. She felt as if they were the last two people in the world.

Kate kept going over and over the sequence of events since Walt had called her, and she was second guessing herself.

Maybe the window had been broken for a week or more. If that were the case, what difference would one or two more nights have made? Why had she raced up here without trying to get more details? It wasn't like her to be so impulsive.

She knew that they probably should have gone to a motel in town, and waited for the daylight, and the police, to give her some help. That might have been a mistake, but it seemed stupid to be stuck in a motel half an hour away from their beautiful cottage. Besides, Kate hated motels, and she knew that Davey would be really disappointed to be stuck in one. He was looking forward so much to being at the cottage – just the two of them.

She just prayed that she hadn't put Davey or herself in any danger, because of the approaching blizzard.

Chapter Sixteen

This being Patrick's first visit to Canada, he was intrigued at how very cosmopolitan Toronto was. It seemed to him that Canada's largest city, as well as being the capital of the province of Ontario, was extremely multi-cultural. Very interesting.

He wondered whether the entire country was this way, or just Toronto. There seemed to be different nationalities represented, wherever he looked. The cab driver had been wearing a turban. The hotel doorman appeared to be East Indian. There were two Asians and an African-Canadian behind the reception desk. It appeared that Canadians took their multi-culturalism seriously.

Everyone seemed friendly and helpful, and Patrick was pleased with his hotel room, which was large and bright. He was expecting a call from the private investigator, so after showering, and lying down on the bed, he closed his eyes, and let his mind wander over the past two years. What had actually happened to bring him to this hotel, in this country, at this point in his life?

He had been living in a paradise of his own making, but it had been a fool's paradise.

At the start, had he been willingly gullible? Yes! Had he experienced some doubts? Yes! By then had he really cared? No!

He, had realized that helping Angel Baby would be a wonderful opportunity to hone his already considerable skills. He would be able to write a paper for the medical journal, and he would be famous, well, more famous than he already was.

That was how it had all started, and it really had been totally innocent at the beginning. It is difficult, however, for two good-looking people to work in such close proximity day after day, without a certain bond being forged. Patrick didn't realize that he was falling in love with his patient, until it was far too late.

Angel knew how to manipulate men – she had been doing it all her life, and Patrick had been ripe for the plucking. Talk about taking candy from a baby! Angel had seduced the doctor before he knew what was happening.

It had been a long healing process for her, with one surgery after another. She was so pathetic and alone, and, of course, he had admired her courage and determination.

Once she was almost healed, she had become antsy and nervous. She needed a lot of cuddling and reassuring, that after all this pain and suffering, she would be truly beautiful.

It became a ritual that he would take her away to quaint little cafés and inns, where they could sip wine, laugh over a cheese fondue, and nibble chocolate truffles, confident that no one he knew would see them. They rarely ever stayed away over night. That would have been too complicated, and would have required too many explanations.

When he decided to buy her the small condo, he knew it was a crazy idea. He knew he shouldn't be spending the money. It was, in essence, stealing from his wife and children. At that point in his life, however, he really wasn't thinking clearly, and couldn't help himself. He had fallen totally under her spell.

Patrick understood that the happier and more relaxed his patient was, the quicker she would heal, and he worked hard at keeping her happy. It had been a time of true magic, as he gradually saw the results of his work. G.B. Shaw certainly got it right, when his Pygmalion fell in love with Galatea. It is difficult not to fall in love with a beauty which one has created with his own hands.

They had wonderful times together, and took outrageous chances. Patrick's wife Lainey, loved him and trusted him, so it was shamefully easy to deceive her. In all that time, however, even after he had purchased the condo for Angel, Patrick had just thought of it as a fling. He hadn't looked too far into the future. He supposed that subconsciously he had just assumed that some day she would go back to Canada, and it would all be just a sweet memory.

He remembered the few occasions, though, when he had seen a darker side of his masterpiece. Once in a small café, the young server had tripped and spilled a cup of hot soup behind Angel. Some of it had splashed on her sweater. Angel had not been burned, or hurt in any way, but instead of realizing that it was an accident, and could have happened to anyone, she had gone ballistic. She had shouted and made a huge fuss, and actually would have slapped the unfortunate girl, if Patrick hadn't grabbed her arm. She wanted the girl fired immediately.

He hustled her out of the café as quickly as possible, after leaving a large tip. Angel burst into tears, and the doctor just attributed it to her nerves, after all the surgeries and drugs which she had endured.

The affair had been a learning experience for the doctor in many ways. He had never done any surgery this intense and complicated, and he had learned a great deal. He hadn't charged her a penny for any of it, rationalizing that he was getting the benefit of the experience, as well as the fun of having this witty, quixotic, loving woman as his mistress.

How could he have been so blind? He kept making excuses for her, blaming her mood shifts and tantrums on the drugs, the pain, the long recovery periods. Too bad he hadn't known that she was an escapee from a psychiatric hospital. He certainly would have viewed these psychotic episodes with a more experienced eye, and would never have allowed himself to become so involved.

Lying on the bed in this Toronto hotel, far from home, he wondered at his own foolishness. She was a taker and a schemer, and he knew now that she could be very dangerous. How had he let himself become one of her victims?

It seemed like a horrible dream. Unfortunately it was all too real. It had taken him these past several weeks to accept that he had wasted all his skills on making her so beautiful on the outside, when she was apparently so rotten inside.

One night, when she had sipped too many wines, and was in a maudlin state of mind, she had ranted on and on about a woman she hated, and intended to kill some day. The woman's name was Kate, and she had apparently stolen Angel's first and only true love, (except for Patrick, of course), she had hastened to add.

She talked a lot about this Kate Chandler, who had been kidnapped once, and left to die in the Everglades. Angel claimed that she had almost caught her in Florida, but Kate had escaped. According to Angel, Kate was a writer and illustrator of books for children, but in truth she was a horrible person, a person who had stolen Mac from her.

To the doctor, the story sounded apocryphal. He hadn't been much interested, because Angel had obviously had too much wine. She sometimes got her dreams or movies confused with reality, so he paid little attention to her ramblings.

It was only after she had destroyed his clinic, and sent the letter to Madelaine, that he remembered her crazy story, and realized that she had likely been telling the truth, when she said that she was going to kill Kate some day.

He was now pretty sure that she had gone back to Canada, not only to hide from him after what she had done, but also, to finally kill this poor unsuspecting Kate.

He couldn't let that happen. She wasn't going to destroy another human being the way she had destroyed him, so he asked his investigator to find out everything he could about Kate Chandler, as well as tracking Angel.

Patrick hadn't slept much on the plane, and it had given him plenty of time to think. He had been emotionally battered from the trauma of losing his wife, his daughters, his practice, his good name, and, of course, his mistress. In fact, his entire life as he had known it, was now gone. He knew that something had to be done. It was just a question of what that "something" would be.

Angel could not be allowed to get away with the destruction she had left behind, nor could she be allowed to perpetrate some nefarious crime against the innocent Mrs. Chandler.

Patrick was beginning to think rationally again. He had rushed to follow Angel wherever she might go, just to seek some kind of nebulous revenge, and keep her from hurting Kate Chandler. It was time to make up his mind as to how he was going to accomplish these two goals.

He was an intelligent man who had made a bad mistake. Now he would begin to put things right.

By the time the plane had landed at Pearson International, and he had settled into his hotel room, Dr. Patrick O'Neal realized that these next few days or weeks could be the most important of his lifetime. He couldn't afford to make any more mistakes when dealing with Angel Baby!

Chapter Seventeen

—————❖—————❖—————❖—————

Sonny Martin and Lester Johnson were two strange friends, out for a little drive on a very blustery night. It just happened to be the same night that Kate and Davey were arriving at the cottage. It was also the same night that Paige had an extra choir practice.

Sonny was an odd young man, seventeen years of age. His friend Lester was twenty-one. The reason they had become friends, was that they both loved dirt biking, and they had spent the previous summer, amusing themselves for hours on end, riding their bikes.

Tonight when Lester had called, Sonny jumped at the chance to go out with his friend, in spite of the rotten weather. He just needed an excuse to get himself out of the house. Sonny's home life was not a happy one. His mother had died of cancer just over a year ago. His father, instead of grieving with his son, had found himself a girlfriend within three months. Not only was she a girlfriend, but she was a young girlfriend, at least she acted very young.

She was a bleached blonde, who liked to lounge around the house in bikini panties and a bra, which lifted her boobs right up under her chin. Sonny never knew where to look. She would get that goofy grin on her face, and shake her boobs at him, saying something like "I bet you'd love to get a nibble of these, wouldn't you Sonny boy?"

Poor Sonny was spending as much time away from the house as possible, but he was afraid that one of these days, he'd break down and ravage her right on the spot. After all, he was only human, he was seventeen, his hormones were raging, and she was driving him crazy. It was a scenario meant for disaster.

His father didn't seem to think there was anything wrong with her parading around half naked in front of his teenaged son, and he was spending money on her as if there was no tomorrow. It was disgusting, and scary.

Sonny had always been a strange young man. With thick glasses, and hair which seemed to grow in several directions, he wasn't exactly a calendar boy.

He was anti-social, and most of the time he felt like a misfit. He wasn't very good in school, but at math he was an absolute genius. He could add, subtract, multiply and divide just as fast as a computer, and numbers were his best friends. He loved them. To him they were like little people, and he had given them personalities.

The number 1 represented anorexic people, very skinny. To Sonny, the number 2 represented inquisitive people. It looked a little like a question mark. The number 3 was a little chubby child, half the size of the obese number 8. Number 4 was an engineer, all straight lines and sharp corners. He always thought of 5's as twins. He couldn't explain it, but he usually saw them in pairs. Number 6 was a pregnant woman. Number 7 was an anorexic person reaching out for help. Number 9 was his least favourite. This was a person with a big head – someone full of his own importance. The zero was the only one which wasn't a real person in Sonny's mathematical world.

Sonny had once tried to explain his "people numbers" to a friend, but she had thought he was crazy, and had avoided him after that.

Being a math genius was tough. He could solve difficult problems in his head, but he couldn't carry on a sensible conversation with anyone. He was dreadfully shy, and full of self doubt, and the new addition to his family – his father's buxom blonde, was driving him round the bend. He needed to get away, but he had no place to go. That was why he had agreed so willingly, to go out with Lester on this stormy night.

Lester Johnson was a whole different package. He had left school at sixteen, and had never held a job longer than a few weeks. He was lazy and slow witted, and he was lonely. His mother had left him and his brother when they were in their early teens. That had triggered something really mean in his father, who had become an abusive drunk. Not a day went by without him hitting Lester on the head a few times "just to keep him on his toes."

Lester knew that one of these days he would punch the old man out, and that would be the end of it. His younger brother had already run away, and there had been no trace of him for over a year now. Lester had no one to worry about, except for himself, and if he could just think of somewhere to go, well, he would go.

Tonight his father had slapped him a few times, for no good reason that Lester could figure, and had kicked him in the pants, as Lester turned to leave. As he had slammed the door, he heard his father cursing and yelling at him that he was not to come back. He figured that his dad would be drunk by the time that he got home, and would have forgotten what he said. Still, it was scary. He had no place else to go.

That was likely why on an impulse, he had stolen the old van, which he was now driving. On a stormy night like this, it was doubtful that anyone would notice it was gone, and certainly the police would have no reason to be looking for it. At least that was what Lester thought.

When Sonny wanted to know where he got the wheels, he simply mumbled that the old van belonged to his uncle. That was good enough for Sonny. He had no idea that the van was stolen. Nor did he suspect that Lester was in a foul mood, just spoiling for a fight. It didn't appear that there would be a happy outcome to this little joy ride, but that wasn't obvious yet to the two friends.

They were in an area of Toronto with which they weren't at all familiar. Actually, they were quite lost. Lester hadn't been paying any attention as they cruised along.

They couldn't decide whether to go to a movie, an arcade, Walmart, or maybe a pizzeria, if they could find one open.

At least the heater worked in the old van. It was actually too hot, and they both had to undo their jackets and take off their caps, as they enjoyed the peaceful feeling of being far away from their respective homes.

"You know, what we need is a couple of broads," laughed Lester, as if the thought had just come to him.

"We need a couple of broads with big hooters and long hair. Man, I love long hair," he added, smacking his lips, as if he had just eaten something delicious.

"Yah, that would be good," agreed Sonny, terrified at the thought of having to talk to a strange girl, no matter how long or short her hair was.

"There won't be any girls out tonight, though, so let's go to Walmart."

Sonny figured that Walmart was a safe place, where he and Lester could spend an hour or so, out of the cold. Maybe by the time Walmart closed, he could go home without running into his dad, and the bitch who liked to taunt him.

The stolen vehicle was coughing and spitting like an old man on his death bed, but the friends didn't notice. They were just rolling along, talking a bit, and peering through the snowy windshield at the white world around them.

Surely they would find something to do. And eventually they did.

Chapter Eighteen

The phone conversation with the private investigator John Chumley, was very illuminating. Patrick couldn't believe some of the information the former detective had managed to compile on both Kate and Angel. Apparently Kate Chandler had a home in Toronto, a condo in Florida, and a cottage in Muskoka. At the moment, according to Chumley's report, she was up north at her cottage, and she had her little boy with her.

As for Angel, well, information confirmed that she was a dangerous and crazy woman. The sooner Patrick was able to confront her, the sooner he would be able to return to Switzerland, and try to pick up the pieces.

According to the investigator, Angel had checked out of her hotel, and had asked the desk clerk questions as to the easiest way to get to Highway 400, and how long the drive would be to Bracebridge.

"Looks as if she's following Mrs. Chandler to her cottage, and she's probably a couple of hours ahead of us, maybe more. Do you want me to try to get back on her trail?"

Patrick didn't know where Bracebridge was, but Chumley told him it was north of the city by about two or more hours. Making a snap decision, the doctor decided that he had to follow Angel himself. If she was driving all the way up to Bracebridge in the middle of the winter, it was pretty obvious that she was chasing the unsuspecting Kate Chandler.

The scary part was that Patrick knew from experience, that Angel was certainly crazy enough, and vindictive enough, to be planning something bad. The good doctor just couldn't let that happen.

Chumley was proving to be worth every penny he was charging. He had managed to get excellent directions right to the Chandler cottage. He even had both the cottage number, and Kate's cell phone number. Patrick was impressed.

Patrick debated asking the investigator to come with him, but decided against it. He wasn't exactly sure what he intended to do to Angel Baby, but he knew he had to see her alone.

In his heart of hearts, he knew that he couldn't hurt her. That just wasn't his style. He might have to rough her up a bit, while trying to stop her from hurting Kate, but that was as far as he'd go.

He was still trying to decide just what punishment the crazy and vindictive Angel Baby really deserved. It certainly wouldn't be murder, even though he had been angry enough those first few days to seriously contemplate it.

Actually, the worst punishment in the world for Angel Baby, would be to cut up her face a bit. He could never do that though. That was something she was more likely to do to the unsuspecting Kate Chandler. No, he could never destroy the face he had worked so hard to create.

Traffic was relatively heavy, and visibility was poor. The doctor was in a strange country, on an unknown highway, on a snowy day.

He couldn't help wondering what trouble he might be bringing down on himself.

Although policemen love to say that there are no coincidences in life, or at least very few of them, (specially in murder cases), there were several coincidences on the highway those two days.

Kate had driven to the cottage on this same highway, the previous afternoon. She was intent on fixing the shattered window. She had been followed by Angel, driving north the next day, on the same highway, toward the same cottage, intent on killing Kate. Patrick followed, driving north toward Kate's cottage, chasing both women. He was intent on stopping Angel, his ex lover, from hurting Kate – a woman he had never met. It was the stuff from which a good movie could be made.

Weather conditions were causing Patrick to go slowly. This, he knew, was likely putting him even further behind Angel. How could he possibly get there in time to stop her from doing whatever it was she intended to do?

Rounding a curve, he saw that traffic was moving even slower than he was. There had obviously been an accident up ahead, and he could see a van overturned on the snowy median.

His heart jumped a bit, thinking that it might be Angel, but then he remembered that she was driving a red Buick, according to Chumley. It never occurred to him that Angel might have been the cause of the accident, rather than the possible victim.

A fleeting thought assailed him. How ironic that would be, if Angel were killed in a car wreck, before he had a chance to confront her. He might not be planning to hurt her, but he certainly hoped to confront her. He wanted to look right into those beautiful eyes, and just ask the one word, "why?"

Patrick was relieved to see that there were no bodies lying around. Police and a tow truck were working to get the van out of the way, and obviously any ambulances were already gone. With the bad weather, clean-up was taking a long time.

As he drove slowly past the scene of the accident, he wondered what type of "good Samaritan" laws they had in Canada. He was relieved that he didn't have to tend to some poor victim. He wouldn't want to open himself up to a lawsuit, but, being a doctor, he would have been duty bound to help anyone who might have been hurt.

He was frustrated enough as it was, worrying that Angel might do something bad to Kate before he could get there. He didn't want or need anything else delaying him.

Passing the accident scene, he thought about the vagaries of life. Here he was – a doctor committed by his Hippocratic oath to saving lives, when, in actual fact, that first day he had returned from Spain, he had actually thought he could take a life! What had he been thinking?

Alone in a rental car, far from home, the good doctor had plenty of time to ponder his situation. He had come all this way to seek revenge on Angel, but what kind of revenge did he want?

Disturbing doubts had filled his head for weeks, bouncing and rolling like tumbleweed at the mercy of a heavy wind. That old idea of murder had raised its ugly head more than once, but he had just kept batting it aside.

"To kill or not to kill." At one point, that had been the question. Patrick laughed. "What a ridiculous figure I've become," he muttered, shaking his head.

He had taken that sacred oath to protect and save lives to the very best of his ability. He was a man whose patients trusted him. He had built up a wonderful practice. He was not capable of murder.

Patrick had started three charities, his favourite being "Patrick's Kids." That one was for babies and children under twelve, who had been born with severe birth defects such as cleft palates. Would it be worth it to throw all that away, in order to get revenge on a deranged woman, who no longer meant anything to him? Absolutely not!

Had he really thought for one moment that he, the famous and beloved Dr. Patrick O'Neal, could actually commit murder? Who had he been kidding? He was furious at Angel. Still, killing her wouldn't solve anything, and he just might have found himself in prison for the rest of his life.

In the solitude and silence of the car, he wondered about Angel Baby and Kate Chandler. How was Angel planning to kill Kate?

Strangling her was likely not an option. Angel's hands were small, and he didn't know what size Kate was. He couldn't imagine one woman strangling another. It just didn't seem feasible.

A gun was the most likely. But where would Angel get one? He didn't think she'd use a knife. That would be too "up close and personal." Kate might be able to fight back, and get the best of her.

He guessed that Angel would give her intended victim an overdose of something. He knew that she had stolen a lot of drugs from his clinic, including Rohypnol. That's more than likely what she would use.

"So there you have it, doc," he said to himself. "You're a bloody wimp, and you couldn't hurt a fly. You might talk big in your head, but you're still a wimp, whereas Angel Baby definitely has the guts to do it!"

Grinning to himself, he said out loud, "Hell, maybe I'll just kick her in that cute little derrière of hers, or shake her till her teeth come loose. That's likely about as vicious and vindictive as I can get!"

Patrick's mind went back to cutting Angel's face, so that she would have to go through the rest of her life truly ugly, ugly as sin. After all, she had proved to be ugly in her heart and soul. Why not give her an ugly face to match?

That wouldn't be difficult to do physically, but as a doctor, would he ever be able to do it? No, definitely not. It might be the perfect revenge, but it wasn't the sort of thing he could ever do. Still, while driving along on this stormy afternoon, it gave him a certain satisfaction just thinking about it.

He wished now, that he had been able to set out earlier. It was not good that Angel could be three or four hours ahead of him.

Hopefully, though, she might get lost, or she might take her time, teasing and taunting Kate, before actually killing her. Yes, that's exactly what she would do.

And now he knew what he was going to do. As soon as he had thought of it, he knew that it was the best and only solution. He would not only get perfect revenge, but he would be doing citizens of the world a big favour. He would make sure that Angel Baby was held by the police, until they could get her recommitted to a mental institution.

This time it would be one from which she couldn't possibly escape.

Yes! If he could get there in time to save Kate, and to send Angel back where she belonged, then this trip to Canada would have been worthwhile.

For the first time in a long time, Dr. Patrick O'Neal felt really good about himself.

After his trip to Muskoka was finished, his next move would be to drive back to the airport, and head directly for Switzerland. There he would concentrate on trying to put his life back together.

It all suddenly seemed very simple, but the good doctor hadn't taken into account the Fates who like to stir the pot. They were up to their old tricks, manipulating mere mortals for their own amusement. At this point, they had something else in mind for Dr. Pat!

Patrick suddenly realized that he was short of gas, and he was thirsty. Fortunately he had only gone a couple of miles further, before he saw the welcome lights of a gas station. With a sigh of relief, he pulled off the highway.

What were the odds that it would be the same gas station where Kate had stopped yesterday, and where Angel Baby had stopped earlier today? Actually, the odds were pretty good, since it was the only gas station for miles, along that stretch of highway.

Patrick asked the young attendant whether by any chance a red Buick had stopped for gas within the past few hours.

"There's a really beautiful woman driving it. I'm sure you'd remember her."

"Hey, you bet," replied the eager fellow.

"She's a knock-out. She wanted help with her map, so we talked for a while. She's visiting someone at a cottage. Crazy in this weather, but she says they've invited her up for a few days to go skiing and skidooing. They won't be doing much of that, until this storm blows itself out. It's supposed to get a whole lot worse before it gets any better."

Patrick mentioned that she was his girlfriend, and that they were going to the same cottage.

"I was supposed to be following her, but there was an accident on the highway, and she got ahead of me. I'm not exactly sure where the cottage is."

Although the doctor had pretty good directions from Chumley, directions which were quite clear, he didn't want to waste any time driving around hopelessly looking for one particular cottage. Why not get Chumley's directions confirmed, if possible, by this young fellow. It could save time in the long run.

"Oh, I can tell you where it is. I know that area really well. Lived here all my life."

By the time Patrick had paid for the gas and a couple of chocolate bars, he knew exactly where he was going. He was clutching a small diagram, which the helpful young fellow had drawn for him. The big question, however, was, would he get there in time?

He had gone another few miles beyond the gas station, when he realized that it would be smart to call ahead and warn Kate. Why hadn't he done it sooner? He did have the cottage phone number, and Kate's cell phone number, and if she wasn't there, he could have left a message.

Well, he would pull off the highway at the very next place which might have a phone.

Chapter Nineteen

Kate thought she had never seen anything so welcome as the cottage, when it appeared out of the darkness. True, it looked cold and deserted, and somehow foreboding, but still, it would be shelter for them. They would soon be warm and cosy.

Somehow it looked so much bigger. with the bare trees around it, and the white snow covering the ground. It was going to be such a great retreat for the family next summer, but tonight, in the storm, it looked unfriendly.

She was certainly thankful, that she hadn't driven up by herself. Davey might be just a little boy, but he was great company, and together, they would snuggle down. Alone, however, she would have been more than nervous, probably hearing strange creakings and moanings, as the wind howled and whined. Strange how just having another human with you, made things seem more safe and tenable.

At the moment, she wondered whether she would ever be warm again. The wind had been bullying them along. It pushed and shoved, showing no mercy, no milk of human kindness. She was sure that she had never been out this long on a night this cold. She was amazed at how well Davey had done.

Since the kitchen was at the back, facing the road, they could easily see the large broken window. The vandal or vandals had done a good job on it. There was quite a big hole in the center of it, but there were still jagged pieces around the edges.

The relentless wind was coming off the lake at the front, so there was no snow blowing through the window at the back. Kate wondered, however, what she would find when they got inside.

At some point, the snow, victim of the raging wind, had drifted into a big pile right against the kitchen door. This had obviously happened since the two Walters had been there. Kate and Davey had to kick with their feet, and dig with their hands, to get enough snow away from the door, so that it could be opened. Davey was good at this, and felt important because he was really helping. In spite of how tired he was, he seemed to revive, and made a game of the snow removal.

To Kate's relief, she found that the power was still on. It was warmer compared to outside, but not by much. They left on their parkas, boots and mitts, as they surveyed the damage.

All she had to do was flip the switch for the heated water line, and they would have hot running water within the hour.

The damage wasn't nearly as bad as she had feared. She had visualized animals taking up residence, but there were no signs of any critters. She had also pictured great piles of snow blown all over the kitchen. Walt and Walt Jr. however, had done a good job of cleaning up the snow and the broken glass. There was some snow in the sink, and some on the surrounding counters and floor, but it could have been so much worse.

Kate had even imagined the vandals coming back to party, maybe even bringing their friends. It was comforting to see that none of her dire fears had come to fruition.

Davey was quick to remind his mother not to touch anything in case of destroying finger prints. Kate grinned a little, as she thought that she had likely created a monster. Davey would be a pain in the butt, constantly reminding her about the fingerprint problem. He was like a terrier, once he got hold of a bone. Actually, he would be a good reminder, in case she got careless.

She got out a pad of paper and a pen, and suggested that Davey follow her, and write down everything they thought was missing. She knew he would love this part of being a detective, and it would help him forget how uncomfortably cold it was in the cottage, or how spooky it seemed.

Once again she realized just how big their newly purchased cottage was, and how quiet it was in the winter, with no other cottagers near by, and no boats zooming around the lake.

"As soon as we've gone through each room quickly, and made note of anything we think is missing, we'll make a big fire and get warm."

"We have to do a really good job, mom. The police will need our help," Davey maintained solemnly, as he dutifully followed behind her.

To Kate's chagrin, she discovered that both televisions, plus the vcr and dvd players were missing, along with the stereo. The cds and dvds, however, were still neatly piled on the shelf. Every bottle of booze was gone, and they had even taken the junk jewellery from the small box in her bedroom. To Davey's great relief, all his paints, brushes and drawing pads, were still there. Apparently they had been of no interest or value to the vandals.

Kate was thankful that, other than breaking the window, the intruders hadn't done any damage. Nothing else was broken or spilled, and the toilet had not been plugged. They apparently hadn't been mean spirited thieves. It seemed that they had only been interested in anything which could be turned into cash. She almost felt grateful to them, which was rather ridiculous.

After they had done their inspection tour, Kate started a fire. Mac had left the wood all set and ready to go, in the fireplace, so that all she had to do was light a match. Sitting in front of it felt wonderful, as the warmth gradually pervaded the room, not to mention their frozen bones. She wished she could have a nice glass of port or sherry to warm her insides, but there was no such bottle to be found. Hot chocolate would have to do.

When they were both warm enough to remove their jackets, Kate said, "Davey, you've got two choices. You can stay right here in front of the fire, and just relax and keep warm, or you can help me. I know you must be really tired, so it's whatever you want."

She knew, of course, what his answer would be.

"I'll help. What are we going to do?"

"Well, I want you to get out the big box of green garbage bags from the kitchen pantry. We'll need those, and we'll need your dad's staple gun. Do you know where he keeps it?"

"Yep. I think it's in that cupboard where the broom and the cleaning stuff belong."

"Okay. You get those things for me, please, while I go get some things out of the old cedar chest. Be really careful, though, that you don't go near that broken window. Those jagged pieces could cut you to ribbons, and you'd never be able to draw again! I'll meet you in the kitchen in a few minutes."

Kate knew it wasn't nice to try to scare the little guy that way, but she also knew that it was one sure way of keeping him safely away from the broken shards.

She had decided that the best way to cover the window tonight, would be to staple the plastic garbage bags all around the frame, then staple more of them to each other, to make one big plastic sheet. Then she would cover that with an old quilt, which she had found last fall tucked away in the cedar chest. It wouldn't keep out the cold, but if the wind shifted, it would at least keep the snow from blowing in. It would also hopefully discourage any animals from trying to enter.

The cedar chest turned out to be a bit of a bonanza. Not only was there the very old quilt which she hated to sacrifice, but also a somewhat tattered blanket, which would contribute slightly to keeping out the cold.

The entire idea was a pretty smart one, but putting it into play was something else again. It took her a while to figure out how to use the staple gun, with the least amount of danger to herself and her surroundings. The darn thing was heavy and unwieldy.

She had to staple the big green garbage bags together, to make the plastic sheet big enough to cover the entire opening. Stapling the plastic to the window frame was difficult and time consuming, and her arms and hands were aching by the time that part was finished. At least she didn't have to battle the wind, while she was struggling with the bags. The unstoppable wind was still coming from the lake, and was giving the front of the cottage a good pounding.

Kate wondered whether any branches might break off and come through a window, or through the screens on the front porch. There were so many beautiful old oak trees surrounding the cottage, that it certainly was a possibility. She didn't want to even think of how they would handle something that serious.

She didn't like having to put staples in the old quilt. No doubt someone had spent many loving hours creating it, but Kate knew it was doing more good stapled to the window frame, than lying forgotten in the cedar chest, which had come with the cottage. Whoever had made it would just have to forgive her!

By the time she was finished, she had done a pretty fine job. The quilt, blanket and plastic bags were pulled tight across the open window, and they were well stapled down. Unfortunately, the window frame would be totally destroyed with all the staples in it. Mac would just have to forgive her for that. You do what you have to do.

Davey kept up a constant stream of suggestions and encouraging words. He made her laugh. What a good little companion he was.

She was glad that she had brought him along. It would have been extremely lonely if she had come up by herself.

Unfortunately, however, it wouldn't be long before she was desperately sorry that she had brought her son with her.

Her call to the police was not overly reassuring. They said that with the treacherous condition of the roads, and the number of calls, they would put her on the list, but it would be the next day for sure, before they could get out to estimate the damage at the cottage.

The overworked officer, who had said that his name was Bradley, seemed to think that she was crazy to have deliberately driven to the cottage in the storm, thus putting herself and her son in danger.

Kate didn't appreciate his snarky tone, but realized that he was likely exhausted in this bad weather. She just hoped he wouldn't be the one to come tomorrow. She had enough on her mind without having to deal with a temperamental police officer.

Chapter Twenty

A call to Jill and the twins cheered her, but also left her a bit concerned. Things were fine at the house. The twins had been studying for their exams the following day, and Jill was baking a cake, (a new hobby), for a post exam celebration.

The only problem was, that Paige said she had to go to a short choir rehearsal. The school choir was performing in a few days, and apparently their music teacher had told them they had to come back to the school that night. She had promised not to keep them late.

Jill was concerned about letting Paige go, as it was such a stormy night. Also, she knew that Paige had to study for the next day's exams. The decision was up to Kate.

At first Kate said absolutely not. It was far too stormy.

Paige wasn't giving up without a fight. "Mom, I have to go. I'll be the only one missing, and I'm the one doing that short solo. I can't let them down. Aunt Jill will drive me, and Amy's mom is going to pick us up, and bring us home.

"Please, mom, you'll make me a total pariah (this was one of Paige's new dramatic words). I'll never be able to face anyone again. I don't mind going out in the storm, and I've really done all the studying I need. I feel good about the exams. I can ace them. Please mom. It's just a little snow. It's not as if we're having a hurricane or a twister!"

Much against her better judgement, Kate finally agreed, then spoke to Jill again.

"I'm sorry, Jill. I hate to ask you to go out on such a lousy night. Do you think it's safe to drive to the school and back?"

"Oh sure, don't worry about it. I'll get her there, and Amy's mom is picking them up, so she'll be fine. Don't you worry."

"Okay, kiddo. I'll owe you a big one. You're the best friend a gal could have."

"Yah, yah," laughed Jill. "You can take me out to lunch when you return, and tell me all your adventures."

Little did she know or suspect, just how many adventures Kate was about to have, in the next twenty-four hours.

Under her breath, Kate cursed the stubborn, idiotic, heartily disliked Miss Lasher, the music teacher. She was filling in for the regular music teacher, who was dearly beloved by everyone, but who was away on maternity leave.

Insisting on a rehearsal, when it was a dangerously stormy night, and when it was the night before the start of mid-terms, was inconceivably thoughtless and careless. Miss Lasher was indeed a royal pain, as all her students claimed, and she should be reprimanded for her cavalier attitude. Kate would definitely speak to her, when she got back to the city. Meantime, she was sure that between Jill and Amy's mom, Paige would be fine.

As she did a few little things around the cottage, Kate gave some serious thought to how lucky she was to have Jill for a good friend. They had been friends most of their lives, even though Jill had led a rather peripatetic existence, spending a lot of time in some very exotic places.

Her father had been a missionary of sorts, and Jill had lived in Tahiti, the Bahamas, Nigeria and the Philippines, to name just a few of her homes away from home.

Each time her father was returned to Canada for a year or two, Kate and Jill picked up their friendship again.

Kate benefited from hearing all the tales Jill had to tell about life in foreign countries. For Jill, on the other hand, it was easier to fit back in with her Canadian peers, with the ever faithful Kate at her side. Kate had complete trust in, and love for Jill, and was never worried when her three kids were in Jill's capable hands. Actually, now that they were in their "terrible teens," the twins seemed to enjoy Jill's company more than that of their parents.

Jill said that the cats were definitely missing Davey, and, according to Peter, all three were sleeping on his bed, waiting for his return. That made Davey smile. He had wanted to bring Tom, Dick and Harriet with them, but his mom had nixed that idea in a hurry.

Since they were inside cats, how would he and his mother have ever been able to carry the three of them from the car to the cottage, without losing at least one of them in the snow? After experiencing the scary and tiring walk in from the road, Davey knew that, as usual, his mom had been right. Still, he missed them a lot.

After talking with everyone, Kate plugged in her cell phone, so that it would be charged in case of an emergency.

She was tired after the long drive, and her struggles with the window coverings. She wondered, though, whether she should go out, and try to start up one of the snowmobiles. She would feel better if she knew that it was cleaned off, and ready to go in an emergency. It didn't take her long to talk herself out of that idea, reasoning that it would be covered with snow again by morning, and it would be difficult to start, no matter when she tried.

Now it was time to get some sleep. Kate wanted Davey to join her in the king sized bed. She didn't like the idea of him sleeping alone in his room down the hall. This was indeed a big cottage, specially with just the two of them rattling around in it.

She knew that, although her make-shift window protection would keep the snow and some of the cold out, it was absolutely no protection from any human who might want to get in. The sad truth was, that they were extremely vulnerable. The question was, how would she persuade her son, who was very independent, and would balk at sleeping in the same bed with his mother. Davey, however, surprised her with a much better plan.

"Well, kiddo, I think it's time for bed," Kate began. "We need to be up fairly early tomorrow, to arrange for the window plywood, meet the police when they arrive, and maybe find time to go for a little skidoo ride, if the snow isn't too deep."

Now came the reverse psychology.

"You'd better sleep with all your clothes on, and I'll try to find a heating pad for you. Being on the lake side, and with the wind blowing from there, it's going to be really cold in your bedroom. You might have icicles on your nose by morning. It's too bad you couldn't sleep in my room. It will be much warmer, and I have that great big bed, but I know you'd never want to do that."

"Mom," said Davey very seriously, "I was thinking that we could pull out the twin mattresses and put them in front of the fire. We could sleep right here, and it would be nice and cosy. We could pretend we're camping out. Don't you think that's a good idea?"

Kate looked at him in amazement.

"Davey Doodle, that's a wonderful idea. We can keep each other company, and we'll be much warmer in front of the fireplace. Man oh man, I wish I'd had you on the island with me. You would have found a way to get us home without any trouble."

Davey basked in his mother's praise, as she continued.

"I like your way of thinking, mister. Wait till I tell your dad what a super idea you've had. Where did I get such a smart kid?

"You know, when you were born, your head came to a big point! Well, not too big, but your dad and I were sure that you were going to be seriously handicapped. You could have plugged the point of your head into a wall socket!! Now look at you. You're the smartest one in the family!" With that she hugged him tightly, and they grinned at each other.

Kate and Mac had teased Davey many times about the shape of his head, when he was first born. The story had become part of the Chandler family lore. Davey didn't mind the teasing, in fact he loved it. The stories always ended with what a smart little guy he had become.

"Just feel it now, oh ye of little faith," he said to his mom. It was a phrase he had learned from his dad, and he liked to use it whenever he could. "It's as round and perfect as a billiard ball."

They were both laughing, as they went off to find the twin mattresses.

Kate knew that they would get things all straightened out tomorrow, and might even have time for some old fashioned fun before heading home. She definitely wanted to take her son snowmobiling down in the meadow, or at least have a good snow ball fight, if the snow wasn't too powdery. She felt that they might as well make this into a real mini winter vacation – one that Davey would remember for a long time.

Well, at least that part was right. Davey would never forget this particular trip to the cottage. Kate might well have some plans which sounded like fun, but, as so often happens, the Fates had other plans in mind.

Chapter Twenty-One

Paige didn't know what was wrong with her these days. She had such mixed emotions about everything, and she felt as if she wanted to argue all the time. Even Peter was a royal pain, and he had always been her nearest and dearest pal. She missed him, but everything he did or said seemed to irritate her.

She knew that kids were supposed to become mean spirited and fractious when they reached their teens, but it wasn't a nice feeling. She wished she could jump ahead five years and be her old self again. She had liked her old self, but she didn't like this new person she had become.

She really did not want to go to that stupid choir rehearsal tonight. Who was mean enough to call for a practice the night before exams? Teachers knew better than that. Miss Lasher was a horrible old bag, but Paige knew she had to go. Everyone else had said they would go, so she couldn't beg off. Blah!

What she'd like to do, was curl up in the big chair in her room, sip a nice cup of hot chocolate, and put in two more hours of review. Then she'd feel really confident that she could answer any questions they might throw at her, in tomorrow's exams.

"Paige, I'll have to drive slowly in this storm, so I think we should go now," said Aunt Jill, coming into the room, with her coat and car keys in hand.

"What's the rush, we've got lots of time," whined Paige, deliberately moving at a snail's pace, from her bedroom to the front door.

"I think you should put on a hat and mitts. It's really windy and cold out there," suggested Jill, with a smile. She knew that Paige was just trying to annoy her, and she wasn't going to play that game.

"I'm fine the way I am," snapped Paige, as they headed to the car. These were words she would soon have to eat.

When they arrived at the school, they found that Miss Lasher was already there – at least her car was in the parking lot, and there were lights on in the main hall.

"Okay, now, you're sure that Amy's mom is picking you up? I'd be glad to come and get you, if you want to call me."

"No, I'll go home with Amy and her mom. You don't need to bother." Muttering a grudging "thanks," Paige hurried up the school steps.

Jill sighed. She missed the old Paige – the one who was so sweet, so obliging, so charming. Puberty was no fun, specially for the adults who had to suffer through it with the teens. She didn't envy Kate and Mac, with three of them to guide through the rough years.

Paige saw that there was only one other singer there, along with Miss Lasher. He was a boy she really didn't like. He was big and roly-poly, and was always sweating. No one liked to sit near him, because he tended to pick his nose and burp a lot. Wouldn't you know he would have a lovely voice!

She had hoped that John McLeod would join the choir this year, but apparently he didn't like to sing. He was tall, with very black hair and long black eyelashes, which any girl would love to have. He had a dimple in one cheek, and it made her feel all tingly when he grinned at her. Wouldn't it have been nice if John was here right now, instead of burping Gerald, and glaring Lasher. Life just wasn't fair!

After twenty minutes, Miss Lasher began pacing around. "No one has called to say they can't come, so where are they?" she grumbled. She hated school, hated being a teacher, and hated her lonely life. She didn't like the kids any more than they liked her, and she couldn't wait for this term to finish. She definitely wasn't returning next year.

After another twenty minutes, it was obvious that no one else was coming.

"I have to go, Miss Lasher. I have a lot of studying to do," said Paige, putting on her coat. She was furious with her friend Amy, who had not called, and who had not appeared. Now she'd have to call Aunt Jill to come and get her, and she really didn't want to do that.

Gerald, the fat boy, jumped into his waiting father's truck, and they took off around the corner. What a pig, Paige thought. At least he could have asked her if she needed a drive. Of course she would never have driven with him. Imagine sitting close beside him, while he picked his nose and burped! Ugh!

Miss Lasher said "You're sure you have a ride?" as she headed for her car. Paige nodded, and Miss Lasher took off around the corner. Now Paige was alone.

As she stood digging into her purse for her cell phone, she realized how cold it really was. The wind was absolutely biting.

Where the heck was her phone? She never went anywhere without it, but suddenly she remembered. She had been lying on her bed, talking with Priscilla, another one of her friends, who was smart enough not to be in that stupid choir. Then Aunt Jill had stuck her head in the door, and said it was time to go. Oh no! She had left her cell phone lying right there on the bed! Now what?

She stayed calm, while she tried to think what to do, but suddenly she realized the seriousness of her situation. Gerald and his father were gone. Miss Lasher was gone. The school doors were locked. She had no cell phone. She was truly up shit creek without a paddle.

Her mom didn't like her using that expression. It was far too close to the truth of what had actually happened to Kate. Still, Paige felt it fitted her situation perfectly at the moment. What in the heck was she going to do?

She knew one thing for sure. When she got her hands on her "former" friend Amy, she would strangle her. Amy and her mom were supposed to drive her home. How could they leave her in this awful position?

Tears came to her eyes, but Paige told herself that she was not crying. It was just the darn wind that was making them water!

Standing on the steps, she looked up and down the street. It had never occurred to her before, but the school was certainly not in a residential area. There were no houses to be seen. There was a church next door, then a lovely big park, then another church. Across the street was a strip mall with an ice cream parlour, a bank, a place to get your nails done, a lawyer's office, and who knew what else. Beyond that was an empty lot, and some other offices.

She had never really paid any attention to the surroundings of the school. Now, with a sinking heart, she realized that there were no lights in the strip mall. It was after 8 o'clock, and everything was closed.

There was absolutely nothing she could do, but walk the eight or ten blocks to the warmth and safety of her home. She wasn't even sure how many blocks it was, but she knew that it was definitely too far, on a freezing night like this.

Oh how she wished she had listened to Aunt Jill's suggestion about a hat and mitts. She'd likely freeze to death, and be found in a snow bank in the morning.

Angry at the world, because she couldn't admit that she was angry at herself, she set out at a fast trot. The faster she went, the faster she would be home.

She kept watching hopefully for Amy and her mom, but no car appeared.

She was barely past the first church, when she stepped on an icy patch, and landed on her backside. Now the tears did come, but they were more tears of anger and frustration than of despair. That would come later.

It was a very dark night. With the snow twirling and whirling around her head, it was difficult to see. The street lights were giving off a feeble yellowish illumination, which didn't help much. It made everything seem ghostly.

Paige thought of every scary book and movie she had ever read or seen. "Nightmare on Elm Street" was right up there, along with "Halloween" and "The Shining". "Tales of the Crypt" wasn't far behind.

She couldn't believe that she had actually come out without her cell phone. Her mom claimed that it was attached permanently to her ear. She had begged and pleaded for it, pointing out that she would be much safer, if she could always call for help when needed.

What a dope she was. She didn't deserve to have a phone, if she couldn't remember to carry it with her. She wondered whether she could pretend that Amy's mom really had picked her up. She could tell Auntie Jill that Mrs. Duncan's car had failed, or run out of gas, part way home, and that was why she'd had to walk the last section of the route.

No, that wouldn't work. Paige was an honest girl, and she couldn't look at Aunt Jill, and deliberately lie to her. Maybe if she just told the truth, and begged her aunt not to tell, her mom would never need to know that she had put herself in a serious situation by being careless. Yes, that was good. That might work.

Her mother would have the worst fit, if she ever discovered that Paige had not only forgotten the cell phone for which she had begged, but she had actually walked home all alone in the dark and cold.

Her nose was dripping now, but she was too cold to stop and wipe it. She just sniffled and kept on going, telling herself that she was fine, and that she could do this.

Just then, a large pick-up truck pulled up beside her. Oh, thank heavens. It must be someone she knew, someone who had recognized her, and was going to give her a ride home. She would be eternally grateful.

She stopped, with a relieved smile on her face, as the window rolled down slowly. A woman with a cigarette hanging out the corner of her mouth, grinned at her.

"Want a lift, honey?" asked the stranger.

Paige knew immediately that this was no one she knew or could trust. She was desperate to get into the warmth of that truck, but she knew the rules about not taking a ride from strangers.

She stepped a little closer, to see if she could see the driver. Maybe he or she was a friend, or maybe they were parents of a friend.

The man driving was wearing a baseball cap, so she couldn't really see his face. He was also smoking. A great cloud of smoke wafted out the open window, mixing with the snow and wind.

"Come on, make up your mind. We're freezing our asses here," shouted the woman with the cigarette and the straggly hair.

These were definitely not people Paige knew. Thinking quickly, she said, "Thanks so much, but my dad's on his way. He'll be here in a second. I was just walking to meet him. It's very nice of you to offer, but I'm fine. Thanks again."

With that, she hurried down the street, praying that the truck would keep on going.

It did.

Now she was second guessing herself. They were likely fine people. She didn't know how she might have squeezed into the cab of that truck, but it would have been so warm. She was likely a fool for turning down the offer. Still, she couldn't take the chance. The woman looked awfully tough and mean. Well, maybe the next car going by would be someone she knew, and her troubles would be over.

Then again, maybe not.

Chapter Twenty-Two

Paige was not only freezing, but she was scared too. She began to think that this was punishment for the way she had been acting lately. She had been awfully nasty to her mom, and to Peter and Davey, and even to Auntie Jill. She loved all of them so much, but they all irritated her these days.

She thought of how amazing her mom had looked the night of the Royal York dance. She had been wearing a lovely new dress, and Paige thought she looked like a movie star. She hadn't said a thing though. She had just been so mean and heartless. She had been mad that she didn't have a beautiful new dress like that, and she had been jealous of the way her dad had been looking at her mom.

What was wrong with her? As soon as she got home, she should call her mom, and tell her how beautiful she had looked that night.

There had been so many other times lately that she knew she had hurt her mother's feelings, but she just couldn't help herself. Mean thoughts kept bubbling up to the surface, and there were days when she hated everyone, even some of her closest friends.

At the moment she hated Amy. How could she leave her in the lurch this way? They had been friends for years – since they started kindergarten together, but Amy had blown her off tonight, as if she was nobody.

Well, Amy could just kiss her cute little behind. They were no longer friends. She didn't need friends like that!

As Paige came to that harsh conclusion, she slipped on another stretch of ice, and down she went. This time she really hurt her wrist, and more tears sprang to her eyes. She would never get home at this rate.

She got back onto her feet, but couldn't use her right hand to dust off the snow. It was smarting, and stinging, and throbbing like crazy, and she wondered whether she had broken it. Standing still, she tried to move the hand around. She waggled it back and forth, and decided that it wasn't broken, but it really did hurt. It was likely strained or sprained. Great! How was she going to write her exams tomorrow if she couldn't hold a pen! Well, maybe they'd let her write them later. That wouldn't be bad at all.

Paige made a very pathetic figure, standing there in the dark, the snow and the wind. There was not another soul on the street, and she felt as if she was the last person on earth.

She had read a really good book about that, but couldn't remember the title. It was something like "The Last Canadian."

In the book, everyone in the world had caught some horrible disease, and they had all died. This guy, however, had been exploring in a cave or something, and had been lost for over a week. When he finally found his way out, everyone he knew was dead.

For a long time he just wandered, looking for another human being, but there was no one. He was able to break into stores to get food, and he used any car he wanted, until it ran out of gas, then he'd just get another one.

In a way it was pretty neat, and she hadn't understood why the man was so indescribably lonely. Now, however, she understood. People need people, and right now Paige really needed a friend.

She was so caught up in the book, trying to remember how it had ended, that at first she was not aware of the van which passed very slowly.

It turned the corner, and was out of sight before she looked around hopefully again for help.

She was passing the big, empty park now, and that was truly scary. It was a huge park, maybe too big to be right in the middle of the city, but Paige knew that Toronto prided itself on its lovely green spaces. In the winter, people often used this park for cross-country skiing, but there was no one foolish enough to be out tonight. It was definitely a night for fireplaces, comfy chairs, hot chocolate, and soothing music.

If it hadn't been for that darn Miss Lasher, she would be home doing all those wonderful things. To be honest, Paige knew that if it wasn't for the cell phone, which was still lying on her bed, she would be sitting in Aunt Jill's nice warm car just about now.

Instead, here she was, still blocks away from home, hatless, mittless, and too darn cold to think straight. She knew that it served her right, after she had been so sulky and sharp with Aunt Jill all day.

Her ears were freezing, so she tried covering one ear for a while, and keeping the other hand warming in her pocket. Then she would bring out the warm hand, cover the ear on that side, and put the frozen hand in her pocket. It was working to a certain extent, but she was getting colder and colder all over. She was still a long way from home, and her right wrist really hurt.

She had finally decided that she would take a chance, and ring the doorbell of the first house with lights on. Of course she still had to get past the large park, then the other church with its big empty parking lot, before she would come to any houses.

When she did get to some civilization again, she would ask them to call Aunt Jill, and she would wait outside on their porch until Jill arrived. There was always the chance that she would be ringing the doorbell of some serial killer, but at this point she was too cold and scared to care. All she wanted was to get home, and she didn't think she'd make it through this storm.

Where were all the city vehicles? Shouldn't there be a snow plough out working by now? A snow plough driver would be great. He'd let her sit in his cab, and he'd have some form of communication, so she could contact Aunt Jill.

When the van suddenly drove right up beside her, it didn't take her long to realize that she was likely in trouble. She didn't hesitate, she just started to run. She had wanted someone to come along, but this was a big van with no windows in the back. She'd heard enough stories, that she knew in her heart, it wasn't there to help her.

"Hey, wait a minute. We just want to give you a ride. Don't run, we're trying to help. You shouldn't be out on a bad night like this."

The words sounded good, but Paige couldn't take a chance. She kept running.

Soon she heard laughing, and footsteps behind her. She knew then that she was likely going to die. Paige Chandler, only thirteen years old, through her own carelessness, had placed herself in a position where she could see no escape. Tonight was going to be the last night of her young life.

She sobbed as she ran. Then suddenly strong hands were grabbing at her arms. It was just about over.

It was Sonny who had spotted Paige first.

"Hey, look at that young girl rushing along. She's almost running. She's got no hat and no mitts. She looks as if she's frozen. Maybe we should give her a lift."

As soon as the words were out of his mouth, he regretted them. He didn't exactly trust Lester, and he knew that the last thing they needed to do was pick up a strange young girl. It just wouldn't be right. Anyway, it was too late now.

Lester slowed down, but kept on going, as he peered out the snowy window at Paige. When he rounded the corner, Sonny was relieved. They were not stopping. Lester, however, sped up as he drove around the large block. He was laughing, and muttering something to himself.

"Don't stop, Les. We'll just scare her. She's likely almost home, or maybe her folks are coming to meet her."

"Oh no. I think we should stop," said Lester, with a grin.

"Not nice to leave a young lady in distress, now is it?" He didn't really expect an answer.

As soon as Paige saw them slowing down and pacing her, she had begun to run. That was probably a mistake. It was like a cat starting to run in front of a dog. There was no way the dog could resist chasing, and so it was with Lester. He slammed on the brakes, and was out of the van, before Sonny realized what was happening.

Now Sonny could see them struggling, and he didn't know what to do. Lester was yelling at him to come and help get her into the van, but Sonny was paralyzed with indecision and good old fashioned fear. He couldn't be part of this. He just wanted to go home and mind his own business. There were times that Lester got a little crazy, and this looked like one of those times.

Paige was putting up a good fight, but she was already so cold and exhausted, that she was no match for the six foot, two hundred pound Lester. Besides, her right wrist, well, actually, her whole hand, hurt so much that it was basically useless. In less than a minute she had been dragged into the van, the doors were slammed, and they were on their way, slipping and careening down the street.

"Hold her down and keep her quiet," ordered Lester, as he rubbed his cheek, where Paige had managed to scratch him with her nails. She was going to pay her for that. He'd make sure of it.

"Sonny, get into the back right now," he shouted at his friend.

Sonny obeyed, scrambling through the middle section. The back seats had long ago disappeared, and Paige was sitting on the floor, but trying to get up on her knees.

"Please don't hurt me," she begged, as Sonny tried to keep her arms from hitting him. She was fighting and yelling, and he was afraid he would hurt her, as he tried to subdue her.

"Sit still. Calm down. We're not going to hurt you. We're just giving you a ride home." Sonny hoped that this was true, but he had his doubts.

"Shut up back there," shouted Lester, scowling over his shoulder. "If you don't shut up, I'll stop the van, and come back there and knock you out. I'm not kidding. Besides, I've got a gun in the glove compartment, and I'm not afraid to use it."

Sonny stopped struggling with the girl. A gun? Lester had a gun? Oh boy. This was bad. Sonny didn't want any part of this!

"Quit fooling, Les. Let's just take her home. Or maybe we should just put her out on the street. She can get home herself. Then you and I can go and have some fun." He couldn't imagine what possible fun he and Lester could have, after this fiasco, but he had to get the girl out of the car.

"Yes, Les," said Paige, picking up on his name. "Please let me out right here. I don't want you to get into any more trouble than you're in already. You can't force someone into your vehicle if they don't want to go. Just let me out now, and we'll all be fine."

Paige was reasoning that since she couldn't fight them physically, she'd have to try to talk her way out of this. She wouldn't let herself think of what Lester might be planning. She just couldn't go there.

It was at this point that she had an almost "out of body" experience. Somehow, from a distance, she could see herself in the back of the old van, small, helpless, scared. She was weeping and pleading with these two strangers.

The man at the wheel was terrifying, and she could easily see him stopping the van, climbing into the back, raping her, then killing her – likely with the gun he said he had in the glove compartment. She could see them throwing her poor dead body out into a pile of snow, in some deserted area. The images were so real, that Paige felt she was going to vomit.

Somehow she kept swallowing until her stomach settled down, and she made up her mind that she would fight right to the bitter end. She wouldn't make it easy for them. If she couldn't talk them into being reasonable, then she would scratch and kick right up to her last breath.

If only she hadn't been so miserable to her family these past few weeks. She had been snarky, recalcitrant, grumbly, really awful. She wished she hadn't told Peter to get out of her room and stay out. She wished she hadn't told dear little Davey that he was a huge pest. Oh, if only she had her mom here now. Mom would know what to do. Together they could fight these two cretins.

Unfortunately, however, her mom wasn't there. She was far away in Muskoka, struggling to keep the cottage nice for all of them. They were all looking forward so much to a wonderful summer at the cottage, and now there would be just four of them, instead of five. How would her beloved twin ever get along without her? She couldn't imagine it. She didn't want Peter to get along without her. She had to get away from these morons, and get back to her family, where she was always safe.

The windshield wipers were old and withered, and they couldn't keep up with the blowing snow. Visibility was limited. Lester was peering out the window, trying to find a place which was quiet and remote. He didn't want people to hear the kid screaming.

When he had first spotted her hurrying along, looking so alone and cold, he had momentarily thought about offering her a ride home. That really had been his first innocent thought. As soon as she had started running, though, he had become very excited. If she was running, he was chasing.

Sonny was putting his finger to his lips, trying to get her to be quiet. He was also whispering "shh" to her, and nodding at Lester. Paige became quiet, and realized that there was likely nothing to fear from Sonny. He might be the goofy looking one, but she felt that it was Lester who was the dangerous one. Maybe Sonny would actually help her.

Lester was quiet now too, as he looked for a good spot to park. Finally, he decided that he would go around the block one more time, and go back to that church parking lot he had seen. That might be a perfect place. It backed onto the big park, and there was certainly no one around tonight.

Lester and Sonny could have all the privacy they needed. The little gal could scream all she wanted, and there would be no one to hear her!

Chapter Twenty-Three

They reached the church property, and were cruising slowly around it. Lester liked what he saw. There were no lights on in the church, so it was definitely empty. He supposed it was all locked up, but he wondered whether he should send Sonny out to try the doors.

If the church was open, they would take the girl in there. It would be more comfortable and warm, and there were lots of nice pews on which they could stretch out, and make themselves at home. Lester giggled a bit at that.

He was very excited now. He just didn't want to make any mistakes. Too bad Sonny was with him. He didn't need Sonny for what he had in mind, although he figured that it wouldn't hurt to let Sonny have a little fun too.

Lester had never done anything like this, and he found that his palms were sweating, and his heart was beating like an old bongo drum.

The girl was talking again, and it spoiled his concentration. He pulled over near the back door, and stopped the van. Then he just sat there, staring ahead through the windshield, which was quickly being covered by the heavy snowfall.

"Sonny, go see if any of those church doors might be unlocked."

"Why?" was Sonny's nervous reply. He didn't like what was happening, or what was going to happen. He just wanted to be safely home and away from all of this, but he knew Lester wasn't going to take him home now.

Shit. Lester was going to take this poor kid into the church and rape her. He just knew it. How could he stop him? Well, for starters, he would tell him that all the church doors were locked. That would delay things for a little while.

Sonny wondered though, if Lester got to rape the girl, why couldn't he? He knew it was just about the very worst thing you could do to another person, but his hormones were raging, and he couldn't get the picture of his dad's girlfriend out of his mind. If he couldn't screw her, then why not this one? Why should Lester have all the fun?

These were the thoughts running through Sonny's head, as he got out of the van, and loped over to the back doors, making a big show of rattling the knobs.

Suddenly he realized that he should be quiet. What if the minister or priest or whoever, was still inside, in a part of the church where lights wouldn't show through the big windows? What if he heard Sonny trying the door handles, and came to see what was going on?

That thought scared Sonny. Of course, he could tell the priest what was happening, or going to happen, and the priest could call the police. That would be really good, except, wait a minute. The police would think that he and Lester were both in on it, and he'd be arrested too. No, he couldn't take that chance.

He hated to have to walk all around to the front of the church. It was a big one, but Lester would just make him go back, if he tried to shirk his task.

He tried the door handle very gently and quietly, and was relieved to find that it was locked.

Sonny wondered whether he should just take off running now. The trouble was, he had no idea where they were. He just knew that it was quite a long way from home. No, his clothes weren't warm enough to be wandering around outside in this weather, and Lester would likely find him and beat him up, so he plodded back to the van. If he was going to be stuck here, he might as well relax and enjoy whatever happened.

Although he told that to himself, he knew he couldn't take part in any rape. He'd be more scared than the girl would be! No, he had to do something, but what?

As he was opening the van door, he looked around to be sure that there was no one watching them. Then he just gawked in disbelief.

There, pulling into the church parking lot, was a police cruiser, lights flashing. Even through the snow, he could see the lights. They were blurry and pretty, but they were definitely cop lights. How had they found them so quickly?

"Lester, it's the cops," he shrieked, badly shaken at the unwelcome appearance of the cruiser. He had done nothing, yet he was almost paralyzed with fear.

"Shit," shouted Lester, looking into his rear mirror. "What do they want?"

Lester had two choices. He could have waited politely for the police to approach. That was the logical, correct thing to do. Even with the girl there, maybe he could have talked himself out of it. Maybe he could claim that it was Sonny's idea to pick up the girl, and they had just been teasing her a bit, having a little fun, before driving her home.

Lester, however, wasn't thinking logically, and he didn't very often do the correct thing. All he could think of was that the van was stolen, and they had a girl in the van – a very young girl, who obviously didn't want to be there. There was only one thing to do.

Lester floored it, and the vehicle fishtailed, then shot out of the parking lot, and headed down the street, going as fast as the poor old van could go.

The police were taken by surprise. They had watched the van circle the church a couple of times, and were curious as to what was happening. They figured that whoever was driving, might be casing the church, preparing to break in, and steal whatever they could find. It was certainly an ideal location for that. No one would hear them breaking a window to get in, and no one would see the old van at the back, looking out onto the park.

Instead of putting on the siren right away, they had decided to hold back and see what the van driver was going to do. When they saw Sonny get out and start trying the doors, they put on their lights, and took off, swiftly closing the distance between them.

The cruiser had two officers in it, and the one had just stepped out of the car, when the van took off. He had to climb quickly back in, losing his hat in his hurry. Unfortunately, they lost a few seconds before the chase began! Those seconds gave Lester a little head start, but it wasn't going to be enough.

Lester was at a disadvantage. First of all, both Paige and Sonny were screaming. Sonny had just been climbing back into the van, when he noticed the cops behind them. Lester jammed it into gear and took off so fast, that Sonny was left half in and half out. With real terror in his heart, he managed to get himself in, and get the door closed.

Lester couldn't think, with all the noise that Sonny and Paige were making. His big problem was that he was totally lost. He had never been in this part of Toronto before, and he didn't know of any places where he might be able to lose the cops, who were now almost right on his tail.

No one in the van was wearing a seatbelt. Lester never wore one, and since the seats from the back had been removed, there were no belts there. Paige and Sonny were being tossed around like two raggedy dolls.

Paige was pleading with Lester to slow down.

"Please stop. You're going way too fast. We're going to have an accident. Just stop and let me out."

She had been so thrilled when Sonny said that the cops were behind them. Now she was afraid that she would be killed, before they could ever rescue her.

Sonny was crying along with Paige. He was begging Lester to slow down before they got shot. He was expecting the police to shoot out the tires, and he knew the van might flip. He was hanging on to Paige, partly to protect her, after all, she was just a little girl, but also just for something to which he could cling.

He cursed himself for ever getting mixed up with Lester. He could be safely at home right now, if he hadn't been so eager to get out and away from his dad's girlfriend.

Inevitably the chase ended in disaster. There was really no logical hope of a happy ending.

Lester looked over his shoulder to see how close the cop car was. That was a mistake. He hit an icy patch on the road, and the van took off, sliding and flying right into a hydro pole. It hit with such impact that Lester became a missile, flying right through the windshield, landing basically on his head. He was dead on impact with a fire hydrant, which was sticking up out of the snow.

Sonny and Paige were luckier. Sonny had put his arms around Paige, and hunkered down before they hit the pole. That likely saved them from flying through the windshield. Sonny's head hit something hard, and he was knocked out. Paige, however, was on her hands and knees, looking dazed and confused, when the policeman finally wrenched open the van door.

To Paige, the officer looked like an angel. He looked like mom and dad, and her home, and a fireplace. He looked like security and safety. He was the most welcome sight she had ever encountered.

"Help me," was all she whispered, as she reached out her arms to him.

Some time later, the first ambulance took Lester's body away. The unconscious Sonny was taken in a separate ambulance. Paige was sitting in the cruiser, huddled under a welcome blanket, which she was clasping tightly around her shaking shoulders.

"Thank you, oh thank you so much. How did you find me so quickly?" she asked.

"Well, to tell you the truth, we weren't looking for you. We had no idea that you were missing, or that you were in that van.

"We saw it go by slowly, and noticed that its rear lights were out. Then we saw it go around the church twice, and we were sure that it was checking out the place before breaking in. That's why we came after it. We had no way of knowing that you were in there, or that you had been picked up against your will, or that the van was stolen.

"What in the world were you doing out alone on this stormy night? Where are your parents, and where do you live?"

Paige couldn't help the tears that started again.

"I was at choir practice at the school, and my friend's mom was supposed to drive us home. They didn't show up, though. Then the teacher went home, and the other choir boy went home, and I realized that I didn't have my cell phone. I wanted to call my aunt, who is staying with us for a couple of days, but I'd left my phone at home."

Here Paige stopped to wipe her eyes and blow her nose.

"My dad's in London, and my mom's up at the cottage getting a window fixed. Someone broke in and stole a lot of stuff. Anyway, I didn't have my cell phone, so I couldn't call for a ride, and there are no houses near the school. All the little businesses in the strip mall were closed, so I had to start walking.

"I was planning to ring someone's doorbell and then call my aunt, if only I had made it to a house. That big guy grabbed me just past the park, near the big church. Oh, and I have two exams – mid-terms, tomorrow, and my wrist really hurts," she added with a sob.

Paige knew she was talking too much, but she simply couldn't stop. It was as if as long as she was talking to the police, she would be safe. They wouldn't leave her. Part of her mind knew that was silly, but the other part just wanted to cling to them. At the moment they were strong father figures.

The officers were looking at her in sympathy, as she told her story. Here was a nice little kid, obviously from a good home, coming back from choir practice, minding her own business, and she was snatched up off the street. If that old van hadn't had broken tail lights, they shuddered to think of what the outcome would have been for Paige. She was one lucky girl.

One of the officers smiled as he patted her gently on the shoulder.

"We'll take you to the hospital for a quick check-up, just in case you're hurt and don't know it. Then we'll take you home."

"My aunt will be so worried. Couldn't I please call her right now and let her know I'm okay?"

Paige had already forgotten about her crusade to be sulky and mean to Aunt Jill. How dumb was that! All she wanted now was to be cuddled and petted, and told what a brave girl she was. She just wanted to go home.

Chapter Twenty-Four

Jill was watching television, when she suddenly realized that Paige should be home by now. She was thinking that she had better call Amy, in case the two girls had gone back to her house. She didn't want to do anything to annoy Paige, however, as she seemed so touchy these days. Just as she decided that she definitely should call, the phone rang.

"Hello Mrs. Bennett. It's Amy. Could I please speak to Paige?"

Jill's heart began beating a little faster.

"Well, isn't she with you, Amy? Your mom was going to pick you up, and drive you both home."

"Oh I never got to band practice. My mom fell down the basement stairs, and knocked herself out, and broke her leg. My dad's out of town, so I had to call an ambulance and get her to the hospital. It was really exciting! I went in the ambulance with her!

"She's been in surgery quite a while, and I've been trying to call Paige, but she isn't answering her cell phone. Isn't she there?"

Jill couldn't believe how calm and matter of fact Amy sounded. She was only thirteen, the same age as Paige, but she sounded very mature. Maybe she was in shock.

"No, she isn't," replied Jill grimly.

"Look, I'm very sorry about your mom, and please let me know if there's anything I can do to help. As a matter of fact, you should come here to spend the night. You can't go home to that big empty house all alone.

"Can you stay at the hospital for a while, until I find Paige, then I'll come and pick you up. Right now, though, I'm worried. She hasn't called me for a ride, so someone else must be bringing her home. Who else is in the choir, Amy? I'm going to have to start making some calls."

Jill was speaking calmly, but her insides were knotting. Paige was her responsibility, and she didn't have any idea where she might be. She didn't want to tie up the phone, though, in case Paige was trying to call her.

First she called Paige's cell phone, but, as Amy had said, Paige wasn't answering it. Finally, Peter stuck his head out of his room, where he had been studying for the past couple of hours.

"Aunt Jill, Paige's phone keeps ringing and ringing. It's driving me crazy. Someone seems really anxious to get in touch with her. Where is she anyway? Isn't she home yet?"

Jill was up the stairs in a shot, opened Paige's bedroom door, and saw to her dismay, that the pink, glittery cell phone which Paige had wanted so badly, was lying on her bed, right where she had dropped it.

"Peter, you stay here and answer the phone. Call me on my cell if you get any news. I'm going to drive over to the school, and make sure she's not still there. If there's been no word from her by the time I get back, we'll have to call the police."

Peter was stunned by this. All of a sudden, he remembered the time two years ago, when his mother had disappeared, and all the frantic calls which they had made.

"Please don't let it be happening again," he whispered, as Jill flew out the door.

Jill eventually returned, almost an hour later, a grim look on her face. It was a brutally cold night – an evil sort of night. She had driven over every street which she thought Paige might have taken home, if she was walking. Jill knew that she would never have taken a shortcut through the park. It would have been quicker, but Paige was too smart for that.

Unfortunately, there had been no sign of her. The school was all locked, and the streets were bare. She hadn't seen a single person walking on this hellish night.

"Oh, why did I ever let her go to that foolish choir practice," she berated herself distractedly. Before calling the police, she decided to call a few of Paige's friends. She suspected that would be useless, though. Paige was not a thoughtless girl. If she had gone to a friend's home, she would have called.

None of her friends had heard from her, and they were all surprised that Paige had even gone to the rehearsal. It seemed that everyone else had decided not to go, on such a miserable night.

At this point, Jill wondered whether she should be calling Kate. After all, Paige was Kate's daughter, and she had a right to know what was happening. Still, Jill didn't know just what was happening yet.

Why call and frighten Kate out of her wits. There was absolutely nothing she could do from Muskoka. She would want to jump in the car, and race right back down to Toronto, but that was a terrible idea. The roads were icy, and likely blocked in places by all the snow. There would be nothing she could do that Jill couldn't do, and she would be putting herself and Davey in danger.

No, the dreaded phone call to Kate would come later, if it was necessary. "Please God, don't let it come to that," she prayed, as she reluctantly picked up the phone again.

She was just dialing 911 when the doorbell rang. Peter raced to it before she could hang up. He was as scared as Jill was. Although he and Paige were squabbling a lot these days, she was still the nearest and dearest person in the whole world to him. After all, she was his twin.

They looked alike, and they thought alike. From the times they had shared a playpen, it had always been Peter and Paige, two against the world. They had an unbreakable bond which joined them forever.

Peter didn't even notice the cop standing there. He just flung his arms around Paige, and dragged her in out of the cold.

His sister was distraught, shivering and talking a mile a minute, with tears running down her face, but she looked beautiful to Peter. The three of them stood hugging and chattering, with no thought of the policeman, who let himself in, shut the door behind him, and stood watching with a wide grin on his youthful face.

It took them a while to get the full story. The policeman, who introduced himself as Officer James Turner, told them as much as he knew. He looked very young, but seemed quite professional. Paige filled in the rest, and as she was feeling much better now that she was home safely, the story became even more dramatic than it had really been, if that was possible.

"It could have been much worse, mam," Officer Turner said.

"If that old van's rear lights had been working, we never would have stopped it. It hadn't even been reported stolen yet. It was just a true stroke of luck, that we were cruising down that street when the van passed us.

"You know, if you're a superstitious person, you might say that the Fates played a big part in this story. If you're a religious person, you should thank God. He really had his eyes on Paige tonight. And, I guess, if you're a practical person, you'd have to say that it wasn't very smart to let her go out on such an awful night."

Jill didn't know whether to laugh or cry, or be offended, at this little speech, so instead, she offered him a cup of coffee, along with her profound gratitude, before he went back out into the cold.

Before he finally did leave, he turned to Paige, and told her that an officer would be around tomorrow to get all the details written down. At this point they weren't sure just what the consequences of the evening's adventure might be. The one perpetrator was dead, and the other was hurt, although no one knew yet just how badly.

He thought that there might possibly be a law suit in the future, depending on how well Paige recovered from her fright. These didn't strike him as the type of people who would sue anyone, but you never knew. If Paige was emotionally scarred, and needed long term medical attention, it could prove costly.

The evening wasn't quite over yet. Before Paige had a hot shower, and a hot chocolate, Jill asked her to write down every single thing she could remember about what had transpired.

"It's easier to remember it tonight, Paige, than it will be tomorrow, and you want to get it all correct," she explained to this teenager whom she loved like a daughter.

After the writing was done, Paige then allowed Jill to tuck her into bed securely, as if she was a little kid. She didn't care. Inside her, she did feel quite grown up, but tonight she needed the pampering.

"You know, Aunt Jill," said Paige quietly, as Jill sat on the edge of her bed, "I was sure that they were going to rape me, and then kill me. I could almost see them throwing my body out into the snow, some place where it wouldn't be found till the spring. I was so scared that I'd never see any of you again. I'm so sorry that I've been such a twerp lately. I promise I'll never act like that again. I know I'm lucky to have such a wonderful family, and I'll never forget it."

The two hugged until they were both crying, and then laughing. Jill kissed her on the forehead, told her she was wonderfully brave, and left just as Peter came in.

He sat and talked with his twin until she fell asleep. He was proud of his sister, who had fought off the two goons.

Then he had a gloomy thought. What would his folks say when they heard about Paige's adventure? They would likely keep the twins under lock and key till they were 18! He knew that his folks weren't really like that, but he also knew that there would be a tightening of the bonds, at least for a while. His mom was going to freak when she heard what had happened.

Jill's night wasn't quite over yet. Once the twins were safely tucked in, she had to leave them long enough to get to the hospital, pick up Amy, and bring her back to the house to spend the night.

Once Amy was settled into the spare room, an exhausted Jill climbed into bed herself, a small glass of brandy in her hand. Up in Muskoka, Kate and Davey were just tucking themselves into their makeshift beds in front of the fireplace, blissfully unaware of the tragedy which had been so narrowly averted.

The Chandlers and Jill were all safe for the moment.

It had certainly been a night to remember, a cold, hellish night. Unfortunately there were more hellish adventures to come, in the next couple of days.

Chapter Twenty-Five

Davey, who had been really tired, fell asleep right away. Kate, on the other hand, lay awake for a long time, wondering whether there were any other humans near by, and if so, would they be friend or foe. It was difficult not to think scary thoughts, while the wind howled outside, and she realized just how alone and vulnerable they were.

She couldn't quite relax, and determined that it was because she was worrying about Paige. Why had she ever agreed to let her daughter go to that foolish rehearsal on a stormy night! That teacher definitely needed a reprimand, and Kate would call her when she got back to Toronto. Well, maybe she wouldn't. She didn't want to embarrass Paige.

She'd talk to some of the other mothers first. She wished now, that she had asked Paige to call her when she got back home safely, but it was too late for that. Jill would call her if there were any problems.

Eventually, warmed by the fire, and thinking how happy she was to be here with Davey, rather than in the Everglades by herself, she fell into a surprisingly comfortable sleep.

She got up once in the night to check on the quilted window, and was pleased to see that it was holding up very well. She and Davey had done a good job.

Sunshine streaming in the living room windows, wakened Kate. The wind had apparently blown itself out, and the world was engulfed in total silence.

Getting out of bed quietly, so as to let Davey sleep, she made her way to a window, and couldn't believe how beautiful and pristine the mounds of snow looked, with the sun shining on them. It was a totally different world, compared to the uncompromising bluster of the previous night.

It appeared that God had not yet decided to paint anything on the heartwarming blue canvas of the sky. There was not a hint of a cloud, not even a wisp. There was just a bright yellow blazing sun, round and beautiful, hanging proudly against the amazingly blue sky.

She couldn't help thinking how romantic and companionable it would have been, if this was just a little two day retreat for herself and Mac. Why did he have to be so far away, just when she could have used his company?

Then, of course, she felt guilty, knowing how much fun Davey was having. She wouldn't have made him miss this for anything. At least that was what she thought at the time. It wouldn't be long, though, before she was desperately wishing that he was safely at home with the twins.

It looked like the beginning of a perfect day. How was she to know that soon, her old nemesis Madison Ramsay, would be setting out for the cottage, planning to kill her? How could she possibly know that in a few hours, a certain Dr. Patrick O'Neal, a man Kate had never met, would also be setting out for the cottage, planning to save her! And, if that wasn't enough, how could she have known that, before the day was finished, she would meet, and say good-bye, to an old school chum, who had always had a crush on her.

She had absolutely no idea just what an extraordinary twenty-four hours she was facing.

After Davey was washed and dressed, Kate made another fire, and they ate their breakfast cinnamon buns in front of it.

"After breakfast, I'm going to try to get one of the snowmobiles started, and if we can get out to the road, we'll be able to jump in the car, and drive in to town. We'll order our window supplies, and see if we can get a man to come and fix it either today or tomorrow. I think we'll be staying till tomorrow for sure. I was hoping we might be able to leave for home this afternoon, but that's just not going to happen."

"Yay," replied her eager son. "It's fun up here – just the two of us. I don't want to go home today. But what if we're in town when the police come?"

"I'm thinking I should call them now, and see if they could give me an idea whether they'll be here this morning or this afternoon. Then we'll know what to do. I'm also going to call some hardware stores in Bracebridge, and see if we can get someone to come out as soon as possible, to fix the window."

Cottages were vandalized or damaged by broken tree limbs all the time. People in the business of replacing windows in cottage country, must be equipped to handle any type of emergency. Would they have a powerful snowmobile with a trailer, which could get right up the road without any problem? They likely would, she told herself.

She was just looking in the phone book for the hardware store's number, when her cell phone rang. It was the police, checking to see whether she was there or not. They were on their way, and thought they would be there within fifteen minutes.

Davey was waiting eagerly for the expected arrival, and when he heard the roar of two snowmobiles coming up their road, he ran to the kitchen door to open it. He had thought the police would be coming in a cruiser, forgetting that the road was still impassable to a car. Sure enough, two big, scary looking creatures in snowmobile suits, parked their vehicles facing back out down the road, and approached Davey. This was better than the movies!

Kate had raced to the door too, thinking that these two apparitions wearing helmets and snow goggles, could just as easily be the vandals returning, rather than the police. How could anyone tell? They looked like creatures from Mars!

Fortunately they really were police, and seemed happy to get in and warm up for a few moments.

Taking off their boots and helmets, they did a thorough walk-through, asking several questions along the way. They were obviously used to break-ins in cottage country.

Davey made a pest of himself, following them, and asking questions non-stop. Finally his mother gave him the evil eye, and he got the hint. He followed them the rest of the way quietly, with no talking.

"We're pretty sure we know who did this," said the shorter of the two officers, whose name was Bradley. He had red hair and a bulbous nose, and looked to be a bit of a drinker. His eyes were small, and close together, and his ears were huge. There was a nasty looking scar across his chin. Actually, he looked like a lab experiment which had gone horribly wrong.

The poor guy was serious, taking notes, and not cracking a smile. He looked as if he was mad at the world, and Kate didn't blame him. If she looked like that, she'd be mad at the world too! He was so ugly that he was scary. He seemed to have no redeeming features. Kate decided she wouldn't want to get on his bad side. She figured that he was the one with whom she had been speaking on the phone.

"It looks like the work of a couple of teens who live here all winter. Their parents have a winterized cottage on the other side of the lake. They're just doing it for money, but at least they never vandalize anything. They really went on a crime spree last week, and broke into at least seven cottages."

"There may even be more," added the second cop, who had introduced himself as Officer DeLuca. He was a tall, good looking fellow with a shock of thick black hair and very dark eyes.

"If people don't have anyone checking their cottages on a regular basis, they might be broken into and not know it for weeks or months. You can really have a lot of damage that way."

"These two kids are tricky," said Officer Bradley. "They've been very smart about not leaving fingerprints."

"Well, if you think you know who they are, is there any hope of getting our stuff back?" asked Kate, hopefully.

"Don't count on it. They've likely fenced it already. They've got their little game down to a science, and they can pick up some nice pocket money over the winter. Just be patient, and we'll see what happens."

Kate gave them some coffee and cookies before they set out again.

"You'd better try to get some boards in here as soon as possible. There's another storm headed this way later today, and they're predicting another two feet of snow."

"Oh dear. I promised to take Davey for a quick skidoo ride. I think we'll do that right now, and then head into town. That's if I can get either of the skidoos started," she laughed.

"Well, we can start one for you before we go. Actually, we'll try them both. It's a good idea to have them available. You don't want to be stranded here."

"That's really nice of you. Thanks so much. Davey, get your suit on. We're going now."

"Just don't go out on the lake," said DeLuca sternly. "There was a big thaw last week, and there's some open water out there. It may have frozen over by now, but the ice will be very thin. A skidoo would go right through.

"It's a mile or more straight out from here, and to the right a bit. The ice is a good two feet solid in most places, but not there. It's basically where the river runs into the lake, and there's just enough current, that with the thaw, it opened up.

"The thaw also caused the surface ice to turn to slush, and then it refroze all bumpy. Then the wind added to the problem, by blowing snow onto some of those bumps, to form small mounds and hills of snow and ice. It's an unusually rough ride out there, and then there's the danger of the thin ice and open water.

"Just stay off the lake and you'll be okay."

"Yikes. Thanks for the warning, but I don't plan to go out on the lake at all. I thought we would just go down to the little meadow near the end of the road. There's about an acre there that's all weeds and wildflowers in the fall, so it should be okay for Davey riding around a bit."

"Sure, that's a good idea. It isn't worth taking a chance out on the lake."

The obliging officers, who didn't seem in any great hurry, cleaned the snow off both skidoos, and started them. They made sure they were running smoothly, and filled with gas before they left.

Davey had a good idea, and decided this was the time to suggest it to his mom. "Mom, could we have a little picnic on the skidoos?"

"A picnic? Sure, why not?" said Kate. "I'm way ahead of you, because I knew that's what you'd want to do. Of course, it won't be a real picnic. We're a bit short of time, kiddo. We'll have a little ride in the meadow, have our picnic, then we've got to get to town, and get back here, before the rest of that storm hits us."

"That's okay. We could just bring hot chocolate and some cookies. I know that it wouldn't be a real picnic, but we could pretend we were eating sandwiches, or cold chicken, or potato salad. We'll eat really fast."

What a little organizer, Kate thought, with a grin. Quickly she found a thermos, made some hot chocolate, packed up some cookies, chips, and an apple cut into quarters, and they were on their way.

It wasn't much of a picnic, but Davey was excited at the idea, and after all, why not? She might as well make this trip as much fun as possible. Life was too short not to enjoy every single day, and it was so easy to put a smile on Davey's sweet face.

Her son, of course, was too small to drive a skidoo, although he was desperate to give it a try. He clung on behind his mom, and she drove up and down and around the meadow, going fast in order to give him a thrill.

Davey, however, was determined to try driving, so Kate decided there was really no danger in the meadow. Changing places with him, she gave him instructions, and let him give it a try. He was fine going straight ahead, but found it awkward turning the big machine. He had fun, though, and did very well. All the while Kate was sitting behind him, with her hands hovering close to the handlebars, just in case.

After an hour of fun, which included the picnic, they parked the skidoo on the cottage road just around a slight bend, where it couldn't be seen from the highway. Kate didn't want to return and find it had been stolen. They walked the short distance to the car, and were relieved to see that it wasn't totally buried in snow. The wind had apparently blown most of the snow off, and they had a relatively easy drive to town.

The hardware people were helpful, but said it was unlikely that they could get in to board up the window until the next day. They would try, but they couldn't promise.

Kate bought some extra food supplies, in case they got totally snowed in for a few days. She considered staying in town over night, but talked herself out of it. She had come up from Toronto to take care of the broken window, and she might as well do it right.

She realized that she was really enjoying herself. The skidooing had been fun, and so was the picnic. The cottage was warm and cozy, and she reasoned that they could carry quite a few supplies on the skidoo, so why not stay? It would be much more comfortable than being stuck in a hotel room, and it would be a memorable little holiday for Davey.

It was probably just as well that Kate didn't know quite how memorable it would be!

Chapter Twenty-Six

Mark Duncan was an excited man. He had just returned from a romp in the snow with his German Shepherd, Kingsley, and he was raring to go again.

He and Kingsley had struggled, thrashed and kicked their way through the drifted snow on his cottage road, and along the regional road. It was a beautiful morning, cold, but sunny, and he had been totally unprepared to see a car sitting just off the highway. He had looked in all the windows, to be sure there was no one in it, before realizing just whose car it must be.

Mark knew that his old school chum Kate, and her husband, had bought the empty Carrington cottage at the end of the road. He had heard about it last fall, when the sale went through. At that time, he just couldn't believe his good fortune.

What little quirk of fate had put Kate back in his life? Was it the malevolent gods playing some kind of mean trick on him, or was it the benevolent gods giving him a huge second chance to get things right? He chose to think it was the latter.

They had gone through high school together in Toronto, and all his friends had known that Mark had a monstrous crush on the delectable Kate. He had asked her out innumerable times, and had finally come to understand that she would always refuse.

That hadn't really stopped him though. In his mind, she was his girlfriend. She was friendly and full of fun, and they quite often did things together in a gang of about ten friends. That, however, wasn't the same as getting her out alone – just the two of them.

There had been times when he had been so frustrated that he could have smacked her, but, of course, he never would. Actually, he had always morphed into a mouse, an insipid, banal child, when he was around her. The witty, clever remarks he could make to her in the darkness of his room, in the middle of the night, flew away into the mist, when he was actually face to face with her.

Somehow Kate had seemed to understand this. She was always kind and friendly when they were together in class. She just would never date him. There had been two or three times over the years, when they had met accidentally at the mall, and she had actually agreed to sit and enjoy a coke or burger with him, but that was the best he had ever done with her.

He had once even driven her home, when she had been caught walking in a sudden downpour, carrying a pile of books. Those times, when it was just Mark and Kate, he thought he was in heaven. Then the times she refused to go to a dance or a party with him, he knew he was in hell.

When Mark thought of high school, he thought of Kate. He had been president of the Student Council, and Kate had been on the executive. Then a terrible thing had happened. Money which had been collected for the Valentine's Dance, went missing. For some reason, everything pointed to Mark as the culprit.

Even though he protested his innocence, no one but Kate believed him. She had faith in him, and had stuck up for him. That proved to him that she really cared, even though she wouldn't date him.

Eventually they discovered the real thief, and Mark was exonerated, but the damage had been done. His reputation was in shreds. He couldn't wait to get away from that school, and to prove his worth to the world.

Unfortunately, Mark had proved to himself that he was just not good with women. Now with three failed marriages behind him, he was once more a free man. The first and third wives were bleeding him dry with their alimony. The second one, however, had been a stroke of luck for him. He still didn't know what had really happened. They had been arguing and struggling at the top of the stairs, and somehow Paula had fallen and broken her neck.

There had been an inquiry, and a lot of gossip, but finally Mark had been found innocent of any wrong doing. Still, there were days when he wondered whether he might actually have given her a little push when they were struggling. He did have a bad temper, and he had been known to lose control and break things on occasion, but could he have actually pushed Paula?

He honestly didn't know, but there were times in the dark of the night, when he could almost picture himself putting his two hands on her back, and giving her a shove. Was that something he had wanted to do subconsciously, or had he actually done it? He would never know for sure.

Anyway, after three marriages which had gone up in smoke, he had been so excited to hear that his old love – one sided though it may have been, had bought a cottage on the same lake, and within walking distance. It didn't bother him too much that she was already married and had kids. He would do it right this time, and maybe he could actually win her over. Somehow he felt that they were meant to be together.

Mark's marriages had all failed because each of his wives claimed that he was too domineering, and a bit too physical. That was irony for you. He had gone from a weak, unsure young boy, to a self-assured, successful, domineering business man.

He may have lacked social skills, but he had been wildly successful in his career in real estate. He had started up a small company at the time in Toronto, when real estate was booming. It had taken off from day one, and he had never looked back. Within four years, he had been bought out by a much bigger company, and was a multi-millionaire by the time he was in his early thirties.

Mark was good with his hands, and could fix or build just about anything. After his third marriage collapsed, he bought himself a small cottage in Muskoka, tore it down, and slowly built a big, beautiful, modern showplace. It was nothing too grandiose. He didn't want it to look out of place, but it was much better than anything he had ever expected to own.

Now, after seeing a car which he figured must belong to Kate or her husband, on the road leading to her cottage, he could hardly wait for her to see his summer place. He would show her what she had missed by always saying no!

Closing his eyes, he remembered the last time they had really talked. He had asked her to the graduation dance, even though he knew that she was going steady with someone else. It was a totally bizarre move, and he just shook his head when he thought about it now.

Kate had tried to explain to him that she wasn't free, that she had a boyfriend, but he was so determined to take her to the final high school dance, that he just couldn't accept rejection. He had called her over and over – wheedling, coaxing, begging, and making a total fool of himself. What a putz he had been!

Finally she had become angry with him, and pointed out that he was almost stalking her. She said that if he didn't stop, she would call the police, and then she actually had done just that.

Unfortunately, that was how things had been left. The police put a good scare into him. After that he had kept away from her, and next thing he knew, she and her girlfriend Jill had disappeared, apparently working in one of the big summer hotels. Then they all scattered to different universities, and got on with their lives. He hated that their friendship/romance had ended that way, but now he would have a chance to fix it.

Two years ago, when all those articles about Kate appeared in the newspapers and on television, Mark's long buried feelings for her had bubbled to the surface. He had read every scrap of information he could find about her, her husband, and her kids. That was why he couldn't believe his good fortune last fall, when he discovered that she had bought the old Carrington cottage so close to his.

Mark Duncan seemed to be at the top of his game these days. He had a beautiful summer home, which he had virtually built with his own two hands. He also had the best friend anyone could ever have.

All the love which he was never quite able to pour out onto a wife, was lavished on Kingsley. He had raised Kingsley, his German Shepherd, from a tiny, roly-poly furball, and they had bonded for life. Where Mark went, Kingsley went. You never saw one without the other.

At the moment, Mark was sitting in his warm kitchen, talking to his pal.

"You know Kings, Kate is likely there with her husband. Can't imagine her coming up by herself in this crazy weather. Actually, I can't imagine why they would come up in the middle of the week, in the middle of a snow storm, for any reason, but it doesn't matter. They're here, I'm sure of it, and I've got to see her. Do you think she's as great looking as she was in high school?"

Kingsley cocked his head and answered with a small "woof." He could tell by the questioning tone in his master's voice that an answer was expected.

"They likely have all their kids with them too, but you never know. I have to go over there and find out. Just imagine if Kate is up here by herself! She could be, you know. All things are possible! She might have come up to have some peace and quiet, while she works on her next book or her drawings. She's become pretty famous these past few years."

Kingsley was now lying with his head on his paws, his big brown eyes on his master's face. He didn't answer this last remark.

"If she's alone, I'd better not move too fast. I don't want to scare her. I think that's why she wouldn't go out with me in high school. If I wasn't being Mr. Milksop I was being Mr. Stalker. No wonder she was confused.

"I'm going to hug her," he declared. "I'll hug her even if her husband is there. He can't do much about an innocent hug. That'll let her know that I'm still interested, and it'll get her thinking a bit. I wonder if she knows I'm a millionaire now? How can I let her know that without seeming to be bragging?"

Just by the sound of his master's voice, Kingsley knew that he was excited, so he got excited too. He jumped up, wagging his tail frantically, and barking hopefully. He was anticipating that maybe they were going to go for another walk.

Mark glanced at his watch, then hurried off to shave – something he didn't usually do when he was at the cottage. He changed his shirt, and put on a red cashmere sweater over it. There now – he looked like money, and was bound to impress her. No, maybe he looked too much like money. He didn't want her to think that he was boasting or showing off. Okay, off came the red sweater, and on went an old navy one that had seen better days.

Staring at himself in the full length mirror, he shook his head. He looked as pathetic as he had in high school. The pale green one was next. It almost won the day, but, finally, he went back to the red cashmere. It cried out confidence and quiet success. Yes, it was definitely the right choice.

Mark was already picturing long summer evenings with Kate, sipping on drinks, and watching the sunset from his screened porch, or from his boat. Surely there would be weekends when she might come up alone. At this point he could only hope and dream, but he knew one thing for sure. This time he was going to give it his very best shot, but there would be no more stalking.

If he couldn't have Kate as a lover, then he wanted her as a friend, just like it used to be in high school.

"Come on, Kingsley. We're going calling."

Chapter Twenty-Seven

Kate and Davey were glad to be back into the warm cottage. They agreed that driving right up to the back door on the skidoo, was much more fun than the long hike they had made the night before, struggling through the snow. Davey had driven up their private road by himself, with Kate sitting behind, ready to grab the handles at a moment's notice. He had done very well, and was as proud as a little peacock.

Now he didn't seem ready to settle down. He wandered from room to room, wondering what to do with himself. What he really wanted, was to be back out on that skidoo. That was the most fun he could remember ever having.

Then he saw the rolling pin in the kitchen, and began using it as a bat. He was swinging enthusiastically, and muttering to himself when Kate walked in.

"What in the heck are you doing?" she laughed.

"I'm practicing my swing for when I try out for Little League," he replied seriously.

Kate laughed again. "Davey, if you get too used to swinging that rolling pin, a real bat will seem too heavy and big for you. I'm not sure it's a good idea."

Undaunted, Davey took a few more half-hearted swings, then, putting the rolling pin back on the counter, he wandered off to do a little drawing.

He was soon settled at the table with his art supplies, and Kate was about to curl up with a book, when the phone rang.

"Hi baby, how's the best looking gal in town?" asked a familiar voice.

"Mac, oh it's so good to hear from you. How are things in merry old England?"

Davey, of course, wanted to talk to his dad first, because there was so much to tell him. Laughing at his youthful eagerness, Kate gave him the phone. She knew he would be a pest, hovering right at her side until he had his turn to talk with his dad. He was excited and anxious to tell him where they were, and what they had been doing. Mostly he wanted to tell him about driving the skidoo.

Finally it was Kate's turn.

"What in the world are you two doing at the cottage all by yourselves? If there was a break-in, why didn't old Walt take care of it?"

Kate took her time, and explained all about Walt's heart attack.

"Davey and I are doing just fine," she said, not bothering to tell Mac about their long and difficult trek the previous night.

"The police came in on skidoos this morning, and took the robbery report, and the hardware people have promised to be here tomorrow, and even possibly this afternoon. So, my darling, all is under control.

"Davey's been a huge help, and thanks to his brilliant idea, we slept on the twin mattresses right in front of the fireplace last night.

It's really been fun. You and I will have to try that some time, if and when we're ever up here on our own, without all our rotten kids, specially that young bratty one."

She added that part for Davey's benefit, and he laughed and shook his finger at her. He was now back at the table, trying to draw a snowmobile.

"Sounds pretty romantic," chuckled Mac. "I'm ready, willing and able."

"I'll just bet you are," cooed Kate, grinning.

There was a five or six hour time difference between Muskoka and London, so Mac had just finished dinner with his old father.

"How's grandpa doing?" asked Kate, who was very fond of her father-in-law. He had an irreverent and sharp wit, which delighted her, and they seemed to understand each other. Kate took an interest in his music – he had played the violin in the London Philharmonic for many years, and he took an interest in Kate's books and illustrations.

"He's looking great, and he seems to keep pretty busy. He plays chess twice a week with an old friend, and he plays bridge once a week in a club. He also gets out and walks around the block a couple of times every day, rain or shine, (mostly rain I think, since it's London), and he treats himself to eating breakfast out most mornings with his pals. I'm really pleased to see how well he's coping."

Mac's mother had died the previous year, and his dad now lived all alone.

"Actually, Kate, I've invited him to come out to Canada for a month or two this summer. I knew you wouldn't mind, as you get along so well with him. He'd love cottage life, and he'd enjoy Toronto too, so he's considering it. I'm pretty sure he'll come."

"Good. That's great. The kids will be pleased, and I am too. He's a darling – much like you. Be sure to give him a big hug from me, and one from each of the kids.

"Now let's get down to the real nitty-gritty. Hope you haven't run into any good-looking women over there. Are you behaving yourself? No dancing with strange women in black dresses, I hope."

Mac just laughed. "You'll never know, kiddo. That's going to be my little secret. Seriously, I really miss you, and wish you had been able to come with me. Are you all set for the big reading and book launch?"

They chatted for another ten minutes, before they could bring themselves to say good-bye. Mac felt uneasy at the thought of his wife and youngest child all alone at the cottage in the middle of the winter. He could think of so many things which might go wrong, but there was no way he could or would envision the most dangerous thing of all, - the unexpected appearance of his old girlfriend Madison, aka Angel Baby.

While Kate was saying her good-byes, she thought she saw some sort of movement out of the corner of her eye. She walked over to the window, but didn't see anything unusual. She wondered whether perhaps it had been a deer going by, but could see no sign of any animal.

Just then, Davey looked up from his sketching. "Mom, could you tell me again about when you were on the island, and you didn't have anything to eat, except for those three butterscotch candies I'd given you?"

This was one of Davey's favourite stories.

Kate ruffled his hair, and pulled him down beside her on the sofa.

"How many times have I told you that story? You should be sick of it by now."

"Just one more time, because I have a good idea, but I need to hear it again. How did you figure out which berries and plants you could eat?"

Kate knew that he could have recited the entire tale by himself, but for some reason he loved to hear her tell it. She knew that as she was telling it each time, Davey was picturing himself alone on a scary island, wondering what he was going to eat.

"Okay, here's the short version. I knew I had to find some source of food, because I didn't know how long I would be there. Would my captor ever come back, or had he just put me on that island to see how long it would take me to starve to death?

"I could never kill an animal for food, so I had to find some plants with berries or fruit on them. But, what if I found some nice looking berries that were actually poison? I couldn't take that chance. I had to stay healthy, so that I could escape and get back to you and your dad and the twins.

"I knew that my family would be searching for me – all except you, of course, who likely didn't give a hoot." Here she tickled him a bit, while he loudly protested.

"So, anyway, I figured out a plan. Every time I found a new bush with berries on it, I would pick about five – that's all. Then I'd eat just one of them. I'd wait for a while and wouldn't eat anything else. If I didn't get any rashes, or my stomach didn't feel sick, or my tongue didn't start to swell, I'd eat a couple more. If I was still okay after a couple of hours, then I'd tell myself that they were likely safe to eat. I knew there was a chance that it could be a slow acting poison, that might take a day to work its way through my system, but I was hungry all the time, so I couldn't wait too long.

"There were a couple of times when I did get sick, once I got the runs, and once I vomited, so I just stayed far away from those devils. I was lucky that there were a couple of bushes there which I recognized, so I mostly ate their berries.

"The best was when I found a leaf that was sort of minty tasting, so I used it as a poor man's toothbrush. I would rub it all over my teeth and my tongue, so that my mouth didn't taste so horrible. Then I would rinse with the rain water which I caught in a pail.

"Doesn't it make you happy that you have a nice tooth brush, and good tasting toothpaste, and you can brush your teeth ten times a day if you want to?"

"Oh, yuck," grinned Davey. "You're goofy, mom."

"Oh, thanks very much. Did you just call your old mom goofy?" She punched him gently on the arm, then added, "now, big guy, you've heard that story for the hundredth time. What have you learned from my foodless little vacation on the island?"

Davey thought about it for a moment. "Well, I know that if I'm ever lost, and can't get home, I'll try to find good berries just the way you did. I'll also carry a big stick in case I run into a man-eating pig or something." He laughed here at the idea of a pig who could eat a man instead of a man eating a pig.

His mom's tales of her adventures were so fascinating, that he almost hoped to find himself in the same situation some day. Almost, but not quite!

"The big lesson that I hope you and the twins have learned, is that you never ever give up. No matter how hopeless things seem, there is always some possibility to help yourself. Don't ever forget that, Davey. Use the brains that God gave you, and do your best."

"Okay," he said seriously, as he stood up and started heading to the kitchen.

"I'll always remember. Now here's my really really good idea. This summer, when all five of us are here at the cottage, some day could we pretend that we have no food at all, and go out looking for food? Could we go the whole day without eating anything but what we find?"

Kate looked at his innocent little face. Only a child could make a game of something which had been a life and death situation for her. In a way, though, it sounded like a good idea. They likely wouldn't last an entire day, but it could be fun, and they were bound to learn some lessons from it.

"You know, Davey Doodle, you're a smart man. I think we could try that, although can you see Peter going an entire day without a can of coke, or a few Oreo cookies? Or what about your dad? Could he get through without a banana or some nuts?"

"Well, maybe there'll be some bananas or some nuts growing near here," said Davey, hopefully.

Kate laughed. "Nuts, maybe, but I think we'd have to go pretty far to find some bananas. Don't you remember that bananas are exotic fruits which don't grow in our country? It isn't hot enough for them."

Davey was still pondering his clever plan, when the phone rang again.

"Good grief, who is it this time? Maybe it's one of your girlfriends," she teased.

"M o m m m!" Davey shouted in pretend horror. "Don't say that. I don't have any girlfriends."

Kate was grinning at her son, as she picked up the phone. It was Jill.

After they had chatted a couple of minutes, Jill, who had been putting off this call all morning, said, "I have something to tell you. It was scary at the time, but don't worry, it had a happy ending – sort of."

"What in the heck are you trying to say, gal? Just spit it out. Has one of the twins been rude or not behaving?"

"No, nothing like that. They're terrific kids. Here's what happened. Paige went to the choir practice last night, and only one other student showed, because it was such a lousy, stormy night.

"The teacher kept them there for a while, but then gave up, and sent them home. Amy's mom was supposed to pick them up, but she fell down the basement stairs, knocked herself out, and broke her leg. Amy got her to the hospital by ambulance, but couldn't get in touch with Paige, because Paige had forgotten her cell phone at home."

"Stop right there. Paige won't even go to the bathroom without her phone, so how did she manage to forget it, and how did she get home?"

"Hold on, kiddo. I'm going to let you talk to her yourself, just so that you know she's absolutely fine. Just in case she wants to embellish the story a bit, let me assure you that everything's okay, but she did have a very scary experience. Now promise that you won't get yourself all upset – because – I swear – everything's fine."

"Jill, you're not making any sense. I'm not going to promise anything. Put Paige on."

Kate was now not only mystified, but worried. What in the world had happened?

Paige, of course, couldn't wait to tell her mom every single detail, which she did, in excruciatingly vivid technicolour. Now, in the safety of her own home, with Aunt Jill and Peter making a big fuss over her, the experience hardly seemed real.

The very worst part of it was to try to understand that Lester was actually dead. One minute he was yelling at her, threatening her, and the next minute he was dead. People in Paige's world just didn't die like that.

He had been a horrible person, but he had died, and in a convoluted way she wondered whether it was her fault. If she hadn't been so stubborn about going to the rehearsal, and if she hadn't forgotten her cell phone, and if she hadn't been walking home, looking so lonely and helpless, would he still be alive? That was the question with which Paige was wrestling.

"Mom, I was wondering whether Peter and I could maybe go and take some martial arts classes? If I had known Kung Fu or Judo or something like that, maybe I could have got away from that bully, before he ever dragged me into the van. I'd feel a lot safer if I knew some self-defense."

"Hey, I think that's a great idea. Maybe I'll come with you. I could have used a bit of self-defense when I was grabbed too. Let's go and sign up as soon as Davey and I get home. Now, listen. Do you want me to come back today?" It's very stormy here now, but if you'd like, we'll just close up and head out. To heck with the window. You're much more important."

"No way. I'm fine. Aunt Jill has been great, and so has Peter. Even the police were really nice. Aunt Jill slept in the other bed in my room, and every time I wakened up, she seemed to be awake too, to talk to me. She was super, and she made me feel safe.

"Honestly, I'm okay now. I just can't believe that Lester is dead. One minute he was threatening me that he had a gun, and the next minute he was dead.

"Sonny was okay. He didn't want to hurt me, and I think he likely saved my life. He hung onto me, and sort of lay over me, as we were flying out of control. He was almost as scared of Lester as I was.

"Last night I made sure to tell the police that Sonny wasn't really bad, and I'll tell them again, if he's in any serious trouble. The poor dumb guy really thought they were just picking me up to drive me home."

Kate smiled to herself. This was vintage Paige, always looking out for the under dog. She'd be inviting the luckless Sonny home for dinner if Kate wasn't careful.

Just before Kate was about to hang up, Paige said, "Mom, I, I'm sorry."

"Sorry for what?"

"I'm sorry I've been such a jerk. You looked awesome in your long dress the other night, and I didn't say anything. I just couldn't get the words out."

"Oh, Paige, honey. Don't worry about it. I appreciate the kind words, but that's the least of the things on your mind right now. We'll talk and hug when I get home. Then you can tell me how gorgeous I am," laughed Kate. She didn't want Paige to know how close to tears she was.

Actually, her knees were shaking, and she felt as if she was going to be sick. Her beloved daughter had come close to being killed, or raped, or both, last night, and she had known nothing about it. Neither she nor Mac had been anywhere near to help her. It was an unbelievable story, and Kate just couldn't quite wrap her mind around it.

Maybe this terrifying experience had helped Paige realize what a good life she had, and how foolish it was to get twisted out of shape because of a zit on the chin, or a certain shirt which was still in the laundry. Death defying experiences did tend to put things in perspective.

Mother and daughter talked for another few minutes, before Jill came back on to say good-bye. The phone was beginning to fade.

The wind was howling and attacking the windows now, and Kate feared that her cell phone might give up. She wouldn't want to be isolated here with Davey. After her Everglades nightmare, and after Paige's terrifying experience last night, Kate knew that it was never a good idea to be too far from help.

Chapter Twenty-Eight

"I've got to go, Jilly-girl," said Kate. I'm afraid this cell phone is going to die, and I'm not sure whether the power is on for the land phone.

"So, it sounds as if Paige is none the worse for her awful experience, and I owe you big time. Thanks so much for taking care of my girl. She says you were wonderful last night."

Kate blamed herself for giving Paige permission to go out on that stormy night in the first place. What kind of a careless mother was she anyway? She also blamed that stupid teacher. She should have either offered Paige a ride home, or waited with her until she had called for a drive. There was no way she should have left Paige standing alone in front of the locked school, in the dark, in a storm.

Kate would set up a meeting with the principal as soon as she got back to Toronto. There was no way she was going to let the incident drop. The teacher needed to be severely reprimanded. What had she been thinking?

After the phone call, she put her cell phone on the table, reminding herself that when she went upstairs, she would plug it in.

She was sick about what had happened to Paige. Her daughter sounded okay at the moment, but Kate knew from her own experience, that something like that wasn't easily forgotten. She just prayed that Paige would not be permanently scarred by last evening's events. She couldn't wait now to get home, and hold her daughter in her arms.

Looking out over the lake, she realized what a miserable day it was becoming. It had been so sunny and beautiful just a few hours ago. Now the storm was really closing in, and the thermometer was dropping. Kate was glad that they were safely back from town. There was no way the hardware people would be here today to fix the window. She and Davey were stuck until tomorrow, or possibly the following day.

They'd be fine, but she was now anxious to get home. She wouldn't even tell Mac about Paige's experience. There was nothing he could do, and it would spoil his trip. He had an important speech to give, and he didn't need any distractions. There would be plenty of time to rehash the entire terrifying occurrence, once he was safely back in Toronto.

Davey kept asking her what was wrong, and she didn't know how much she should tell him. Finally she decided that he was old enough to hear the truth. There were several good lessons to be learned from Paige's experience. Besides, Davey, at five years of age, had known all about the kidnapping of his mother, her weeks alone on the island, and the wild rescue.

Actually, he had been with her on a shopping expedition, when, turning his back for a minute, she had completely disappeared. He still remembered clearly his part in the rescue, so now, two years later, he could certainly handle the story about Paige's misadventure.

After giving him a shortened version of the experience, Kate said, "Now, Davey, how do you think Paige did last night, in the van with those two guys?"

"I know what you mean, mom. You mean did she help herself. Well, yes she did. She scratched them and yelled at them, and asked them to be nice, and not hurt her. Right?"

"Right," she grinned, hugging him until he yelped.

It was at that point that they were both startled by a pounding on the back door.

Davey got to the door first, and swung it open. He seemed to have forgotten that he had been taught never to open a door unless he knew who was on the other side. Kate made a mental note to go over that rule with him as soon as they had a quiet moment.

They were both surprised to see a woman standing there smiling at them.

"Oh, thank goodness there's someone home," said the stranger, walking right in without being invited.

"Well, do come in and make yourself at home," said Kate with a grin, but the slight sarcasm seemed lost on the woman.

"Whew! That's a long walk. It's snowing, and the wind is so strong. It felt as if the temperature was dropping with every step I took."

She shivered and rubbed her pink cheeks. "My face feels as if it's frozen. I doubt that it ever gets this cold and windy even in Alaska!"

It occurred to Kate that it would be nice to have a woman with whom she could chat by the fire for a while. Davey was a great companion, but it was always fun to have a gal with whom to gab. She wished that she had bought some wine while they were in town.

Before shutting the door, she looked down that long empty road. There was no skidoo, and there were no skis or snowshoes, so the woman had definitely walked.

"Where in the world did you come from?" she asked, with a slight frown.

The stranger ignored the question. She was too busy putting down the hood of her parka, and opening it. That was when Kate was able to see just how lovely she was, with her red hair, pink cheeks and big brown eyes.

"Man, I'm so cold. Do you mind if I just warm myself by the fire? It looks so inviting."

She didn't wait for an answer, but went to stand in front of the fireplace, without even removing her boots. They, of course, were covered with snow, which soon melted all over the floor.

"I'm afraid that I'm a bit lost," she finally said, giving them both a dazzling smile. "I'm on my way to visit some friends for a few days, and my car is stuck in a snow drift. I saw a car parked just off the main road, and decided that there must be at least one human close by. I just followed the skidoo tracks, where they hadn't been covered in by the wind. It's a long way, though."

Kate asked quite a few questions, but she got very few answers. This person, who said that her name was Angel Baby, seemed more than a little vague, when asked about her destination.

"Who are the friends you're visiting? We can give them a call, and at least let them know you're safe. They might be able to come and get you by skidoo."

Kate felt that she had to offer this solution, although she really did feel like having a little company. She had been wishing that Jill could have been here with her. She would be quite happy if it turned out that Angel had to stay overnight with them.

"Uh, their name is Woods – John and Mary Woods. I'm pretty sure, though, that they don't have a phone. They've just bought the place."

Angel Baby was sorry now for not having thought this out more clearly. At least she should have come up with a more believable name than John and Mary Woods. Well, thank goodness she hadn't said Smith or Jones!

"Surely they have a cell phone?"

"No, I don't think so. They like to get away from all civilization – specially cell phones and computers."

Kate thought this was a little strange, but her kind nature demanded that she be hospitable.

Davey wasn't saying anything, but he kept looking at the woman with a puzzled expression. There was a frown on his face, as he stared at Angel, and it was making her nervous.

"So, how are you, D – uh, dear boy?" she inquired, turning on her most dazzling smile again. She swallowed hard as she realized that she had almost called the little bugger "Davey." She had to be more careful. She was supposed to be a stranger, but she and Davey had spent quite a bit of time together in Florida, when Kate was missing. This would be a great test of her new appearance. She just had to remember to keep her voice low and slow.

She and Kate had never met face to face. Well, that wasn't exactly true. They had come close to a meeting in the Everglades just before all hell had broken loose. She, however, didn't think that Kate had been in very good shape to take much notice of her size and shape, in that short moment in which they saw each other.

"My name's Davey," he said shortly, "Davey Chandler, and I'm fine." Then, turning, he went back to his drawing. He kept glancing her way, though, as she made herself at home. He knew instinctively that he didn't like her. Somehow he understood that she was dangerous, but he didn't know why he knew that. There was something about her hands. They flapped like little broken wings when she talked. Who else did he know who did that?

Kate frowned at her son, indicating she didn't like his rudeness. What was wrong with him? Davey was always a well mannered little fellow.

She offered to make Angel a cup of tea, but the uninvited guest said that she'd rather have a glass of wine.

"Sorry, there's no booze of any kind in the cottage. We had a break-in a few days ago, and they took all the booze. We don't leave wine here over the winter anyway, and Davey and I certainly couldn't carry any in with us. We made that long walk in the cold and dark last night. It wasn't easy," she added with a laugh.

"I must admit, though, I would have really enjoyed a good drink once we got here safely."

"The police were here, and they said it was teenagers who took all our stuff and broke our window." Davey liked having such exciting news to share.

"The police!" Angel looked at least startled, and possibly frightened at that, but she immediately put her head down, and began taking off her boots.

"Oh dear. Look what I've done. I've dripped melting snow all over your floor." She said this without any apology in her voice. She was simply making a statement.

"That's okay," said Kate graciously. "It's easily wiped. Davey, could you get me a cloth from the kitchen closet where the rags are kept. Thanks, hon."

Over a cup of tea, the two women chatted, while Davey tended to his art work.

"Is there a Mr. Chandler?" asked Angel Baby, looking directly into Kate's eyes.

"Yes, indeed," laughed Kate. "He's not here with us this time, though."

For some reason, she felt reluctant to divulge too much information about her family. She was a little doubtful now, about this stranger. Her story about the friends sounded suspicious. How many people in this day and age would come up to a cottage in the middle of the winter, with no means of communicating with the outside world? Besides, this exotic beauty sitting in front of her didn't look like the type of girl who was good at "roughing" it in the middle of winter, in some elusive cottage.

Her hair was a lovely shade of red, and Kate wondered whether it was dyed. It didn't look like a colour one normally saw on red haired people. She studied it for a moment, thinking that she had seen hair like this quite recently, but where? Maybe at the hair salon, she told herself.

Kate had the feeling that there was something odd about her unexpected visitor. Trying to pin her down, however, was like trying to have a conversation with a bowl of Jello. She managed to slip and slide and change the subject at every turn.

"I must say that you look pretty, sitting there with your rosy cheeks. You're a very beautiful woman, but I'm sure you know that."

Angel Baby preened. "Yes, I know. I really am beautiful, and because of that, I could get any man I wanted. When a woman is beautiful, men just fall at her feet. Don't you agree?"

Kate grinned. "Well, I'm not sure about that. Don't you think it's more important to be beautiful inside? Just because a gal is a raving beauty doesn't mean that she can't be wicked, or dumb, or crazy. Good looks don't ensure good personality and character, unfortunately."

She regretted having mentioned Angel's good looks, but the woman was truly lovely.

"Well aren't you the smart one, with your Muskoka cottage, your big Toronto home, and your condo in Florida," said Angel with a smirk, changing the subject. She was annoyed that Kate had said looking good on the outside, didn't necessarily mean that you were good on the inside. Was she some clairvoyant thinking she could look right into Angel's soul? Phooey on her. Oh how she hated this woman!

Kate stared at her in amazement. How did she know that they lived in Toronto, and had a condo in Florida? And what did she mean by saying that Kate was "the smart one?" She might have been good looking, but she was unbelievably rude.

Kate had now decided that she was not so interested in entertaining this stranger, and giving her a warm bed overnight. She could just go back out into the wind and snow for all Kate cared.

"How in the world would you know all that?" There was a coldness in her voice, which told Angel she might be coming on too strong, too quickly.

"Oh, I'm sorry. You've misunderstood me. I didn't mean that to sound insulting. I'm sure it's wonderful for you that you have a handsome husband, and all these lovely homes. I guess maybe I'm just envious. These are all things I would have had too, if it hadn't been for a few twists of fate.

"Anyway, I recognized your face as soon as you opened the door," Angel Baby replied, thinking quickly.

"I've read all about you and your books and illustrations, and your fancy living, and, of course, I think it's wonderful. It's the kind of life that anyone would love to have."

She didn't sound the least bit sincere, but before Kate could think how to answer her, Angel managed to drop her mug of tea onto the carpet.

"Woops. Silly me. Now how did I do that?" asked Angel, with an innocent look.

The mug was one of a set of four fine china mugs which Jill had given Kate. Each mug had a Glen Loates painting of animals on it. This one was Kate's favourite. It depicted a black bear with her two cubs.

The mug shattered into several pieces, and Kate felt sick. How had that happened? It had looked to her as if this stranger had dropped it on purpose, but surely she was mistaken. She knew one thing for sure. Angel Baby was a walking disaster, and she didn't think that she liked her much.

Kate was mentally ticking off reasons in her mind. The woman had appeared from nowhere. She had told some unlikely story about friends expecting her – friends who had no means of communication. She had marched in and across the room, wearing her snowy, dripping boots, and she had deliberately dropped the mug on the wooden floor, where it would be sure to shatter. Then she had made the rude comment about Kate being so smart having all these nice things. This had all happened in the first fifteen minutes. What else should Kate expect?

She had gone from welcoming the woman warmly into her cottage, to a sick feeling in the pit of her stomach, that there was something wrong with this picture.

Somehow she knew that she and Davey had been far safer before she had opened the door to this beautiful visitor.

Chapter Twenty-Nine

Angel Baby was sizing up the situation. It was a piece of good luck that Kate and Davey were definitely all alone here. Mac was far away, and there were no neighbours anywhere to be seen. Of course, in this storm, it was difficult to see beyond a few feet. Still, she was confident that they were by themselves.

She had thought about this day for ages. All the feelings of hatred and jealousy which had been partially buried these past two years in Switzerland, were bubbling to the surface, and Angel Baby had the almost irresistible urge to leap at Kate, and scratch her eyes right out of that lovely face. That would just be for starters.

Angel was confident of her own ravishing good looks, thanks to Patrick's work, but she had to admit that the "oh so elegant" Kate Chandler, was too darn attractive for comfort. With her reddish-blonde, shoulder length hair, perfect English rose complexion, long eyelashes and high cheek bones, (not to mention her slim figure and long legs), there wasn't a man alive, who wouldn't give her a second or third glance.

Angel had always wondered whether maybe Kate was actually better looking than she was. She had asked herself whether that was why Kate had been able to steal Mac from her so easily. Men were such easy pickings for a good looking gal.

Well, now she would do the same to Kate. She would steal Mac back. Angel Baby was a beauty, thanks to Patrick, and Kate was still just your above average, good looking woman. It wouldn't even be a fair contest, after she was through with Mrs. Mac Chandler. By the time she was through with her, Kate wouldn't look appealing to any man – specially Mac.

Angel knew that the most fun and the best revenge, would be to leave Kate horribly disfigured, but still alive. That way she would go through the agony of losing Mac and even the kids, who wouldn't be able to stand looking at her.

The problem with that scenario, however, was obvious. If she left Kate alive, Kate would tell them who had attacked her, and Mac would be on her trail forever. No, she had to have time to cut Kate's face to shreds, but slowly and deliberately, in order to draw out the terror and suffering. Then she would kill her.

She had thought about this so many times, while locked up in that hateful place, and she liked to go over it in her mind.

Finally, she would kill Kate either with a few knife stabs to the heart and neck, or with her little Montreal special. Maybe one shot right between the eyes would finish her. No, somehow a bullet was too quick. She wanted Kate to suffer! She'd have to stab her.

Suddenly she began to giggle. She had just thought of the perfect weapon, an icicle! A big sharp icicle would be fantastic! It would melt and leave no evidence! She loved it. Then she realized the problem with that brilliant idea. Could she be sure of finding one when she needed it? Didn't icicles only happen when the snow and ice were thawing? Phooey, back to the gun or knife.

What she wanted to do, was to tease and terrorize Kate, who would be tied to a chair, for several hours. Then she'd take a break, and have a little sleep. If Kate was still alive by morning, she would cut her some more, just for fun, then kill her, and leave before anyone arrived. Revenge was going to be oh so sweet!

She didn't know what to do about Davey, though. He kept looking at her strangely, as if he was trying to remember something, and he was making her nervous. Maybe he was recognizing her voice. She was trying to keep it low and slow, but when she got excited, she tended to forget.

Oh well, she suddenly realized, once she had Kate safely tied to a chair, she would want her to know that she was really Madison. It wouldn't matter then, whether Davey had figured it out or not.

Okay, when the time came to play games with Kate, she would slip Davey some Rohypnol – enough to put him away for good. It would be the kindest thing to do. Then he wouldn't have to see what she was going to do to his mother, and he wouldn't be left alone in the cottage with a dead body. After all, she told herself that she wasn't a monster, and she did have some kind feelings toward the kid, even though he was a pest.

She could see that Kate was looking puzzled and annoyed now. Well, she hadn't seen anything yet, thought Angel. They had the entire afternoon and night ahead of them, and she was in charge. The gun in her purse made her top dog, but first she wanted to have some fun.

"Looks like you need some more wood for the fire. If you give me an axe I'll go and chop some for you. If I'm going to be here all night, I'll want lots of heat. I love sitting in front of the fire, don't you?"

There was something manic about her. She seemed full of suppressed energy, as if she was going to fly apart at any moment.

Kate noticed that there was something odd about her voice too. One moment it was quite low and sultry, then, the more she talked, the higher it became, and the faster the words came. What was going on? Kate was uneasy now, but she couldn't yet identify the reason for her unease. Maybe she was just over sensitive at the moment, after hearing about Paige's near miss last night. Maybe the entire world seemed dangerous at this point.

The strange thing was that it really looked to Kate, as if Angel had deliberately dropped that mug, but why would she do such an incomprehensible thing? Why deliberately try to antagonize your hostess? There was definitely something here which Kate was missing.

"Oh, no, thanks. Davey and I can get some from the shed. I think we likely have lots out there." No way in hell was she going to put an axe in Angel's hands.

"Come on, Davey, put on your boots and jacket, and find your mitts. We'll go get some wood. The thermometer says it's twenty-seven degrees below freezing. It's even stopped snowing now, because it's so cold. That's likely the very coldest you've ever experienced, so bundle up. A little bit of fresh air will do us good."

"But mom, we're just going to the shed. It's not very far. I don't want to put on all that stuff. I'll just have to take it all off again when we come back in."

"Davey, just do it. You'll be glad you did once you get out in the cold."

Kate had no idea just how glad Davey would be!

Turning to Angel, she said, "You sit there and relax. You must be tired after your long walk up the road. It won't take us long out there."

I'll kill her with kindness, she thought to herself, with a little grin.

"That's fine with me. I don't want to go out in that cold again. If you don't mind, I'll just use the washroom while you're outside," said Angel. "Which way is it? This is such a big cottage that I hope I don't get lost!" she added gaily.

Kate and her son put on their jackets and boots, hats and mitts, and headed to the shed. Davey gathered some kindling, while Kate picked up three large pieces of firewood. She was dismayed to see that there was very little firewood left. She would have to chop some, but not right now. Actually, she didn't think that she had ever used an axe before, and she wasn't eager to start. Oh well, one has to do what one has to do, she thought grimly.

At the moment, her priority was to figure out what to do about Angel. Was she just rude, or was she a little bit unhinged? Kate knew that the best thing would be to find Angel's friends as quickly as possible, and then get them over here to pick her up. That was if there actually were any friends!

"I don't like her," said Davey firmly, as they walked back from the shed.

It was so cold that they could see their breaths, and when they inhaled, their nostrils stuck together. The wind was howling, and the freezing cold penetrated right to the bone.

"Why do you say that, hon?" asked Kate. "Why don't you like her?"

"I don't know, I just don't like her," he shrugged.

"I feel as if I know her, but I don't," he tried to explain.

"Did we maybe know her when I was just little, and that's why I can't really remember her now?"

"No, I'm sure we've never met her. I'd remember if we had. She certainly is pretty.

"I want you to be polite to her, Davey. Don't let her know you don't like her. You'll either hurt her feelings, or she may even get mad at you."

Kate wasn't sure why she added that little bit.

Davey frowned, but said no more, as he tried to open the door.

The door, however, wouldn't open.

"I think it's stuck," he said, wrestling with it, and trying not to drop his kindling pieces.

Kate had the three large wood pieces in her arms, placed so that they were nicely balanced, so she tried to open the door without putting them down.

"Oh for heaven's sake, it must be frozen shut," she said in disbelief.

Reluctantly putting down the wood, she tried again.

The door didn't budge.

Kate grabbed the knob and twisted it back and forth.

She felt like kicking it, but didn't want Davey to see her do such a childish thing.

"What the heck is going on? It's definitely not frozen. The darn door is locked! She's locked us outside.

"Why would that woman have locked the door?" cried Kate in disbelief and disgust. "She's crazier than a bedbug."

Davey laughed at that. He hadn't yet realized the seriousness of their situation.

Kate's mind was racing. What if Angel left them out there forever? They would freeze very quickly. They could take shelter in the shed, but it wasn't any warmer than the outside, except that it would keep the wind off them.

"Hello," she called, as she began pounding on the door. "Angel, let us in. The door is locked!"

It was unbelievably cold. Thank God she had insisted that Davey put on his hat and mitts. Ordinarily she would have just run out with her jacket and boots on, leaving the hat and mitts behind. She had wanted to set a good example for Davey, however, so she was as bundled up as he was. Still, she was terribly cold, and knew that he must be too. The brutal wind was bringing tears to their eyes, and the tears were actually solidifying on their cheeks.

They were in serious trouble!

"Hey in there," she called again, pounding harder. "Angel, please open the door. We're freezing out here."

Davey started pounding on the door too, but the more they pounded, the more quiet it seemed inside the warm cottage.

It was as if they were the only two people left in the entire frozen world.

Chapter Thirty

Kate felt ridiculous pounding and yelling. The pair of them must have looked like idiots. Still, what else could they do?

"Davey, you go try the front door. No, wait a minute. We'll both go."

She hated to go around to the front of the big cottage. The wind was blowing in right off the lake, and it would be even colder out there. Still, they had to find a way to get inside.

As with many Muskoka cottages, there was a large screened porch, which ran across the front. This allowed cottagers to sit out on the porch at night, sipping a drink or a cup of coffee, and just enjoying the beauty of the night. There were always fireflies, flying squirrels, and raccoons to be enjoyed, with the screens for protection against being eaten alive by those vampirish Canadian mosquitoes, or the man-eating blackflies.

Kate was sure that the screen door and the main front door were locked. She had checked them both last night, but it was worth a try.

She didn't want Davey to go alone, though. She was now very wary and unsure of their strange guest, and she could picture her grabbing Davey, then locking Kate out. She mustn't let that happen. She didn't want Davey alone in the cottage with this Angel person. She was trouble with a capital "T."

The wind was howling like an animal in pain, and it was beyond freezing. Without protection for their faces, they wouldn't last very long.

Davey was shivering, and his lips looked blue. "I can't hold these, mom," he cried, dropping the kindling into the snow, and trying to stuff his hands into his jacket pockets. He was hopping from one foot to the other, and looking at her with pitiful eyes.

This made her think of Paige last night. Poor Paige, with no hat, no mittens, and no one to help her. She had been all alone on a deserted street in the dark. That must have been terrifying for a thirteen year old.

As suspected, the front door was also locked, and Kate began to think that they would have to break a window. How ironic that would be! They had come all the way up here from Toronto to fix a broken window, in order to keep snow and animals out. Now they were going to have to break another one in order to let snow and these two human animals in!

Immediately she realized what a ridiculous thought that was. The cold must be getting to her brain. They already had a broken window! It was still securely closed with the plastic bags, blanket and quilt, but she could rip her way through those if necessary. After all the time and effort it took last night to close off the window, it would be a shame if she had to tear it apart today.

"Come on, Davey. Don't worry, we'll get in. We'll go around to the back, and if we still can't get the door open, we'll just break through that wonderful barrier we made last night. What an adventure! The twins will be so disappointed that they weren't able to come with us."

She was trying to keep things light, so as not to frighten her son. She didn't want him to know how baffled she felt. Why would Angel deliberately lock them out? Was she just playing a game? Didn't she realize how cold it was outside? Did she need time to do something inside? Had she locked the door, then fallen asleep?

If she hadn't had Davey with her, she would have gone in there and accosted Angel, telling her that she had to leave. With Davey here though, she had to protect him and make sure that he was safe. She didn't want to rile Angel, and maybe push her into doing something bad.

They had just rounded the corner, and started pounding on the door again, when it suddenly opened.

"What's all the shouting? Did you lock yourselves out?" smiled Angel innocently.

"No, we did not lock ourselves out. You locked the door. Now why would you do that?" asked Kate angrily, as she pushed Davey into the relative warmth of the kitchen. She would worry about the kindling and firewood later. If anyone went to get it, it would be Angel. Kate would make sure of that.

"Don't be silly. I would never do such a thing. My goodness I owe you a lot. You're being so hospitable to me, letting me stay here out of the storm. I'll be forever grateful.

"I'm so sorry. I was up in the washroom, and I guess I didn't hear you shouting at first. I came as quickly as I could. Don't make a big fuss now. You haven't been out there that long. Goodness, what would you have done if I had been taking a little nap?"

She giggled and shook her head as if picturing this funny possibility.

In spite of herself, Kate almost laughed. This woman was unbelievable. What a cocky little twerp. She had nerve, that was for sure. Was she nuts or just into practical jokes?

Kate couldn't understand her. When they went out, the door was unlocked. It wasn't the type which automatically locked itself, therefore Angel had locked it. But why? Did she just do it as a joke which got out of hand, or did she have an agenda? For about the umpteenth time now, Kate asked herself who Angel was, and what she wanted.

The atmosphere in the cottage was now extremely frosty, and it had nothing to do with the weather. Kate was furious, and worried, but there was no point in trying to argue with this strange woman. She was sitting there rocking in front of the fireplace, apparently very happy with herself.

Actually, Angel was enjoying herself tremendously. This was fun! Never in her wildest imaginings had she thought she would get a golden opportunity like this. She had Kate Chandler alone, well, except for Davey, at a remote cottage in a winter storm. What could be better!

Locking the two of them out had been hilarious! She should have left them out there longer, until they really were half frozen. Oh well, it had still worked. Kate was becoming unhinged, at least she looked a bit frazzled. That was good enough.

Davey was a worry, though. The little punk kept staring at her as if he knew her. Hell, he'd only been five when they were last together. She'd had to babysit him a few times when Kate was missing, and she had been trying to ingratiate herself with Mac and the twins. She would have to get rid of him, before she really started on Kate. She didn't want him to figure out who she was, not yet anyway. That would spoil all the fun.

It was lucky that in those years when she had been stalking them, she and Kate had never actually come face to face. There was no way that she would recognize her as Madison, not until she, Angel Baby, was ready to tell her.

Oh what fun that was going to be, to see the terror on Kate's face, when she realized that she was all tied up, alone, helpless, with her old nemesis Madison. She'd likely be crying and begging for mercy.

She'd likely say "You can have Mac. Just let me live, and please don't cut my face!"

Angel Baby grinned at the thought. She'd talk to Kate, tell her of all the wonderful things she and Mac would be doing, while poor ugly Kate would be cold in her grave.

She would be sure to mention that the first thing they would do would be to get rid of the three kids. They'd send them far away to some awful boarding school, and they wouldn't let them come home for holidays. Ha ha. That would drive Kate crazy. She thought she was such a perfect mother, and she and Mac seemed to dote on those kids.

If Kate had been looking at Angel just then, she would have seen the evil grin on her face, as she pictured the fun she was going to have during the next 24 hours.

Kate was now concentrating, and staring at Angel Baby. If she had been able to get herself out of a dreadful situation in the Everglades, she should be able to easily outsmart this mean-spirited mystery woman.

Should she have a weapon handy, just in case? Well, yes, that would be nice, but what weapons were there? All she could think of were scissors or a kitchen knife. They would be useful in a pinch.

Thinking about weapons reminded her of the frightening days on the island. She had made herself a weapon out of a shard of broken glass, with a bit of towel wrapped around it for a handle. Thankfully she had never had to use it, but she had carried it with her at all times, just in case her kidnapper returned.

Then it came to her. Somehow she had to call the police, and it had to be done without alerting Angel. She would take her cell phone off the table, as surreptitiously as possible, and make the call from her bedroom.

"Angel, would you put the kettle on please. I'm going to run upstairs and find myself a warmer sweater. I'm still frozen, and a cup of tea is just what we need."

"Sure," said Angel, jumping up, and heading for the kitchen, almost too eagerly. It was as if she had been waiting for an excuse to go in there.

Kate looked around hastily for her cell phone, but it wasn't on the table where she had left it. Now what? Where was it? She looked on the floor, and on the big table, but there was no cell phone.

"Davey, have you seen my cell phone?" she whispered.

"No," he whispered back, shaking his head.

Damn that woman. Obviously she had taken it while they were locked outside. Kate's heart sank.

Should she confront Angel, and ask for her phone, or should she pretend she hadn't noticed? Which would be better? She wasn't sure.

Okay. She'd just wander into the kitchen, pretend to check the window, to see that the quilt was still well in place, then casually pick up the land phone and try to dial 911. She wasn't even sure whether it was on or not. Mac might have cancelled the phone for the winter months. Well, she'd have to try.

She'd be ready in case Angel attacked her, or tried to stop her. She'd bop her on the head with the phone, and yell for Davey to look for her cell in Angel's tote bag. She was taller, and looked stronger than Angel, so she should be able to subdue her somehow. She would just have to hit her hard enough to knock her out.

If Angel didn't seem to be worried when she picked up the phone, that would be a big relief. That should mean that she wasn't planning anything bad, and that she didn't care whether the police came around or not.

If the phone was actually working, Kate would ask for the officer, tell him her name, and say she needed help. Oh shoot, they'd ask what kind of help, and what could she say with Angel standing right there? Well, she'd just say, "please hurry, we're in trouble," and hang up. At least the police would come as soon as they could. Yes, that would work. Angel wouldn't try anything if she knew the police were on the way, but if she was totally innocent, she'd certainly think that Kate was weird.

It would make Kate look stupid and paranoid, but at this point she didn't care. She just had a bad feeling about Angel. If Angel was planning to hurt Kate for some unknown reason, then she must be planning to hurt Davey too.

There was no way Kate was going to let that happen – not while there was any breath left in her body.

Chapter Thirty-One

Walking quietly into the kitchen, Kate said, "I thought I'd get out some more cookies. I'm sorry that the cupboard is so bare. We couldn't carry much in, and we certainly weren't expecting visitors!"

Angel, who had been fiddling at the sink, seemed startled. She gave a little jump. Kate couldn't see what she was doing, but she did see her quickly shoving something into her pants pocket, before turning around.

Now what was she up to, wondered Kate. She definitely was not going to drink that tea. The woman might be planning to drug her or poison her. What could she possibly want? Was she going to rob them? That was a laugh. There was really nothing left to steal. Could she be planning to kidnap Davey? That seemed doubtful. She hadn't really paid any attention to him since her arrival.

These thoughts were flying around in her head like confetti in a wind storm. She grabbed the phone, but her heart sank as she realized that there was no dial tone.

Oh no, she muttered to herself. The friggin phone is dead. Isn't that just beautiful! Either the storm had knocked out the phone line, or Angel had cut the line before coming into the cottage, or Mac had cancelled the phone for the winter months. Anything was possible.

Kate remembered seeing some movement by one of the windows shortly before Angel came pounding on the door. Could it have been Angel, making her way around the house to find the phone line and cut it? Could she have been peeking in the window, to see if Kate was alone? Kate had been talking on her cell phone with Jill.

Of course it was possible that the land line had been dead since last night, and she just hadn't been aware of it. Any calls had been on her cell phone, and she hadn't had any reason to check out the land line. She shouldn't be blaming Angel for the dead line, yet it seemed plausible that she might have cut it.

Kate didn't see any need to tell Angel that the phone was dead. That would be her little secret. If Angel knew that Kate had no way of calling for help, she might be even bolder in whatever she was planning, if, of course she was planning anything.

"Who were you trying to call?" asked Angel nosily.

"Oh, I was just going to call the hospital and ask how old Walt, our caretaker is doing, but I don't think I will."

Good, that sounded fairly plausible.

"By the way, I've changed my mind. I really don't feel like tea right now. Make some for yourself, but I don't want any, thanks."

Kate was going over in her mind what it was about Angel that scared her. To begin with, she didn't like the fact that she had likely been peeking in the window before announcing her presence. She didn't appreciate that Angel had marched in uninvited, across the rugs and floor without removing her snowy boots. She didn't like that Angel had been so evasive when answering her questions.

Also, Angel had mentioned that she walked up the long road. Well, why wouldn't she have gone to the first cottage at the end of the road? It had lights on last night, so surely there was someone there today. Wouldn't it be logical to go there first before coming all the way along to here? It seemed that this cottage had been her actual destination. If so, why?

Kate was sure that Angel had deliberately dropped the mug on the floor, breaking it, and spilling the tea. Was that just to annoy her, or to get her flustered?

Of course the biggest thing which worried Kate, was the indisputable truth that Angel had deliberately locked them out. But again, why?

Had she needed time to search the cottage for something? Well, the cell phone had been in plain view, and she had apparently taken it, but why go to all that trouble? Obviously it would be to keep Kate from using it, but once again, she had to ask herself why? Was it because she didn't want Kate able to call for help? Help from what?

At this point Kate didn't know whether she was letting her imagination run wild, or whether there truly was a potential problem. She had to be cautious, if only because Davey was there.

She had a tiny little plan forming in her mind, and she thought she would give it a try. She was feeling sleepy after coming in from the extreme cold outside, to the warmth of the cottage inside. Maybe Angel would be getting sleepy too. If only she could get her to lie down and have a sleep, Kate would get herself and Davey out of here.

If they could get to the skidoo while Angel slept, they would head for town, and they'd be safe. They wouldn't come back to the cottage without a police escort. That was a wonderful idea, and so simple. All she needed to do was get Angel to sleep.

Unfortunately she knew that there were no sleeping pills or anything that she could have used to put in Angel's tea. She would have to rely on the body's natural instinct to sleep, after coming in from the cold. Angel had walked from the end of the road, or so she said, so she should be tired.

"Come on. I haven't been very hospitable. Let's go sit by the fire and chat. Tell me a little bit about yourself, and about these friends of yours."

Angel looked at her suspiciously, but Kate seemed to be sincere, so she followed her back to the living room, and sat once again in the rocking chair by the fire.

To someone looking in from outside, it was a picture perfect scene, something reminiscent of Norman Rockwell. There it was – a lovely old cottage, a blazing fire, snow falling against the window, two women conversing, and a child drawing at the table. It made you feel nostalgic, all warm and fuzzy, and gave no hint of the incipient evil waiting to pounce.

Kate couldn't help looking at Angel's lovely red hair. It was such an unusual shade. Where had she seen someone with exactly that shade of red? It had been just recently.

Suddenly it came to her. The dance at the Royal York! Mac had danced with that woman in the amazing black dress. She had red hair just like this. Surely it wasn't the same woman! Surely she didn't have another stalker on her trail!

Kate was just about to ask Angel Baby whether she had been at the Royal York dance, when she realized that the warmth of the fire was finally making her guest sleepy. Yes! Her eyes kept closing, then popping open again. This was good news for Kate.

Angel realized just how tired she was. She hadn't had a good night's sleep in a long while, and after the drive, the long walk through heavy snow, and now the warm fire, she simply couldn't hold her eyes open any longer.

Seeing that Angel's head was nodding, Kate suggested casually that Angel might like to lie down for an hour.

"After all, we're going to be stuck here for tonight and maybe even tomorrow. Without a television, maybe we'll want to sit up and play cards or something. I'd like a little snooze too, so why don't we all have a nap now."

Davey was about to protest, but his mom gave him another one of her looks, which Davey called her "stink eye," and he obediently remained silent.

Fingers crossed, she prayed that Angel might like the suggestion. Angel considered it, and surprised herself by agreeing to a short nap. Just half an hour would do her a lot of good, and then she could get to work, so to speak. She felt quite safe here. They had no idea who she was, and no idea of the danger lurking. When she got up all refreshed after a nice nap, she would make cocoa or something for Davey, and lace it with enough Rohypnol to kill a horse.

She would give Kate just enough to put her out. Then, while she was unconscious, she would tie her to a chair.

Angel could just imagine the desperate look on Kate's face, when she wakened to find herself all trussed up like a turkey, and Davey out cold. Angel could have some fun with her, using the scalpel she had stolen, among other things, from Patrick's clinic. If only the plan didn't involve a fair amount of blood. Angel Baby tended to get faint and nauseous at the sight of it. That was something she hadn't really factored into her plan.

She would then take a skidoo, and go back to her car, which was partially hidden at the end of the road. It wouldn't be long before she was out of the country, or at least on a plane to somewhere safe. When things eventually cooled down, and she was sure that they weren't looking for her, she would return and start her campaign to get Mac back in her arms. Dancing with him the other night had felt so good. She couldn't wait to do it again.

It was a fairly good plan, and she thought she would have all the time she needed. She didn't really believe that the police would be back, but if they did show up, she would just stay out of sight till they left. She hadn't done anything wrong – so far – so they would have no interest in her. Woops, no, that wasn't exactly right. Once they discovered the murders, they would remember her, and be very interested. She would become that dreaded "person of interest."

No, she must not, under any circumstances, let the police see her.

Right now, though, she really had to sleep. Then everything would be clearer in her head.

"Okay, I'm ready for a nap. We shouldn't sleep for more than an hour at the most, though," said Angel, heading up the stairs.

As soon as Kate had got her settled in her room, she hurried back down to the living room.

Without looking up from his drawing, Davey complained, "I don't want to have a nap."

"Shhh, she might hear you," cautioned Kate in a low voice.

"I just made up that part about snoozing. You and I are going to get into our skidoo suits and boots, and we're going to head out to the car, then to town.

"You have to be the most quiet you've ever been, Davey. She might get really cross if she thinks we're trying to fool her."

The thought that Angel Baby might have been dancing with Mac at the Royal York ball, had serious implications. Who was she? Why was she pretending that she didn't know Mac or anyone in the family? Why would she be dancing with Mac a few nights ago, and then show up at his cottage a few days later? What was the connection?

Kate just knew that she had to get Davey and herself safely away. There would be time later to solve this mystery.

Davey was solemn as he thought about this. "I wish I could remember who she is," he whispered.

"Are you really, really sure we don't know her from a long time ago, when I was just a kid?"

Kate shook her head, but had to smile at Davey's impression of himself. Apparently, in his mind, he had been "just a kid," a long time ago. What did he think he was now – a teenager? It was funny in a sad sort of way. Her baby was growing up way too fast.

"No, I don't think we've ever known her. I'm sure I'd remember her. She's quite an unusual person.

"Now hurry, and get your clothes on. We're out of here."

As so often happens, however, the Fates decided to step in and stir the pot a bit. Before they could get their warm clothes on, they heard the pounding on the back door.

Whoever it was, Kate said a silent thank-you. There was usually safety in numbers, and Kate expected and hoped to see the police or the hardware men at the door.

Chapter Thirty-Two

Mother and son looked at each other, and Kate thought, Great, we're saved. Whoever this is, it's someone who can help us. It will now be three of us against one.

Peering out the door window first, she saw a man who didn't look familiar. She knew it couldn't be a policeman, or the man from the hardware store with her window boards, since there had been no sound of a skidoo approaching from the road or the lake. It wasn't Walt Jr. either, which was too bad. He could have fixed the window. Whoever it was, must have either plodded through the woods, or up the road.

She hesitated before opening the door. What if this guy was Angel's partner? What if Angel had come first, to see if she and Davey were alone? What if she had called him with Kate's cell phone, and told him it was safe to come now. He could have been waiting in a car at the end of the road.

No, that wasn't likely. Angel hadn't acted as if she was expecting anyone.

Kate just had to have a little faith here.

Whoever it was, he could very well be the answer to an unspoken prayer, the man who was going to get them out of this sticky situation. She couldn't just ignore him, or shut the door in his face.

"Davey, get the rolling pin," she whispered.

Davey did as he was told, without asking any questions. He seemed to understand the problem right away. Was this man good or bad?

Finally Kate opened the door a crack.

The man, tall and good looking, pushed back his hood, and gave her a huge grin.

"Hi Kate. Oh my, you're just as lovely as ever. The years have been really good to you."

Kate stared at him, recognition coming slowly.

"Kate, don't you recognize me? It's Mark. It's Mark Duncan from high school days. Don't tell me I've changed that much!"

"Mark, I don't believe it!" Kate smiled and opened the door wider.

A big German Shepherd danced around in great excitement, and wagged his tail frantically.

Yes, indeed, she did remember Mark Duncan. The last time she had seen him, she had threatened to call the police, and tell them that he was stalking her. She finally had called them, and had always regretted it.

Shortly after that, she and Jill had left to start their summer jobs, and then they were off to university, so she had never seen or heard from him again.

How in the world had he tracked her to the cottage? Was he here to hurt her? Was this some kind of revenge he was finally taking, because she had given him the brush-off, and called the police about him?

If she let him in, and he wouldn't leave, what could she do? He looked to be big and strong. There was certainly no one nearby she could call for help. Heck, she couldn't even find her cell phone!

Then she realized with shame, how utterly paranoid she was being. She was becoming too cynical! She didn't seem to trust anyone any more.

Mark looked good, and she had always liked him as a friend, until he had gone off the deep end, calling and calling several times a day, pleading with her to go to the graduation prom with him.

He had become a terrible nuisance, and she just hadn't wanted anything more to do with him, so she had called the police. How awkward. She hoped he had forgotten the incident, and if it wasn't forgotten, she hoped at least that he had forgiven her. After all, they had been teenagers, with all the usual angst that entailed.

He was standing patiently, smiling at her. If he thought it was strange that she was holding a rolling pin, he didn't say anything. The dog was now sitting at her feet, looking up at her hopefully with his big brown eyes, and woofing as if he was trying to tell her something.

Mark seemed to sense her confusion, and he laughed.

"Don't worry, I'm not here to invite you to the prom. Actually, I'm a neighbour now, and I was so pleased when I heard that you had bought this place. My cottage is the first one you pass when you get off the main road."

Kate was looking at the dog. She couldn't resist him. He was almost human, the way he was cocking his head from one side to the other, and looking so eager.

"Well, please come in. I guess it was your cottage which had the lights on last night, when Davey and I arrived. I was tempted to go to your door, but was a little afraid. I decided to save our energy to make it to our own place.

"Actually I was expecting the police when I heard you knocking. That's why I'm so surprised to see you. It's darn cold out there, come on in."

"Is it okay if Kingsley comes too? He's pretty well behaved, and I don't like to leave him out by himself in the cold too long. He'll be hurtling himself at the door to get in. He doesn't like to miss the action."

"Sure," she laughed. "Why not? My son will be delighted. He's a great animal person, and so am I."

Mark took his snowy boots off right at the door, and placed them on the little mat. He cautioned Kingsley to be quiet, and to behave, then walked into the kitchen.

"Oh oh, what happened to your window?" he asked, examining the quilt which was still in place. "Is that why you said you were expecting the police?"

"Yes, we had a break-in recently. They stole a lot of stuff, but didn't harm anything except the window, so I guess we were lucky. Davey and I came up to get it fixed, since our man who checks the cottage is in hospital with a heart attack."

"That would be Walt Sr. I heard he was hospitalized. He's really reliable, and so's Walt Jr. Fortunately they say he's going to be all right."

Kate brought her old friend to sit in the living room in front of the fire.

Kingsley and Davey took one look at each other, and became instant pals. They were soon engaged in a wild game of chase around the cottage.

"Wow, Davey, slow down," cautioned his mom. She didn't want Angel to waken up just yet. First she'd like the chance to tell Mark the situation, and ask for his help and advice.

"Why don't you put on your skidoo suit and boots, and go play in the snow with Kingsley. It's cold out, but you'll be warm if you're running around. There are a couple of balls in the closet. I'll bet he'd love to chase them.

"Stay at the back of the cottage, though. Don't go down by the lake. You can watch for the men from the hardware store."

Kate wasn't sure why she threw that in. There was no way that the hardware guys would make it here today, not on this stormy afternoon. Maybe she wasn't quite sure about Mark yet, and wanted him to think that there would soon be other men, even police here at the cottage. That would stop him from trying anything.

She made them some coffee, and sliced some of the lemon loaf which she had brought back from town.

So far, Angel had not appeared.

"This is a busy place today" said Kate quietly. "A couple of hours ago, a woman came knocking at my door. She said that she was lost, and was looking for the cottage of some friends, but she doesn't seem too concerned. Actually, she seems to be settling in for the duration of the storm. She's upstairs having a little sleep right now.

"You know, something else is bothering me. Why didn't she stop at your cottage first, instead of struggling all the way up here. Your place is so much closer to the main road."

"Well, maybe she did stop at my place. I was out for a couple of hours with Kingsley. We had a long walk and play in the snow. Maybe she came, and no one was home, so she had to continue on to here."

That did sound reasonable, so Kate put it aside.

She was a bit reluctant to delve into her concerns about Angel just yet. She thought it would be better to talk with Mark a few minutes, to get an idea of whether he was likely to help her. She also wanted to satisfy herself that he wasn't somehow connected with Angel.

"What have you been doing since high school? You were taking business at Toronto University, weren't you?"

"Yes, you've got a good memory. I started a real estate company which did pretty well. I sold it a while ago and made a ridiculous amount of money, so now I just dabble in a few things. I suppose you'd call it an early retirement, but I don't think of it that way."

He seemed so confident and sure of himself that Kate could barely believe he was the same shy, self-conscious guy who had followed her around like a puppy. She figured he had done pretty well for himself. He was far too young to be retired, and that was a gorgeous red cashmere sweater he was wearing. This guy had money, no doubt about it. How nice for him.

"I can't believe that after all these years, we would have cottages almost next door to each other. What a coincidence!" Kate was shaking her head in amazement.

"Isn't it though? When I read all about your experience in the Everglades, and then how well your children's books are doing, it reminded me of all the good times we used to have. We had a good gang of friends, didn't we? I couldn't believe it when I heard you had bought this old Carrington place. It's a great old cottage, but it needs a fair amount of work."

"Tell me about it," laughed Kate. Then, changing the subject, she queried, "Are you married?" She was hoping that he was. He would be more likely to not become a pest, if he had a wife to keep tabs on him.

"Not any more," he laughed, shaking his head. "Three strikes, and I'm out for good. I think I'm better with animals than I am with women," he added ruefully.

"Probably it's just that the right woman hasn't come along yet."

These could be dangerous waters, Kate thought. She didn't want to give him the wrong impression, any ideas that she would be open to a little hanky-panky, with Mac so far away. Of course he had no idea that Mac was away in England, and she wanted to keep it that way.

Before she could say anything, though, Mark continued. "I've made so darn many mistakes in my lifetime, but I'm trying to make up for them. I give away a lot of my money, and that makes me feel good. I started a program for rescuing animals lost after disasters.

"You wouldn't believe how many poor little creatures get separated from their owners during a hurricane or a tornado. It's sad, but it's so great when you can reunite them, or find them a new home. I get a lot of pleasure out of that program," he said proudly.

Kate was feeling more relieved by the minute. Mark was a good person, and she was sure he would help her.

Standing up, she said, "I'm going to get us some more coffee, and also check on Davey and Kingsley. They're likely having fun, but that wind is making it awfully cold. I don't want either of them to get frostbite."

Actually, she just needed a moment to make up her mind about telling him all her concerns. She was hoping that he and Kingsley could get them safely away from Angel, but on the other hand, if Angel turned out to be harmless, she didn't want to look like a paranoid fool.

Chapter Thirty-Three

"Davey, do you want to come in now?" asked Kate, holding the door open just enough to stick her head outside.

"No way, mom, we're having fun. Watch Kingsley. Look how fast he can dig the ball out of the snow!"

Kate watched for a moment, then said, "He's a pretty smart dog, isn't he? Okay, you can stay out for a while longer, but as soon as your toes or fingers start to get cold, you come in. We'll make some nice hot chocolate."

Davey and the dog were having a riotous time in the snow. They had obviously bonded.

"Looks as if they'll be friends for life," she laughed, returning to the living room.

"I can't get over the coincidence of us both ending up here after all these years," repeated Mark.

"You haven't had time to experience a summer here yet, but I know you'll love it.

"What about your husband? What's he like? Is he the type who likes to tinker and fix things, or will he be boating or lounging around on the dock, with his nose in a book, while he pays someone to do the work?"

"A little bit of both, I guess. I'm sure he'll be busy teaching the kids to water-ski, and he does like hiking, so we'll all do some of that. We're new at the cottage game, so it's going to be a learning summer for all of us.

"Actually we plan to do some serious renovations. This old cottage must have been beautiful in its prime. The bedrooms upstairs are huge, but there's only one bathroom! That's our first priority." Kate laughed and shook her head.

"We all get along pretty well, but I think the five of us contending for one relatively small bathroom, would put some serious strains on the family. We plan to put in two good sized washrooms for starters, and then we'll see what's next, so it should be fun."

"Well, let me know if there's any way I can help you. I mean it Kate. I love building and repairing. That's my main hobby now. I'm the world's best tinkerer, and you'll have to come over and see some of my work.

"Plumbing doesn't interest me much, but I'm really good at carpentry. I've built some cupboards which I think are pretty nice, and I built a really beautiful table and hutch for the dining area. My cottage is pretty big. It just keeps growing." He laughed and shrugged his shoulders like a big kid.

"It'll soon be as big as this old mausoleum."

"I understand that there's quite a history about the Carrington family. Are you aware of it?"

"I know some of it I guess. Old man Carrington, the grandfather, made all his money in bootlegging and lumber, back in the twenties and thirties. His wife was the spoiled daughter of a lumber baron from British Columbia. Between the two of them, they had more money than brains I think. Anyway, they apparently built three different cottages in Muskoka, and when they were using one cottage, the other two just sat empty. What a waste! One burned down back in the fifties, and one was sold and turned into a small resort.

"When the old ma and pa died, their two kids began fighting over this one. It had been left to both of them, but they never got along, so the case was in court for years. Neither would agree to sell, so instead of coming to a compromise, it just sat empty.

"Finally, about two years ago, the son died under mysterious circumstances, and the daughter finally got her greedy hands on it. Unfortunately, by then she had been diagnosed with cancer, so she put it on the market, and some family from Toronto bought it. Then, apparently they won the lottery, built a huge mansion over on Lake Joseph, and put this one up for sale. That's when you and your husband stepped in and bought it."

"That's fascinating," said Kate, shaking her head a bit.

"What a sad history it's had. Well, we plan to make it a happy family retreat, and we're looking forward to many wonderful years here. Thanks for filling me in on the story. We had heard bits and pieces, but never the entire tale. I'll have to tell Mac and the kids. They'll be so interested."

While Mark had been talking, Kate found that she was gradually remembering all the things she had liked about him in high school, at least until he had become a royal pest. She was glad to renew the friendship.

"We're so anxious to spend out first summer here. How early does the ice in the lake go out?"

"Well, that depends on a lot of things. It's usually around the middle to the end of April. That's when I come up and take the winter shutters off. I don't put the boats into the water, though, until well into May. You'll know when the time feels right.

"By the way, shutters would be a great idea for this place. That would prevent the break-ins. I'd be glad to help your husband with those."

After chatting another twenty minutes or so, Mark stood up.

"Guess I should be going. Kingsley and your son must be getting pretty cold and tired by now. I'd almost forgotten all about them out there. I hadn't meant to stay so long."

"Listen, before you go, I want to tell you something." Kate was speaking very quietly, and looking up the stairs as she spoke.

"Let's go into the kitchen for a moment."

Mark looked intrigued as he followed her.

"What's the matter?"

"Well, this woman I mentioned, showed up a couple of hours ago, claiming to be lost. There's something suspicious about her, but I can't put my finger on it. I had just been trying to talk her into taking a nap, when you knocked on the door. I was hoping that while she slept, Davey and I could go out on the skidoo, and get to town. I'm uneasy about spending the night here alone with her.

"It likely sounds stupid, but I don't feel safe with her. I'm so glad that you came when you did, and I wish you would stay a little longer. I'd like you to meet her, and let me know whether you think she could be dangerous. Honestly, I just feel so much more secure having you here."

Kate hoped fervently that this didn't sound like a "come-on". She didn't want Mark to think she was flirting with him, but she felt much safer with him in the cottage.

"What makes you think that she's suspicious?" asked Mark with interest, also speaking very softly, and moving closer to Kate.

"It's just a lot of little things, which may sound dumb to you. She says that she's on her way to friends, but she seemed vague about their name, or where exactly they are. It was as if she was making it up as she went along. Then she locked Davey and me outside when we went to get some wood. She swears that she didn't, but the door didn't lock itself, and when we came in, my cell phone had disappeared.

"Now, one other thing has me really worried. We went to a dance at the Royal York last week, and a beautiful red head asked Mac to dance. I didn't see her face, but her hair was such an odd and lovely shade of red, that it stuck in my mind. Angel Baby has that exact same hair! There's something else too. She knew Mac's name, and my name, yet Mac said that night that he has never met her before. He couldn't figure how she knew our names.

"Doesn't it seem strange to you that she would show up here, but not acknowledge that she was at the dance, waltzing around the floor with my husband?

"I know you likely think I'm paranoid, but I just have a bad feeling about her. Davey keeps saying that she's familiar to him, but he can't remember where he might have seen her. He instinctively doesn't like her, and kids are usually pretty good at sizing up people."

"That does sound a bit strange. Do you have any enemies from the past who might be after you? You know, someone who's jealous of you, or some crazy who doesn't like the books you write, or, I don't know, maybe an old girlfriend of your husband's?"

That struck a chord with Kate. She was shaking her head, when she suddenly stopped and stared at him. "No, it couldn't be. No, definitely not."

"What?" asked Mark

"Well, my husband had an old girlfriend who stalked us for years, and then tried to kill me again a couple of years ago, but this is definitely not she. This woman is much better looking, although she is about the same size.

"Oh shit! I wonder whether that's why Davey keeps thinking he knows her? Oh, my God. Could Angel Baby really be Madison with a new face? Could that be possible? No, I don't think so. As far as we know, she's still locked up in a psychiatric hospital out in B.C."

Kate was talking to herself, but talking out loud.

"A psychiatric hospital? That doesn't sound good. Yes, I'll definitely stay until she gets up, and I'll see what I can get out of her. There's no way now that I'm going to leave you here with her, until we figure out who she is, and what she wants."

That was reassuring to Kate, and she took a big breath, and smiled at her old friend.

"Thanks, Mark. I appreciate it very much. You've put the idea in my head now, though, and I can't stop wondering whether it could be Madison. She's a bit of a bitch like Madison, and there's something strange about the look in her eyes. I wonder whether you'll notice it too.

"By the way, she calls herself Angel, or Angel Baby. It's just the kind of thing she might do, you know, changing her name when she changed her face.

"She barged in here, tromping all over with her snowy boots, she deliberately broke a lovely mug and didn't apologize, she seemed to know a lot about me, and I thought that she had almost called Davey by name when she first came in, but then she quickly covered up. There are so many little things which are just the kind of thing she used to do when she was stalking us. But how in the heck would she have known I was up here all alone with Davey?"

Kate didn't want to believe it could be Madison, yet it was looking very suspicious. The fact that Davey instinctively disliked her, added to all the other small things, plus the way she had locked them out, made a rather convincing case.

Kate and Davey were stuck in a cottage far from home, in a brutal winter storm, with a possibly dangerous, certifiably crazy woman. Thank God Mark was here! He would be able to help them.

Or would he?

Chapter Thirty-Four

Around the time that Kate was realizing this could be her old nemesis Madison Ramsay, coming back to make another attempt on her life, Angel Baby/Madison decided she needed to know what those two were doing downstairs.

She could no longer hear them talking, because they had moved into the kitchen. Why were they whispering? That really annoyed her. She hated secrets, if she wasn't in on them. Was there anything suspicious about this old school friend showing up now, just when she had Kate all to herself?

Angel Baby could feel her brain getting "fuzzy around the edges." That's what she called it, when reality and imagination began to merge. She had to stop it happening before she got really confused. There was no room in her murderous plans for confusion.

She had really needed a little sleep, and was just dozing off, when she heard the pounding at the door. She feared it was the police, and considered going out a window, but was afraid of falling. She had been listening to the conversation from the top of the stairs, but now she couldn't hear them.

Digging her nails into the palms of her hands, and taking deep breaths, she concentrated on what she should be doing.

Of course she still felt that she had the advantage, but not by much. At least Kate didn't know who she really was, and no one knew that she had a gun. Those were two big points in her favour, which put her out ahead of them. What they didn't know could definitely hurt them, she giggled softly.

Now was the time to make her move, before any more people arrived. She couldn't hide up in the bedroom forever. She needed to see this man face to face, and decide how much of a problem he might be.

She knew, however, that letting him see her, was going to be a mistake. He could be a witness later on, after the killings. That was why she had stayed upstairs in the first place. She hadn't wanted him to see her, and she hadn't realized that he would stay so long.

Maybe he was deliberately waiting to get a look at her. Maybe that's why he and Kate had been whispering in the kitchen. She realized that she had to go down and assess the situation. She would drive herself crazy otherwise. Angel Baby didn't realize just how ironic that thought was. She didn't realize, or want to admit that she was halfway there already.

Was he a threat to her plans? Yes. Should she get rid of him? Yes. Okay, Angel Baby, how do we do it?

Splashing water on her face, she patted it dry, then took a moment to fluff her hair, straighten her clothes, and admire herself. Yes, she was still gorgeous. Eat your heart out, Kate, she thought, as she headed down the stairs.

Kate stared at her, as she made her slow descent. Could this possibly be Madison with a new face? It sounded too much like science fiction to be true, but she was the same size as Madison had been, and it was just the kind of insane plot that a crazy person would like. All the little annoying and mischievous things she had done were definitely "Madison type" things. Even the fact that her voice kept changing was suspicious.

Kate had only seen Madison in person on one occasion, but she had heard her on the phone years and years ago, when she and Mac were first married, and she had seen pictures of her. Angel certainly didn't look anything like Madison, and Kate couldn't remember what her voice had been like, but obviously Davey felt he knew her from somewhere. Maybe it was her mannerisms which he recognized.

Mark and Kate stopped talking, as Angel came slowly down the stairs. They both watched her silently as she approached.

"They've been talking about me," she told herself, as she gave them one of her winning smiles. "I'm about as welcome as a cow pie at a bake sale." This thought made her smile even more.

Angel had a good, off the wall sense of humour, and she often laughed at her own jokes. That was something Mac had always liked about her.

As Mark watched her with interest, he couldn't believe how good looking she was. She was beautiful, and you could tell that she was totally aware of her good looks. He told himself that no one that beautiful could be bad, at least that was what he would like to think.

She certainly didn't look anything like an escapee from a mental hospital. Now that he could see her, he doubted very much that there was anything sinister about her. Kate was way off the mark. Still, he should make sure, before leaving his old friend alone with her.

He wondered whether he should invite them all over to his place for the evening. He had a gun stashed away in his bedroom nightstand, and Kate would feel more secure, knowing he'd be able to protect her. Well, he'd wait a little bit, then suggest that they all go over to his cottage.

Angel was still wondering what these two had been doing in the kitchen. Had they been simply doing a little hugging and kissing, and didn't want her to hear them? Or, had Kate been whispering about her?

Maybe she had been asking Mark for help, asking him to stick around, and stop Angel from hurting her. No, that wasn't likely. She didn't think Kate was really suspicious yet. Still, they had been talking very quietly. Why?

Who was he? Was he really just an old school friend of Kate's? That's what it had sounded like from upstairs. She had been able to hear most of the conversation, when they were in the living room, and it really had nothing to do with her, nothing suspicious. He didn't look like a cop, but she couldn't be too careful. She had to cover all possibilities while her mind was still pretty clear.

Well, one thing for sure, he was certainly handsome. But no, dammit, this was all wrong. There wasn't supposed to be anyone here except Angel, Kate and Davey. Now what? How was she going to get rid of him without him getting suspicious?

"Oh, Mark, this is Angel," said Kate, noticing that Mark was looking at Angel with great interest and admiration. Men were all the same. They were all suckers for a pretty face.

"She got lost looking for her friend's cottage, and she's staying here till we can get in touch with them."

Angel tried to be polite, but her mind was swirling, and it was difficult to concentrate. She had looked forward to this revenge for a very long time. She had gone through all that surgery to change her appearance and give herself a new start in life. It had all been done to keep herself out of another psychiatric hospital, and, to snag Mac again. She wasn't going to let some creepy neighbour spoil everything, no matter how good looking he was.

He was asking her something, as she stood and looked at him appraisingly.

"I said, what's the name of your friends?" he repeated. "I know most of the people on the lake, so I can likely give you directions, or take you over there on my skidoo. It's back at my place, but that's no problem. I can easily walk back and get it. Do you have good directions to their cottage?"

Mark, of course, was just saying this to try to get some useful information out of her. If she was able to tell him how to get to the friend's cottage, or if by chance he actually knew the people in question, then he'd assume that she was not dangerous, that she was telling the truth, and was just lost, as she claimed.

Angel's mind went blank. What names had she made up about her fictional friends? They were simple names, but what were they? Was it Smith – Jim and Betty Smith? No, that didn't sound quite right.

Come on, Angel, think. It was Brown. No, it was Young. Yes, that's it, Anne and Bill Young. NO, that didn't sound familiar.

With them both staring at her, she said, "You know, all of a sudden I'm feeling a little woozy. I must have slept wrong on the pillow, or I just stood up too quickly. I haven't had much to eat today, and I'm diabetic. Just let me sit for a minute."

She, of course, wasn't diabetic. She just threw that in to make herself look rather helpless and weak. If she didn't appear dangerous, it would throw them off guard. Also it was a good excuse to give her a few moments to remember the names of the supposed friends. Good for her! Her mind was still working quickly and rationally.

She could beat these two any day of the week, with one hand tied behind her back. The very thought made her smile inwardly. When push came to shove, she wouldn't be the one with her hands tied behind her back. Of that she was very sure.

Chapter Thirty-Five

Angel Baby was nervous about Mark, and her mind felt sluggish. If she could only remember the names of her fictional friends, which she had mentioned, when she first arrived. She couldn't think well, while they stared at her, and at this point she had no idea what names she had so blithely imagined.

She sat quietly in the chair, with her head down. She didn't want them to see her face just now. They might guess or realize that she was concentrating, trying to remember those stupid names. If Kate remembered the names, and if Angel came up with something different, it would be ball game over. Kate would know she had just made them up.

Kate hurried to get her a mug of coffee, making sure to put it in an old mug which she didn't like. There was no way Angel Baby was getting her hands on any more of the pretty mugs Jill had given her.

Kate was thinking it was strange that Angel had eaten that lemon cake, if she was a diabetic. She shook her head, and muttered, "She's no more diabetic than I am." Why had she lied?

Meanwhile, Angel sat quietly with her head in her hands, hoping that this would all go away. Things weren't happening quite the way she had planned, but she could handle things. She was so much smarter than these two amateurs.

What in the world were those names? She vaguely remembered that they were simple, and had some reference to cottage country. Was it Waters, or Lake or Woods? YES, that was exactly right. It was John and Mary Woods. Still, she wouldn't mention them unless Mark asked again. He seemed to think that he knew everyone on the lake, so he'd be suspicious that he had never heard of them.

Feeling much better, she turned her most seductive smile on Mark and said, "So, Mark, I take it that you live around here. Do you stay here all year long?"

"No, I live in Toronto, but Kingsley and I come up here a lot. Kingsley's my dog. He loves cottage country."

"Where is he now?" Angel looked around uncertainly. She wasn't too fond of dogs. She had heard Davey and the dog chasing around the cottage when they first came in, and it sounded as if it was a big dog. Now there was a strange man, plus a dog, to screw up her plans. How could one small woman cope with two adults, a child, and a dog? She didn't like the odds.

Her mind was beginning to whirl, like an out of control merry-go-round. She could handle it, though. Yes, she could. She took some big calming breaths as inconspicuously as possible.

"Kingsley's outside playing in the snow with Davey," answered Kate.

"They're having a great time, and they're watching for the hardware men. They'll likely be arriving shortly to fix the window."

Not in this storm, they won't, thought Angel Baby, glancing out the window. She was sure that there'd be no hardware men today.

Kate was ridiculous the way she kept mentioning them, as if they would be her saviours. No, Angel Baby just had to worry about this Mark character, his dog, and maybe the police.

She sighed to herself, as she realized that she should likely be speeding things up a bit, and finish what needed to be done, before anyone else arrived, and before she lost total control. This darn cottage was busier than the Toronto airport.

Mark was talking again.

"I'm president of the Cottager's Association, so that's why I know just about everyone on the lake. Now who did you say your friends are? We can give them a call, and let them know that you aren't lost in a snow bank."

Angel was ready for him this time, and let the names just roll right off her tongue.

"They're John and Mary Woods, but they've just bought the place, so you likely wouldn't know them." It sounded lame, even to her ears.

"They're a lovely couple, full of fun." Her mind was still racing, but she was hanging on. She mustn't lose control. If she started hallucinating or fragmenting, she'd be in a hell of a mess.

Gradually she realized that she didn't feel so good. Maybe she should have had a sleep. Her mind was "fogging." Plans were crumbling and whirling, like grains of sand in a dust storm. She should not be sitting here, talking with a potential witness to the crime which was about to be committed. She should cut her losses and leave right now, aborting the entire scheme.

At the moment, that sounded like a good idea, but she hated to give up. This was such an ideal location for a murder, at least it had been, until Mark had appeared. Besides, how long would she have to wait to get Kate alone again, without her kids and Mac around her?

No, there would never be a better time than right now. Mac was away in England, the twins were in Toronto, Davey and the dog were out in the snow. If she could somehow incapacitate Kate and Mark, she could lock the kid and the dog outside until they froze to death. Perfect.

The time had come, but how was she going to do it? Her head felt all weird, as if it was stuffed with those white Styrofoam peanut shaped packing pieces. Bits of ideas were slamming around, but that was the problem. They were just bits. There was no solid idea there.

Mark was talking again, and she tried to appear normal, while she schemed and planned.

"I was saying that I read everything I could about Kate, when she was kidnapped and left in the Everglades. Had you heard about that?"

Was he trying to trick her? Did he suspect who she was? Did he know what part she had played in Kate's adventure? No, that was impossible. It was just coincidental that he was asking about the fiasco in the Everglades.

"Oh, of course I've read about it. Actually I was in Florida when all that happened." Oh, oh. Why had she said that? She was getting careless. They were both looking at her in a funny way now.

"I was just spending a couple of nights on my way to the Bahamas, for a much needed vacation. I was with a couple of friends." There, that sounded plausible. That should throw them off the trail. She certainly had a lot of fictitious friends these days! She let out a nervous giggle, and quickly cleared her throat to cover it.

"I think I'd better get Davey and Kingsley in now. They've been out there a long time, and it's unusually cold today." Kate headed to the back door, just as Angel frowned and said, "Oh no, please, don't let that beast in here. I don't like dogs."

At the annoyed look Mark gave her, she added. "I mean I love dogs, but I'm very allergic to them. I don't like what they do to me. That makes me sort of scared of them." She was blithering and she knew it, but she was getting confused. Everything had been working out so well before this guy had arrived.

She had really looked forward to having Kate all to herself tonight. Now it was somewhat messed up. She was reluctant to kill Mark, but it looked as if she would have to.

But what about the dog? He might jump at her throat, or bite her arm or something. She'd better sit here quietly, until she could think of how to get rid of him.

Mark was asking her something.

"Angel, you must know where the cottage is, if you were heading right there this afternoon. If I go and get my skidoo, do you think you can guide us there without getting lost? They must be so worried about you."

What was this guy – some kind of a bulldog? Why was he pressuring her this way? Why was he so eager to get her out of here? Oh, wait a minute. Maybe he had the hots for Kate, and he wanted to make a move on her. She looked from Mark to Kate, and then back to Mark before answering.

"I'm sure I could find it under normal circumstances, Mark, but just look out the window. Look at the way the wind is blowing the snow all over the place. I'd be afraid to go out on a skidoo right now. We might get lost and freeze to death. I think I'll just stay here nice and warm tonight, and tomorrow I might ask the police if they can help me."

She had no intention of going anywhere near the police, but it sounded pretty good to her ears, and she thought that Mark and Kate were buying it. It would have been sort of fun, though, to go on a skidoo ride with Mark. He was quite attractive.

At that point Davey and Kingsley came bouncing in. The dog was shaking himself, and the snow was flying all over the room.

"Kingsley, sit down boy," said Mark quietly and firmly.

"Kate, if you've got an old towel or a clean rag, I'll dry him off, rather than have him shaking the snow all over."

Kate found an old towel, and Kingsley had a good rub down. He then plopped himself down in front of the fireplace, and promptly went to sleep.

"Well, he's certainly worn out," laughed Mark. "What did you do to him, Davey?"

"We just had fun. I threw that ball about two hundred times, and he found it in the snow every time. He's a great dog. I hope I can play with him this summer when we're all here."

"Sounds like a good idea. He's smart in the woods too. If you want to go walking and exploring, Kingsley never gets lost. He'll keep you safe."

Angel was now feeling extremely antsy. She just wanted to get on with the "let's hurt Kate" party.

Finally she made a decision. It was now or never. She had to make a move before Mark and the dog left. Mark had seen enough of her to be able to give a good description to the police. She had to take care of him, but that just meant extra work for her, and more opportunity to make a mistake.

"Excuse me a moment, please," she said in her sweetest and most friendly voice. "I forgot something in my room."

"Oh just sit a minute. You looked quite woozy when you first came down. Climbing the stairs might make you dizzy again," said Kate. "Is it something I can get for you from your room?"

She was thinking that she might be able to retrieve her cell phone, which she assumed was in Angel's room.

Angel, however, needed desperately to get away and calm herself. She needed to find the cool nerves of steel which she always had, when picking up men, and taking them to their rooms. She was always so calm and purposeful with strange pick-ups, so why was she getting so confused and anxious here?

"No, I'm fine now, thanks, and I'll be right back down. I need to get some of my medications from my bag, and I want to throw a little water on my face."

Mark and Kate just looked at each other with puzzled expressions.

Chapter Thirty-Six

Patrick was becoming sick of his own company. He wished now that he had brought the private eye, John Chumley along with him. He was tired of asking himself the same question over and over. Was he doing the right things for the right reasons?

He honestly didn't know. He just knew that Angel couldn't be allowed to get away with the terrible things she had done to him, and she couldn't be allowed to kill a completely innocent woman, for no reason other than jealousy and revenge.

As he chomped on one of the chocolate bars he had purchased at the gas station, his thoughts turned once again to Angel Baby, and the way she had acted during most of the two years they had known each other. He had liked her light-hearted attitude towards life, and her sense of fun. He had appreciated her courage and determination, and most of all – he had loved her.

Who can ever explain why we choose to love one person and not another? Why had he been so drawn to her? Was it just because she was his own creation? She was smart, and a lot of fun, but so was Lainey.

Angel was beautiful, but so was Lainey. Angel loved him (at least he had thought she did), but again, so did Lainey. What then had been the attraction? With a sigh, he realized that he would likely never know.

All the snow around him, on the highway, coming down from the sky, and piled on the median, made him think of the time he and Angel had gone for a long skidoo ride in the moonlight. He couldn't remember what excuse he had given his wife about coming home so late, but whatever it had been, it had worked. Lainey loved him enough to trust him, and that made him feel so ashamed.

How despicable he had been, letting lies roll off his tongue as easily as rain drops dripping from a roof. He had betrayed her trust over and over, and now he was paying. Ouch, how he was paying!

He hadn't been a very nice person these last two years, secretive, deceitful, eating breakfast with one woman, but anxious and excited about being with another. With the advantage of a little bit of time, he could look back, and see how bewitched he had really been. He realized that he had unthinkingly stolen time from his wife and kids, and had wasted it on someone who hadn't been worth it.

He felt somehow that Angel hadn't been a real person. She was just a dream he had created with his own hands. She had been every man's dream, but there had been no substance to her. She was just a beautiful illusion.

As he drove along, Patrick snorted, and shook his head. What a dork he had been! Well, actually he had been an Irish dork, and that was even worse.

The great, renowned Dr. O'Neal had been taken in so completely by an escapee from a psychiatric hospital! "Well, look at me now, ma," he said to the empty car. "Your little boy was bested by a beautiful psycho!"

She really had him bamboozled, and the sad part was, that he had loved every minute of it! He had never suspected that he was in way over his head.

Anyway, that particular moonlight skidoo trip, which had just popped into his mind, had been exciting, romantic, and hilarious, all at the same time. It had only been when Angel Baby insisted on taking a turn driving, that things had gone a little crazy. They were on a skidoo trail going through the woods, but it wasn't very well groomed, and there were lots of bumps of ice and snow, as well as several sharp turns.

Angel was driving much too fast, but she wouldn't slow down, and Patrick didn't care. He was in love, and he was having fun.

At one point, he had taken his arms from around her waist, and leaning back, had taken a light hold onto the back strap. This gave him more wind in his face, and a sense of almost flying. Suddenly, however, they really were flying! Angel had hit a large bump on the trail, and the skidoo had momentarily taken off through the air.

Patrick, who was barely holding on at all, flew backwards into a snow pile. He wasn't hurt, and was laughing so hard that he could barely get his breath. He realized two things at the same time. The first was that he only had one glove. The other one must have been caught on the seat strap, and pulled right off when he flew backwards. The second thing he realized was that Angel wasn't stopping to wait for him.

Getting to his feet, and brushing off the snow with which he was covered, he began to hurry along. At that point it still seemed pretty funny. After ten minutes, however, with no sight of Angel ahead, it began to seem slightly serious.

What in the world was she doing? The trail had several twists and turns in it, so he couldn't see very far ahead. Besides, without the bright headlight of the skidoo, the woods were black. He couldn't see where he was going, and it was difficult to follow the trail.

He realized that she wasn't coming back for him, because he couldn't see that bright skidoo light, and he couldn't hear the roaring of the machine. Where the devil was she?

There wasn't much point in shouting, but he did, just in case she might hear him. His shouts, however, were met with silence.

Where was she, and why hadn't she waited for him, or come back for him? Surely she realized that he was no longer sitting behind her. If this was her idea of a joke, it was getting stale fast.

Was she hurt? Had she hit a tree and knocked herself out? Dammit, what was going on?

He was cold, and he was out of breath. After half an hour of hurrying along, peering into the blackness, and becoming more anxious at every step, he rounded a turn, and there she was. Struggling valiantly, she was trying to get the skidoo out of a shallow ditch.

"Where have you been?" she yelled, half crying and half angry, as she looked up, and saw him approaching.

"Did you fall off, or did you jump off on purpose?" she asked accusingly, as she stopped her efforts to move the heavy snowmobile.

"All I found was your glove, still hooked under that back strap. There was no place to turn around, and I had to keep going a long distance. Then I tried to turn here, and it was a ditch, and the skidoo went right down into it."

By now she had really begun to cry, and looked so pathetic that Patrick couldn't be cross with her.

He put his arms around her, and started to laugh, and soon Angel Baby was laughing too. They flopped down into the soft snow, and sat there laughing like two fools, two fools in love.

Eventually, when they were exhausted from their hilarity, it took them another half hour of wrestling with the recalcitrant skidoo, before they could get it out of the ditch, and turned around on the trail. It was time to get home before anything else went wrong.

Patrick drove back, and Angel kept her arms firmly wrapped around his waist.

It had become one of their favourite stories, but, of course, there was no one with whom they could share it. Inevitably, they told it to each other, over and over, laughing every time.

Patrick shook his head, as he remembered how much fun they had experienced during their short but intense romance. Why had it gone so wrong? At the beginning there had been no indication that Angel wasn't playing with a full deck. What had triggered her psychotic break?

The big factor had obviously been when Patrick told her he would never leave his family. Looking back, however, he realized that there had been several small incidents which should have alarmed him, but which he had ignored. There is so much truth to the old adage that 'love is blind.'

Coming back to reality, the good doctor noticed a sign which indicated that he was 50 kilometers from Bracebridge. He knew that Kate's cottage was apparently half an hour beyond Bracebridge, so that was good. He would stop at the first place he could find open, and he would call to warn her. Once he warned her, there would be no need for him to go all the way to her cottage. Of course, there was still Angel Baby. Was he going to pursue her or not?

He would decide that after the phone call. If Angel Baby was already there with Kate, he would definitely try to get there as quickly as possible. If, however, Kate was alone, he would warn her, and leave it at that. He could still talk to the authorities, and set them on to Angel, without having to drive all the way to the cottage. That might be preferable. It would preclude him doing anything to Angel Baby, which he might regret later.

It was at that point that a car switched lanes right ahead of him, with no warning. Patrick stepped on the brakes, and the rental car fishtailed on the icy surface. It was totally out of control, and, after hitting the left side of the rear bumper, it went careening onto the snowy median.

The airbag deployed and smacked him in the face. It took Patrick a few minutes to assure himself that he wasn't hurt, although his nose felt as if it had been punched by an iron fist.

His next problem was that the car refused to budge.

It had come to a stop on a pile of snow. The median was loaded with snow and icy chunks, which had been cleared from the highway, and the car looked as if it would be grudgingly lodged there until the spring thaw.

"Dammit" roared Patrick, as he watched the traffic going by. What was wrong with these Canadians? Weren't they willing to offer help in an emergency? Wasn't anyone going to stop?

Finally a car pulled very carefully onto the edge of the median, and the driver put the window down.

"Need some help? What's wrong?"

It's pretty obvious what's wrong, the doctor thought, crossly, as he made his way gingerly through the snow, to the stopped vehicle. His nice shoes were not quite up to the job in all this snow. He'd never be able to make it into the cottage without boots, so that meant another delay. He'd have to try to find a store in town, and buy a pair.

"I'm afraid it's hopelessly stuck," he explained to the elderly gentleman.

"Do you have a cell phone? If so, I could call for a tow truck. I'm new in the country, though, and I don't know whom to call."

The old man very obligingly made a call for him, and then continued on his way.

Patrick could do nothing but wait. He was fuming, frustrated and frantic, as he waited what seemed like hours, before the bright lights of the tow truck appeared.

He had a sick feeling in the pit of his stomach that he would be far too late to do any good for the unfortunate and unsuspecting Mrs. Kate Chandler. Why hadn't it occurred to him to call hours ago? He had been concentrating too much on what to do with Angel, and not enough on how to help Kate.

As he waited impatiently for the tow truck to appear, he wondered whether he had over-reacted, when he heard that Angel was heading north to cottage country. Maybe it was a legitimate visit to a friend. Dr. Patrick O'Neal wanted desperately to believe that he had jumped to the wrong conclusion. He wanted to turn around and go back to the airport. He wanted to forget the whole ugly mess.

Still – what if he had been right the first time? What if Angel really was on her way to kill an innocent woman? Could he live with himself if he didn't at least try to warn Kate? No, of course not. He couldn't turn back now. Trying to persuade himself that Angel was not on a murderous mission, was just plain wishful thinking. It would be like trying to persuade himself that hummingbirds don't fly.

Dr. O'Neal had always been a man of action. He couldn't stand himself these days, with his wishy-washy approach to a serious matter. It was so out of character for him. He had to get a grip!

Now, to make matters worse, he was stuck on the highway, far from any civilization as far as he could tell, and he had no way of even getting to the nearest town.

Finally he saw the flashing lights of the tow truck. It didn't take long to pull the car back onto the highway, but there was more bad news. Dr. O'Neal knew nothing about cars, except that they were good for getting you from one place to another. He therefore, had to take the tow truck driver's word for it, when he explained that the right front wheel was bent, and the car was not driveable.

It looked as if Patrick's journey had come to a sudden and ignominious halt. He had been derailed, at least for now.

Chapter Thirty-Seven

Kate and Mark were chatting in low voices. Angel Baby was still upstairs supposedly getting her medications.

Kate was more convinced now that this could be Madison in disguise. Well, it wasn't exactly a disguise. If it was Madison, she must have had some serious surgical work done on her face, and she must have had a very skilled doctor.

There were no scars visible. Kate had seen pictures of Maddy, when she was much younger, and was first dating Mac. There was no resemblance whatsoever, except possibly for her actual body size. Also, as far as Kate could remember, Maddy had not had the big boobs which she now possessed.

"I'm not sure about her, Kate," frowned Mark. He was whispering, and looking up the stairs as he spoke, making sure Angel Baby didn't catch them talking about her.

"She's nervous with us, which is odd, but if she is a diabetic, and just had a little spell, that would explain her nervousness or shakiness.

She does know the name of the people she was supposed to visit. I've never heard of them though, so she might have just made up the names, but why? What would be her reason?

"Do you think that she could really be your husband's old girlfriend? And even if she is his old friend, why would she be wanting to hurt you? That certainly wouldn't endear her to him. That would be totally crazy."

"That's just it, Mark. She is crazy, and to her, it likely seems sensible. I'm thinking it's possible, except that as far as I know, Madison is locked up safely in a hospital in British Columbia.

"Still, Davey has an uneasy feeling about her, and I do too. Also, she made some strange remarks when she first arrived, that in retrospect were just the type of thing that Maddy might say. I can't believe that she would have been let out of the hospital, but maybe they thought she was all better, or maybe she escaped. She's very crafty. She stalked us for years, and the police couldn't find a thing to pin on her.

"The point is, if it is Maddy, she's definitely out to kill me. She's tried it before – just two years ago, when she teamed up with the guy who kidnapped me. She's got this mad idea that if I'm out of the way, Mac will go back to her."

Kate shook her head as she continued.

"In some crazy way, I feel sorry for her. Mac says she was a really sweet, fun girl when he first knew her. It's not her fault that she's got a few screws loose. It's hereditary.

"After the years of stalking us, when she was finally put away, we discovered that there was a history of psychosis in her family. It apparently skipped her parent's generation, but both her grandfather and an uncle ended their lives in mental facilities. She's dangerous, and I don't want her anywhere near Davey.

"Do you think that maybe you and I could take Davey over to your place for a while?"

"Sure, I guess so, or, even better, we could go right in to town to the police station, but in the meantime, what would we do with her?"

"Well, could we tie her up and leave her here? Then we'd be free to go to town and get help."

Mark thought about that for a moment.

"You know, that could work. Of course, if she isn't Maddy, and if she is actually harmless, she'll likely sue us, but what the heck, we won't hurt her. Have you got any good rope or anything we could use to tie her?"

Mark was serious, and Kate was beginning to feel better. He would help her. Now she wouldn't have to spend the night here alone with Maddy or Angel or whoever she was.

Between the two of them, they should be able to subdue her. Unfortunately, as far as she knew, there was no rope or anything which they could use.

"All I can think of is maybe a couple of cords from the lamps. They do that in the movies."

"Well, I've certainly got lots of rope at my cottage, but I hate to leave you here with her. Maybe we should all move over to my cottage, and we'll tie her up there, and call the police."

"Wait a minute, we're being stupid. Why don't we go right this minute, while she's upstairs. We'll take out two skidoos, and head out to my car."

Mark laughed, "Of course. That's the answer. We'll have to take Kingsley home first though, and lock him safely in my cottage. Then we'll head to town. Come on, let's do it."

Before they could move, however, Angel came down the stairs.

"I'd really like a cup of hot chocolate now. I feel so much better. Could we do that Kate? I'm sure that Davey and Mark would enjoy a cup too."

"Well, if you're diabetic, Angel, are you sure that you should be having hot chocolate?" asked Kate, crossly. "Do you have your insulin with you?"

She was very disappointed that they had wasted so much time, and hadn't managed to get away. Now they were stuck here with her.

Angel just looked at her, trying to think of an answer. Finally she said, "O.K. You've got me there, Kate. What a smarty you are. Of course I'm not a diabetic, but I felt embarrassed at being so woozy and light headed in front of you two, so it was the first excuse I could think of. Silly me. I just didn't want you to think that I'd been drinking, or to guess that maybe I'm pregnant."

She seemed sincere and truthful, and it was difficult to find fault with her story.

"Pregnant?" cried Kate.

"Yes," nodded Angel. "I haven't told anyone yet, and I'm not very far along, but I've been having dizzy spells, and I'm sick in the mornings. I'm so excited, though." Here she patted her stomach gently. "Even his or her daddy doesn't know yet. He's out of the country, but he'll be home soon."

The words were flying out of her mouth, and she had no idea what she was going to say next. She just knew that they wouldn't expect violence from a small, helpless looking gal, who was pregnant.

Oh no, thought Kate. If she's pregnant, how can we possibly tie her, and leave her here while we go for help? On the other hand, is she really pregnant, or is this a convenient lie, like the one about being a diabetic?

Mark was thinking much the same thing. Their plans to hold her down, and tie her tightly seemed a bit barbaric.

Angel was thinking how smart she was. She had them well fooled.

"Oh, I feel so silly now. I really hadn't planned to tell anyone until I tell the father. Please let me go and make the hot chocolate. You two sit and catch up. This storm is here for good, so we might as well enjoy ourselves. Aren't we lucky to have a big strong handsome man to keep us company!"

She smiled flirtatiously at Mark, and was out to the kitchen before Kate could protest.

Mark grinned at her and shrugged again. Then he mouthed the words, "Now what?"

He was very annoyed with himself for not getting Kate and Davey out of here sooner. They had wasted too much time gabbing.

Kate wasn't sure what they could do now, but she knew that there was no way she was going to drink any hot chocolate, or anything which was prepared by Angel's hands. How could she keep Davey and Mark from drinking it, though?

She whispered to Mark, "Don't drink it!" and was on her way over to whisper the same thing to Davey, when in the distance she thought she heard a phone ringing.

She rushed to pick up the kitchen phone, but the line was still dead.

Going back into the living room, she stood and listened, but there was no more ringing. Had it been her missing cell phone which she had heard? If so, where was it? It must be upstairs in Angel's tote bag. She had been so right when she suspected that Angel had taken it.

She was still pondering how she was going to broach the subject, when Angel returned from the kitchen with a tray of steaming mugs.

Mark pretended to take a sip of his, then put it down, saying "Ouch, that's really hot. I'll just let it cool a bit."

Davey was sitting at the table, drawing as usual. Kingsley was at his feet. Angel put the mug down on the table beside his drawing book.

"Drink it all up, Davey. It's so good for you. It gives you energy, and makes you strong. You'll be able to go back out in the snow to play with Kingsley!"

At the same time, Kate hurried over to the table, saying, "Oh I must show Mark some of Davey's drawings." As she reached the table she knocked over the steaming mug of cocoa, spilling it all over Davey's drawing book, the table, and the floor.

"Forgive me, Davey," she said silently, as he jumped up in dismay.

"Mom, look what you did. You've spoiled all my drawings."

No one noticed Kingsley lapping up the hot chocolate, as fast as his tongue could go.

Kate hadn't thought of that possibility, and tried to shoo the dog away from the spill. Kingsley was determined, though. The hot chocolate was delicious, and, ignoring Mark's shouts, he finished lapping every bit of the liquid. If it was drugged, as Kate suspected, the poor dog was going to be the victim.

Angel Baby looked annoyed, but secretly she was pleased. What a perfect way to put the dog out of action. She had wondered how she was going to get him locked outside or into another room. She had thought about trying to entice him out with some cookies, but that would have looked suspicious to Mark and Kate.

Seeing him slurp up the drugged cocoa was perfect. Thank you Kate! She had put enough in it to kill Davey, or at least put him out for quite a while, until everything was all over. She wondered whether that same amount would kill the dog.

Mark would also die from an overdose, but she had put just enough in Kate's to put her to sleep for a while. She had other plans for Kate, and she needed her awake to suffer through them.

While Kate was busy trying to wipe up the spill on Davey's drawing book and the table, Angel was encouraging Mark to drink his cocoa. Mark, however, was frantic about Kingsley. If the cocoa was indeed drugged, had his dog lapped up enough to hurt him? Would it kill him or just put him to sleep? Was there really a drug in the cocoa, or were he and Kate being paranoid?

He raced to get a bowl of water for Kingsley. Unfortunately, the dog wasn't thirsty now after the hot chocolate. Mark forced him to drink some, as he knew that chocolate was really bad for dogs, even if it wasn't drugged.

He felt angry and frightened, and watched the dog closely. If anything bad happened to his old friend, he couldn't imagine what he might do.

Angel, however, knew exactly what she had to do. She had to go to plan B. It would likely work just as well, as soon as the dog fell asleep. If he didn't, she'd have to play it by ear. She was more afraid of the darn dog than anyone else.

Within ten minutes, Kate had cleaned up the cocoa mess, Mark had forced Kingsley to drink some water, and had poured more all over his paws to force him to lick it off. That hadn't worked, however. Kingsley had simply shaken the water off his paws, and slumped back down.

Davey had grudgingly forgiven his mother for ruining a couple of pages of his art book, and the dog was now sleeping peacefully on the floor. Mark tried shaking him, and talking right into his ear, but Kingsley was down for the count.

Just then, they could hear a phone ringing again. Angel knew the phone in the kitchen wasn't working, so it must be Kate's cell phone. She had taken it while Kate and Davey were locked outside. She had hoped that Kate wouldn't notice that it was missing, but now the darn thing wouldn't stop ringing.

She tried to talk louder to cover the sound, but Kate held up her hand to shush her, and said, "That sounds like my cell phone. Could you get it for me Angel. I assume it's in your tote bag or somewhere in your room. It could be important, and if I don't answer, whoever it is will just keep calling. Anyone who would be calling me, knows that Davey and I are supposedly up here all alone. They'll think there's something wrong, and will likely call the police."

By then the phone had stopped ringing, but Angel knew it would likely start again. This was all going wrong. It looked as if she was going to have to act now or never.

It's like crossing the Rubicon, she thought. I think I'm just passing the point of no return. She realized that she couldn't wait for Mark to drink his hot chocolate, and either fall asleep or hopefully die. He was too concerned about the dog, and was ignoring his drink.

Too many things were going wrong. She would get the ball rolling right now. "Lacta alea est" she muttered. "The die is cast."

Standing up, she walked to within two feet of where Mark was now sitting on the floor beside Kingsley. He was petting the dog, shaking him, and talking loudly, but his efforts to waken his beloved companion were doing no good.

Angel gave him her most attractive and flirtatious smile. The unsuspecting Mark smiled back rather grudgingly. If she had hurt Kingsley with her damned hot chocolate – drugged or not, he didn't know what he would do, but killing her was a distinct possibility.

Without hesitation, without even drawing a deep breath, without considering consequences, before Mark could even stand up, Angel Baby pulled the little "Montreal special" out of her pocket, and, smiling sweetly, she put a bullet right between his eyes!

Chapter Thirty-Eight

The only good news for Patrick, late on that cold, blustery, Canadian afternoon, was that the tow truck driver was a friendly and helpful man. When he told Patrick that he owned a small garage in Bracebridge, and he would be happy to tow the car there, the frustrated and discouraged doctor was relieved.

There was really no choice, and he was grateful to have the help. It had been a piece of luck for him when Bob Garland came along.

Patrick didn't want to get into the details of his journey, so he simply said that he absolutely had to get to a certain cottage, to help a certain woman, who might be in trouble.

Whatever problems the stranded doctor had, sounded mysterious to Bob Garland. He was intrigued, and wanted to help any way he could. After all, there wasn't much excitement in his life, and this good looking fellow was very likeable. Also, he had the slight remnants of a lilting Irish accent, which Garland found most appealing.

Patrick was relieved once they reached the garage. After getting approval from the rental company, with whom Garland had worked before, it was agreed that the mechanic would keep the car, and work on it the following day. In the meantime, he would lend Patrick his big old skidoo machine, plus an old skidoo suit and helmet, so that Patrick could try to make it to the cottage.

The plan had a lot of problems which they tried to resolve, but it was the best that Garland could concoct, and Patrick was glad of any help. He realized that meeting this generous and friendly mechanic might have been a huge stroke of luck.

Patrick called Kate's cottage, but there was definitely no one answering.

There was either no one there, or for some reason, they couldn't or wouldn't answer. Patrick didn't want to think about what that reason might be

Now there were three important players in this part of cottage country. One (Kate) simply wanted to replace a broken window. Two (Angel Baby) wanted to commit murder and mayhem, and three (Patrick), was the only one who had a somewhat altruistic goal. At least he was hoping to save a life. Each had his or her own agenda.

Would they actually meet at some point, and carry out their plans, or would Mother Nature step in, and create a totally different scenario? Only time would tell.

Patrick hoped that the phone wasn't working because of the storm, but he wondered whether Angel Baby had arrived safely at the cottage, and had snipped the phone wire to keep Kate from calling for help. Still, Kate had a cell phone, so that wouldn't have been a problem.

"Don't worry. Our power here in cottage country goes out quite often. With the wind blowing the way it is, it's no surprise that the phone lines might be down. These are almost gale force winds."

Bob was trying to offer a little encouragement. The doctor seemed unduly upset that he couldn't get through to the cottage. Bob wondered what was so urgent.

Trying to divert Patrick, the mechanic said, "Tell me, doc, why would a nice Irish boy leave his homeland, and go to live in Switzerland?"

While he was talking, he was busy uncovering his high-powered skidoo, and filling it with gas. He'd had it a few years now, and it had the power to get through heavy snow, which smaller, less powerful machines just couldn't handle.

"Well, my wife and I met when we were at university. She and her family always vacationed in Switzerland, and the first time I travelled there with her, I fell in love with it. It's so clean, and so beautiful. It's perfect for skiing and skidooing, my two favourite sports. Besides, it's not far from Italy and Spain and Greece – all wonderful vacation spots. It's got everything, as far as I'm concerned, and it's a laid back, gentle sort of life. We just decided that when we graduated and got married, we'd make our home in Switzerland, and we've never regretted it."

"Good for you. Maybe when I decide to retire and sell this business, I'll come and visit you." The mechanic snorted and gave a little chuckle at his own humour. He had never travelled anywhere outside of Canada, and had no intentions of doing so. Muskoka was his home, and Muskoka was where he planned to stay.

He was a trusting soul, so he felt sure that he would eventually get his skidoo back without any problems. Besides, Patrick had assured him that he had done plenty of snowmobiling in Switzerland, so he knew how to handle the big machine properly.

The two men were about the same size, so the mechanic brought out his old skidoo suit for Patrick. It was a spare he kept for emergencies, and this certainly appeared to be an emergency of some kind. The poor doctor seemed almost distraught, when no one answered his phone calls.

Bob Garland didn't like to pry, but he would have loved to know what or who could be dragging the doctor out on this miserable night. It was dark now, which made visibility even worse.

"Don't even think about coming back here tonight," he said to Patrick.

"I'll be closing up within the hour, and going home. Anyone who gets himself into trouble after that, will have to take care of himself. I have my own family to look after.

"I'll be here all day tomorrow, though, if I can get back into town, that is. I live on the lake myself, and it wouldn't be the first time that I've been snowed in." He hesitated and looked at Patrick, struggling into the skidoo suit.

"Say, where is this cottage anyway? If it's out my way, we could put the skidoo on the pick-up truck, and get you a lot closer to your destination. It's really dangerous for you to be snowmobiling along the edge of the road on a night like this. You can't tell what's the road and what's the edge. There are a few deep ditches in spots too, so it's just not a good idea.

"Are you sure you can't wait until tomorrow? The police will stop you for sure, if they see you. As I said, I'm not going to close up for a little while, just in case someone else needs help. That means that if you want a lift, you'll just have to wait for me. I can't go yet.

"There could be more stranded motorists out there, and I hate to close up too early. It's way too cold for anyone to spend the night in a car. I'm telling you lad, you need to wait until tomorrow. You should get a room in a motel right here in town. If it's not a life and death situation, then you should just stay put."

Patrick saw the good sense in this, but he knew he had to press on. He had driven all the way from Toronto for one purpose. Now he simply had to get to that damn cottage, because he suspected that it actually was a life and death situation.

He dug out the piece of paper on which he had Chumley's directions, and those of the young gas attendant. Bob got out his glasses, and stared at the paper for a couple of minutes.

"By gosh, you're in luck. I go almost right past the end of that road, to go home. If you're determined not to wait till tomorrow, then we'll set out within the hour. I'll take one more call, and then I'll close up for the night.

"You can help me put the skidoo on the pick-up, while we're waiting for any more calls. It'll save time in the long run."

"That sounds good, Bob. I'm not too keen on driving along an unknown road in the dark, and in a storm like this one.

"If we're not going for a while, though, I might as well take this suit off again. I'll be too hot. I can't believe you'd put yourself out this way. It's good of you. Are all Canadians so generous and willing to go the extra mile?"

Patrick was impatient, and wanted to leave right away, but he didn't fancy driving on that unknown road, specially if the police were likely to stop him. He didn't like the idea of being picked up and possibly fined, when he was just trying to do a good deed.

On the other hand, if he did get stopped by the police, maybe he could get them to go into the cottage with him. That would be the perfect solution.

Actually, he was having more and more doubts about what he was trying to do. Was it really any of his business? If he could get through to Kate, and warn her of her danger, and then just forget about Angel, would that be good enough? No, not really. Angel could not be allowed to get away with what she had done, and what she was planning to do.

Patrick wondered whether Kate might already be on her way back safely to Toronto. What would he do if he got to the cottage, and it was all locked up, dark and empty? Where would he go?

He'd have to find shelter for the night. The more he thought about it, the more he realized that it was a ridiculously dumb idea. He wasn't really in any position to help anyone. He needed help himself.

Little did he know just how much help he would need, before the night was over.

He went back and forth in his mind, trying to make a decision. He hadn't considered the possibility of arriving at a lonely cottage at night with no one there – except maybe a dead body – and then having to turn around and get himself all the way back to shelter. He had thought he would arrive in the afternoon, do whatever he had to do, then head back. It had seemed simple when he first thought of it, and there had been no blizzard in his plans.

While they sat down and waited in Bob's little office, the mechanic said, "I'll give you my cell phone number anyway, and you can call me tomorrow, when you're ready to come back, if the power is back on at the cottage. If I'm not out towing someone, I'll come and get you. You'll just have to get yourself back out to the end of the cottage road, and wait for me.

"Now if there's no working phone at the cottage, we'll have a problem communicating. Maybe you can use the lady's cell phone, if she has one. Otherwise, you'll just have to get back here on your own I guess. Once the storm stops, it won't be too bad along the main road, but you'll have to be careful.

"Hopefully the cops will be too busy to notice you. Ha ha. I'll be holding your rental car for ransom, so you'd better show up!" He laughed, and smacked Patrick on the back.

Bob got one more call for help, and by the time he returned to his garage, Patrick was dressed again, and ready to go. He had tried calling Kate's cottage one more time, but with no luck.

Bob had a little ramp he used to get the machine into the back of his small pick-up truck, and they finally set out.

The blizzard had not let up. If possible, it might even have become more cold and blowy. It was a terrible night. Only an idiot would deliberately go out into a storm like this, thought Patrick, with a sinking heart.

He had never thought of himself as an idiot, but tonight might prove him wrong.

Chapter Thirty-Nine

As Angel pulled the trigger on the little gun, she marveled at how easy it was. It was just like a toy, but it seemed to have put a real hole in Mark's head. He was sitting, slumped against his dog, with a neat, bloody hole between his eyes. It made her want to giggle.

While Maddy stood there, staring at her victim, Kate couldn't believe what she had just seen. It was the action of a mad woman, a crazy person. It was the action of a psychotic killer, possibly a pregnant psychotic killer! Angel Baby might be all of those things, and maybe more.

Kate yelped as if she had been kicked from behind, and jumped up, making a move to go to Mark. She felt a helpless and hopeless terror take hold of her mind. Were she and Davey next?

Angel whirled on her, and pointing the gun right at her, said, in a calm, cool voice, "Sit down and shut up, Kate." Then with a little giggle, she added, "Simon Says sit down. Davey gets the next bullet, unless you do exactly as Simon Says."

Kate wondered whether Madison, aka Angel Baby, had faded into a strange world of her own. She had shot Mark without hesitation, then slipped into the old childhood game of Simon Says.

"Madison, we've got to help Mark. He may still be alive."

So, Kate knew! Instead of calling her Angel, she had called her Madison. Just like that, all of a sudden, Kate knew that she was Mac's old girlfriend Madison. How the heck had she guessed? Maybe that little punk had told her. He was too smart for his own good.

"I'm not Madison. I'm Angel Baby," she yelled, wildly waving the hand holding the gun.

"You sit right there, and I'll check on the handsome Mark. He had a really killer smile, didn't he? Yep, he had a killer smile that could break your heart, but I have a killer gun which just shot him dead," she mused, as she looked down at him.

She was trying to focus on Mark's mouth, and not the bullet hole between his eyes. Angel Baby really didn't like the sight of blood!

"I'm not kidding though. If you move, I'll put a bullet right between the kid's eyes. Come over here, Davey, and stand beside me."

"No, I won't," said Davey, in the bravest voice he could muster. He looked to his mom for help, but at the moment she was helpless.

The little boy's eyes were the size of two fried eggs, sunnyside up! They seemed to take over his entire face.

He had heard his mom call the woman "Madison." So that's why she seemed so familiar to him. She was Maddy! But how could that be? She didn't look the same, except that she was the same size. What kind of magic was this?

All Davey knew was that he had hated and feared Maddy in Florida, and he sure enough hated and feared her here. She had maybe killed Kingsley, she had shot Mark, and now she was going to kill him and his mom. Oh no she wasn't! He had outsmarted her before, and he could do it again!

On the floor, poor Kingsley hadn't moved. The sound of the gun had made both Kate and Davey jump, but the dog hadn't stirred.

He must be dead, thought Kate with a sinking heart. If she hadn't knocked over that mug of cocoa, Davey would have been drinking it, and there might have been enough poison in it to kill him too. It made Kate weak and angry to think of it.

If Kingsley was dead, who was going to help them? If only he was alive, he would likely know instinctively that Maddy had harmed Mark, and he would have attacked her. Come on Kingsley old boy, waken up, she prayed silently. Then she turned back to the crazy woman brandishing the gun.

"Madison, don't be foolish. You know you wouldn't hurt a child. Davey's done nothing to you. He's just a little kid, and he can't harm you. Please don't hurt him. I'll do whatever you say, but just leave him out of this."

Kate couldn't believe what she had just seen, and she didn't know how to handle Madison, without getting her more angry or confused. Why in the world would she have killed Mark? He wasn't threatening her in any way. Actually he was being very nice to her.

It occurred to her that maybe the gun just had blanks in it. Maybe Mark was just knocked unconscious. The gun was so small. You could barely see it in Madison's hand. Could it have really killed him? Yes, apparently so, judging by the hole in his forehead.

Angel Baby was surprised too. Had she actually just killed a man? Was it really that easy? Wow, that little Montreal special was something else. It was powerful. She was powerful!

One of Angel's problems was that she knew there had only been one bullet in the gun. She mustn't let Kate know that. As long as Kate thought there were more bullets, she'd do whatever Angel said, just to keep Davey safe.

What was her next step? Well, she couldn't leave the body there, propped against the dead dog. At least she assumed that the dog was dead. She had no idea how much Rohypnol it took to kill a little boy, and she had no idea how much of it Kingsley had consumed. She had put a lot into that cocoa, though, just to be sure.

Angel felt as if Mark's eyes were upon her, and they made her nervous. He seemed to be accusing her. She either had to throw something over his face, or get him out of here. She and Kate had to drag him away some place, but where?

"We're going to have to hide him, or bury him, Kate. Any ideas about a good spot?"

She was acting as if this was an every day occasion. Actually, she felt quite calm inside. It had been so easy.

Kate just stared blankly at her. What did she mean by "bury him?" The ground was frozen solid out there. There was no question of burying him. Madison was certifiably crazy.

Kate had a fleeting question about how Mac could ever have loved this person. Of course, according to him, she only started showing signs of dementia towards the end of their relationship. Still, Mac was always so sensible. This nut case didn't seem his type.

Staring at Madison, Kate was trying to decide whether she was really pregnant. She prayed that she wasn't. Kate knew that there was no way she could hurt a pregnant woman.

Had Maddy just thrown that suggestion out as a ploy to put them off guard, and get their sympathy? Likely. Actually, it was pretty smart of her, but Kate wasn't falling for it.

Meanwhile, Angel was trying to decide what to do with Mark.

Should they just drag him out into the snow? No, that would be useless. If the police or the window men did come around, they'd spot him for sure. She and Kate would never be able to get him up the stairs, so a bedroom was out. A closet might work! If they took all the brooms and things out of a closet, they could stuff him in there!

Smiling, Angel said, "Where's the biggest closet you've got on this floor, Kate?"

Kate understood right away what Madison was thinking. She was either going to stuff her and Davey in a closet, and take off, or she was going to hide Mark in a closet, and then, who knew what she would do with her and Davey?

It would be preferable to have Madison try to drag the body upstairs. If she could grab Mark's head and arms, and go up the stairs first, Madison would be in a vulnerable position, holding up the legs. She would be below Kate on the stairs, and if Kate got the chance, she could push Madison down the stairs and maybe grab the gun.

She was trying to stay calm. That approach had usually worked in the Everglades. She had to keep Davey safe no matter what. Right now she didn't have the luxury of being scared or falling apart. She had to keep her wits about her, and get themselves out of this mess.

There was no time to grieve over Mark. That would come later. At the moment, she couldn't make herself understand that he was dead. Just a few minutes earlier Mark had offered to help her. Just a few minutes earlier Mark had told her about his realty company, his passion for making beautiful furniture, his love for his dog.

Now this tall, handsome man, who had come back into her life after all these years, was dead, and it was somehow because of Kate.

She had to shut those thoughts out, and save them for another day. Today she had to help this vile, foolish, crazy woman, stuff her innocent old friend into a closet. It was incomprehensible.

Angrily, she said, "Really, there aren't any big closets on this floor. They're all upstairs."

"No, forget that. We're not dragging him upstairs. Come on, where's the broom closet?"

"Well, it's in the kitchen, but it's full of junk. You'd never get him in there."

"Okay, Davey. Make yourself useful. You go and start taking everything out of the broom closet. Don't try anything smart, or I'll shoot your mom, and then I'll really hurt you. Simon Says, just throw the stuff on the floor, and come back here fast."

Davey looked to his mother for help. Should he do what Maddy asked, or should he stand up to her? For some reason he didn't really feel so scared of her now.

He had built a little shell around himself, and was trying to hide inside it. Actually, he was trying to make himself invisible to the crazy Maddy. It was his own personal coping mechanism.

Kate nodded her head at him, and he unhappily shuffled off to the kitchen.

"This is a total waste of time, Madison. Even if we could stuff Mark into the closet, - I presume that's what you're planning, - the door won't stay quite closed.

"To hide him properly, you'll have to get him upstairs. That kitchen closet door can swing open at any time. The catch on it is damaged, and the floor tilts a bit. Remember, the police and the hardware men will be here any time now."

Kate tried to make this sound as believable as possible. She hoped that Madison wouldn't wonder why she was being so agreeable about helping her.

Kate truly didn't want to hurt Angel. She just wanted to get her out of their lives. She wanted her back in the hospital, where doctors could help her, and where she could not terrorize the Chandlers.

She knew that Angel couldn't help being the way she was. She had something missing or loose in her brain. It made her smart and cagey, but it also made her mean and dangerous.

Kate wondered whether she could actually outsmart this vile woman, before she did them any serious harm. She hoped it wasn't going to be an epic battle to the death.

Chapter Forty

Angel Baby spent some time thinking about Kate's suggestion. If the cupboard door wouldn't stay closed, there wasn't much point in trying to hide Mark there. It seemed to make sense, that they should drag him upstairs, and hide him in a bedroom closet.

This was a huge old cottage, and there were likely some great hiding places up there.

She hated the work that was going to involve, though. Which would be easier, dragging him through the snow to the wood shed, or bumping him up those stairs to a bedroom?

The shed would likely be easier, but it was so darn cold outside. By the time she got into her jacket and boots, all the while holding the gun, it might give Kate a chance to jump her and take the gun. No, they'd stay right here where it was warm and safe, and somehow, they'd get the guy up those stairs.

All the time she was considering the choices, she was keeping the gun pointing at Kate. It was a damn nuisance. She'd like to put it down now that it was empty, but she needed Kate to keep thinking that there were more bullets in it.

"Don't call me Madison any more," she ordered in a calm, cool voice.

"I'm Angel Baby now, and there's a doctor in Switzerland who would gladly swear to that."

Well, Patrick might not be exactly glad to reinforce her statement, but it sounded good.

Aha, thought Kate. So that's what happened. She must have either escaped, or been released from the psych facility, and had gone to some cosmetic surgeon in Switzerland to change her face. Actually it was quite brilliant. He had done a fantastic job.

Right at this moment, however, she looked like a child about to have a tantrum. Was she finally wigging out completely, and, if so, was that good or bad?

"I went through two years of agony to get this beautiful face, and I'm now Angel Baby. There is no Madison. She's dead and buried. Now repeat after me – there is no Madison."

Kate didn't say anything to this. She just looked at Angel with disgust, then decided that maybe she should reply.

"Well, Madison may be dead, but it appears that Angel Baby is alive, and just as bad. How could you kill Mark? He wouldn't have hurt you in any way.

"How could you try to drug an innocent little boy? Were you planning to kill him? Was there enough drug in that cocoa to kill the dog? What was it you gave them, Angel? Was it some kind of date rape drug like Rohypnol, or was it some other evil drug straight from the hospital pharmacy?"

Angel Baby ignored these questions. She simply shrugged her shoulders, then said, "You know, you might be right about putting Mark upstairs. Come here, Davey. Leave the closet and come and help us."

Davey returned to the living room, dragging his feet. He had never seen a dead body, and he didn't want to look at Mark. He also couldn't believe that Kingsley could be dead. He was so lively and so much fun just a little while ago. He didn't want to see him lying there so still. He must be dead though, or he would have wakened when the gun went off. He averted his eyes as much as he could, and went to stand by his mom. He grasped her arm as if he would never let it go.

"Now here's what we're going to do. Kate, you grab him under the arms. I'll take one leg and Davey will take the other. That way I can keep my gun on you."

"No way. Davey is seven years old, for heaven's sake. You're not making him drag a dead body. Forget it."

Angel Baby laughed. "Kate, you're in no position to say "no" to me. You will do as I say, or as Simon Says," here she giggled again, "or I'll shoot you, and then have some fun with Davey. Now what's it going to be?"

Kate was in an untenable situation.

"Look, Angel," she said, using the name preferred by this maniac. "I'll help you any way I can. I have to, since you have the gun. But, please don't make Davey try to help carry Mark. This could traumatize him for life. Anyway, he's too small. He wouldn't be able to carry enough weight to make it worth our while. He'd just hinder us. You and I can do it. We don't need any help.

"I remember Mac telling me what a sweet and loving person you were, when you two were together. How do you think he would feel if he knew that you forced his little son to actually touch and try to carry a dead body? Do you think he'd ever look at you with anything but disgust after that?

"You've done enough damage already, trying to poison or drug him with the cocoa. Do you think Mac would be happy about his ex girlfriend poisoning his beloved little boy?"

This seemed to get through to Angel. She looked almost embarrassed as she turned her gaze on Davey.

"Oh, Davey, I was just kidding. I guess we don't need your help. You can go and put all the stuff back in the cupboard. If we have any unexpected company, we want the place to look nice, don't we?"

"Thank you Lord," Kate said silently.

"Come on, let's go. You take his armpits and I'll take his feet. Too bad there are so many stairs. This is going to be tough. Just don't try anything, Kate. I'm putting my gun in my pocket, but I can get it out really fast."

Then she suddenly remembered something, and began to laugh.

"You don't even know it, Miss high and mighty Kate, but Mac and I danced together last week at the Royal York. It was wonderful. He told me that no one fit into his arms the way I do. He loved my dress too. He said I was the best looking woman in the room. We laughed at you, sitting at the table, looking so dumb, while your husband and his lover whirled around the room.

"Did you notice my dress? Wasn't it gorgeous? I bought it in Montreal. Those silver shoes made me nice and tall too. I was perfect in Mac's arms, just the way I've always been."

There was a dreamy and wistful expression on her face, as she remembered the night at the Royal York. In her mind, it had been much more than just a short dance with Mac. It had been an entire evening of fun and glamour.

"You know, I think that somewhere in Mac's heart, he knew that he was dancing with his own beloved Maddy."

In your dreams, lady, thought Kate. To her it seemed that Angel couldn't stop talking now. It must be some kind of nervous reaction. Kate just let her babble on, while she tried to figure a way out of this mess. She stared at her, though, remembering the woman with whom Mac had danced.

She had never seen the woman's face – just her back. Yes, she had been right. That beautiful red hair belonged to Angel Baby. What nerve! Too bad Mac hadn't recognized her. Then he would have called the police. She would have been sent back to the mental ward, and Mark would still be alive.

Angel Baby was still babbling.

"You shouldn't have let Mac go off to England, Kate. By the time he gets back, you'll be dead, and believe me, you're going to be a really ugly corpse. I'm going to cut up your face till it looks like stewing beef. That's how he'll always remember you, ugly and dead."

She gave a fiendish little grin as she said this, but in her mind, she was wondering whether she could really do it. Angel Baby had always been afraid of the sight of blood, and somehow, she had never really considered that cutting Kate's face would entail a great deal of blood. She wasn't too sure now that she could actually do it. Damn, it had seemed like such a great idea, but what if she fainted after the first cut?

Davey was glaring at her, as she threatened to cut his mom's beautiful face.

"Stop it right now. Don't talk like that in front of Davey. You're not going to harm us in any way. Deep down, you're way too nice a person, Angel."

Kate was laying it on a little thick, but anything that might soften this murderess should be tried.

"Mac would be devastated if you do anything to any of us, and I know you don't want to hurt him. He would know that you had done it, and he would never forgive you, so you'd be hurting me for nothing.

"You need help, Maddy, and you know that Mac would be happy to get you the best care possible. He still worries about you, you know."

This was such an out and out lie, that Kate could barely look at Angel as she said it.

"Don't call me Maddy." She actually stamped her foot like a spoiled child.

"I told you. I'm Angel Baby now. Madison is dead. Come on, we've got to move this corpse."

It took them forever to drag Mark across the living room floor, and over to the bottom of the stairs. This was not easy. Kate was trying to be gentle with her old school friend, but Angel was bumping him along in an indifferent manner, and trying to keep her eyes averted from his bloody face. He might as well have been a bag of coal, or a sack of potatoes, for all the respect she was showing him.

Kate backed onto the first step, then the second, and then the third. By then she realized how difficult her feeble plan was going to be. She would have to make her move about three quarters of the way up, if she had any hope of knocking Madison out by a fall down the stairs. Flimsy as it was, it was the only idea Kate could think of at the moment.

She felt as if she was doing all the heavy work. Madison seemed to be just following along. Mark's bottom was bumping on the stairs, and Kate was saying a silent "please forgive me" to her old friend, as they struggled with him.

Weren't there serious laws about doing harm to a dead body? She was pretty sure that there were, and she knew that Mark's body would have some horrendous bruises before this was finished.

She had to do something before they reached the top, but what the heck could she do? She had little or no hope that her pathetic plan would work. If she tried to push Mark into Madison, and Madison didn't lose her grip and fall, she would undoubtedly shoot Kate. That mustn't happen. She had to get Davey out of here safely before she became the "target du jour."

Anger and fear were like fuel flooding her veins. The question now was, what would be the smartest move to get the upper hand, without getting herself or Davey shot?

If only she had a weapon! Angel had the best weapon, that childish looking little gun, and Kate knew she had to take it from her.

They were both busy now, sweating and heaving the body around. If only Mark would waken, miraculously open his eyes, and grin at them.

Better still, maybe Kate herself would waken, and discover that this was all just a frightening nightmare!

Chapter Forty-One

True to his word, Bob managed to drive Patrick right to the end of the cottage road. It was actually such a black night, and the visibility was so poor, that they drove past it, and had to back up quite a distance. That was no mean feat on a night like this.

The next annoyance was the trouble they had getting the skidoo off the back of the truck. It was like a big animal hunkered down, not wanting to go out into the blizzard. Well, who could blame it for that?

Patrick had the fleeting thought that perhaps the Fates were trying to warn him not to go any further. Maybe they wanted him to turn around and head for home.

Bob felt badly about leaving Patrick, but, judging by the map he had seen, the cottage wasn't too far along the road. He had faith in his old skidoo, and he knew that it could master many deep piles of snow without getting stuck. He just hoped that Patrick was the experienced driver he claimed he was.

The two men shook hands, and Bob waited till Patrick had the machine running. Patrick waved, as he took off into the night. Almost at once he disappeared from sight, lost in the swirling, twirling, mad dance of the wind and snow.

The strong skidoo headlight lit up trees along the roadside, laden and bent low with the weight of the snow. On a calm night it would have been an extraordinary fairyland, but in this blizzard, it was the most uninviting, frigid, barren, lonely landscape one could ever see. No person in his right mind would willingly venture out into it.

Bob said a little prayer for his new friend, the Irish doctor from Switzerland. He wondered if, by offering the use of his skidoo, he might just have signed a death warrant for Patrick. He had a very bad feeling in the pit of his stomach, as he climbed back into his truck and headed for home.

Patrick, on the other hand, was excited. The waiting had made him tense and hyper, but now, out in the darkness of a miserable night, he felt exhilarated. He was finally going to confront Angel, and meet her intended victim, Kate. The sooner he got this done, the sooner he would get back to Lainey and the kids.

He wondered what Angel Baby would say, when he appeared at the cottage door. She wouldn't believe her eyes. Would she try to bluff her way through the meeting? Would she put her arms around him, and pretend to be happy to see him? This was going to be interesting.

The machine roared, as it ploughed along through the deep snow. Patrick thought he could see the outline of a cottage, but there were no lights visible. He knew from the map that this wasn't Kate's cottage. Hers was farther along this same road.

The old helmet Bob had found for him, should have been retired years ago. Its face guard had been lost, and the wind was blowing the snow right into Bob's eyes. With the darkness, the snow slapping and whipping at his face, and the frigid air making his nostrils stick together, Bob was trying to go slowly and carefully. That turned out to be his first mistake.

At the slow speed, the skidoo got bogged down in a pile of snow, which turned out to be in a ditch. Somehow, he had driven off the side of the narrow road. On this dark night, in this blizzard, it was impossible to tell where the road ended, and the ditches began. Bob had warned him about the ditches, and he thought he was being careful, but visibility was non-existent, and he had driven right off the edge of the road.

Patrick had to get off the skidoo, and try to lift its front end out of the snowy trap. In spite of the low temperature, he was sweating inside the skidoo suit, by the time he managed to clear the snow from the runners, and heave the heavy front end of the machine back onto the road.

He wondered what Lainey would think if she could see him now. What was she doing right at this very moment? What were Shannon and Maureen doing? Did they miss him? Were they still taking music lessons, Maureen on the piano, and Shannon in the dance studio? Did Lainey have any second thoughts about maybe taking him back?

That lovely world seemed a lifetime away.

Patrick was colder than he had ever been in his life. He was sure that it never got this cold in Switzerland. A few minutes ago he had been sweating inside the suit. Now, however, the piercing, relentless wind was cutting right through that same suit, and turning that same sweat to ice water. He knew well how quickly someone could die outside, on a night like this. Hypothermia could strike with little warning, and he was alerted to his condition, when he realized that he was getting sleepy.

He tried talking to himself, but that didn't work well. Every time he opened his mouth to say something, it filled with snow and wind, and almost choked him. The cold was making him feel almost light-headed.

The cottage had to be close now. Surely he hadn't passed it. He considered shutting off the skidoo, and walking the rest of the way, but was hesitant. First of all, he didn't know how much farther he had to go. It might be a lot longer than he expected. He felt too tired, after battling with the skidoo in the ditch, to walk very far in this deep snow.

On the other hand, he didn't want to broadcast his arrival, with the roaring of the snow machine. He wondered whether the howling wind would muffle the sound of the motor, and decided that it likely would. So – he would keep on driving until he could at least see the cottage.

That decision made, Patrick tried desperately to wipe the snow and ice off his eyelashes. He had to take off his mitts again, old crumby things which Bob had found for him. They made his hands feel dirty.

It was difficult trying to clear his eyes and lashes, and keep control of the machine, all at the same time.

That was undoubtedly why he was going a bit too fast, with a bit too little concentration, when he rounded a sharp bend in the road. There, lying across his path, was a large tree branch, which had been brought down by the weight of snow, and the force of the wind.

Patrick had no time to stop, or even to veer out of its way.

One thin, pointed limb of the large tree branch was weighed down by its burden of snow. When the skidoo hit it, however, the snow shook loose, and the sharp pointed limb, freed from the weight, sprang up, and by some malevolent turn of fate, it pierced Patrick's neck, actually impaling him. It was as if a large icicle had been thrust into his neck, except that this icicle was attached to an immovable tree.

The freak accident happened so quickly and unexpectedly, that at first Patrick didn't realize what had occurred. He thought he had been shot. All he felt was the awful pain, as the sharp end of the limb, plunged into the only part of his neck which had been exposed.

It took him a few seconds to realize that he was actually impaled on the point of a thin tree limb. He could feel the warm, steady trickle of blood begin running down his neck.

Patrick knew that he was in a bad predicament. Actually, he was suddenly in the fight of his life. Screw the cold and the wind! They were bad, but this could be a death blow. This was as bad as a bullet to the throat, possibly even worse.

He sat there, totally stunned. How could this have happened? What were the chances? He was badly, maybe mortally wounded, on a deserted road, on a freezing night, in a far away country. He needed help, quickly.

Obviously there was no help coming. He would have even been happy to see Angel Baby struggling down the road! He was more alone at this moment than he had ever been in his entire life. The truth was, that his life was now in his own hands.

Somehow, he had to break that tree limb. There was no way he could pull it out of his throat. He wasn't sure how far in it had gone, but he knew he could do severe damage, trying to pull it out under these circumstances. Already he was having trouble swallowing, and, although the cold was slowing the bleeding, he could still feel a steady drip.

He needed a hospital with warmth, bright lights, sterile conditions, and trained doctors. All he had was a dark, freezing, deserted road, his own not too clean hands, and whatever skills he possessed.

Telling himself that it might not have penetrated too far, he tentatively tried very slowly, to inch it out. Unfortunately, it felt as if it was pretty far into his throat. The pain was severe, and he could picture it tearing some muscles, or rupturing something important. It seemed stuck in there, and didn't want to move.

The snow machine was roaring, as it tried to get loose from the tree. Patrick hated to do it, but he shut it off. He couldn't risk it finally getting free, and jerking ahead. With him still impaled on the tree limb, it would tear his throat apart.

It was just then that Patrick thought he heard a scream. It was very faint, but it definitely had sounded like a human scream. Oh God, was that Angel Baby killing Kate?

He had come all this way from Switzerland in order to save Kate, and now he was impaled on a tree – totally helpless. It was so ludicrous, that he would have laughed, except he felt more like crying.

At this moment there was absolutely nothing Patrick could do to help anyone, not even himself.

His situation seemed hopeless, but Patrick was a fighter. It was then that his pragmatic nature and medical training kicked in. There was no choice, really. No time for a pity party. It was obvious that he had to break the limb off somewhere close to his neck. He couldn't just sit here on the skidoo, attached to a big fallen branch, and waiting for help which would never come.

Breaking it, however, was much easier said than done. Gently taking it with his two hands, and trying to break it, without causing it to move in his neck, was next to impossible. His first attempt caused excruciating pain, and he had to stop and take some deep breaths before trying again.

He mustn't cause himself to pass out, not here, not now. He had to concentrate, and use his skilled hands to perform the most difficult of operations. He had to break off that sharp limb, so that he was no longer impaled on it, and in a way that didn't push it further into his neck, possibly doing irreparable damage.

Unfortunately, his bare hands were so darn cold, that he could barely feel them, let alone get much strength into them.

He lost all sense of time, as he made another couple of futile attempts to break that invasive limb.

As he was working on it, as gently as possible, he thought he heard another couple of screams. This was horrifying. He could do nothing to help, yet someone was likely being killed or tortured.

Sweat broke out on his forehead, and immediately froze. Finally, totally exhausted from blood loss, extreme cold, and a terrible dread of the outcome, he told himself that he would make just one more try. Then maybe he'd just close his eyes for a second. He was getting so sleepy. He knew that it was hypothermia making him sleepy, yet the will to keep his eyes open was fading.

Forcing his frozen fingers to put as much pressure as possible on the limb, and gritting his teeth with the pain, he heard the "snap," as the sharp tree limb finally broke into two pieces.

Unfortunately, the one piece was still in his throat, sticking out about three inches.

Fortunately, however, Patrick could not see the bloody, jagged tear, which was the result of all his efforts.

Chapter Forty-Two

While Kate and Angel Baby were shoving and pushing the unfortunate Mark around on the stairs, Davey had disappeared. Kate was glad to have him out of Angel's sight. She hoped that the old adage – "out of sight, out of mind," – would apply. She didn't want Davey annoying Angel Baby in any way, or even attracting her attention. She was so volatile, that she was liable to shoot first and think about it later.

Angel had put Mark's legs down, and was trying to get a better grip on them. She hated this, and was thinking that she would just like to get on that skidoo, and get the hell out of here. That wasn't a possibility, though. She had to finish this blasted job, get rid of Kate and Davey, and then leave.

Kate spotted Davey first. He was tip-toeing out of the kitchen. She could see that he had removed his shoes, and was being as stealthy as a little cat, about to pounce on a mouse. She could tell by his eyes, that he was frightened, but determined. In his hand was that crazy wooden rolling pin, and his mother knew in an instant just what he planned to do.

She was frightened for him, but hopeful as well. She didn't think he could hit Angel hard enough to do any damage, but if he would just whack her on the wrist, she might not be able to pull the trigger. Davey likely wouldn't think of that, though.

Kate held her breath as he got closer. He was almost right behind Angel now. "Please God don't let her see him," she thought frantically.

Angel Baby was scowling up at Kate. "Come on, Kate. You're not lifting him properly. I've got all the weight in these big legs of his," she complained. Her own voice was covering any noise which Davey might make inadvertently.

Suddenly, swift as a cobra, her beloved little boy, who was gentle, artistic, funny, and loving, sprang to the side, and just a wee bit ahead of Angel, and brought the bat down across her shin bone.

Angel Baby screamed, and dropped Mark's feet. She bellowed like a moose with its antlers stuck in a tree.

Davey didn't hesitate, bringing the bat back again for a second go at the target, he struck her on the head.

Angel Baby folded like a cheap lawn chair.

Kate dropped Mark's body, and muttering, "Sorry, Mark," she scrambled down the stairs, and began digging in Angel's pocket.

At the moment, Angel wasn't putting up much of a struggle. She seemed to be out cold!

The gun was there, and now it was in Kate's hand, instead of Angel's!

Turning to Davey, she hugged him fiercely. "You wonderful, clever, brave boy. You've just saved our lives."

Davey looked dazed, and he was now clinging to the rolling pin, as if it was one of his beloved cats.

"I think she killed Kingsley," he whispered, tears in his eyes.

Kate realized that was how Davey had found the courage to do such a brave and foolhardy thing. He was distraught about his friend Kingsley.

"Maybe he's just drugged, hon, and he'll waken up after a while."

"Well, who's gonna tell him about Mark?" Davey wondered. "He and Mark were best pals."

Then he began to sob.

Kate needed to hug him, so she very gently put the gun into her jeans pocket, and cradled him in her arms, whispering soft soothing sounds to him. She didn't know anything about guns, and had never even touched one, so she hoped that she wouldn't accidentally shoot off one of her toes.

They cuddled like that for a few minutes, till Davey stopped crying. Then Kate checked to see whether Angel Baby was still breathing. Although she seemed out of it, she was still breathing regularly, and might waken at any time.

"We have to get out of here, Davey. We're going to get on that skidoo, and get the heck as far away as possible. You go get into all your gear as quick as you can. Don't forget your mitts and hat. I'll do the same, and we'll just leave these two for later.

"No, wait a minute. Run upstairs first, and see if you can find my cell phone in Angel's room. It's likely in her big tote bag. If you find it, call 911, tell them there's been a shooting, and tell them where we are. If you can't find mine, use hers, but don't waste any time. I'll get my things on, and get the skidoo started. Hurry now."

Davey started up the stairs, trying not to look at Mark, who was resting uncomfortably with his head on one step near the top, and his legs and feet resting on another step further down.

"Mom, what about Kingsley? We can't just leave him here."

"We have to leave him for now. He's sleeping too soundly to waken him. We'll be back with the police by the time he wakens. Don't worry, Davey, he's going to be fine."

Kate hoped that she was telling the truth. Kingsley was in such a sound sleep, that she wasn't sure whether she could see him breathing or not. He might already be dead, but there was no time to check.

She was bent over, putting on her second boot, when Angel dove at her from behind, knocking her against the counter.

What was going on? Had Angel been playing possum at the foot of the stairs? Kate was disgusted with herself for being so careless. She had really thought Angel was unconscious, and had let down her guard.

This was as ridiculous as those movies in which the heroine turned her back on the villain, who was supposedly unconscious or dead on the floor. The villain always reached out a hand to grab the victim's leg, or suddenly pounced from behind, just as Angel Baby had done.

"I'll kill you, Kate, and I'll kill that brat of yours too. He nearly broke my leg, and my head is throbbing. The two of you don't know what you're up against now."

Kate groaned. Angel was like the Energizer Bunny. You just couldn't stop her.

She frantically dug in her pocket, and brought out the little gun.

"Back off, Angel or Maddy or whoever you think you are. I've got the gun now, and the tables are turned. Don't go threatening me or Davey. At this point I'd be quite happy to put a bullet in you, but I won't do that in front of Davey, so we'll let the police handle you. They're on their way."

Kate didn't think that was true, but it might scare Angel Baby.

Angel started to laugh. "Oo, I'm so scared," she said. "Please don't shoot me Kate. I promise I'm sorry, and I'll be good."

She was grinning and laughing, and Kate knew that there was something wrong. Why wasn't she frightened? She had either gone totally Looney-Tunes, or she knew something that Kate didn't know. Then Kate guessed it, and her heart sank. She wondered whether there were any bullets in the gun. Was that why Angel was laughing so hysterically?

At this point, she saw Davey coming as quietly as possible, and pointing to something on the counter. Angel wasn't aware of him, because he was still in his stocking feet, and she had seen him going upstairs. Her laughing covered any noise he might be making.

Kate glanced sidewise at the counter, and immediately saw what Davey had put there. It was a large can of hornet blaster. He must have found it in the closet, when Angel sent him to clean it out. Well, if the gun was no good, the hornet blaster might give them a slight chance of getting away. It was worth a try.

Switching the gun to her left hand, Kate quickly reached for the can. Angel, however, reached just as quickly for a sharp knife which was sitting there. Davey had put it there as well, just in case they could use it against Angel, but this time his plan had backfired. Angel got it first, and plunged it into the back of Kate's right hand.

The next few moments were chaos. Kate screamed, dropped the gun, and clutched her hand, which now had a big knife sticking out of the top of it.

Before bending down to pick up the gun, Angel twisted the knife in Kate's hand, then, with a fiendish smile, she pulled it out.

The pain was beyond excruciating.

Davey pushed his mom aside, grabbed the hornet blaster, and sprayed it directly into Angel's eyes.

Now it was Angel who dropped the gun, and was screaming, as she clawed at her eyes, dancing in a circle of fear and pain.

This was Davey's night. He was a one man tornado. His mother was screaming, Angel was screaming, and he seemed to be the only one who knew what to do. This awful Maddy person, who called herself Angel Baby, had likely killed Kingsley, and had stuck a knife in his mom's hand. She wasn't going to do any more harm, not while Davey was around. He figured he was just as smart, and he knew that he was a whole lot quicker.

He got right up to Angel, and sprayed her eyes again, even though they were closed. She now had spray on her forehead, dripping down into her eyes, as well as on her beautiful face. She seemed in such agony, that she could do nothing but twirl blindly, and finally fall on her knees. She was in too much pain to even think about trying to wash the repellent out of her eyes.

Kate forced herself to take several deep breaths, before reaching for a clean tea towel. She pressed it on the large wound, and tried to staunch the flow of blood.

Then she remembered an old sweater in the closet. It had a wool belt on it – just the thing for a makeshift tourniquet.

Davey wasn't quite finished with his James Bond act. He grabbed the handy-dandy all purpose rolling pin, and whacked Angel right on the wrist. That was just in case she tried to pick up the gun again. Then he very carefully handed the gun to his mom.

Kate didn't know whether to laugh or cry. Her little fellow was a hero, and she had to get him out of there before Angel was back in action.

"Oh, Davey you're a miracle. I owe you big time. Now, get into your boots and stuff. We've got to get out of here. No telling how long it will be before she's at it again. She's just too dangerous for us to stick around. Hurry, hon."

"Okay, but do you really mean that you owe me big time?" he asked, as he struggled into his boots.

"Of course, you know I do. Now hurry."

"Oh, that's great, because I want to keep Kingsley, if he's alive. He'll be so lonesome without Mark, and who else would take him? He might be given to somebody who would be mean to him."

Kate thought about their precious three cats at home. Tom, Dick and Harriet were much beloved by all the family. Would they tolerate a big dog? Would he tolerate them?

It wasn't the time for a debate. Kate's hand was radiating pain right up her arm, and she couldn't get her mind to focus clearly on cats and a dog. She needed to get them out of there.

"Davey, we'll try. If he doesn't hurt the cats, he's welcome to stay. Everyone will love him. If he makes their lives miserable, though, he'll have to go. I won't have him disrupting their happy home. We had them first, and it wouldn't be fair to them.

"That's all I can say now. Come on, we've got to go."

"Yeah," crowed Davey, pulling on his cap. "I know he'll be good to them. He'll play with them, you'll see."

It was good to see a smile on that precious little face, Kate thought. She was worried that Davey would be totally traumatized by what he had seen and done tonight. If Kingsley died, he would be devastated. She told herself that her son was strong and smart, and hopefully this evil night wouldn't leave a lasting impression.

She checked Angel, who was still cringing and moaning on the floor. She didn't even seem to be aware of them.

The ideal situation would have been to tie Angel securely before they left, but Kate had no time and no rope.

If only she had known that there was a would-be guardian angel in trouble just down the road, things might have been very different. Kate would have gone to help Patrick, she and Davey would have been down the road with him when the police arrived, and, together, they would have been able to handle Angel Baby, without any more harm to anyone.

Unfortunately, of course, Kate didn't know Patrick, and certainly didn't know that he was on his way to help her.

So, motioning to Davey to be quiet, they slipped out the door. She just wanted to get them to safety, someplace where there was no corpse lounging on the stairs, no comatose dog lying in front of the fire, and no insane woman, huddled on the floor, rubbing and clawing at her eyes.

If there hadn't been such a blizzard, and wicked wind, they might have even seen Patrick, sitting on his skidoo, bent slightly forward, as he sat, still attached to the tree.

Even if Patrick had spotted them coming out the back door, he couldn't have yelled at them. The stick in his throat was stopping any form of vocal communication.

Again it seemed that the Fates were up to their old tricks.

In her haste to leave, she never thought to ask Davey if he had called the police. She was pretty sure that he hadn't, or else he would have told her.

If only she had thought to ask him, and had discovered that Davey actually had called 911, she might have decided to stay. If she had stayed at the cottage, waiting for the police, the rest of that cold night in hell would have turned out very differently.

Kate, however, was totally focused on getting Davey to safety. If it had been just Kate against Maddy, that would have been a different matter. Kate was resourceful and relatively fearless, but with Davey in danger, she had to be much more circumspect.

As they hurried out of the cottage, neither of them noticed the key to the second skidoo. It was hanging right there on the hook by the door – hanging where anyone could find it!

Chapter Forty-Three

Kate's hand was throbbing, and she could feel it swelling under the tea towel, which was wrapped around it. She couldn't get the mitt over the towel, and knew that it was going to be really awkward trying to drive.

Blood was pouring out of it, and Kate realized that she might very well lose consciousness, if she didn't get some medical help. Hopefully the freezing air would help to slow the bleeding.

She wondered, with despair, whether she might lose the use of the hand for good.

Kate knew that she should hold her right hand up, to slow the blood loss, but that was almost impossible, as she struggled into her boots, jacket and helmet. Hopefully the tourniquet would help.

"Davey, you sit in front of me, and put your hands on the handlebars. You're going to be driving, with a little help from me. Isn't it lucky you practiced out in the meadow today."

Kate was trying to keep it light, but she knew she was putting a great deal of pressure on the seven-year old.

"We're going to go down the hill, and out onto the lake. We'll follow the shore. There are several cottages all close together, around that first bend. Surely there'll be a light on in one of them. This way will be faster, and hopefully safer than going down the road. Also, we'll be able to see if Angel starts following us."

She had absolutely no idea what they could do, if Angel did manage to pursue them. They'd just have to play it by ear, and hope that God was keeping an eye on them.

The first problem was that the skidoo didn't want to start. It was just too cold, but after what seemed like several minutes, and was likely only moments, it started with a jump, and a great roar of enthusiasm. They took off down the bank, with little Davey steering.

The cold air felt good on Kate's hand under the cotton towel. She hadn't had time to think about the wound yet. She knew it was deep. The knife had almost gone right through her palm, but then Angel had actually twisted it as she pulled it out. What an evil woman!

Kate had been determined not to faint, but felt extremely light-headed. She had to remain calm for Davey's sake, but what she really wanted to do was just lie down and make all this horror go away.

How would she do her lovely illustrations, if her hand lost its flexibility and dexterity? It was a thought too horrible to contemplate. Could she learn to use her left hand instead?

At first Davey was too excited to be scared. After all, he was the one driving the skidoo, and getting them out of danger. He wished Kingsley could have come with them. He also wished he knew how far away that open water was.

He remembered the policeman talking about it this morning, and telling his mom not to go out on the lake. He had to admit that the thought of dark, freezing, open water scared him, but mom must know what she was doing. Mom was smart.

With the wind howling and swirling, it was difficult to see any distance ahead, even though the snow machine had a good headlight. Kate knew that the open water was just beyond the turn into the bay, but she hadn't anticipated that in this blizzard, it would be almost impossible to see ahead. If they missed the turn, they would plunge right into that open water.

Taking a quick glance over her shoulder, her heart almost stopped beating. She couldn't believe it, but there – quite a distance back – she could see the headlight of a skidoo. It was coming right in their direction. It must be Angel. She must have rinsed her eyes to the point where she could see again. She had the determination of the devil!

It was then that Kate realized the mistake she had made. She had left the key to the second ski machine right on the hook. If she had taken it with her, there would have been no way for Angel to follow them.

There was no sense berating herself, but Kate felt that she had let Davey down. He trusted her implicitly, but he had been the one making all the smart moves tonight.

"Let's go a little faster, Davey. I think Angel's behind us."

"But mom, what about the water?" he yelled over his shoulder. His arms were getting tired now, but he couldn't tell her. She couldn't drive with her hand all cut up, and there was no one else to help them, so he was it. He sure wished they'd had time for supper, though. He was so hungry. Man, a hot dog would taste good just about now.

"We're not anywhere near it yet. It's at least a mile away, but keep looking straight ahead, and slow down if you see where the snow gets darker. That will be the open water. It's going to be tricky, but the two of us can do it. We have to do it. We can't let Angel catch us. She has the gun, and she may have put more bullets in it by now."

She didn't want to scare Davey, but it was best if he knew exactly what the situation was. They were in serious danger.

"When I yell 'turn' you've got to turn the machine really fast to the right. When I yell, it will mean that we're almost to the water, and you can't delay a moment. That's really important. I'll try to grab the handle with you, to help turn it, but my right hand is pretty well useless, so it's going to be up to you."

Kate remembered that earlier today, when they had been driving the skidoo in the meadow, Davey had trouble turning the big machine. Now their very lives might depend on him being able to do it. Blast that damn Angel, sticking the knife into her hand!

She was yelling all the instructions into Davey's ear, and she prayed that he understood the danger. Poor little guy. All he wanted to do was play with Kingsley, and draw in his art book. How had they gotten themselves into such a mess!

Davey just nodded his head, and kept staring straight ahead. This wasn't fun any more. It was scary, and his arms were too tired, but he would never admit it.

It was difficult yelling at each other over the snarling of the wind, so they were both silent, as they peered anxiously ahead. Every once in a while, the wind seemed to stop to take a breath, and there were a few moments of calm. During those times, they could see further ahead, and so far there was no black water.

There were, however, some big chunks and mounds of ice in certain places. They looked like big eruptions right out of the lake. Davey wasn't always able to miss them, and there were places when they were almost airborne, as they bumped and bounced over these impediments.

Kate had chosen to try to escape across the lake for several reasons, one of them being that it would be nice and flat, and easy for Davey to drive. Maybe she had been wrong, but she didn't think so. She knew how badly the snow had drifted in spots on the road. They might not have been able to get through to the highway. At least there was plenty of room to maneuver on the lake.

It seemed as if they had gone a long way already, and she wondered what they would do if their machine ran out of gas. She also wondered where the heck that bay was.

It was uncomfortable reaching her arms around Davey, so that she could grab the handles in an emergency. Her right hand was throbbing and burning, and she couldn't squeeze it. It would actually be useless if she had to grab that right handle and put any pressure on it. She figured she could, however, use her good left arm and hand, to give Davey some help in making turns.

She prayed that Davey's much smaller hands and arms wouldn't give out on him. They must be tired by now, considering the workout they had been given.

Davey had been practicing driving the skidoo earlier today. That would tire his arms. He had also been swinging the rolling pin vigorously, not only practicing with it, but actually using it to whack Angel several times.

Then, of course, there was the dreaded hornet blaster can, which he had so cleverly used as a weapon. He had been pretty darn amazing and resourceful, but his tired arms must be ready to fall off just about now. Wait till she told Mac how terrific his little son had been. That is, if she ever saw Mac again, she thought grimly.

After Kate's Everglades adventure, one kind reporter had written that she was the poster girl for courage, tenacity, and determination. Well, seven year old Davey was certainly the poster boy for those same traits. The little guy had been a marvel today.

Then she remembered that he had also been outside playing in the snow with Kingsley, tossing the ball over and over. Good grief, he should be out cold by now, but here he was, doing his best to drive this big machine, and keep them out of the water.

Kate could see the possibilities of a disastrous ending.

The next time she looked over her shoulder, it was obvious that Angel was gaining on them. She was on the newer and more powerful of the two machines which the Chandlers owned. It was

Mac's skidoo, and they had bought a bigger one for him, so that it could drag a little trailer behind. They had been looking ahead to winter weekends, when they would be able to bring supplies in to the cottage. Kate wondered whether that would ever happen now.

So much had happened today – none of it good, that she was feeling pessimistic, and just plain scared. Was Angel going to catch them before they could get to a cottage with lights on? And if she did catch them, what defense did they have against that damn gun?

If only Davey had been able to call the police, they might be on their way by now. They would have gone to the cottage, and found no one there but a dead Mark and a comatose Kingsley. After searching, and seeing signs of a struggle, they would likely have followed the skidoo tracks out onto the lake.

Wait! Maybe that was a policeman following them now. Maybe it was actually someone who could help them! Oh wouldn't that be wonderful!

Kate turned to look over her shoulder again. Well, whoever it was, they were definitely catching up. If she knew for sure that it was the police, they could stop and wait, but she couldn't take that chance. If it was the police, Angel would have told them that Kate shot Mark, drugged the dog, then blinded her with hornet spray. Kate would have to do a lot of talking to get herself out of that! The police could be on their way to arrest her!

Leaning close to his ear, Kate shouted at Davey, "Did you find my cell phone?"

"Yep. It was in her big bag, just like you said." Davey shouted this while still looking straight ahead. He was afraid to even blink. They seemed to have been riding for a long time, and he was sure they must be near the water by now.

"The police said they'd be there fast as they could," he added. He didn't say that maybe they should have stayed at the cottage and waited for the police to arrive. It might have been safer, and it sure would have been warmer. In spite of the helmet with the face guard, Davey's face felt frozen. It didn't seem to move when he talked.

He remembered that when he had been running around outside with Kingsley, it hadn't seemed to be that cold, but now on the skidoo, his face was stinging, and even his feet were starting to ache. He hoped they didn't freeze solid by the time they finally got inside someplace warm.

Kate gave him a one-armed hug, whispered "you're the best," into his ear, and turned to have another look at the pursuing machine. All she could see was a bright headlight doggedly pursuing them!

Chapter Forty-Four

Patrick realized that at the moment, he was too weak to even get off the skidoo. He had to just sit there quietly, after breaking off the killer limb. There was a three or four inch piece of it still protruding from his neck. He knew that pulling it out, could open the floodgates, and do unimaginable damage.

The scary thing was that if he should happen to fall on it, he could shove it right through to the back of his neck. No telling what damage that would do! He had no idea just how far in it was, but it would have to be removed in a hospital with proper tools.

He was worried about the screams he had heard, because now things seemed ominously quiet. All he could hear was the howling of that malevolent wind.

He found himself getting quite sleepy. His eyelids just didn't want to stay open. Unless he started moving, he would quietly fall asleep, and freeze to death. Not a good alternative. He was determined that he would not fall victim to hypothermia.

Even getting himself off the skidoo was an effort, and he had to be so careful not to let anything touch the offending branch, which protruded like a handle on a pot.

How vulnerable he was! If Angel Baby could see him now, she would likely take the palm of her hand, and shove that stick till it came out the back of his head. What a picture that presented! He shuddered, as he took his first tentative step into the deep snow.

If he could just get himself to Kate's cottage, then she could call for help, and he might have a chance. Of course, that would mean that the screams he had heard were not from Kate.

Time and luck were the big factors. All his grandiose plans for saving Kate, and somehow making Angel face up to what she had done, were gone with the wind. Now all he could do was concentrate on getting help for himself.

He couldn't die in Canada, a beautiful country, but so very far away from Lainey and the kids.

Staggering a bit in the snow, he got his balance, and took another few stumbling steps. This was going to be a marathon, and he shouldn't have any trouble keeping awake.

He noticed that it had stopped snowing. It was just the wind which was making life unbearable. At least between the gusts, he could look ahead, and watch for some sign of the cottage. He couldn't be that far from it now.

"Just another few steps, Pat, just another few steps." This became his mantra, as he plodded on.

Sharp spears of pain were now emanating from his throat. Swallowing was almost impossible, and he realized that there must be serious post trauma edema. He had to keep spitting the accumulated saliva. He was not a man who would ever spit in public, but tonight, with no one around, it was the only thing he could do.

Maybe coming to Canada, and seeking revenge, hadn't been such a good idea. Probably the idea of revenge is evil in itself. Maybe this was his punishment for planning to hurt Angel Baby in some way.

As he plodded along, he tried to keep his mind off his throat, and think of some of the things he had read about revenge over the years. One quote which sprang to mind was "to take revenge is often to sacrifice oneself." Man, how true was that one! If he hadn't been out here for revenge, this would never have happened to him.

Of course, his main purpose had become an effort to save Kate, but he doubted that he was up to that now. It might turn out that Kate would have to save him.

Another quote he remembered reading was "Nothing good ever comes from revenge." He wished he had paid attention to that one. Whoever said it, was pretty smart.

His stomach was feeling queasy, but, in spite of the brutal wind, he felt quite warm. He knew that was the hypothermia attacking with a vengeance, and he felt a rush of relief, when he thought he could see the cottage in the distance. It still seemed a long way, but he could make it. He had no choice. He either made it to the cottage, or he was a dead man.

He stepped into some sort of a hole, and his leg sank right to his knee. Panic took over. He raised his head as high as he could. He was terrified that something would hit that damn stick, or the stick would hit something. In either case, it would be not only excruciating, but likely lethal.

When he heard two skidoos roaring up behind him, he thought he must be hallucinating. He told himself that it was just a roaring in his ears.

Then his heart gave a leap of gratitude, when it occurred to him that it must be his friend Bob, coming to look for him. Part of him knew that didn't seem likely, but it was still a wonderful hope.

"Police. Stop right there," said a gruff voice, as both men stopped their machines and got off. With skidoo suits and safety helmets, they looked like men from Mars. Of course, Patrick realized that he would have too, if he hadn't removed his helmet to protect the protruding stick. The chin strap had been moving, and pushing against the stick.

Wait till they got a good look at him, with that damn limb sticking out of his neck!

"Who are you, and what are you doing here?" asked one of the men.

Patrick pointed to the stick and shook his head. He didn't know whether he could speak or not, but he wasn't going to try. No telling what damage could be done. He was hoping to come out of this not only alive, but relatively unharmed, and still able to speak and swallow like a normal person.

"What the hell!" exclaimed one of the policemen, shining his big flashlight right into Patrick's face. "What happened to you? Is that part of a tree limb? Good God! Who did this to you?" Bradley couldn't believe his eyes. He'd never seen anything like this.

Nick DeLuca, the second officer, guessed what might have happened, since they had passed the skidoo stuck on the big tree branch.

"Did you fall on a branch, and it penetrated your neck?"

Patrick didn't want to nod, but he tried to show with his eyes that that was just about it. He was trying to keep his head as still as possible.

"Do you know the people in this cottage?" asked Bradley.

Patrick wasn't sure of the correct answer. He knew Angel Baby, but wasn't sure that she actually was in this cottage. He didn't know Kate, but again, he tried to indicate a "yes" with his eyes.

"You need to be in the hospital. I'm going to call for an ambulance, but I don't know how they'll get you back out to the road. They won't be able to drive in here, obviously."

Patrick almost shook his head "no" before he remembered the new appendage.

He grimaced to indicate a "no," but found even that small facial movement used muscles, which tightened the throat, and made the stick move. This was impossible!

"We've got to get to the cottage, someone's in trouble. A little kid called us a while ago, and said he and his mom were in danger, and that someone had been shot. What a night! We've had more calls tonight than we've had in a month.

"Has anyone passed you on this road, maybe going the other way?"

Again Patrick tried to indicate "no" by frowning slightly.

"I'll call the ambulance, and you can wait here for them, while we go in and have a look. Will you be okay?"

DeLuca didn't want to leave Patrick, but he didn't know what else to do. He figured that the 911 call which they had received from Davey, should take priority, but this poor bugger was in serious condition. They had to get help for him.

This was frustrating. Patrick wanted to tell them that he had heard some screams, but there was no way he could talk. He shrugged slightly. One thing he knew damn well. He wasn't going to wait here and freeze his butt. He'd follow them, but couldn't indicate that too well.

True to his word, the cop called and relayed the problem. He warned that the two paramedics would have to leave the ambulance at the end of the road, and carry the stretcher to the patient. It wouldn't be easy. Maybe Patrick should start walking out to meet them.

"Look, just wait here, or start walking out, whatever suits you. We'll see what's going on in the cottage, and then one of us will come back, and take you the rest of the way on the skidoo."

With that declaration, the two cops started their machines and went roaring towards the cottage.

Patrick felt abandoned, but he kept plodding along. He felt better, knowing that help was coming, even though it would be a while.

He wondered with dread what the cops would find.

Chapter Forty-Five

By the time Patrick finally made it to the cottage, the two policemen were taking notes, as they inspected the scene. He peered through a window first, before heading to the door. He wanted to have some idea of what was happening in there, before stepping into something bad, although with the police there, things should be under control.

Would Angel Baby be holding a gun or knife on Kate? Would Kate already be dead? What would Angel do with Kate's little boy? Surely she wouldn't hurt him too. The good doctor, who was barely hanging on, had no idea what he might see, but he certainly hadn't expected the tableau laid out before him.

He could only see a little corner of the living room, but it looked as if there was a dead man sprawled on the stairs, and possibly a dead dog stretched out on the floor. What in the hell had happened here? Where were Kate and Angel Baby? Who was this dead guy, and what did he have to do with anything? Was this even the right cottage?

Patrick had to get in out of the cold. Although the big lacy snowflakes, which had been parachuting down all day, had finally stopped, that was not the end of the story. The cruel wind had picked up in velocity and noise. It bellowed like a sick cow, then hissed like a party of snakes, as it blew in, directly off the lake. It was biting and relentless in its ferocity, seemingly having a mind and spirit all its own. It was alive, and it made anyone foolish enough or unfortunate enough to be out in it, feel frightened, helpless, and hopeless.

Patrick leaned against the window for support, as he watched the two officers search the crime scene. Of course, it wasn't the broken window, which was still covered with Kate's home repair blankets, but a smaller window which gave a bit of a view into the kitchen and down the hall. He was panting from his efforts struggling through the deep snow, and he wanted to get his breath before going in. He was way past the point of exhaustion.

The one officer was standing looking at the body, and shaking his head, and Patrick knew that the man, whoever he was, was dead.

The other cop was bending over the dog, feeling his chest. Patrick could faintly hear him say "This poor fellow's drugged or poisoned. He's alive, but his heartbeat is fast and irregular."

Eric Bradley hated his job. He had been on the force for almost three years, and if he had been able to think of anything else to do, to make a decent wage, he would have quit long ago. He hated spending his days dealing with drunks, domestic violence, bad car wrecks, and vandalism. Most of all, he hated being ugly, and he hated his life.

Anyone who had to deal with Officer Bradley, made sure that there wasn't a second time. He was not a compassionate man.

On this hellishly cold night, he wanted to be home in bed with a beautiful blonde. The dream would be even better, if she happened to be blessed with big hooters. Of course, he didn't have anyone in his life like that, but that was his dream. Instead, he had two old dogs, a German Shepherd and a Golden Lab, and it made him furious to see this poor dog, unconscious on the floor. How could people treat an animal that way?

He didn't care a shit about the dead guy on the stairs, but he'd like to get his hands on whoever had drugged the dog.

Feeling exhausted, shaky, and light-headed, Patrick leaned against the window, catching his breath. He couldn't help noticing how very ugly this cop was. He had red hair and a drinker's nose, and his cheeks were covered with deep acne scars. The fleeting thought came to the doctor that it was so sad to have to go through life looking like that. He could have fixed the poor guy's nose, and the rough skin, easily. Well, maybe not easily, but it certainly could have been done.

He wondered, as he supported himself against the window, whether being so ugly had affected this cop's personality. It had been his experience that people who were truly ugly, were often affected by their appearance, and developed a hatred for mankind, and life in general.

DeLuca was now standing still, looking around the living room. In his own quiet way, he gave the impression that he didn't miss much.

"What do you think has happened to the kid who called 911, and where's the mother? When we were here today, she seemed like a pretty nice woman. I don't think that she killed this guy and then took off."

"Maybe he's the guy who came to fix the window," suggested Bradley, still petting Kingsley, and trying to waken him.

"I don't think so, Bradley," said DeLuca, shaking his head in silent disgust. This guy was as dumb as a bag of bricks. Thank God he wasn't his usual partner.

"There are no boards around, and the window obviously hasn't been fixed yet. Besides, there was no skidoo out there, so this poor guy and his dog must have walked from nearby.

"The kid on the phone didn't say they were in danger from any man. He said that there was a strange lady here who was trying to hurt them, and that there had been a shooting. He also said that she had locked them out in the cold for a while."

DeLuca had walked right through the kitchen when they first arrived. The door had been unlocked, and after knocking loudly once, he had simply entered, calling out to Kate as he strolled through the cottage. Now it was time to go back, and have a good look.

They made note of the bloody knife on the counter, plus the blood. It was obvious that there had been a struggle of some kind. The rolling pin was on the floor, along with the hornet blaster can.

"Hey, look here. There's blood all over the counter and the floor. Someone's wounded.

"What the hell happened, and how did the dead guy fit into it?"

DeLuca was talking to himself, as well as making notes. Bradley wasn't that interested, but he did admire how serious DeLuca was about his job. He wished he could be like that.

"I'm worried about Mrs. Chandler and her boy. They're not upstairs, so where the hell are they?" asked DeLuca.

"I think you'd better go back out, and wait with that poor man with the stick in his throat.

"I hope it doesn't take the paramedics too long to get here. That tree limb sticking out of his neck, was just about the worst damn thing I've ever seen."

"You're not kidding. I wanted to pull it out for him, but I guess that's not the right thing to do," muttered Officer Bradley.

Patrick realized that he had to get in and get warm. He also had to see for himself what had happened to Kate. Had Angel Baby killed her, and taken off?

Pushing himself away from the window unsteadily, he turned to make his way to the door.

Unfortunately, the good doctor had lost a bit too much blood, and was now way too shaky and cold. He was going into shock. Circumstances worked against him, and Patrick plunged face down into the snow. As he lost consciousness, he made an effort to turn his head, trying to keep the stick from hitting anything.

Neither cop was close enough to hear his little moan, and neither had any idea that he was now lying out there in the snow and cold, slowly freezing.

For DeLuca and Bradley, this was a huge mystery.

In the lovely little vacation town of Bracebridge, there are very few murders. There are so few, in fact, that many of the policemen on the local force, and on the provincial force, have never worked a murder case.

These two officers at Kate's cottage had never been called to a murder scene, and the little that they knew, came from television shows. They spent their days investigating break-ins, fender benders, and boating accidents, with the occasional drowning thrown in.

DeLuca was thrilled to be involved with a real murder, and didn't want to make any mistakes. Bradley couldn't have cared less.

Chapter Forty-Six

The highway was almost impassible in spots, and the ambulance took a lot longer than it normally would have. The capricious wind had blown the snow into huge mounds in some places, and had swept the road clean in others.

The paramedics parked beside Kate's car, at the end of the cottage road, and got the portable gurney out of the back. Its legs on rollers would be no use tonight. They realized that they were going to have to carry the victim out through this storm, through places where the snow was piled high, blown there by an unforgiving wind.

This was going to be a 'tour de force,' and each paramedic wished silently that he could just jump back into the ambulance, and take off to somewhere warm.

"Shit, it's colder than a witch's you know what," grumbled Shorty Sanders, who looked down at the world from a height of six feet six inches. Years ago, some wit had thought it would be funny to call him Shorty, and the nickname had stuck. The deep snow wouldn't be too much trouble for him. Jimmy Ostrander, his partner tonight, was only five foot eight, and they looked like Mutt and Jeff, struggling along.

It was so dark, that in spots they couldn't tell whether they were on the road, or off on the edge. The flashlight wasn't much help. They struggled along in silence, because the wind seemed to blow the words away, before they could be heard.

This was a total nightmare. As Jimmy fell to his knees for the second time, he wondered how they could possibly carry a patient out, without doing him harm.

When they finally got to Patrick's skidoo, which was still entangled with the big tree branch across the road, there was no sign of Patrick.

"What the hell? Didn't that cop who made the call, say that the guy would be waiting right at his skidoo?" asked Shorty, with a frown.

"Yep, but I thought that was strange. They wouldn't leave him out here alone on a night like this. They must have carried him into the cottage, so that he wouldn't freeze," was Jimmy's reply.

"They couldn't very well leave him out here by himself, with a tree branch sticking out of his neck."

Neither paramedic could really picture what the officer had tried to describe.

From the abandoned skidoo, they could now see the cottage, which was still a good distance away. Their hearts sank, as they realized how difficult it was going to be, carrying out the patient.

They were still resolutely striving to get through the snow, carrying the empty stretcher, when Shorty stopped to catch his breath, and said, "Oh oh. What's that lying in the snow right close to the back door?"

Without another word, they tried to run, an impossible task.

At that very moment, Bradley was coming out the door, heading back to the skidoo, where he thought Patrick would be waiting.

"Shit, what now?" he muttered, as he almost tripped over the seemingly frozen body of Patrick, now partially covered by the blowing snow.

It took the three of them to lift the doctor, and get him into the cottage. When they turned him over, and saw the limb still sticking out from his neck, they grimaced in horror.

"Oh God, that must hurt," said Jimmy, screwing up his face, as he looked at Patrick's neck. It was no longer bleeding, but there was a lot of frozen blood, along with a fair sized tear in the flesh, around the entrance wound.

DeLuca and Bradley watched, as the two paramedics took Patrick's vitals, confirmed that he was still alive, but barely, and began the slow process of trying to warm his frozen body. The thought of taking him back out into that freezing night was frightening, but what else could they do? They had to get him to the hospital as quickly as possible, if he was to have any chance of surviving.

Before they left, Bradley asked them to take a look at the dog. It was still sleeping, but had made a couple of snorting sounds, as if it was trying to waken up.

Jimmy and Shorty both took a look at him, and declared that he had definitely been drugged.

"His breathing seems pretty good. I think he'll waken up eventually. Someone likely tried to give him enough to kill him. Poor fellow. I wonder if he belongs to the guy on the stairs. When everything gets straightened out, if you find that he has no home, let me know. I'd be glad to have him," said Jimmy, patting Kingsley's head.

Bradley had already made up his mind that if no one wanted the dog, he was going to take him, but he nodded, as if in agreement.

By now DeLuca had called his supervisor, described the situation, and been ordered to stay there until reinforcements arrived.

He watched patiently, as the paramedics quietly went about their work. They were anxious to get Patrick to the hospital, but bundling him up sufficiently to keep him warm, was the challenge. They had him almost wrapped like a mummy, with extra blankets taken from Kate's supply, but they had to leave the neck exposed, where the tree limb was protruding. It was tricky.

The long trip, stumbling through the snow, carrying the doctor out to the waiting ambulance, was one those two paramedics would never forget. It was the most macabre, challenging, and exhausting trip they had ever made, and they would tell the story for years to come.

DeLuca, not one to waste time, decided to take a walk around the outside of the cottage, to see if there were any footprints visible. He knew it was a forlorn hope, but had to try. To his amazement, he found some relatively clear skidoo tracks heading down to the lake. It looked like they came from two skidoos.

Stopping to ponder this, DeLuca remembered Kate talking about taking the little kid for a skidoo ride down in the meadow that morning. Did they go on two skidoos or one? Was the little boy, Davey, big enough to handle a skidoo by himself? Could these skidoo tracks have been made by Kate on one, and Davey on the other?

He didn't think that was likely. Why would Kate have taken her son out onto the lake? He remembered specifically telling her not to go out there, because of the open water. Where was the strange woman Davey had mentioned on the phone? Was she on one skidoo and Kate on the other? Had she chased Kate onto the lake?

God help us all, he thought, as he raced to zipper his suit, and put on his helmet.

His supervisor had told him to stay put, but someone had to follow those skidoos. Whoever was on them, could be heading for disaster, and if it was the murderer, he or she could be getting away.

"Bradley, I'm going to follow these tracks. Someone's gone out on the lake, and I suspect that it's Mrs. Chandler chasing the woman, or the woman chasing her. You stay here till the reinforcements arrive, and help them any way you can. I'll be back soon."

Under his breath he muttered, "If I get back at all."

The thought of going out onto that dangerous lake was not appealing, but the thought of Kate and Davey being chased out there by someone with bad intentions, wasn't good either.

DeLuca revved up his machine, and took off, fearing that he might be too late to help anyone.

Was he doing the right thing? Could he have pretended that he didn't see those skidoo tracks? How was it all going to end?

Chapter Forty-Seven

When DeLuca first hit the lake, he couldn't see anything ahead of him, except for the occasional skidoo tracks. The wind had erased them in many places, but in others they were still clear.

He was on a powerful snow machine, a bigger and faster one than either of the Chandler ones. He knew that, because he and Bradley were the ones who had cleared and started both of the Chandler ones this morning for Kate. That seemed a long time ago.

He was relieved when he finally caught sight of a skidoo far ahead of him. When it veered slightly to the right or the left, he could see a bit of its headlight illuminating the snow. Now the question was, who was riding that skidoo, and what were they doing out here on the lake? What about the other skidoo? Where was it? There had definitely been two tracks leaving the cottage.

DeLuca wondered whether he could reach them before they got to the open water.

Riding at full speed, he had little time to think of anything except the danger which lay ahead. Thoughts of his family, however, kept creeping into one part of his mind. He and Cheryl had a brand new baby – little Mikey, just two months old. They also had a toddler named Susie. What a perfect family. He and Cheryl had been high school sweethearts, and, although they did their share of fighting, they still had a lot of fun together.

Cheryl wanted him to get out of the police force and take a job in her father's shoe store in Bracebridge. He, Nick DeLuca, prisoner in a shoe store, fitting shoes on big smelly feet all day long? No thank you. They fought about it all the time, but, although he loved her, this was one time he would not give in to Cheryl's pleadings. He was a cop at heart, and always would be.

Usually he didn't think of his job as being dangerous. After all, ninety-five percent of the time he was dealing with petty criminals. Most of them were just dumb school drop-outs, too lazy to get a regular job. Tonight, however, was a different story. He actually had a murder on his hands, and a man with a terrible neck wound. That was just for starters. Now he was doing something truly dangerous. It was foolish to be out here in the dark, in the middle of a blizzard, with open water somewhere ahead.

If the unknown woman was the person who had shot the man back at the cottage, she likely still had the gun. He'd have to be careful with her. A cop shouldn't usually make snap judgments, but after meeting Kate Chandler this morning, he was pretty sure that she wasn't the one who had shot the guy between the eyes. It just didn't seem her style.

Besides, on the phone, Davey had said that a "bad lady" was trying to hurt him and his mom, so he was pretty sure that it was the "bad lady" who had likely shot the man lying on the stairs. That meant that Kate and Davey had managed to get away on the first skidoo, and the "bad lady" was chasing them.

He had read all about Kate in the Toronto Star, and even the local paper had carried the story, when she bought the old Carrington place. He knew she was an artist, and a writer, and he knew that she had survived all by herself on an island in the Everglades, against terrible odds. The kidnapping and her amazing escape had made all the papers. There was even talk of making a movie about the adventure.

Speaking with her this morning, made him think that, although she was strong and capable, she was still just an ordinary housewife and mother. She was too gentle, too refined to be a killer. DeLuca was good at judging character.

De Luca was pleased to see that he was catching up to the skidoo, and he thought now, that he might be seeing a bit of light, which could be the second skidoo up ahead of the one he was following. Were there now three of them out on the lake?

Angel Baby had just looked over her shoulder, and couldn't believe her eyes when she saw the headlight of a skidoo, which was obviously following her. Who could it be? She knew that Mark was definitely dead – too bad about that. He had looked good in that red cashmere sweater. He had likely just been a nice guy, in the wrong place, at the wrong time.

If only she could have trusted him not to point the finger at her, after the murders of Kate and Davey were discovered. It was almost a sin to kill such an attractive man, specially one with money!

Huh, the murders. What murders? Everything had gone wrong. That little brat Davey had been her undoing. Imagine a little kid like that being so resourceful! He had just about broken her shin bone, when he hit her with that rolling pin, and then that hornet blaster had nearly blinded her. It had been more painful than all the surgeries she'd had.

He had been like that horrible little Chucky doll in the movies. A little snort of laughter escaped her lips, as she thought of Davey, running around, attacking her at every turn. It was as if there had been at least three of him!

No, she wouldn't have any problem now killing that little monster. The question was, how was she going to do it? She had rushed out so quickly to follow them, that she had no weapon with her. At least she could have grabbed the knife with which she had stabbed Kate's hand. Forget the hand, she should have plunged it right into her heart!

A feeling of panic swept over her. If and when she managed to catch up with them, what in the world could she use to kill them with no available weapons? That burdensome question kept prodding her. There were two of them, and only one of her, and Davey counted for two all by himself!

And now there was someone chasing her. That someone must be the police, but how had they become involved? Oh, of course, Davey, the little whirling dervish, the annoying little white knight, had likely called them. He had been a busy boy.

She should have tied him up to begin with, or given him more Rohypnol, and forced him to drink it. Kate had deliberately knocked his cocoa over. She must have suspected something at that point.

Angel could feel her head starting to buzz again. That was always a bad sign. She was still pretty sure that this was happening, and that it wasn't just a dream. Or, wait a minute. Was this just a movie which she had seen recently? It had a beautiful woman in it, and a handsome man. The woman had just walked up to the man, and she had shot him between his nice green eyes.

How had it ended, though? She couldn't remember anything after that scene in which the man named Mark had been killed. The woman had a neat little gun in her hand, and Angel Baby remembered that she was truly beautiful.

Pictures were flying in Angel's head like colours in a kaleidoscope. The whack on the head, which Davey had given her with the rolling pin, hadn't helped any.

With a real effort, however, she somehow managed to get her thoughts in order. Maybe it was the cold air which helped to clear her pounding head.

Too bad for her, but that killing scene was no movie. She remembered now very clearly. She was the one who had shot Mark, no doubt about it. That meant that if she couldn't get away, she was going to be caught and put in prison for killing him. And, if she wasn't put in prison, she'd be sent back to the nut house, the psychiatric hospital.

No, that would never happen. She would kill herself before she ever allowed that to happen. She could just imagine what life would be like for her in prison, or in the hospital. It had been bad enough before, but now that she was so truly beautiful, she would be the helpless victim of every disgusting pervert in the place, male or female.

She had to get herself out of this somehow. There had to be a way. She had an entire lifetime ahead of her to spend with Mac. She had gone through so much to change her appearance, all in order to get Mac back into her life. But what could she do with no weapon to kill Kate, and no way of defending herself against the police?

It occurred to her that if only she had stayed with Patrick, none of this would be happening. Dear Patrick. She had loved him those two years. She had managed to put Mac on a back burner temporarily, and she had been divinely happy with Pat in Switzerland.

Why hadn't she left well enough alone? They could have gone on the way they were, for a very long time. Eventually he would have left his wife and kids. She knew he had loved her, and their lives together were wonderful. Why had she been so stupid?

Right this very minute, they could have been cuddling in her lovely condo, sipping wine in front of the fire, and whispering loving things to each other.

If only, if only.

Well, she could give up chasing Kate and Davey for now. She could go a different direction and get herself off this cold, foreboding lake. She would head back to Toronto, and get a flight out of the country before anyone could find her. She would go someplace warm and sunny. She needed to spend some quality time on a beautiful beach in Bermuda, or the Bahamas, or maybe even Tahiti. Yes, the farther away the better. She liked that idea, a beautiful woman on a beautiful beach. That worked for her!

How sad that she hadn't thought of that pretty plan a little bit sooner!

Ahead of Angel, Kate and Davey were struggling. They were cold, they were tired, and they were both having trouble hanging on. Davey's arms were about to give up. They were aching, and felt like two floppy noodles. There was no strength left in them.

Kate's hand was throbbing, and sending piercing shards of pain right up her arm. She could barely close it to grasp the right handlebar. They were both weak from hunger and exposure.

She told herself that if she and Davey got themselves out of this mess, she would coax Mac to take her for another one-nighter at the Royal York. Hell, they'd stay there for a week!

As for Davey, well, she would do everything she could to ensure that he could keep Kingsley. He deserved that, after all his bravery and ingenuity. He had done as much tonight, as most men would have done.

When Kate cast a quick glance over her shoulder, she could see that Angel Baby was much closer. She was likely within forty feet of them, although Kate wasn't a very good judge of distance. All she knew was that Angel was practically right on their tails.

She also saw with surprise, that there was another snow machine behind Angel. Was it the police? Oh, please God, let it be the police. Who else could it be?

Turning forward again, Kate saw a sight which made her heart leap right into her throat. For one frightening moment, despair and fear encircled her mind and body, like strangling hands.

The black open water was directly ahead!

All that stood between them and that watery grave, were some big lumps and small hills of snow and ice. They formed almost a little edging along that evil black water. They actually hid the view of the open water to a certain degree, and if she hadn't been warned about it by the policeman, she might not have realized what it was.

"Turn, Davey," she yelled, as she grabbed helplessly for the right handlebar. The pain was excruciating, and her hand was a big shapeless lump, but somehow, she managed to put it over Davey's little hand, and, together, they yanked that machine to the right.

The blessed beast obeyed them. It turned almost easily, and now they were running parallel to the open water, rather than right at it. They drove into the bay and stopped, before Kate dared to take another quick peek over her shoulder.

Later she would wish with all her heart that she hadn't looked back. The tragic and terrifying sight, would give her nightmares for weeks to come.

Chapter Forty-Eight

Nick DeLuca knew that they were getting dangerously close to the thin ice and black water. He was so horrified at the thought of someone plunging into that death trap, that he was sweating inside his suit.

The powerful machine was running full out. He had to reach those skidoos and stop them, before a real tragedy occurred.

What would he do, if one or both of them plunged into the icy lake.? Would he be brave enough to go in after them? He wasn't sure, but his heart was beating, as if looking for an escape hatch.

Now he could only see one skidoo ahead of him. What had happened to the first one? It could have gone around the bend into the safety of the bay, or it could have gone straight ahead into the water. He didn't dare to guess.

Just as he was wondering whether his insurance was paid up, he saw several things at once.

He saw the bumps and berms and small piles of snow and ice, which were indicators that the open water was just beyond. He also saw the only skidoo ahead of him, hit the berms, and take off, airborne momentarily, before landing with a huge splash, and slowly settling into the water.

At that moment the wind died right down, as if holding its breath.

He could hear the unearthly screams, as whoever was riding that skidoo, began sinking out of sight.

Nick was pretty close behind the hapless snowmobiler, but not close enough. He still had a short distance to go, but he was afraid to drive the machine any closer, in case the ice was too thin to hold it.

Meanwhile, Angel had been thinking how unbelievably cold she was. She didn't have a skidoo suit. She was just wearing a good pair of slacks, a sweater and a warm jacket. She had no skidoo helmet for safety. That meant that there was absolutely no protection for her beautiful face, and it was freezing.

She hadn't known she was going to go out on a snow machine on this frigid night, and she certainly wasn't dressed appropriately. Although she did have a cute little cap which pulled down over her ears, her gloves were next to useless. Basically, she was cold all over.

Angel Baby had not been at the cottage in the morning, when DeLuca told Kate about the open water, and the subject had never come up when Mark was there. Angel, therefore, was blissfully unaware that there was any danger ahead.

She was still thinking of the lovely, sunny, warm beaches in Tahiti. She would buy herself a couple of great bikinis. She would definitely get one in hot pink. She looked amazing in pink. For the second one, she might try either red or aqua. She would have to see what was available. In any case, she would look so luscious in a bikini, that she would likely have to fight the men off with a stick. Lovely! Just what she needed to perk up her spirits.

She was getting tired of the scam she had been pulling in Montreal, Hamilton and Toronto. The men were so stupid – cheaters every one of them. Mac would never have been a cheater, nor would Patrick. They were good men, beautiful men.

Yes, technically they were both cheaters, but she had forgiven Mac a long time ago. As for Patrick, well, he had cheated on his wife in Angel Baby's favour, and that had been lovely. Of course, eventually he had gone back to Madelaine, but that wasn't really cheating, or was it?

This was confusing. It was likely because she was so cold that she couldn't think clearly. Oh, if only she could get off this blasted lake!

Angel was within a few yards of Kate's machine, when she looked over her shoulder again. That darn skidoo behind her was really gaining.

Because she was looking back, she didn't see Kate's skidoo, as it suddenly veered to the right. When Angel turned around again, it was too late to make the turn. She had no idea that there was danger ahead, so there was no reason in her mind, to make such a sharp turn.

She did try following Kate, but she was going too quickly. She bumped over several small frozen piles of snow, and was suddenly airborne. Even when she landed with a splash, she didn't realize at first what had happened.

When the icy cold water began creeping up her legs, however, she knew.

Even the wind seemed momentarily silenced by her desperate wails.

Angel screamed and screamed, while she frantically tried to get off the skidoo. She wasn't going down with that thing, not without a fight.

Unfortunately, one sleeve of her jacket had somehow caught on the left handlebar. She knew she was caught, but she didn't know where, so her struggles were in vain.

Being so heavy, and having hit the water nose-down, the skidoo, with Angel's added weight, sank quickly.

The shock of the icy water was instantly debilitating. Strangely, it felt as if she was on fire. She gasped for air, but swallowed water. Over and over she gasped and gulped greedily, for that lovely cold air, but inhaled and swallowed more of the deadly, freezing water.

She tried to hold her breath, but couldn't help gasping, which only drew more water into her mouth, up her nose, and into her bursting lungs. She tried to open her eyes, to see something familiar in her last conscious moments, but she was surrounded by blackness.

DeLuca leaped off his machine, and ran to the edge. The ice was thin, and breaking under his feet, so he didn't want to get too close, yet he knew he had to. He couldn't stand there and let that person drown, no matter who it was. He knew though, that his efforts were going to be futile. The poor bugger, whoever he or she was, had already disappeared into the blackness.

"Sweet Jesus help me," he muttered, as he prepared to ease himself down into that black death. The ice, however, was too thin, and, giving way with one loud crack, it caused Nick to plunge straight down. He gasped as the relentless icy water crept into, and soaked through his heavy skidoo suit. The shock to his system was instantaneous. Nick knew he was a dead man.

He ducked his head under, kicked his feet wildly, and felt around with both hands, but there was nothing. He came up for air, and forced himself to go down again, a bit deeper this time, knowing he might not have the strength to get back to the surface. He had to try, though.

The third time he came up, he knew it was hopeless. If he didn't get out now, he would never get out.

Trying to climb back onto the icy edge was almost impossible. It was thin, and kept breaking under him. Finally he hit a solid piece, and slowly and painfully hefted himself out of the water.

It was only then that he realized someone was trying to help him. Kate was leaning over, grabbing his hands, and slowly dragging him safely away from the edge.

"Come on, there's a cottage with lights on just round the bend. We'll get warm there," she pleaded.

Kate was crying. She had seen Angel Baby go right into that black hell, and it had been a shocking sight. Poor Angel Baby. She hadn't been a bad person, just a very sick one. She hadn't deserved this horrible ending. She had needed help, both for her mind, and now for her body. Kate knew that this police officer had done an amazingly brave thing, as he had pushed himself down into that frigid water over and over.

Now Nick just lay on the ice, trying to catch his breath, and shivering uncontrollably.

His body ached with the cold. It felt as if there were hot needles piercing him all over. He couldn't move, nor did he want to.

He didn't realize that he was crying, not only for the person who had died, and for the fact that he hadn't been able to save a life, but also because he hurt so much from the hypothermia.

"Come on, DeLuca," begged Kate, trying to get him into an upright position. "Think about your family. They expect you to come home tonight. I'll bet you've got little kids, and a beautiful wife. You can't let them down.

"It's just a short way into the bay, and we'll all be warm and safe. Please sit up. I've left Davey waiting on the skidoo by himself. He'll be frozen by now. I need your help. Please get up. You have to get on your skidoo and follow me to that cottage."

DeLuca just kept lying there, shivering as if every bone in his body would shake loose.

"Damn you," yelled Kate.

"I'm going to leave you here to die, if you don't get up right now. You're causing my little son to freeze, just waiting for us. If you don't come now, there'll be three more dead people out here on this blasted lake."

That seemed to get Nick's attention. With a huge effort, he got to his feet. He staggered, and would have fallen again, but Kate was there to help him.

"Good for you," she encouraged, soothingly.

"Now it's just a few steps to your skidoo. I know you can do it. They might even have a phone in that cottage. You'll be able to call your wife, and tell her you're okay. You're a hero, you know. You tried more than anyone would have, to save her life. Maybe you don't know it, but she was going to kill Davey and me, and she's already killed my neighbour. She was crazy, poor thing. Anyway, you did your best."

Kate kept babbling, just to keep Nick awake and lucid. She was terrified that he would pass out, and she would have to leave him here.

Nick's head was a bit too muddled to really understand what Kate was saying, but he understood that he had to get on his skidoo, and get off the lake. He would worry about the rest later.

Chapter Forty-Nine

———⟫•◦•⟪——— ———⟫•◦•⟪——— ———⟫•◦•⟪———

They were three exhausted, and frozen strangers, who came to the cottage door that stormy night.

When Joanna Springfield and her husband Joe opened the door, they couldn't believe their eyes. They had been playing bridge with their friends, the Thompsons, and had been both surprised, and a little frightened when they heard the pounding and shouting.

As far as they knew, they were the only two couples on this side of the bay, that weekend.

Kate knew they had to get into that warmth, and quickly. Nick just couldn't stop shivering.

"Please help us," begged Kate, when the door opened, and the warm air came drifting out.

"Someone has gone through the ice on a skidoo, and my friend here – he's a policeman – went into that freezing water three times trying to rescue her. He must be suffering from hypothermia, and we need to get him to the hospital. I think my son has frostbite too."

Kate hadn't noticed that in all the excitement, she had lost the tea towel, which was supposed to be protecting her hand. Now they could all see the swollen, misshapen hand, covered with dried blood, with a gaping hole almost through it. Kate felt faint when she looked at it. With a sickening feeling, she realized that she would likely never draw again. She could have cried, but she was too tired and traumatized.

Davey seemed almost catatonic. He hadn't said a word, since Nick had splashed into the water, trying to save Angel Baby.

The Springfields and the Thompsons couldn't have been nicer. They took the three survivors in, called 911, and made some warm milk for Nick. Kate knew that he shouldn't be given caffeine, and she knew that he mustn't drink anything too hot, so warm milk seemed appropriate, although he balked at drinking it.

The two men stripped off his wet clothes, and found warm, dry ones for him. Both Springfield and Thompson were shorter than Nick, so the pant legs were too short, and the sweater was a bit tight, but they would do.

Then they had him lie on the couch, under several blankets.

Kate held the mug of milk, and helped him sip it, all the time hoping that this was a proper treatment for hypothermia. Nick was dizzy, slightly confused, had shallow breathing, and couldn't stop shivering. These were all symptoms of hypothermia.

She wondered how he had managed to drive his skidoo behind her the short distance to this cottage. The guy was certainly made of strong stuff! Because he hadn't been in the freezing water too long, Kate was sure that he would be fine.

Once they got their skidoo suits off, and were sitting in front of the fire, Kate and Davey seemed to be okay. Their clothes hadn't been wet.

The Thompsons had one little girl named Becky, who was ten years old. Her mom ran to their cottage next door, and came back with a pair of her jeans and a sweater for Davey, just in case he wanted something warmer. Davey, however, protested loudly that he didn't need any girl's clothes.

Kate was thankful when he put up the protest. He had been totally silent, but now he seemed to be recovering his speech.

The cottages along this stretch of the bay, were all built close together, and also close to the road. The ambulance, therefore had no trouble getting right to the cottage. All three patients were crowded into it, as it took off for the hospital.

This was the same hospital to which Patrick had been taken earlier. Although it was late on a stormy night, business was booming.

The emergency room was a bustling hive of activity. There were nurses, doctors, a few technicians, patients, and friends and relatives, all sitting, standing or pacing. There were gurneys and wheelchairs coming and going. There was continual noise from equipment, televisions, nurses conversing, and patients calling for help and attention.

It was an interesting area to observe, but an unpleasant place to be, if you were a patient.

After Patrick had been treated for hypothermia, and the stick had been removed from his throat under anesthesia, it was decided to move him by ambulance to a bigger hospital in Toronto, where there would be a specialist who could repair the complicated damage to his throat.

When the accident happened, Patrick's first thought was that the limb might have punctured the carotid artery, in which case he would have exsanguinated rapidly. Because of the placement of the limb, however, he realized that hadn't happened.

Unfortunately, he also knew that there were many bad things which could happen to his esophagus or his larynx, pharynx, or trachea. There were so many important tubes in the throat to help him eat, breathe, talk etc. If that piercing limb had managed to avoid everything in his throat, it would be a miracle.

He needed to see a specialist who could repair any serious damage, and was grateful that they were sending him to a bigger hospital.

Strangely, just as Patrick was being taken out by ambulance, to be transferred to Toronto, Kate, Davey and Nick, were arriving by ambulance. They actually passed in the emergency corridor.

Patrick had come all this way from Switzerland to confront and possibly take revenge on Angel Baby. He had also wanted to save or protect Kate. Now Angel Baby was dead through no fault of his own, although he wouldn't hear that information for another 24 hours. At this point, he had no idea of what had transpired on the inky black lake. He just knew that he hadn't been able to do anything to help Kate, if, indeed, she had needed help.

Patrick would eventually learn that his entire trip had been futile. Not only had he failed in his mission, but he had managed to seriously hurt himself in the process. In retrospect, he would have been much better off, if he had stayed in Switzerland, and minded his own business.

At the hospital, Nick DeLuca was taken away quickly. He was obviously in the worst condition.

Kate insisted that they check Davey, before she showed them her hand. Davey was actually in pretty good shape. He had a bit of frost bite on his cheeks, but it was easily remedied.

Joanna Springfield had made toast and peanut butter for them, when Davey mentioned that he was starving. Now he was feeling pretty good, except that he was very worried about Kingsley. Had he wakened? Was he sick? Was he looking for Mark?

He wanted to go right back to the cottage, but that just wasn't going to happen.

Kate's hand caused a lot of concern. It was a mess. The doctors did the best they could, cleaning it and padding it, and applying ice and antibiotics, but they knew that Kate required the services of an excellent surgeon.

Ironically, just as in Patrick's case, it was decided that Kate had to be transferred to Toronto, where she would get the best care possible. Since she was going by ambulance (no way could she drive a car), Davey had to go with her.

Kate had to make some sort of arrangements before being shipped down to Toronto. After thinking about it for a few minutes, she came up with a good idea. First she inquired as to the condition of Walt Sr., explaining the reason for her interest. It was all good news as far as Walt was concerned. He was recovering very nicely from his heart attack, which had now been classified as "mild." He had not required surgery, and was going to be released the next day.

In spite of how very late it was, Kate decided that she had to call Walt Jr. She explained the situation to the very sleepy young man, and asked him to contact the police. Hopefully, they would give him permission to go into the cottage, likely with an attendant officer, since the cottage was now a crime scene. Kate wanted him to check on the dog, and get him to a veterinarian right away.

If Kingsley was fine, she wanted Walt to look after him, until she or Mac could get back up to the cottage in a few days, to get him.

She was quite sure that the Springfields would step up and take care of the dog, but thought it would be better to ask Walt Jr. first.

Walt was so happy that his dad was coming home, that he was quite willing to do this favour for Kate. He was also excited that there had been a murder at her cottage, and that he would be talking with the police. This was the most thrilling thing that had ever happened to him, and he was going to enjoy every moment of it.

That taken care of, Kate asked if she could see Nick, before leaving the hospital. She was happy to see that he was doing well. His body temperature was slowly coming back up to normal, and, although extremely tired and a bit shaky, he would eventually be fine.

They talked a bit, and Kate thanked him for coming out on the lake to try to save her and Davey from Angel. He had been an extremely brave man, and she felt that she owed him a great deal.

Who knew what might have happened, if she and Davey had been alone out there with Angel, and if Angel had not fallen through the ice.

Nick had to be honest, and admitted that he hadn't had any clear idea of just what had been going on. He had been looking for a murderer, as well as trying to find Kate and Davey.

She told Nick exactly what had happened when Angel shot Mark. Nick explained that she would have to come back up to Muskoka, to answer a lot of questions for the investigation, and Kate assured him that she would be available whenever they called her.

Davey was sure that Kingsley was alive, and he was happy to know that Walt Jr. would take good care of him, until Davey and/or Kate and Mac could get back to the cottage.

The blizzard seemed to have finally worn itself out. It was no longer snowing, and the wind was no longer blowing. The roads were gradually being cleared, and it promised to be a decent drive to Toronto.

After a call to Jill, to tell her how and why she was coming back to the city in the middle of the night, Kate was suddenly overwhelmed by exhaustion, both emotional and physical. With Davey safely tucked into the ambulance at her side, she suspected that they would both sleep all the way to the hospital.

The three main players, Kate, Patrick, and Angel Baby, had come to cottage country for different reasons. Now two of those three players were leaving cottage country, wounded, but alive, while it appeared that one would be staying.

Kate had a seriously damaged hand. Patrick had a serious hole in his throat. Angel Baby, had taken a serious, and unexpected dive, into frigid waters. She wasn't going any place.

It seemed that the cold night in hell was over.

Epilogue

It was almost six months later, July1ˢᵗ, Canada Day, and the Chandlers were throwing a party at their newly renovated cottage. Well, in actual fact, renovations were still in progress. It was a very big cottage.

The weather was co-operating beautifully. It was a pleasant 80 degrees, with just a slight breeze to ripple the navy blue water, and make its way through the whispering pines.

There were a few wispy white clouds on the blue canvas of the sky. It was, in fact, a typical summer day in Muskoka.

The party had started at noon, and looked as if it was going to go on well into the evening. Although there were lots of nibbles, along with cold drinks, beer, water, wine, and pop, the actual barbecue wouldn't start till around 4:30.

At that time, Mac would be cooking the usual hot dogs, hamburgers, and sausages, to go with the potato salad, and hot beans. If anyone had room for dessert, there was a big Canada Day cake.

There were even special doggie biscuits for Kingsley, who was now an important part of the family.

While the cottage improvements were being made, Mac had asked the workers to put up a tall, white, flag pole.

Today at noon, when all their guests had arrived, they raised a big Canadian flag, amid cheers and toasts, and it was now flying proudly on the front lawn.

At the moment, Mac was driving the boat. The twins, Peter and Paige, were the watchers, along with Kingsley. Davey was enjoying his first actual ski. He had tried several times that summer, but, although he could always get up on them, popping out of the water like a little cork, he couldn't manage to stay on them.

He had taken some bad spills, but was determined to master the sport. Kate was sure that his arms were three inches longer from being dragged by the tow rope! He would not give up, though, and today was the day. Davey was grinning from ear to ear, and Kingsley was barking fiercely from the boat, ready to jump in at any moment.

Everyone on the dock and lawn cheered too, as Mac proudly towed his youngest son, not too far from the shoreline. Mac had taken Davey right past the dock, and had slowed down, so that Davey could just let go of the bar, and sink gently into the water. Davey, however, shook his head, and wouldn't let go, so Mac was taking him around again.

There was no happier young man on the lake that day than Davey Chandler, and he wasn't about to cut his ride short.

Many good changes had been made to the old Carrington cottage. It was sporting a fresh new coat of paint. They had also had heavy white shutters made for every window on the first floor. When winter came, those shutters would be closed and locked. No vandal or thief would have a hope of breaking in to this cottage, unless they carried a ladder, and managed to climb to the second story.

It made Kate feel somewhat depressed, when she thought about those shutters. Mark had kindly offered to help make them, just before Madison had killed him. His death was still unbelievable, and so unnecessary.

On gloomy days, Kate couldn't help spending some time playing the "if only" game. If only Mark hadn't arrived when he did. If only Maddy hadn't had that wretched gun. If only they had managed to tie her, and get away.

Unfortunately, the game never had a different outcome. Mark was dead, Angel was dead, and there was nothing more to be said.

Two extra bathrooms had been added to the cottage, and there were more changes to come.

The old place looked elegant and charming, and the Chandlers loved it.

Jill was there with her new boyfriend, Steve. He owned a small publishing house in Toronto, and he and Jill were so happily matched, that they were planning a wedding in September.

Tall, with reddish hair, green eyes, and a crazy grin, Steve was loved by the entire Chandler family. He played soccer for an all-star Toronto league, and they all went to see his games as often as possible.

Davey was even thinking of joining a soccer team now, rather than playing baseball. This summer, however, they were all spending so much time at the cottage, that he hadn't played either sport.

Jill and Steve were hoping to be married on the beach at Edgewater Beach Resort, in Florida, where Kate and Mac owned their condo.

Paige had recovered nicely from her dreadful fright, on that cold night in January. The experience seemed to have caused her to mature very quickly. She jumped right over the terrible teens, and had become a serious, thoughtful young girl, still full of fun, but not full of the angst, and deliberately sullen attitude, adopted by so many teens.

Lester's sudden death had given her bad dreams for weeks, but that was all behind her now. She was growing more like Kate every day, both in looks and in attitude.

Officer Nick deLuca and his wife Cheryl had been invited to the July 1st celebrations. After the terrible accident on the ice, Nick had suffered debilitating nightmares. He dreamed over and over that he had gone down in that frigid water with Angel Baby, and, although he would waken up soaking wet, it was from sweat, rather than lake water.

He was over the night terrors now, though, and back to work. Actually, he had become a bit of a folk hero in the area. What he had done was considered bravery beyond the call of duty.

Kingsley had spent two days at the vet's hospital after his ordeal. The Rohypnol and the chocolate had nearly killed him. He was a strong dog, however, with a strong will to survive.

Strangely, when the Chandlers brought him home to Toronto, their three cats accepted him without much fuss. They made it clear who would still be boss, and Kingsley seemed to understand. He was the interloper, so he trod very carefully, where the cats were concerned.

Little Harriet, the smallest of the three cats, took a great liking to him. When he slept, she would snuggle up between his paws. One day she had the entire family in hysterics, when Kingsley walked into the family room, with Harriet sitting nonchalantly on his back. She looked like a little circus performer sitting on an elephant. Kingsley looked a bit sheepish. Davey rolled around on the floor with laughter. Peter had run for the camera.

Each time they went to the cottage for a weekend, Kingsley would race down the road to Mark's cottage. He would circle it several times, sniffing and barking. Then, realizing that Mark wasn't there, the dog would hurry back up the long road, back to Davey, for a game of ball, or a boat ride.

As far as Kingsley was concerned, that boat was his, and he howled if it left the dock without him. He also thought the canoe was his, but that was another story.

It broke Kate's heart to see him still looking for Mark, but he seemed happy with their family, so in time, she hoped he would stop looking for his old friend and master.

Mac's dad Martin, had come out from England for a visit, and was loving every moment in Canada. Kate was trying her best to persuade him to move there permanently, and she almost had him convinced.

Old Walt Sr. was well recovered from his heart attack, and he and his son Walt Jr. were once again looking after many of the cottages in the area. They had been invited to the party too. Kate liked them both, and she figured that the nicer she was to them, the more care and attention they would give the Chandler cottage.

Patrick had returned to Switzerland, but he and Kate had become email pals. When Patrick had been in hospital in Toronto, Kate had been there too. Somehow, through the hospital grapevine, they heard about each other.

Although Kate was discharged the next day, Patrick was there for a week, before being able to return to his home.

Kate visited him, and learned about his effort to try to save her from Angel Baby. She was grateful to him, and felt guilty that he had been hurt, while trying to help her.

He couldn't believe that Angel had died. He hadn't wanted that for her. He was relieved, however, that Kate hadn't been hurt.

His voice was gradually returning, although it sounded very husky now. Once in a while he called Kate, but mostly they communicated by email.

Patrick's wife Lainey had been distraught, when she learned of his accident, and the cold war between them was gradually thawing. He had confidence that he would eventually get his family back. In the meantime he was rebuilding his clinic.

Kate's hand had healed beautifully. She would always have a scar to show for that hellish night, but the hand was improving every day. After weekly physio sessions, and many exercises, she had 90%

mobility in it again. The important thing was that she was having very little trouble doing her illustrations. She felt blessed and grateful that Angel Baby hadn't done more damage with the knife.

The skidoo had been recovered from the water, but there was no sign of Maddy. The experts seemed to feel that she must have been swept down the river, where it was very deep.

Kate knew that Maddy was dead. No one could have survived that plunge on that frigid night. To do so, she would have had to somehow climb back onto the ice, and then make it to a cottage for help.

The Springfield cottage was the nearest one occupied that night, and she certainly hadn't appeared there. Still, the fact that they couldn't find her body was unnerving.

Co-incidentally, someone had broken into a cottage four lots down from the Springfields, that same hellish night. Warm clothing and a blanket, along with a bottle of rye, were missing. The fact that no other cottages had been vandalized along that strip, seemed strange.

In Kate's darkest moments, she wondered whether Maddy could possibly have escaped. In stores or on the street, she found herself looking suspiciously at any woman who was about Maddy's size.

She didn't tell Mac or the kids of her fears, because they would think she was crazy.

Most of the time, she just enjoyed her life, and her wonderful family.

Occasionally, though, she got a weird feeling that someone was watching her. She knew it was just her over-active imagination, and yet - - - - - - - -

The End

CPSIA information can be obtained at www.ICGtesting.com
Printed in the USA
LVOW11s2007061014

407521LV00001B/2/P

9 781491 745960